- *Praise for Critical Care* -

"…easy to read; lots of action to keep the readers' attention…a few serious thoughts keep one pondering the deepest meanings of life." Greg Burliuk – The Kingston Whig-Standard

"…filled with suspense and intrigue….the more I read the harder it was to put down." E.F.

"…a quick note from the Dominican Republic to say that your book is sooo good. **I LOVE IT!**" J.F.

"…I could not put your book down. I absolutely loved it and am waiting for your next installment."(email from a reader)

"…I have started reading and have not been able to put it down. I have read many books from the likes of John Grisham, Fern Michaels and James Patterson and Phillip Brown has won me over with his book." (email from a reader)

"… I really enjoyed the book; I loved the flow of the father going through his life and wanting to make it right. I hope you might write again; about this family or in the same style about another." P.C.

"…I would first like to compliment you on a marvelous book "Critical Care". It was hard to put down and I enjoyed it from beginning to end." G.P.

"…you must buy Critical Care and read it. Phillip Brown has a remarkable style. I lost two days and part of a night of my Christmas Holidays. Critical Care is a *"can not put down read…"* A.D.

That man is the richest whose pleasures are the cheapest.

— *Henry David Thoreau*

It is my pleasure to thank the many people who
both encouraged and assisted me with Critical Care.
Please accept my humble gratitude.

— *Phillip Brown*

- Preface -

By the mid 1990's the struggle of life's journey had taken a toll on almost everything about and around me. Perhaps it was a mid-life crisis or perhaps it was a calling but I was heading to the Dark Continent called Africa. I had stuffed my life into one of those modern backpacks and was ready to go.

It had taken six months to prepare. My two brothers, who were also my business partners, seemed supportive enough so I had worked to delegate the duties of my job in such a way that if I didn't come back it wouldn't much matter. The rest of the family, friends and relatives were, in varying degrees, rooting me on.

After much anticipation and many tears, I settled into my seat on the evening flight heading east from Toronto, Ontario. When the door of the aircraft closed and I realized that, short of a crash en route, I was fulfilling the commitment I had made to myself to make the trip.

Little did I know how impactful this journey would be. I was about to empty the accumulated contents of my life's vessel over the hills, plains and dusty roads of East Africa and have it refilled with the magic of renewal and awareness that awaited me.

I tell you this not so much because it sets up the story *Critical Care* but moreover because this was the time I read a wonderful book by John Grisham called *A Time To Kill*. The book was good; very good actually. But it was his introduction on the cover that kindled a spark whose ember warmed a thought.

I seem to recall that Mr. Grisham told of how he decided to write his first novel and that he was encouraged to, "Just write one page each day and in a year he would have written a novel."

He did just that, and so have I.

For all of you who have penned a poem or a story or been told that you should write more: keep on writing. One day you may follow in the footsteps of Mr. Grisham and write a book one page at a time.

I believe much of what we experience comes to us because we are ready for it or because we are vehicles of receipt and delivery of a message. The story, *Critical Care*, and all of its characters was certainly the case for me. During the process of writing *Critical Care* I had begun with the kernel of an idea and started typing from there. All else just flowed through me and on to the pages. The story and characters were waiting to be introduced to you through me. I was quite amazed and humbled to meet each character when they revealed their identity and story to me and how they would fit into the novel.

So please, turn the pages and meet them…they and the story they tell are waiting for you. I truly hope you enjoy reading *Critical Care*. I certainly enjoyed writing it.

- Introduction -

Life had seemed so easy for the wealthy and proper Douglas family of Boston until, on a chilly Fall morning a shocking event changed all of that forever.

Short of the usual family and social challenges, patriarch Peter Douglas had provided for all the material needs of his offspring. His second marriage was joyful, his kids were healthy, the transition of the family corporation was complete and life was good. The family reputation was golden but Peter had yet to realize much was still missing.

Little did he know what awaited him on the other side.

What other side you ask?

You know – the side we dream about and wonder about when something unexplainable happens.

The side we hope may be better when and if we get there.

Peter awakes to a new day. The first day in his new life of discovering that there was more to life than what met his eyes.

His son Brian takes the lead in a race against time on the death clock at his Father's bedside. He goes head to head with the astute and deceptive Dr. Joseph Zalkow who wants Peter Douglas dead. Can he hold the family and business together? Will he be able to withstand external evil forces that work against him. Will his family support him?

Was this a test or was it real? You decide…

- Chapter 1 -

"Hey boy, ya comin' in the car this morning?"

Peter Douglas embraced this routine, albeit brisk, Monday morning in October while he enjoyed a brilliant sunrise.

Sunshine had been rare over the past few weeks. Record-breaking fall rains soaked the ground and had swollen local rivers.

Peter felt relaxed. A weekend at his home in the country near Westwood, just southwest of Boston and the joy of his usual brisk walk with Schebb, his loyal blond Labrador retriever, had that effect.

Thoughts of many such similar mornings, when he'd contemplated all his business and personal matters or threw unanswered questions to Schebb, were prominent today.

"Life's mysteries. What do ya think fella?"

"You love that dog more than me." His first wife had always accused him. In the end she was right; but that was history, and his new wife seemed too busy most of the time to notice either of them.

Enjoying a morning meal on the sunny deck, he read the business section and the obituaries, while Schebb gnawed on an old slipper.

Peter felt the soft fur. He stroked Schebb's head periodically causing him to look up. Peter adjusted his position to rise. Simultaneously Schebb sat up, wagged his tail, unaware that the vet was awaiting him for his fall check-up and grooming. Many leather seats in Peter's cars had been scratched from the same struggle that would take place in the vet parking lot today.

Schebb's early life had not been easy, and at the end of his first year as an abused pup he found himself strapped to the vet's table about to be put down.

Peter had stuck his head in the door to say hi to his veterinarian friend who was just filling a hypodermic needle. Schebb let out a whimper for help, beckoning with his brown eyes. Peter was about to excuse himself.

"You're not in the market for a dog, are ya, pal? I'm afraid this one's goin' down."

Peter winced, but when he looked in the dog's eyes something captured him. A connection had been made. An hour later Peter had a freshly shampooed, de-fleaed, clipped, manicured and immunized, albeit scrawny, pup wrapped in a blanket on the seat of his car. The Caring for Your Pup book had been a bonus, with the chapter on food already marked. Peter spent $324.97 on his new dog that day, but many times he had said, "Best darn investment I ever made."

Peter cruised out through the gateway of their boulder fence, enjoying the colorful maples that overhung the narrow side road that led from Peter's secluded neighborhood toward town. He watched Schebb sniff the air then bark out the window when they passed the horse paddocks where the four-legged residents took little notice. Peter scanned the beautiful barns and large yellow house that sat on a small hill overlooking acres of shorn grass where the purebreds ran.

Schebb settled back onto his seat. The futile barks stopped. He seemed used to car rides from Peter's country home to somewhere. They were usually longer than short and almost always ended somewhere nice. On occasion though he would end up at someone's home where kids would torment him for an afternoon and feed him all the things he seemed to love but shouldn't eat, which made for a tired evening and numerous trips outside.

Today, Peter steered the car toward Carl Nathan's estate. Peter figured Schebb would have a good run chasing cows and horses, and a swim in Small Pond before he went to the vet in Needham. Schebb rested his head on Peter's lap; a little head rub rewarded him. Peter tuned the radio to a world news station, put Schebb's window up halfway and enjoyed the shared time.

Peter frowned while he listened to the news.

"Why doesn't someone invent a good news-only station?"

The relaxing head massage continued.

"I'll have to suggest that to Carl about GBC when we see him."

Peter picked through the radio stations and finally settled on soft classics. He massaged his own forehead and temples firmly then squinted, trying to relieve some tension that had built since he got back from his walk.

At sixty-three Peter stayed focused on being a picture of good health. He was proud that his heart had fully recovered from an episode years earlier and he had pledged to keep it that way. He now kept his six-foot-two frame in peak shape. He ate well, worked out and even meditated. He had his drinking well in hand now, adjusted dramatically downward, since his father had died in a car wreck, while under the influence, many years earlier. His thick brown hair was just starting to show some gray. His face belied many years of working and playing very hard.

It had taken a nervous breakdown at forty-four, after losing his Dad, and a minor heart attack in his fifties to get the message through. Once Peter Douglas made his mind up about something though, there was no looking back for himself or those around him. One either bought in or moved on. Most of his friends from the youthful days had moved on or burned out.

Peter enjoyed the resplendent beauty of the leaves in transition. Driving a little faster than normal today on the quiet road, he felt the wind passing smoothly through his car and messing his hair. His mind wandered.

Thoughts of an Asian woman named Choy played a short film in his head. He reflected on his divorce and the conclusion of the transition of his business empire to his first-born son, Brian. He remembered the strain on his family and himself at that time and his decision to pack one bag and board a plane to South East Asia for an indefinite sabbatical.

Choy was then a newly divorced freelance journalist who sat beside him on the plane to Hong Kong. The silence between them was broken only by courteous exchanges for the first two hours of the flight. It wasn't until the flight attendant drenched them with two glasses of red wine that the tension turned to humor and then to friendly conversation, which turned to Peter and Choy spending nine months traveling, writing, photographing and generally loving life and each other. During their time together Choy also exposed Peter to the teaching and knowledge of deep meditation and explored with him the idea of conscious realms beyond ones physical presence. Peter still had her silk blouse and she his white shirt, both bearing the blood-red stain of their first meeting.

Peter felt his face beginning to quiver and then tighten into an uncontrollable grimace. The back of his head exploded with pain. He watched the fall colors ahead melt into a psychedelic whirl. His body stiffened. He drove the accelerator to the floor.

Schebb jumped to his feet and started whimpering at his master.

The car accelerated down the open road.

Peter's arms stiffened like steel rods. His nails shattered when the increased pressure of his grip caused them to break through the covering on the steering wheel. Blood oozed from his cuticles. His jaw clenched powerfully in response to the shock. He ground his teeth tightly, breaking several, mixing enamel slivers with the saliva and blood.

His twisted mouth now oozing.

Schebb barked and licked at Peter's foaming mouth.

The wind through the car mingled with Peter's loud groaning.

The hair on Schebb's back stood straight.

Peter's head pressed back hard against the rest. His stiffened legs drove his body deeply into the leather upholstery. Muscles and tendons in his hips, shoulders and neck tore under the strain of superhuman effort.

Peter felt utterly out of control, bathed in a wash of pain.

He heard no sound. He saw no color. His reality was gone. Now just blackness.

Calves knotted and thighs bulged with the effort his body was generating.

Nose bleeding steadily; tiny, bloody tears ran down his face.

Neck, forehead and temples swelled with twisted, bulging veins.

The ninety mile-per-hour wind now blew matted hair, sweat and rose-colored foam from his face.

Schebb was suddenly hurled to the floor.

The car launched off the asphalt curb, tore through the guard rail and severed an old sign. Both front tires exploded. The engine revved uncontrollably, free from the resistive pavement.

For a few seconds Peter drifted high above the scene. He watched his car fly several hundred feet out into the open woods before starting its decent into the river. A billow of steamy, greasy, smoke forced its way out from under the hood.

Peter felt calm and detached.

He observed this oddity from a painless floating plane well above the calamity.

Schebb was pinned in place. Peter's body strained up and out against his seat belt and billowing airbag. The force of the exploded bag pushed the air from his lungs, and in a great burst he had expelled fluid from all orifices of his body.

A foamy red spray painted the billowing cloth. Blood was everywhere now.

A great bellow of gas exploded beneath him taking with it a day's excrement which mixed with a release of urine.

The crash of snapping branches echoed through the car. Each took a role in decelerating this forest intruder.

The nose of the car had tipped forward.

The descent continued.

Glass shattered and protruding car parts were ripped away from its body.

Each tree imposed its share of punishment.

The car's dive followed a predetermined arc through the wooded ravine.

The engine sizzled when it plunged into the swirling Charles River, the foaming water cushioning the vehicle's sudden, but soft, landing.

Peter became briefly conscious but then his odd flight above the scene abruptly ended, slamming him back into his unconscious reality.

The slowing effect of the trees, the turbulent water, had spared much of the impact. The swollen river covered most of the rocks which could have been the final resting place for Peter's car.

After the initial dunking the car bobbed up. It began a journey down river.

Schebb's eyes bulged and slobber dribbled from his mouth. He gasped for air.

Cold water leaked into the car, flooding the floor where he lay.

Clambering up onto the seat he licked Peter's face, nudging him forcefully.

Peter didn't respond.

A raspy bark echoed in the car.

It filled, accelerating down river toward the waterfall.

Peter was limp. Each collision with a wave or submerged rock threw him about.

Schebb stood on the passenger seat barking out the window.

The approaching exposed boulder meant nothing to him. When the car smashed into it, broadside, the wet dog was hurled out of the window.

The pointed rock was just slightly higher than the car door. Schebb's head banged against it. He was plunged, stunned, into the rapidly moving water.

The car took a solid hit, crumpling a door, throwing Peter against his belt before it rounded the obstacle, continuing, toward Schebb. The cold water swirled to Peter's waist. Diverted by the seat belt, it flowed in through the window rushing around Peter's chest and neck, washing his face clean. Periodically the car tires grazed submerged rocks.

The mist of the upcoming falls loomed ahead.

Schebb yelped when his body was forced against another boulder. The rushing river pinned him in place.

Floundering, he coughed water from his lungs.

The face of this long-time friend came bobbing toward him. Schebb barked.

The car approached.

The front quarter panel stopped and crumpled first, forcing the back end to swing closed against the rock like a vise with Schebb in its jaws.

He yelped and thrashed when the vehicle started to squeeze him. The vise gripped its prey, but it also forced the rapid flow of water to bulge outward: the final effect – Schebb was squirt twenty feet away from disaster toward shore.

He paddled wildly.

Peter was now awash. His car remained pinned.

The dog's feet scraped bottom, claws dug in, creating forward motion. Once on shore, he turned, shook the water from his fur. Schebb barked weakly toward the odd sight in the river.

Peter's head was hanging forward, to the side.

Schebb turned, without stopping, ascended the forested bank to the road.

He came out several hundred yards around the bend from where the car had been launched. The sound of an oncoming car wasn't a deterrent. He made his way onto the road then stopped, placing himself directly in the path of this one.

Joel, like Peter earlier, eyed the rush of color and sniffed the sweet air while he drove his family through the countryside. He guided his car casually around a curve. Music from the radio entertained his wife and two kids.

Another golden lab was perched in between Joel and his wife.

At his first sight of another canine on the road he was jarred when his dog, Amber, barked loudly.

His startled passengers were jolted to attention. Joel felt his nerves fire from a shot of adrenaline being released.

All eyes were now on this dog poised in the middle of the road, staring at the approaching vehicle.

"Daddy, watch out."

Smoke spiraled up from the screaming tires. The car careened to a stop just feet from the dripping lab.

Chaos broke out.

The children shrieked.

Amber clambered to get out of the window.

Joel's wife beckoned him to pull off the road.

He instinctively pressed the buttons of the power windows to secure the car, which had stalled from the force of the screeching halt.

His heart raced. He stared, wide eyed, while this wet muddy lab barked viciously, then leapt up at his window spewing drool at him.

Amber growled and barked near Joel's ear.

The children's screaming dizzied him. He felt his face sting; sweat breaking out across it.

The car wouldn't start. The engine seemed dead.

The lab jumped onto the hood of the car continuing to bark and growl, seemingly, at the family.

The panic level inside the vehicle increased.

Joel yelled for his wife and children to get down.

He fumbled with the ignition key.

Amber responded viciously by pressing her muzzle against the inside of the windshield in response to this external enemy.

The children wailed. Their mother leaned over the back of the seat trying to calm them.

Joel cringed at the noise. His stomach felt sick and impulsively tightened.

Then he saw a blur.

A thick leather belt slapped down on the hood of the car.

A slice of pain ripped through his chest in response to this gunshot like sound.

The lab yelped then heeled back just missing the swing of the burly, bearded man who yelled at him to get down.

Joel, instinctively, glanced in the rear view mirror now filled with a gleaming chrome grill.

"You folks okay?" Joel heard the man yelling through the muddy glass.

Joel looked at him. He felt pale; fear filled, he nodded.

He felt his wife's grip when she clutched him. The children sobbing quietly in the back brought water to his eyes.

Amber growled lowly at the newcomer over Joel's shoulder.

"I'll take care of the mutt."

Joel watched.

From the back of his pants, the man drew a small, silver hand gun then aimed it at the lab that had retreated down the road.

The dog flew over the wooden guard rail when a bullet ricocheted into the trees. His barking seemed to taunt the bearded truck driver. A second shot seemed to narrowly miss him, ripping through an overhanging branch.

Horns honked when two cars from the opposite direction screeched to a halt. A man jumped out. The trucker stood tall, unmoved.

"Are you looking for it?"

"Looking for what?"

"There's been a crash back there. A car must be down in the river."

The trucker ran for his cab.

"Breaker, breaker, this is The Bearded One, does anybody copy?"

"Copy that, this is Snake. What's goin' on Fuzzy?"

"I'm just south of Needham at the Mill Street bridge. I think we got a serious accident on our hands. At least one vehicle over the edge, likely down in the Charles River. I gotta dog here, barkin' like crazy. I bet people's hurt. Get us some help."

"Roger that. I'll make the call."

The Bearded One made a quick beeline toward Joel's car.

The electric window went down. Joel stared.

The trucker made a quick apology for their scare.

"You folks best get the kids outta here. I'll take care of this. I think there's been an accident down the road aways. Could be a car in the river. It won't be pretty."

"My car won't start."

Joel watched the trucker eye the red lights of the dash, then the console. His long arm reached a gloved hand through the window, over Joel, then slipped the gear shift into park.

Joel frowned. He felt his face redden.

The engine came to life.

Joel looked back.

The red plaid shirt of the gun-toting trucker was gone.

- Chapter 2 -

He stretched his hands and cracked his knuckles, relieving some of the tension from hours of typing. Matt Douglas was pleased with his first morning's work. He felt the click when he gently closed the lid of his laptop computer. The story had finally begun.

He stared out over the green ocean, then slid open the wide screen door and walked from the balcony, through sheer white curtains, toward the bed where he flopped onto his back. Staring up, the whirling fan mesmerized him. His mind drifted while watching the carved wooden blades shadowed against the white stucco ceiling. A soft breeze cooled his body. He could hear the curtains wafting back and forth, making a swishing sound that neither disturbed nor stimulated. His nose tingled with sweet and salty tropical scents that floated on a melody of waves rolling and crashing on the beach and rocks below. His mind drifted in tune with the sound of the running shower. He began to tingle elsewhere.

Matt knew this feeling well: the crisp sheets of a king-size bed against his back, soft pastel colors, a well-appointed room with several telephones, flat screen televisions and tasteful lamps. A silver ice bucket bedside, dripping rivulets down its side onto a white cotton napkin, busily chilled a dark green bottle bearing the name of a famous French vineyard. He couldn't help but smile, lauding his good fortune.

He then heard every sound, envisioned every action. The shower had stopped. The glass doors glided open. He could hear her feet when they met the floor, the sound of her towel while she dried herself. He felt a heat come over him when she entered his view. She wandered his way.

Cara Walters was stunning. A five-foot-nine summer blonde; girl next door type. At twenty-two she was almost eighteen years his junior.

This seemed all too perfect. Disbelief of her presence there had him doubting his own reality.

What was the catch this time?

"I finished with cold water."

"I can tell."

Her small breasts stood pert. Her goose-bumped flesh was taut on her lithe, toned, frame.

Matt cringed inwardly.

For the umpteenth time he contemplated his age and the mileage lines she must now be observing on his face.

Character, he told himself.

His eyes locked on hers.

She smiled while she dried her hair. The towel around her waist loosened and dropped to the floor.

The staring contest continued.

He lost.

His gaze fell, drawing a line down between her breasts to her stomach. He paused at her navel and looked at a small tattoo of a dove in flight that graced its rim.

"A souvenir from a summer in the Greek Isles," she once told him, "Where everyone on the beaches is naked."

Greece was definitely on his travel agenda.

His eyes followed the outer V of her lace panties then drew together to focus on a damp crease in the fabric. Her perfect trim was just visible through the delicate material.

Matt wanted her now.

As if by mental command she crawled gently across the bed and gave him a soft, open-mouthed kiss; wet and sweet. With her tongue she traced the L-shape of a scar that ran down from the right side of his lower lip.

He quickly moved her hand, gently shook his head, don't; embarrassed by the scar of a childhood operation.

She took her cue.

Matt calmed.

I really like her.

He closed his eyes. Her left hand slid down his chest, over his stomach, into his silk boxer shorts. He felt her lips kiss then smile slightly; she slipped away to pursue her adventurous hand.

It was moments like this that made all the effort at the gym seem worthwhile. He had a well-defined chest and arms. He was able to show a full set of abdominal muscles if he flexed a bit. Sure, he drank, but otherwise tried his best to keep his diet simple and healthy. It was a matter of economics to him.

The less junk he ate, the less time he'd have to spend working it off and more time for this.

He slid a hand over her back and down into her underwear. Evidence of her excitement slipped between his fingers. Cara looked up and smiled a glossy wet smile. The fan blew her soft long hair toward him. The light scent of her perfume took over. He pulled her to him and kissed her, at the same time slipping her panties down her legs. With one finger he launched them into the air. The blade of the fan spun them around a few times then gently propelled them onward. They landed on a pearl-white telephone which rang on cue.

Her nails dug in gently. She was oblivious to the phone.

His mind started to race.

The telephone persisted; so did Cara.

He was losing the battle.

Her hands were warm.

He reached for the telephone.

She pulled his arm back. "It's definitely not someone calling to offer us a better time than we're having now."

The urge was overwhelming. A creature of habit, slave to the telephone, Matt knew the only two people with this number were his brother and his pilot.

He rolled onto his side, she slid off, he grabbed the phone and cradled it between his shoulder and ear. He could feel her, hot and damp, against his side while he listened.

"Are you kidding me? Shit!"

Matt sat up abruptly, sending Cara rolling.

"I'll get back to you...soon!"

He hung up the telephone just short of slamming it down. That was saved for the office. He looked at Cara, whose now-doleful eyes stared at him. If one could be indicted with a look he was staring at it.

"You were right. It's my Dad. But this is serious. There's been an accident. He's in critical condition. Everyone's being called to the hospital."

Matt rose, totally distracted now, and headed for the shower. He looked back. Cara pulled one of the cotton sheets over her. The breeze from the fan pressed it to outline her shape. He wondered if her body was still alive with anticipation.

He cracked open the shower, stepped in; immediately he was lost in thought under the warm spray. He felt a familiar wave of guilt churn in his stomach. The moment was shattered. Every self-doubt he ever had seemed to surface. He knew his father wouldn't approve. In fact he had never approved of him.

Why was he always off doing something his father would scorn, just when important things were happening?

Matt punished himself mentally. There was very little sunlight in his father's shadow. He faced the flow of water. His eyes stung with tears welling beneath his eyelids. His head pounded. Passion subsided.

The sound of the sliding glass doors didn't bring him back, but Cara's hands on his hips did.

"You've been in here forever." She stood with her front curving against his back, resting her head between his shoulder blades.

"Sorry, I guess I was lost there for a while."

"Where'd you go?"

"To hell and back." Matt swallowed hard. "But heaven here on earth is nicer...especially when I've got my own angel."

Cara's hands wrapped around his chest.

"Give me the soap."

He obliged and relaxed a bit when he felt her soapy hands massage his back and buttocks. She wrapped her long arms around him, soaped his chest and stomach. He raised his arms overhead and leaned forward against the wall as the beat of the shower splashed in all directions. His mind was just slightly ahead of her hands and his response just slightly behind, but respond he did when she made her way down to his upper thighs and groin. His mind either cleared or fogged; he was never quite sure which when the brain became unidirectional and eliminated all traces of rationality. The feeling was an old friend, though a friend he mostly welcomed since it had provided many escapes over the years. The absurdity of the moment was lost. Now it seemed very clear what he should do.

Yes, a familiar friend.

He turned. Then, with a single motion bent and hoisted her up around his waist. She reached for the shower rod with one hand and towel rack with the other. Matt pressed her back against the wall. A selfish thought about not having to perform passed through his brain, but passion overtook him when he felt her legs squeeze around his waist. His hands under her bottom. Water splattered against his back. He gazed at her beautiful body while they united and then continued to watch her while she rode effortlessly and rhythmically with him.

Cara's eyes were closed. Her head fell back. She flexed every muscle.

He could feel her quiver. His legs stiffened followed by a deep moaning.

Both panting, muffled only by the sound of falling water.

Her cheeks felt like hard, round melons in his hands. His thumbs cupped the indentations on each side, his fingers buried in their slippery spread.

In a swooping motion she undid her grip and flung her arms around his neck. He felt her teeth sink in; she groaned deeply, wrapping around him with what seemed like every ounce of her strength. It seemed she'd break if he squeezed her any harder. His legs shook when he let loose a deep, almost painful release. Matt sucked Cara's protruding neck muscle, listening to her fading moan, lost in pleasure. They slowed; neither spoke, neither looked. Lost to the world of make–believe; then reality flooded in.

He slid her gently to the floor of the over-sized tub and let a plume of water come over his shoulder onto her head. His legs and arms quivered with fatigue. He had always been amazed at the gymnastics and feats of strength he was able to perform in these circumstances.

Cara sat, knees drawn, head down. Was she sad about something?

She smiled that wicked white smile at him.

"Wow, that was fun…again?"

Matt rolled his eyes and smiled. "You're beautiful. I love you."

The words came so easily from one who rarely felt them.

He slid the doors back and emerged into the marble bathroom. He admired himself casually in the steamy mirror.

I wonder how long I can keep doing this? I wonder whether I'll ever settle down? So many women, so little time.

"I have to go back to the mainland for a few days. I want you to stay here and relax. Actually I think I'll lock you in our room until I get back!"

"Matt!"

"I'm just kidding. You have some fun. Go diving, do some wind surfing, spend some money."

"I like that part."

"I must be crazy, leaving you here in Bermuda with a hotel suite and a credit card."

"You are crazy, remember?"

"Yeah, crazy about you."

Cara stood, closed the door to the shower. The warm water rained on her breasts.

Matt watched through the foggy glass.

I must be crazy.

He walked into the main bedroom then picked up the telephone.

"Hi, Captain, it's me, I've got bad news for us. It's the old man…there's been an accident. Comb your silver hair. Drop off your date if you're with one. We're leaving right away."

Matt paused for a moment when the line went quiet. He hoped that his pilot Captain Robert Hoskins would buy his bravado yet wondered why he even bothered trying with someone who knew him and cared for him and his father's family so well.

He heard an incoming beep on the phone line, went to press the cradle to connect, then paused. Listening to the little inner voice that he usually ignored…this time he hung up the phone.

Matt dressed quickly; loafers, linen pants, polo shirt done up at the collar, a light raw silk sports coat, all set off by a subtle tan that he felt gave him that youthful look he liked. He mussed his hair, now with lingering summer highlights; it fell naturally. He splashed on some cologne, grabbed his garment bag, stepped onto the balcony to grab a parting kiss and a touch of Cara's soft, warm, body.

His armor on, he was composed.

"Remember that thought," cooed Cara, when Matt pressed her close and moaned slightly in her ear.

"I'll see you in a few days, sweetie. I'll keep in touch. Stay safe, okay?" Matt closed his eyes. He kissed the top of her head, breathing in her scent.

The concierge greeted Matt with warmth. A treatment saved for all her favorite guests who appreciated privacy and tipped well.

"I need a lift to the airport, Miss Dugas."

Matt took the small sealed envelope that she delivered with an extended arm and a big smile.

"For you."

He gently reinforced the message, with casual formality that he was not for her. A subtle advance, noticed by her boss, during a hotel tour a few months earlier had nearly cost her job. Matt had covered for her with her boss Steven Merck. She owed him big time, but Matt had only ever smiled when Merck asked; a story not to be shared.

Matt walked into the back office to have a word with Merck while the car was summoned. He informed him that he had to leave for a few days, that his friend Cara would be staying on as his guest, that he wanted her kept secure and happy. Merck smiled at Matt and assured him that all would be in good hands.

He was the premium guest's best friend. He would ensure all that Matt had requested and would also keep him informed of any unusual developments. Matt trusted him with this privileged task and Merck knew it. That would be considered in the generosity that Matt would bestow on the appreciative staff. Merck had earned Matt's trust one time earlier when a not-so-loyal female friend tried to take advantage of a similar situation. That woman found out that Bermuda was not only dangerous at times, but could close its doors very quickly to an unwanted visitor.

Matt let the sea air fill the car. He breathed deeply and sighed. The drive to the airport allowed him a few minutes to catch his thoughts; not an easy task for a man whose mind never stopped racing. Even a single day of relaxation left him feeling like his mental engine had slowed.

The Mercedes taxi navigated South Road with ease. Scooters, bikes and islanders on foot shifted aside to let the speedy white car drive by.

They split the two golf courses and joined Harrington Sound Road. The taxi crossed the Causeway to Kindley Field Road. Matt took a final, long draw of salt air and hoped it wouldn't be long before he returned. He envied the sailors, skiers and boaters frolicking in Grotto Bay.

How simple their lives are.

His car came to a stop on the tarmac just feet from the stairs and open door.

"We all set to fly, Captain?"

"All set boss."

Matt recognized the look from his captain, who he generally call Bob. A look that said thanks for ruining another date.

Matt smiled and raised his eyebrows. He and Bob exchanged knowing looks that only two lost souls can exchange.

The turbines began to whir. Bob sealed the door and took the left hand seat in the cockpit.

Matt plopped into his usual seat. He fingered the waiting beverage. He dialed his brother in Boston. While waiting for the ring, he casually opened the envelope from the hotel and read two words on the vellum. He felt his palms moisten and his chest squeeze a bit tighter... *Susan called*.

- Chapter 3 -

Despite being teased all his life about his Polish ancestry, Wilton (Fuzzy) Polonski was as docile as a lamb, although a massive lamb. He was the son of Wilma and Anton Polonski. He'd been pulling rigs for years, had come across every sort of accident. He'd helped many people and had little to show for it, but that's the way he liked it.

Not knowing exactly what to expect, he opened a storage compartment, shouldered two coils of rope and grabbed a small duffel bag packed for such emergencies. He headed for the guard rail.

Two cars had stopped.

"Grab some flares and mark the highway."

The dog was back, barking excitedly at this man from below.

Fuzzy worked his hands deftly, looped the rope around the rail, heaved the coil down the bank toward the water, grabbed it; then in awkward, grunting strides, he coaxed his six-foot-six, three hundred and fifteen pound frame to the bottom.

He heard the dog barking feverishly. He looked up river toward the barking. There was the car, trapped.

He assessed the situation.

He saw a man visible through the rear window of the car, now rocking back and forth against the boulder in a precarious contest with the flowing river.

His stomach knotted at the thought of the angry river he would have to face.

He found a level area; grabbing up a few large rocks, he tested his arm to see if he could hit the car.

The first one bounced off the roof.

The second smashed through the rear window.

The dog whimpered.

He reached inside his duffel bag and quickly fished for a small three-tined grappling hook.

With his thick fingers, he tied one end of the rope securely through it.

"Stand back there, fella,"

He swung it overhead…

Both stood motionless, watching closely.

After a long, hopeful arc, the steel claw glanced off the edge of the roof and splashed uselessly into the rapids.

Like a fisherman reefing in a net, Fuzzy dragged the hook ashore.

He tried again…again…

He tongued the dripping, salty sweat from his lips.

"Fucking thing…"

Fuzzy looked to the dog for support or forgiveness. He wasn't sure.

He grunted again, swinging toward the target.

Finally, the steel projectile slid over the hood and grabbed firmly onto the bumper.

Fuzzy tied the rope around a sizable tree nearby, then stared at the choppy, swirling water.

His knees quaked with the chill when the water wet his ankles. He began his trip along the rope towards the car.

He felt the heavy buffet of the white water against his body, which carved a swath in the river.

His feet slipped, his throat tightened, his hands ached from squeezing the life line.

He leaned hard into the current to counter its force. He could now see the dashboard through the open window.

He gripped tighter, feeling his feet slipping from beneath him.

He was floating horizontally, gasping for air.

Choking and panicky now, his shirt billowing with frigid water, skin tightening against the cold, jeans and boots tugging at his legs and feet.

I can't swim!

The dog was frantic, rushing up and down the bank, but stayed on shore.

The sensitive balance that had been struck between the car, the rope, the boulder and the rushing water was undone with this sizable human anchor.

Fuzzy struggled to get control.

The car was beginning to slowly rotate and break free of the rock.

The rope stiffened in his hands.

The car spun toward him.

The driver's side window came into his view, a head rolled back and forth while water filled around the body.

The dog barked wildly.

Fuzzy's panic increased.

Is this it? Am I a dead man?

The car was breaking free but paused in complete equilibrium; held by friction from the rock, the rush of water, the rope tension and Fuzzy's drenched and floating mass.

He churned his feet, feeling for the river bottom.

Frantically, looking back and forth, choking time and again.

His ears deafened with pounding blood, veins popped with adrenaline.

Forces undone – nature in charge.

Fuzzy was suffocating.

He held his breath and gripped the rope.

The car released and started to move.

The pounding pulse in his ears scared him.

The waterfall loomed.

One hand was snapped away from the stiffened rope that now vibrated with the strain. The grappling hook lodged behind the bumper was now holding the total force of the car, water and Fuzzy. The rope caught on several other protruding boulders between Fuzzy and the shore, the car's run to the falls had stopped...for now.

His hand ached as he clung to the rope and wavered with the car in this deluge that strained to push him and this other man to certain disaster.

He sputtered and gasped; he moved his other hand back in place and made his way along the remaining length of the rope until he reached the grill of the car.

Panting, he looked around. He braced himself.

Think man. Think.

Through watery eyes he inspected the rope and hook.

Not much time.

He glanced at the shore and realized that the car had moved far enough down river that he was now at the point where he had descended the bank, which was substantially closer to the shore.

He lunged; feet touching the bottom giving him just enough of a grip to make steady progress. Flailing, his arms and legs thrashed against the pressure of the water.

Spent, he fell to his knees, sodden, on the rocky shore.

His guts contracted, hurling water and vomit on the dry, grey rocks.

He grabbed the extra rope and lumbered to the nearest tree.

A quick loop and knot around a tree gave him the purchase he needed for his plan. Back into the frigid water, thrashing toward the flooded vehicle.

He could feel the blood pressure in his face.

He lunged with raw aggression.

Feet just skimming the riverbed, he pressed forward and grabbed the taut rope holding the car. The extra strain drew a high-pitched squeal from the rope and chrome bumper.

He pulled himself to the hood of the car, letting the water pin him against the grill. He quickly stuffed the loose end of the rope through the grill, reached under the bumper to pull the excess around and out.

With fat, numb, fingers he tied the quickest knot he could.

The straining grappling hook released and flew upward, grazing his forehead then blurring his vision with blood.

The car, the man and Fuzzy all bobbed further downstream.

Then the car stopped abruptly, the second rope had taken over. Fuzzy slammed against the grill.

With blurry eyes he looked at the sapling on the shore, seeing it bend with strain.

He rested, choking for air.

The air exploded with a thunderous sound.

Fuzzy was jolted to attention.

A single rotor medi-vac chopper appeared above the falls a few hundred yards away.

He struggled to hold himself in place against the hood of the car.

Frozen but delighted, he waved frantically at the gleaming white chopper.

Even through blurred vision he read a bold red cross and "72X" on the tail.

It hovered.

Fuzzy pleaded silently.

C'mon, baby, c'mon…

The door slid open.

Two overhead booms extended from the top of the opening. He watched a figure in a green flight suit, life vest and helmet being lowered in a sling to just above the roof of the car. Upon contact the rescuer raised their visor.

A woman?

Fuzzy was dazed but acknowledged her thumbs-up sign. He nodded agreement to her request for patience with an open extended palm. She yelled into a small microphone in front of her mouth. Her face was set, her eyes focused. They darted over the situation, gathering as much information as possible. She swayed back and forth in the rotor's air currents.

Fuzzy's ears ached with the deafening sound of the rotors. The helicopter rocked above the water. Then with a downward lurch the woman landed on the roof of the car. Her cable went slack but stayed connected. She was now close enough that Fuzzy could make out her words. She quickly told him the plan and asked for his assistance.

She had pretty eyes, white teeth, reddish lips, with a bit of frothy saliva in the corners of her mouth, and some blemishes on her cheeks.

He agreed and followed her look skyward seeing a stretcher being lowered from the second arm.

His remaining task was to somehow get a soaking wet body out of the car and onto the stretcher. He pulled a hunting knife from his waist sheath and cut a length of rope from a coil his rescuer handed to him. He fastened a loop around his girth, then onto the knotted loop he had made through the grill. Fuzzy let the water take him alongside the car. He unlatched and pulled hard on the door. It didn't budge.

No way. Too much water.

The man would have to come out through the open window.

The stretcher dangled overhead, the wind from the rotors stung his face with water.

The paramedic, perched on all fours on the roof, barked some words into her mic. The stretcher lowered a few feet more until it was floating beside Fuzzy. He cut another piece of rope from the loose end, tied the floating stretcher to the door handle.

Fuzzy grimaced each time his body pounded against the car. He was numb.

With awkward saw strokes from the knife across the seat belt straps, Fuzzy cut the man free to float in the car. Now the current worked to Fuzzy's favor allowing the body to drift into place on the water-soaked stretcher,

Lying on her stomach, the paramedic attempted to help Fuzzy with the limp body. He heard her words.

"Great work...that's it...we can do this."

A warmth of pride momentarily girded him against the cold.

The rope around his waist cut the flesh but the chilled water provided a numbing anesthesia.

Uncontrolled barking echoed from shore while a prone body lay on the stretcher.

Fuzzy tried in vain to get at least one belt across the limp body when a lurch from above ripped the door handle from the car and pulled the stretcher skyward.

Submerged, he gasped for air. Water blurred his vision.

Coughing, scanning the sky, he watched the stretcher and paramedic quickly rise to safety.

Fuzzy pulled himself forward; gripping the shore rope firmly, he slashed the one from his waist.

Now moving hand over hand until he could stand in the waist-deep water.

Chilled from head to toe, exhausted, he stopped to look back at the bobbing car, then up at the hovering helicopter.

The door slid shut, safely encasing the rescued and his savior.

With a single tired wave, he motioned them to get going.

Responding with a quick pivot the chopper dropped its nose.

Moments later it was out of sight.

Only the flooded car and the barking of a Golden Lab remained to attest to the events which had just taken place.

Fuzzy slashed the rope and watched while the car made its way silently down river, over the falls into shallow water below.

Thank you Jesus, that could have been me.

The medi-vac chopper would make the trip from river to hospital in about twelve minutes, flying high over the twisting roads, traffic, countryside and city.

It was hot, noisy and far from steady in the 8'x8' rear cabin.

The lady medic worked frantically to stabilize the victim's body on the stretcher, now locked in place. A neck collar was fastened on.

With her tiny cold hands, she quickly tightened straps across his chest and legs to protect his back. Then a wide band of tape was stretched across his forehead to fasten him to the stretcher. Head and neck were immobilized.

She radioed a preliminary report to the chief trauma surgeon in charge of receiving the case.

She looked up at her partner then cupped a hand near her mouth to be heard.

"We have a heart beat!"

She flashed a smile, then back to the task at hand.

"Pulse and blood pressure low, airway partially blocked with mucous, breathing weak but adequate."

She suctioned his throat, slid an elliptically shaped tube deep down into his neck to immediately clear and support his airway, allowing an unrestricted flow of precious air to his lungs. With a flexible rubber pouch attached, she assisted the first few breaths.

A heart and blood pressure monitor were attached. A warm intravenous solution now dripped into the pale, chilled arm.

Finally, she swaddled his body with pre-warmed blankets. The heat on her hands felt good.

Her stomach was tight with a woozy claustrophobic feeling in the now 90 degree cabin. She felt the urge to strip the sweat-drenched, uncomfortably tight flight suit.

Her hair was wet, matted, and hung down her face.

Forcing calm and focus she breathed deeply, remaining huddled over the precious cargo.

She watched her partner medic extract a soggy wallet from the patient's pants and hand it forward to the pilot who flipped it open to inspect for ID.

They both waited and listened.

"Medic control this is 72X, the victim is Mr. Peter Douglas. Repeat the victim is Mr. Peter Douglas."

- Chapter 4 -

A hand came in from his left side. The appearance of the pink memo slip did not disturb Brian Douglas as much as the shaking hand that was holding it.

Brian looked across the long, polished, board room table at the two executives from Kyoto Corporation of Japan.

A smile parted his lips.

He was about to award their firm a one-billion-dollar, multi-year contract to manufacture electronic equipment for his company.

He was calm, holding the slip in his lap below the table.

Heat radiated from Marjorie's body and, more oddly, her hand was on his shoulder.

Brian glanced down, then imperceptibly stiffened when he read the two words on the note: YOUR FATHER!

His mind raced across early efforts, working with his father, to significantly expand the company from a local paging and cable television business to a multi-national media and telecommunications giant. Now, Chairman and Chief Executive Officer of the Douglas Corporation, this senior son had big shoes to fill and family relations, strained by the transition, to heal.

Marjorie's hand slipped off when Brian abruptly stood.

She had rarely touched him; a thought that registered somewhere deep in his racing mind.

The men from Kyoto also jumped up quickly, not really knowing what was happening.

" Sorry, ah sorry, very sorry. I must leave at once. Don't worry, we will finish this – promise."

They bowed politely when the translator delivered the message.

Brian's back disappeared through the boardroom doors.

Brian saw Marjorie's eyes well with tears when she explained that the hospital had called to say that his father had been in an accident and flown to the trauma center. Details were sketchy. She apologized for her lack of information. Brian's car was waiting downstairs. He paused to hug her, a moment longer than casual.

"Things will be fine. Promise," Marjorie comforted.

"Better cancel today's stuff…"

He squinted, eyes now stinging.

"…and tomorrow."

"I'll call the moment I have some news…Marj, please give my apologies…" he thumbed toward the boardroom, "… to the boys. Tell them I'll be in touch."

They both managed a smile.

– Chapter 5 –

Fresh fingers of ocean air on her legs gave her dreams a sensual theme when the salty breeze fluttered the linen dress. The daily pool side nap was a daily routine for Mrs. Marion Douglas. The beach home, with pool, was just one of the assets she now enjoyed since her painful divorce from Peter Douglas. Once divorced she had moved to get away from her previous high profile life in the big city, yet her anonymity didn't last long in West Palm Beach Florida. She was amazed how quickly she had become popular in the social circles of her new home town.

After many months of persuasion she had convinced her recently widowed mother to make the pilgrimage from the family potato farm in Idaho to sunny Florida. At eighty-four, Emily still played a mean game of gin rummy. She also waltzed better than most.

Marion enjoyed their beach strolls in the morning, afternoons by the pool, evenings off at one social event or another. Her mother's vision was fading but her views and values were stronger than ever. Marion looked up to mother, who had guided her well. Today her company helped keep her away from the habits to which lonely divorcees can easily fall prey.

Her small farm upbringing, learning to run a home, combined with active study and extracurricular activities had reinforced the notion she tried to live by: one gets out of life as much as one puts into it.

In her senior year of high school, with a straight 'A' report, she accepted a trip to Boston to meet with the admissions committee of a prestigious East Coast girls' school called the Hélène Marie Women's College. Her family couldn't afford the tuition, but her scholastic abilities had made her eligible for scholarship funding. Marion had never been out of Idaho and as with many trips in life; this one would have a profound impact on hers.

Marion made the trip to the College with several other girls. Faculty interviews, school tours and sightseeing around campus and area were all on the agenda.

The formalities ended on Friday when the visiting co-eds had been invited to attend the Spring Dinner Dance that evening.

Marion felt out of place and innocent with the two out-of-state seniors she was bunking with, though these moneyed two seemed to find her innocence seductive.

She did let them outfit her from their ample closets while listening to promises of having the time of her life. The silk and other fabrics pressed next to her tanned skin started to convince her that these older two may know some things she didn't.

She blushed.

The sight in the mirror of her bare cleavage was totally unexpected.

Although with fair hair tumbling in curls around her firm shoulders, framing her perfect skin, she had never felt or looked so beautiful.

"All of us will be dressed like that."

Their promise, albeit from knowing smiles, convinced her it would be alright – this time.

"Besides, how else will you catch a man?"

Those last few words jolted Marion's thoughts.

Boys? In an all girls school?

She felt her skin moisten. A flush heated her body. Her knees quaked ever so slightly.

Marion nibbled carefully on some unknown delicacy.

She gazed across the ballroom filled with one hundred and fifty young women dressed in every color of the rainbow.

She giggled.

The chatter in the room was pulsating.

She sipped her single glass allotment of red wine.

They were told it was to help their digestion and initiate them in the ways of formal functions.

It took only minutes for a full-blown black market to strike up once the precious liquid had been served. Money, faux jewelry, IOUs, promises of pay-back were immediately exchanged for the wine of the less inclined.

It seemed odd to her that the most obviously shrewd in business quickly became the most intoxicated making it seem like they were almost encouraging this sort of commerce.

Marion could see that her escorts were slated for great business success.

She felt privileged and exclusive by the attention that the male waiters surrounding tables and senior school staff gave her table.

The first glass of red wine warmed her all over. The second made her lips numb and she felt herself smiling an unusually broad, happy smile.

Her dinner conversation flowed, interspersed with waves of giggling.

She could feel the heat of her two hosts; each on one side, legs pressed against her, chatting, giggling and reaching across.

It all seemed familiar and comfortable to her.

Marion kept them guessing when they tried, without luck, to embarrass her with questions and teasing about her body, boys, sexual experience or lack thereof.

Marion forced herself to keep sitting proper despite the warm buzz and desire to slouch.

She liked these two young women and the attention.

Concentration on dessert and her third glass of wine was broken by the squeal of a poorly adjusted microphone.

"Ladies, it is now time to move to the ballroom for the evening dance. The gentlemen from the Notre Dame School will be arriving shortly."

The room echoed loudly with chatter and giggles.

"May I remind you that you are all Hélène Marie ladies," the voice continued, "…virtue once lost can never be regained. Our pride and reputation are built upon the decorum with which you present yourselves to the world at large, including the gentlemen from Notre Dame."

"Ladies, enjoy your evening. Remember, the regular eleven p.m. curfew has been extended to midnight at which time all of you are expected in your dorms for bed check."

At that last comment Marion joined the women en route to the ballroom.

She watched them while they preened, giggled, smoothed dresses, adjusted body parts and did their best to proceed in an orderly fashion.

She also steadied herself against the effects of her first alcohol experience.

The broad smile remained.

Marion joined a row at precisely seven o'clock when the Hélène Marie ladies were instructed to create two lines down the middle of the ballroom facing each other.

The band struck up.

Grand doors to the ballroom swung open.

One hundred and fifty jacketed and tied young men made their way down the middle of the lines.

Marion's eyes darted at these handsome, impeccably dressed boys, trying to get a glimpse at each one.

These were not farm boys.

Her skin moistened again and her face reddened when the men strolled by the young women. Marion had never seen so many handsome men and she wondered whether they been hand-picked for the occasion.

A mixture of cologne, cigarettes and liquor permeated the air.

She stood straight.

The gentlemen stopped abruptly. Each extended a hand to introduce himself to the girl in front of him.

The band changed tempo.

She felt his hand squeeze hers.

She was dancing.

Marion was more overwhelmed by the organization of it all than with the first gentleman that she was dancing with.

When he turned her, Marion caught the gaze of a different young man who was staring past his dance partner at her.

She lowered her eyes and heard her mother's voice in her mind.

Now don't be bold.

She looked up anyway to stare straight into the eyes of yet another handsome young man.

"Where are you from?"

"Pardon? Oh um sorry – pardon me – what did you say?"

The music stopped for a brief second, then started.

Another hand was in hers. The first boy was gone.

The second boy spun Marion in a different direction.

A new hand…another…another.

She realized that no one was left standing alone the way she had sometimes been back home.

Several men asked if they could remain for a second dance.

Marion caught on quickly to the laws of supply and demand.

It seemed every switch was to be done with the party to the right when the music stopped, thus the object was to position yourself near someone who you fancied a dance. Poor positioning could merely be overcome by declining a switch.

Marion liked the attention.

Where was that first boy?

Marion declined numerous invitations to sneak one of the many refreshments or other temptations that these boys offered.

"My name is Peter Douglas. Would you like to dance?"

Like before, when she first spotted him, her eyes met his.

Marion smiled.

She took the offered hand.

It was firm.

Peter asked if she would decline a switch.

She relaxed.

The second time she declined without being prompted.

She felt comfortable in the arms of this boy named Peter.

She held her own in the easy conversation between them.

"I'll be right back." Peter held her hands in his. "Next dance when I return, okay?"

She smiled slyly at him. "If I'm still available."

Marion accepted the next offered dance.

He was no Peter Douglas but, in his absence, she wasn't about to wait either. So on she danced with new partners enjoying her new found popularity.

"May I?"

Marion turned then raised her eyebrows inquisitively at her dance partner who abruptly acknowledged Peter's return.

He courteously shook her hand then passed it to Peter.

"By the way, my name is Carl, Carl Nathan. I hope we can dance again."

Marion smiled uncomfortably. Carl eyed Peter steadily, then backed away.

"What did you do, pay him?"

"No, but I would if I had to."

Marion blushed when he leaned in.

Struck by the smell of cigarettes and alcohol, she stepped back.

She now understood why so many people were departing the building for fresh air.

"Sorry, everyone's doing it."

"You struck me like more of a shepherd than a sheep."

"You're right. I'm sorry okay?"

They danced and chatted.

Marion recounted her years growing up on the farm while Peter responded with stories of life on the bustling Atlantic coast.

She felt they seemed worlds apart, yet a comfortable bond had been made.

"I leave for Idaho in the morning. Although if I get the scholarship…"

She felt his lips press gently against her neck.

"…we could write." She shivered now.

He leaned back slightly.

She stared into his eyes then closed hers.

His mouth was wet and warm.

Girls' voices in each ear shocked her back to reality.

Her two roommates with their two male friends accosted her.

The four reeked of booze and smoke.

They hatched a plan about sneaking onto the bus for a ride over to Notre Dame. Marion's hand felt Peter's squeeze.

He caught her eye.

Marion picked up on his cue and encouraged the girls to keep moving. "Great idea. We'll meet you all outside in ten minutes."

Peter kept her hand in his. "I have no intention of trying to smuggle you on that bus. Besides, there's a guy on each bus to stop that anyway."

"And if he wasn't there?" She looked at Peter.

"Who knows?"

She smiled inwardly. "Yes, who knows."

Nice job girl.

She and Peter squinted suddenly.

Last song. Lights on.

Couples locked in tight embraces or other compromising positions quickly righted themselves. Those who had not been matched marched toward the grand doors.

Peter and Marion lingered.

His hand squeezed hers. "Someone has to be last."

She liked the feeling.

The two were met with a bustling scene in the foyer of the school.

It was bursting with energy.

Pairs said goodnight. Friends exchanged versions of evening stories.

Kisses goodbye. Overheard promises of calls or letters.

Marion agreed to walk Peter to his bus after a bit of convincing.

The cool evening air dizzied her.

She took his arm, then pressed close for the short walk. She paused.

This time, when she saw Peter look into her eyes and move toward her, there was no interruption.

The warmth of his wet lips touched hers.

She felt like the earth had left her feet.

Her body temperature soared. She melted in his arms and mouth. The pulse in her ears blocked out all sounds when the feel of Peter's strong grip surrounded her. She could feel every point of contact against his body including what she knew was his full arousal against her upper thigh.

For an instant she dreamed of a crowd roaring.

Flustered, she realized that the sounds were not a dream. Cheering and cat-calling actually coming from behind her.

The last pair to exit the school were now the object of attention for three buses of young men.

Marion, bidding Peter a quick farewell, made a bee-line for the steps and up toward the big doors of the building. She didn't look back.

"I'll write," he called.

Smiling, she hoped he would.

Peter lingered, letting the attention subside before heading to the first bus in the line of three. It was the farthest away; hopefully the least interested in his activities.

Peter rounded the front of the bus, nearly colliding with two of his classmates; one emptying the contents of his stomach, the other watering the front bumper.

He steered wide. Neither noticed.

When he spotted the bus driver and chaperon standing near the rear having a pre-boarding cigarette he relaxed, no trouble tonight.

He glanced at a number of young men in the bushes responding to various calls of nature.

Peter reflected on Marion's brief lesson about sheep and shepherds.

He plopped down beside his roommate Edward who had saved a seat near the front for him.

Howls and whistles were targeted toward him.

He felt his cheeks redden. The darkness of the bus made for good cover.

The bus rocked with the horse-play of the chaps in the back that he could see in the mirror.

His nose flared with the smell of cigarette smoke drifting forward. His stomach knotted at the sound of someone vomiting out of a side window.

He felt an eerie sense, a heighted awareness of the activities going on around him.

It felt good to be Peter Douglas.

Sheep and shepherds. He would have to remember that one.

Definitely a shepherd, Marion. Definitely a shepherd.

"How was it?"

Peter was oblivious, trying to lock every tiny detail into his brain for later recall.

Her smell...the body heat...the crinkle of her dress...her breasts...the taste of her lips.

"Come in Peter, do you read? Well, how did it go?"

"How'd what go?"

Peter shoved Edward's pointed elbow out of his ribs.

"C'mon, you were with her all night. I saw that action on the lawn. So did half the school."

"That wasn't action, asshole. Marion's a nice girl. She's not like that. I just kissed her goodnight. She's leaving tomorrow."

"Ooh, a little touchy are we?"

"You wouldn't understand. You wouldn't know romance if it fell on you. When's the last time you kissed a girl ... or should I say the first time?"

The two went silent.

Edward Smarton Barkley turned away to stare out the window.

"Hey, sorry, but you were buggin' me. I like her, okay?"

Peter returned the elbow jab to the ribs.

For friends, he and Edward couldn't have been more dissimilar. When Peter arrived at his appointed dormitory room two years earlier, he was surprised to see that his roommate, Edward S. Barkley, had already settled in.

He was even more surprised that, even though he was second on the scene, all the best drawers, closet and bed were still unclaimed.

He knew that many fist-fights had been wagered and friendships broken over the golden rule of dormitory life: first come, first served.

Peter had arrived early on the day of check-in.

Edward was absent, so Peter settled himself in, filling the prime spaces with his belongings.

He noticed that Edward had brought only the basics.

Peter had everything he needed to customize his domain for the school year.

An hour later this block-walled room was his home.

The first flush gave him a sense of ownership. The pin-up poster on the back side of the door gave him a sense of masculinity.

He was ready to stake out and defend his turf even if it meant sharing the showers down the hall with nineteen other dorm-mates.

The sound of cutlery and talk was loud when Peter approached the dining hall.

He scanned for familiar faces. No one he recognized.

A hundred or so clean-cut boys. All similar, yet all different. All trying to fit in, somehow, to the unwritten hierarchy of college life.

Though he was a sophomore, this was Peter's first year at the Notre Dame School. He had spent his freshman year at a different school that was not to his liking. After much coaxing, he'd convinced his parents to get him transferred.

He loaded his plate with the evening meal, added two glasses of milk to his tray and a generous serving of chocolate cake. His mouth watered with hunger.

He ambled through the tables to one with some empty seats.

He scanned the others at the table.

There was a leader in every crowd, it seemed; even when the crowd was only two, there was always someone in charge. Normally that was Peter, but for now he accepted the nod of approval from the young man who stared at him from across the table.

Peter listened, eating his chocolate cake first.

"Did you see the cripple?"

"Ya, he's got one shoe the size of a football."

"He's got a cane, too."

"No! Where?"

"Over there, in the corner by himself. He's been over there since we got here."

"Maybe he's deaf and dumb too."

The boys chuckled.

Peter smirked, but tried to focus on his food.

He gazed across the room to the fellow eating alone at a table in the corner. He looked normal enough. He wasn't quite as white as Peter and his table-mates. He dressed a little poorer, but he looked okay.

"You should see him walk. He kind of limps and leans on his cane."

"He had to make four trips to the food line to get all his stuff to the table."

A bread roll arced high over Peter's head and bounced off the lone diner's table.

"Nice one Zalkow."

The skinny little fellow smiled proudly when the room erupted in laughter.

Peter chuckled, but he didn't find it funny.

The boy in the corner never looked up. His back was turned slightly more to the crowd. He ate in silence.

A few more projectiles landed near him.

Suddenly all was quiet.

Eyes focused on the main door at the tall, hefty, man who was staring at them.

"I am Richard Pringle. Unless I get a call from an NFL team this Fall. I will be your best friend if you need one or your toughest coach…if you need one."

He made the customary announcements about friendship, studying, co-operation, proper meals and hot water.

He had a good sense of humor. He joked about sneaking in or out of the building, with or without a girl. That brought a loud round of hoots, cat calls and blushes from the group. He promoted sports and studying and spoke of the fun and hard work he'd been through on this campus himself. He finished by telling everyone that his door was open 24 hours a day, if there was anything they wanted or needed to talk about.

Peter noticed that the room was silent with respect.

Aah…another shepherd.

Normally lights were out at ten, but tonight Richard threw in a one-hour extension as a welcome gift.

Peter and his new buddies made a full tour of the campus along with many other small packs of adventurous young men. The various groups exchanged information when they re-grouped and talked about neat buildings or alleyways or a window to peek in at a neighboring house.

Across the river was the Hélène Marie College. It was a place much talked about by all the boys. The place of legendary stories which Peter doubted had any truth to them.

Peter's group had the big scoop of the evening when they came across a parked car with two amorous couples in it.

Music from the radio, giggles, moans and foggy windows were everything the boys needed to put together a fantastic story. The four crouched in silence behind a hedge, straining to see something to support their vivid fantasies.

Peter wondered if the others had erections too.

The toll of a church bell startled them into leaving; some knew they would now miss the best part, other weren't yet sure what that was.

Each of the boys backed away from the hedge and walked a bit farther apart than usual. Pocketed hands and other body language confirmed Peter's surmise. They ran in silence back to Appleton House where they were greeted by Richard tapping his watch and muttering something about it being fast. None spoke to him. They had just gotten their first break.

All was quiet when he made his way down the hall. Only the night lights were on, which let the bulb of any room light blaze a signal under the door onto the hall floor. Peter realized then how the don always seemed to know who was still up without opening the doors.

He smiled to himself. Life's little secrets.

There was no beacon from under his door so he entered quietly, trying not to disturb his anonymous roommate.

Enough light from the street streamed in for Peter to make out the far side of the room. He could hear the breathing of someone sleeping so he quietly shut the door.

The introduction could wait until morning.

Three quiet steps into the room his ankle and foot made contact with something firm yet light. There was a second of silence.

Then the unmistakable sound of a cane landing on the floor.

He froze, flashed back to the cafeteria, and hoped that Edward would not awaken.

Perspiration formed on his brow. Seconds passed. Edward mumbled, rolled over, and settled back into a rhythmic saw.

Peter inched his way to the far side of the room.

He skipped his bathroom duties, slipped out of his shoes and trousers, eased into bed.

Peter's first year at the Notre Dame School was off to a very interesting start.

Giggling girls still lingered near the college doors, exchanging stories of the evening.

The chaperones milled about, trying to disperse them all to their rooms.

Marion passed quickly through the foyer. She relaxed hearing the door close behind her, drowning out the noise of the other girls. The air was warm and damp. The back garden was empty. It reminded her of summer evenings on the farm when she would go for long walks at night and think about her future. Now she walked and contemplated the present. The muffled sound of the buses departing from the front of the school disturbed the quiet thoughts.

He's on one of those buses. Good night.

Ambling along the stone path through the gardens, she smiled when the ducks and crickets seemed to greet her. She admired the maze of manicured bushes, replaying the entire evening again and again while she sat on one of the stone benches, wishing she had said this, or not acted like that, wondering if Peter felt any of what she did or if she'd ever see him again.

She put her hands to her face; breathed deeply…she could smell him.

She stood to continue her walk, smoothed her gown, and adjusted the low bodice. Removing several hair pins she ran her hands through her hair, looking up at the brilliant display of stars overhead. Her skin felt cool, moist, goose bumps ran up her legs.

Her chest tightened, nipples reacting to the chilled air and her warm thoughts. She ran her hands from the back of her neck down over her shoulders and her breasts, pausing, then firmly squeezing through the satin material with her thumb and forefinger. She let her hands slide down to her stomach, over her hips and thighs.

Her body was electric.

She thought of Peter pressing firmly against her while they danced and when they kissed.

The current increased. She could feel a blush rise to her face.

Marion bent her head, following her hands the length of her legs to her ankles.

Her body shivered.

Blood rushed to her face.

With a long breath she stood, throwing her hair back gazing again at the bright sky. She felt her face tighten when a broad smile spread across it.

She shuddered momentarily, regained herself, then started the stroll back to the college dorm.

At the entrance, Marion was met by a uniformed night-security man who stared out at her. He peered at her for some moments before his ring of keys jangled. He retracted the dead bolt and eased the door open a foot.

"You almost spent the night out there, young lady."

The hallway was dark save for reflected moonlight.

His weathered face peered at her through rheumy eyes. A distinct smell of alcohol permeated the air.

"You're looking very pretty tonight, my dear."

Her pulse raced. She placed a hand over her chest.

"Are you going to let me in?"

"How about a little stroll in the garden, my sweet thing?"

"How about you open that door right now before I scream, you creep?"

"Oh, you won't do that. You're out past curfew. You'd be expelled. No one would believe you. I know your type."

Had he been watching her?

Her stomach tightened, her system now fully adrenalized. One hand on her chest, one hand on the door, she pulled.

"Let me in. Let me in."

"How about one little kiss? An admission charge."

"Let me in or I'll scream, I swear it. I'll scream"

"You're a feisty one aren't you?"

She tugged hard on the door, throwing the guard forward off balance. She realized this advantage and pushed back against the door. The guard rocked back. She saw surprise in his face.

She was strong.

With a final pull toward her, the door swung open, bringing the guard with it.

A shove to the right and he swayed sideways enough for Marion to get by.

"Stop. Don't touch me."

She grabbed his arm and threw it aside. A throaty laugh was the last sound she heard before bursting into the hall and running squarely into the path of an oncoming female chaperone.

"Oh my Goodness. I am so sorry"

"My Lord child, what are you doing?"

Marion smoothed her ruffled dress and hair. A dead bolt around the corner snapped into place.

"Who is that? Seymour?"

Marion spun around to stare directly at Seymour.

He was out of breath. His cap was skewed to one side.

She spun back, "Madame I was…"

Seymour quickly interrupted, "I just saved this young one from the night goblins. She was locked out in the garden, M'ame."

Marion faced this woman, who looked inquiringly at her through pouched, watery eyes. Her gray hair was pulled high up on her head. She wore a white blouse, buttoned to the neck, which was covered by an evening sweater. Her straight beige skirt went well below the calves, bi-focal glasses hung from her neck on a beaded gold chain. Her sagging jowls vibrated when she spoke.

"You are our guest here, young lady. Whatever are you doing up this late? Don't you know that curfew was an hour ago? Carry on, Seymour. Thank you."

"But I was…"

"Young girls like you should stay away from men like Seymour. He gets some strange ideas late at night. Now go to bed."

Marion turned. Seymour was ambling down the hall.

"I just wanted…"

"Go."

Angry and embarrassed now, Marion turned toward the dorm and walked briskly away.

The stodgy chaperone walked in Seymour's direction.

Her room was the last door on the right at the end of a long dark hall. The left-hand side of the building backed onto the garden where she had walked. The right side faced the front of the school, looked out over the lane way and the wooded front entrance. Along the hall there were two lounges whose windows let moonlight stream in.

She was startled when her shadow appeared on the wall to her left. It disappeared when she passed the lounge and made her way further down the hall. The next lounge allowed another bath of moonlight to capture her image on the wall.

She stopped.

She viewed her outline.

Head perched on a slender upper body, curves of her chest giving way to a flat tummy, the billowing of her dress.

Marion swayed back and forth, watching her shadow move in response. She imagined how she must appear to others, wondered if they found her attractive.

She feigned a dance with Peter shadowed on the wall.

At the click of a door far at the end of the hall, she hastened out of the light toward her room. She stopped in the darkness and pressed against the wall to observe the source of the sound.

They moved quietly.

They won't come this far; probably girls heading to the toilets.

Marion relaxed, then stiffened, when the two were caught in the moonlight of the first lounge.

She was wide-eyed.

A young woman, naked except for her panties, was escorting a disheveled boy into the first lounge.

They tiptoed into the lounge out of Marion's view.

Her pulse quickened, breath shortened.

That charged, excited feeling was back.

She eased her way along the wall toward the lounge.

Her throat was tight, body damp again.

By the time she was at the edge where the wall met the glass of the lounge she could clearly hear the sounds being made by the young man and woman. It was not a familiar or single sound, but rather a chorus of breaths with moans and sighs, a few indiscernible words. The sound of kissing was very distinct.

She wanted, in the worst way, to peer around the corner and witness exactly what was happening. She felt a funny combination of guilt and curiosity. Her imagination was running wild.

Two shadows on the wall in front of her gave her a start. The pair must have been sitting down or on the floor because now both were in plain view, albeit projected on the wall. She watched carefully, determining quickly who was who.

The boy seemed to be aggressively fondling the girl who made no resistance. They kissed, then wrapped their arms around each other, only to separate and fondle some more. The girl actively caressed him.

Marion felt dizzy, amazed at the shadowy display of passion.

The boy bent down removing the girl's underwear. Then he quickly undressed.

He pulled his shirt over his head. She undid his pants. He kicked off his shoes and his trousers dropped to the floor. He then danced on one foot while awkwardly pulling them off.

She held back a wide smile at this funny, odd scene.

Marion could sense the heat in the air and within herself.

She could periodically see the outline of the girl's breasts and round buttocks when she stood sideways to the moonlight that reflected them on the wall.

She found herself staring, almost in horror, when she realized that she was staring at the shadow of an erect penis. The boy and girl stood facing each other, hands on each other's shoulders. A perfect outline was sculpted against the wall.

Marion followed the young woman's curves starting at her head. She was as tall as the boy. She drew a visual line along the contours of her face, onto her chest. She captured the image of the girl's round, pointed breasts. Her eyes carried on down past her stomach, over her pelvis, down her legs to the floor. She then drew a similar line up the young man's legs to his groin. The portrait of his arousal was imposing. She wondered if that was for real or an illusion of some sort caused by the reflected light.

Her pelvic muscles tightened. All of that inside?

The visual tracing was interrupted when the pair embraced again, then separated. A shadowy hand from the young woman reached out, gripped, then commenced rapid movements.

Marion was mesmerized.

He kept his hands on her shoulders; let his head roll back like a wolf howling at the moon.

Another click down the hall jolted Marion. She held her breath and stayed pressed flat against the wall. A flood of light illuminated the end of the hallway. The blue peaked cap of Seymour protruded. His head twisted right then left, paused, then retreated back to where it had come from.

Marion sighed.

These two, no, these three could be caught in the act.

The adventure had overwhelmed any sense of fear.

It was suddenly crystal clear that passion outweighed any sense of reason one might possess at that instant.

All those love stories studied in English literature class were suddenly relevant.

The shadows continued their dance. Like so many performances that intensified when the act played out, these actors too were increasing their motion and intensity.

He stood with his body fully extended, chest pushed out and head rolled back. She moved closer, her rapid arm movements a blur on the wall. His throaty groans increased in rhythm and intensity. It was getting so loud Marion felt sure someone would hear, but like a movie house horror show, although she didn't want to watch the scary parts, she did want to see how it ended.

A profound sense of curiosity kept her eyes glued to the screen. The howl from the wolf seemed to reach a crescendo, the female shadow dropped to her knees. Marion covered a gasp. The girl's body moved in rhythm with his for a few seconds.

Then both froze.

He stood tall, head rolled back looking up; his hands on her shoulders.

She knelt still.

A few painful moans from the boy echoed in Marion's pounding ears... then subsided.

Marion swallowed hard, took a deep breath and looked at the floor. She could feel the pounding beat of her heart from head to toe.

Silence filled the hall.

The one shadow stood and embraced the other.

The boy quickly donned his clothes.

The girl stood naked, watching.

He danced on one foot, trying to put his shoes on without success, then pulled his shirt back over his head.

Now collected…a short pause… then out the window, he was gone.

She watched the naked girl, with underwear in hand, run from the lounge, feet quietly padding the carpeted floor. Her white bottom jiggled when she ran.

Marion, now alone. The movie was done.

It all seemed humorous in an odd way.

She leaned against the wall, stared where the two had danced minutes earlier. A sense of wonder overcame her.

She gingerly made her way into the lounge.

Sniffing the primal smell in the air, she went to the open window to witness the place of exit.

He was gone but where did he go?

Marion faced the wall, then walked forward until her projected size was exact.

She stood in the precise spot where the performance had taken place then paused. The room was vacant and quiet.

Leaning back, she pushed her fingers through her hair then locked her hands behind her head. She extended herself onto tip toes and rolled her head to one side to observe her profile on the wall. She imagined the other two shadows dancing around her.

She closed her eyes, imagining herself and Peter performing on a wall sometime in the future.

When she opened her eyes the moon had slipped behind a cloud and bade the shadows goodnight. Marion tiptoed quietly to the end of the hall. She made a stealthy entrance into her room closing the door silently behind her. She did not want to risk awakening her two friends who would want her to explain her whereabouts for the past several hours.

At the end of the room was a tall, curtained window. Two bunk beds and two study desks lined one wall. A full-length mirror, a studio bed, a coffee table, a pedestal sink and closets occupied the other. The walls were white but the tapered beam of light coming past the curtain left the room mostly black.

When Marion made her way toward the window her feet rustled against something on the floor. She felt the velvet of one of the girl's dresses.

Marion slipped off her shoes to avoid the sound of heels on the wooden floor. Her bare feet crushed a second dress when she stepped.

Her eyes adjusted to the light.

Shoes, stockings, slips, bras and panties carpeted the floor.

She was relieved to see the bulge of a sleeping woman in the lower bunk.

Two dresses meant that neither girl had ventured back to Notre Dame.

Marion opened the curtain, allowing moonlight to bath her body. She stuck her head out into the evening air, breathing in the pine scent of the treed school grounds.

She turned and faced herself in the long mirror.

Standing barefoot, she admired her perfectly formed dress. The bell of the lower half was cinched at the waist and rose tightly up her abdomen. The moon highlighted only one side of her so she turned and faced the window to illuminate a full front view. No longer a shadow, she admired the mirrored image of her breasts pushed high by the garment. She brushed her hair with her fingers, letting it fall onto her shoulders.

She liked what she saw and realized that others did too.

Her dress was buttoned up the front with twenty small buttons.

Marion undid the first few. Without their support her bosom overwhelmed the dress and the pattern of her brassiere was clearly visible. She watched sideways in the mirror while she continued to release the buttons. She imagined a time when a handsome husband like Peter would do this for her. Once the dress was unbuttoned to the waist she slipped it off her shoulders then let it slide to the floor. The smooth material rustled softly as it piled around her feet. She delicately stepped out, moving it to one side.

She peered at herself, eased her slip down her legs and over her feet. She had declined the earlier offer of nylons and a garter belt, preferring to have her legs free to feel the air under her dress, which she pointed out, was long enough that no one would notice

Now she stood bathed in moonlight in only underwear and her bra.

She felt beautiful.

She *was* beautiful.

Her long muscular legs matched a firm set of shoulders and well defined arms. She recalled being called boyish, but Marion did not envy the milky, fleshy bodies of most girls her age.

She reached behind her back and undid her bra.

Her breasts barely moved.

She bent slowly, slipping out of her underwear to stand naked in the moonlight, cool breeze passing over her tightening skin.

Marion painted beautiful photographs in her mind, tingling from head to toe.

She stood frozen like a statue.

Listening to the breathing from the bunk bed behind, realizing her nervousness, she calmed.

They're sound asleep.

She stood naked, still motionless, feeling newly confident, unlike a few hours earlier.

There was something different about the breath of the sleeper behind her. She listened intently, still frozen like a nude statue in the moonlight. It took her a few moments to realize that there were two different breathing noises coming from the lower bunk.

Marion quietly drew the curtain back the rest of the way to let more moonlight beam into the room.

The lower bunk was definitely occupied. The upper one looked undisturbed.

What else could this night possibly present?

She knelt beside them, listening to the sound of slow, thick breathing.

The room was bright.

She stared at the face of the girl sleeping closest to her. Thick wavy hair, undone, now tumbled over her face and bare shoulder.

Marion listened to every breath.

She gently lifted the upper edge of the sheet and gradually drew it back until it was at the bottom of the bed.

The girls lay peacefully, both on their sides.

One cuddled up behind the other, arm wrapped around her partner. Their legs were perfectly meshed, bent at the knees.

Marion was neither surprised nor offended at the sight. Instead she observed the beauty in this picture of innocence and serenity.

She didn't dwell on how or why they ended up there together.

A few minutes passed.

Marion quietly drew the sheet back over her friends.

After one last gaze at the moon, a last moment of evening breeze, her reflection in the mirror, she drew the curtain.

She had always worn bedclothes at night, but tonight the thought never crossed her mind. She slipped between the cool, pressed sheets of the roll out.

Her body shivered.

She could feel the contact of the cotton at every point that it touched her.

Her mind retraced this most unusual evening.

She thought of her two friends lying naked together just a few feet away.

Her hands found their way over the most familiar and sensitive parts of her body the way they had done so many late nights in Idaho.

Taut, mesmerized by the intensity, Marion held her breath for what seemed like minutes.

The waves subsided.

She eased the air from her lungs.

In a dizzy flight of mind and body, she slipped into a deep sleep.

- Chapter 6 -

The medivac helicopter pilot saw the tiny spots of faces that watched, without consideration, of the essential nature of his machine. He noticed the usual collection of faces peering out from their offices and apartments. He wondered about them and their thoughts about him.

Did they think, that tomorrow, it could be their lives or the lives of people they loved that he was rushing to a hospital for life saving care?

If they did, would they burden the system with noise complaints?

He steered 72X confidently around the perimeter of the downtown high-rises. Hopefully they looked on with admiration and would commend him on his efforts, if they had the chance.

He thought of the wife he had lost while he was overseas doing battle for his country.

From his glass and metal capsule, cocooned by instruments, he descended toward the roof of the hospital. The wind from the spinning blades buffeted the white coats of the awaiting medical team. Another delivery, executed with speed and efficiency.

What are those Doctors doing on the roof? That's breaking some rules.

He thought of lifting bodies from every type of disaster imaginable. Always waiting for his crew to give him the signal that all was secure for transport.

From his perspective, a hundred feet or more above the scene, it always looked familiar: faces torn with anguish staring up at him like he and his craft were an apparition of God himself.

This delivery was simple.

One tour of duty in the Air Force and four years flying for the U.S. Drug Enforcement Agency in and around Central America made life in the USA flying a medi-vac chopper seem like child's play.

He spotted two news helicopters hovering in front of him.

Outta my way guys.

He looked at several radio-toting, blue-suited constables, four men in green and the three in white coats all straining to watch his descent.

A stiff breeze buffeted his machine when it broke across the edge of the building and became turbulent. The striped wind-sock stood straight out, indicating a wind speed of at least 15 knots.

The five-ton flying machine pitched and yawed, yet its pilot eased it gently onto the painted white H.

The bump of contact with solid ground felt good.

Well done.

The flying was easy. Most of the risks lay in the invisible space two hundred feet above the surface when taking off or landing. A sense of safety lay in either seeing the ground well below him or feeling solid contact.

"This is 72Xray down and clear."

He could feel the action behind him. The chopper's side door slid open, a burst of fresh air filled the interior which he knew, from other flights, the medics appreciated.

The stretcher was quickly shifted to a portable gurney waiting on the rooftop.

Less than two minutes after feeling the touchdown, the pilot watched the men in green, followed by the white coats, scurry to the waiting elevator.

"Ground to 72Xray."

"72Xray, go ahead."

"We have a boating accident in the harbor near …."

His crew took only seconds to prepare for departure. As quickly as they had delivered Peter Douglas to this rooftop, they were off to assist other unknown victims in need of help. The helicopter lifted from the roof, scattering debris in every direction. He noticed a few birds nestled low that seemed to watch this iron sister lift effortlessly into the sky.

"I've got clear breathing, a light heart beat."

The elevator was jammed with people surrounding Peter's stretcher. One attendant held a bag of clear fluid high in the air, letting it drain slowly into Peter's arm. A Doctor pressed his stethoscope against Peter's chest while another rolled his eyelids back and flickered the beam of a penlight into his pupils, hoping for a response. Both Doctors made eye contact.

"I'm getting nothing inside. I'd say he's in really deep or…"

The third Doctor scraped his fingernail along the soft underside of Peter's foot. There was no reaction.

Had Peter's toes curled downward in response, the Doctor would have deduced that his neurological functions were normal. If his toes had turned up, brain damage was indicated. No response left them guessing, but it likely meant that Peter's brain was functioning nominally or not at all.

Peter's wet clothes, stained with blood, soaked the blankets placed over him in the helicopter.

His skin was a pale shade of blue.

His lips were swollen.

A Doctor started to speak into a walkie-talkie, but stopped when the elevator doors slid open. They burst into the corridor and ran with the stretcher.

"Trauma two…" The lead Doctor yelled commands when they passed the control desk. Still gaining numbers, the entourage made the gallop with their distinguished patient. The focus of the entire floor had been galvanized. Peter Douglas's day, which had started out idyllic, was now in the hands of one of the country's finest medical teams.

"This first hour will be critical," the Doctor declared.

The lighting in the trauma room was focused around the bed of the new arrival. It seemed that every specialist in the Boston Trauma Center had been called to attend. The shadowed, secure room concealed the motion of nurses and attendants rushing in and out of the area. The green and red hues from data screens were the light show for an orchestra of tones and beeps that echoed the numerous vitals being monitored. Clear liquid now filled tubes that delivered precious, sustaining fluids to Peter's body.

"Everyone, this is our hospital's chairman, Peter Douglas. Need I say more?"

The enduring Douglas family of Boston had built or substantially funded the building of a number of wings at this prestigious medical institute. Their historic and current community and political activism was a boon to any cause that engaged any of the passionate Douglas clan.

Amongst many of his corporate and philanthropic board positions around the country, the much honored Chairman Peter Douglas was completing his final year on this hospital's board. His connections alone had green-lit projects and brought in millions every year; a source of support too important to lose.

A family not to be disappointed.

- Chapter 7 -

The ringing of the poolside telephone had not awakened Marion, but Emily's tap on her shoulder did. When Marion opened her eyes, she focused gradually on her elderly mother sitting close by on an upright chair.

"Dear, it's Peter. There's been a terrible accident. He's unconscious. They're trying to save his life. I think you should call Catherine."

Marion questioned her mother for more information, but quickly realized that the call from Boston held little in the way of detail.

She sat up, smoothed her hair. She was no stranger to crisis. She took a long sip of the tepid fluid in her cocktail glass. She closed her eyes for a moment, letting the soothing qualities of the contents settle over her.

Her mind skipped over a lifetime spent with the man now in question. She usually tried not to think about him, but few hours went by that their life together didn't haunt her with the reminder that she was now alone. Marion was almost startled at the nature of some of her thoughts.

What was that part of her that would welcome his death, and yet still long to be held in his arms?

How odd that love and hate were so imperceptibly separated. How is it that the person that provided so much love could invoke such pain?

Evil and good fought for control of her mind, quickly turning her feelings into a pool of mixed emotions.

The telephones at the luxurious Paris Continental Hotel were unique. The first two rings were a strobe light, the third like a cat purring, the intensity increasing with every following ring. She rolled off him and answered after the first purr.

"Catherine Douglas... Mother, what is it? Daddy? Where? How?" She paused to hear the few facts that her mother was able to convey.

"I'm almost finished here. I'll catch the next possible flight. I love you too. See you soon."

Catherine reached for a heavy black plastic hair cleat that sat on the night table. While twirling her bright red mane into a manageable rope at the back of her head, she looked at the man with her in bed.

No words were exchanged. This evening had just come to an end.

Catherine was a plentiful woman who made the best of her assets. She had a great smile, a freckled face and a beautiful head of red hair that drew attention to her wherever she went. No one could explain how Catherine had ended up with bright red hair since there wasn't any in her father's or mother's families.

What had once been a source of boys teasing and insecurity when she was young was now one of her "tools of seduction," as she called it.

People everywhere now noticed Catherine Douglas when she walked into a room "hair first." She was radiant, exotic in a way, dressed to kill, with a personality to die for.

Men loved her.

Though she lacked a perfect body, she exuded sexuality and backed it up with enthusiastic performance.

The door clicked shut. She sighed and let a wide yawn escape. She paused, closed her eyes, let the feel of precious sexual relief waft through her for just a few moments.

Eyes opened.

Naked, she bolted for the phone to call her assistant.

"Something's up back home with dad. I need the next flight to Logan."

Her day had been a whirlwind of meetings. She'd prowled the Paris collections, sketching the latest trends which her company would have copied and hung on the racks for sale, at half the designer prices, in less than twelve weeks. Catherine's eye for fashion and artistic talent had led her to the top of the fashion buyers' world. The perversity of her industry was that the designers actually wanted to be copied. The more people saw of any specific style, the more credibility the designers achieved whether it carried their label or not. She walked a fine line and remained friends with the top models, designers and fashion editors, yet stayed loyal to her company and buying public.

Catherine's assistant called back with the flight details and took notes while Catherine dictated a series of tasks that needed to be done in her absence. "It's all yours from here, okay?... You can handle this and remember to have fun...two more days of shows...not too much fun...no you are not like me...be good...huh?...no you can't have his number. Sketch well. I'll catch up by phone and email...thanks...yes thank you...I hope daddy does too."

- Chapter 8 -

Nothing registered.
It seemed normal.
Peter hovered.

A movie of his life played through his head at a remarkable speed. The clarity was astounding: pre-natal life, the slap of a hand at birth, his first breath, baby years, young boy and adolescent traumas, first sexual experiences, near death experiences along the way, young adulthood memories, thoughts long forgotten, middle years of family and friends.

Voices played through his consciousness.

Visions played out in his mind's theater.

Peter felt peaceful floating over the hospital room scene.

Where am I?

No one yet knew that he was caught in a perfect balance between life and death.

He watched the Doctors work frantically, trying to restore life to his lifeless body. Peter now viewed his entire life from a unique perspective; sometimes reliving the previous experience, another time observing from above, life then and now carrying on below. He witnessed his many youthful risks and saw the ripples of his actions wash across the pond of his life and affect others. He felt the mixture of emotion for which he was responsible oscillate through positive and negative waves while the movie played on.

Peter saw that he had become a kind and giving man in his latter years but he could easily see in the review of his time that in his early life he had been completely self-centered. He witnessed the hurt reactions of family and friends as he doggedly pursued his single-minded quest to build his business. This contrasted dramatically with his more recent times when, as a volunteer and philanthropist, he brought help and comfort to those who were in need. He was shocked at the lack of family members reaping the benefits of his softer nature.

The many negative actions in his life inflicted a punishing sorrow, countered by the overwhelming joy of the positive ways he had affected people. Inventory was being taken. Judgment was upon him and he was the judge. The pressure mounted; the review continued. A void inside him opened wider, seemingly making room for his own final assessment of the life he had led. He floated and watched, reliving, yet totally detached and objective. Expectation tormented him.

His life played out; strands of which began to separate before him. The intensity grew. Positive events spun off into one direction, the negative another. Faster and faster his existence whirled by, repeating before him time and again. Each event elicited an automatic reaction which sent it spinning off in one direction or another. Positive or negative. Good or evil. Peter was his own critic. Impartial, unbiased, his response to his own life was determining his destiny.

Episodes continued to scroll passed; Peter tried to justify his actions.

"I'm not bad – evil – I'm human dammit. I've made mistakes – I can fix them – give me a chance."

He shouted out justifications at the negative and boasted at the positive. He tried to reach in and make repairs. Panic overcame him while he struggled to right the wrongs of his life.

"Another chance," he yelled. "Give me another chance... please."

Tears propelled by a lifetime of regrets wet his face.

The pull from each side grew stronger. More and more of his life was weighed. His darkest secrets were revealed; the things he'd done and said, assuming no one would ever know about, were bared. His deepest, blackest mysteries posted for all to read. The feeling had been barely perceptible at first, with the positive aspects of his life eliciting a warm response, the negative something cooler. As the judgment continued, the polarization between positive and negative intensified, sometimes represented by feeling, sometimes by sound, then color, light, pain, pleasure and a host of other sensations. Peter could feel the opposites tearing at him, stretching his soul in two directions as though at any time he might rip in two, split apart forever, never to be whole again.

"Help me – I am sorry…I can do better…give me a chance."

Try as he might to influence his judgment of himself, he could not stray from a set of pre-conceived rules or principles which he seemed compelled to follow. These rules, he realized, had been with him since birth. A purity of mind and spirit had been in place to govern his lifelong actions. Principles, which he could see had always been there to rely on, but at times had been ignored or displaced by allowing his desire to outweigh his will.

What had started out as a broad overview of his life continued in greater and greater detail. Around and around this movie of his life spun. Peter could feel growing negativity within himself, the inevitability of which was that he, as his final judge, would not be kind. What had taken a lifetime to live was being played out before him in a measure of time so small that it could not be determined by any earthly means. The entire contents of his being were unraveling before him like some great computer downloading its constituents to one final and painful conclusion.

Peter could feel an inevitable doom come over him while the negative force of his judgment tore away at the remainder of his soul. It seemed that, try as he might to plead for charity, his pleas fell upon deaf ears: his own.

He felt stretched out like he were being sucked down into some black, bleak abyss. A fear like none he had ever experienced was overtaking him.

"Heeeeelpp meee…"

Excruciating agony rose to a crescendo. Sounds from beyond any worldly making roared in his head.

He squeezed his eyes against a blinding white light that exploded before him.

The movie was over. Like the bright light on an old home movie screen, the reel of his life had spun to an end.

All was silent. All was white, like a flash of lightning that didn't fade after the thunder clap.

Beep, beep, beep, beep.

"Clear."

"Aaaaaahhhhhh…"

A jolt of electricity contorted his body, it bounced on the table.

He felt no pain.

His mind burst wide open. Reality poured in.

"We have a heart beat."

Half a dozen masked faces stared down at him, eyes all twinkling. A white blaze of overhead halogen lights pierced the group. Spurts of congratulatory remarks arced between the gang of six. The rough action of moving his body from stretcher to bed, combined with his hypothermic condition, had caused his heart to go into fibrillation, then stop. Several jolts of electricity through the paddles of the defibrillator had reinstated a regular heartbeat.

Peter's life, now a green line with regular spikes, played out on a small screen to his left. Two clear bags of fluid hung on his right. A third and a fourth bag of thick red liquid flanked the two. Figures in the background moved about quickly. Someone wiped his brow and face with a damp cloth, removing dried blood and saliva. His face molded like soft putty when the pressure of the cloth moved his loose skin from side to side.

"Am I alive?" Peter asked aloud. The sound of his voice echoed within his shell failing to be heard by anyone but himself.

Someone peeled back his eyelids and flashed a bright beam directly into each eye. Another hand raised his limp arm and pinched his hand forcefully in hopes of a response.

"No pain response."

"No pupil constriction."

"Pulse accelerated but steady, blood pressure 80 over 50."

"Rectal temperature 28 degrees."

"Vitals stable."

"Tuck in those warm blankets. Open the two warm IV."

"ECG recording."

"EEG recording."

"CAT scan in fifteen."

Peter heard the sliding door of the glass-walled room hiss open and shut.

"Hello? Hello?"

His words echoed again. No one noticed.

"I can hear you."

His voice surrounded him. He looked right, then left, trying to get someone's attention, but the activities around him continued. To the outside world, his eyes hadn't moved.

"I'm okay, I'm here. I can hear you ... can you hear me?"

Nothing.

Someone wiped his dripping brow again. He felt nothing, no external sensation of temperature or touch. He tried to sit up. He felt pinned in place. He felt confused and dazed. Claustrophobia engulfed him.

What was happening?

His mind raced.

"Bring those blankets up to temp slowly."

Peter felt nothing.

He worked his mind: his name, date of birth, nine times nine equals eighty-one, Mississippi: M-i-s-s-i-s-s-i-p-p-i.

He scanned his life: childhood, adolescence, young adulthood, adulthood, girlfriends, school, work, marriage, family, and career. It was all there.

"Schebb," he yelled.

He could hear the barking, feel the cold water, the sounds of the helicopter, a bearded, panicked face. A feeling of flight lifted him. The rest became crystal clear. He hovered over the highway, watched again when his car launched off the curb into the air, down into the river.

A momentary white flash blinded him.

Once again he was looking up at people with masked faces while they manipulated his cold body.

His eyelids were peeled back again and probed. His limp arm was raised and pinched.

"No pain response."

"No constriction."

"Pulse accelerated but steady, blood pressure 80 over 50."

"Rectal temperature 29 degrees."

"Schebb, I am so sorry."

Then nothing. Just silence and sorrow.

- Chapter 9 -

World Politics class was nearly over when the Dean peered through the blind. Sarah Douglas stared off into space, twirling a newly dyed, long, thin, braid around her fingers. Pink braids were not in the dress code, but Sarah had cleverly pulled hair from underneath so that the outer layers usually camouflaged it. It was her own little rebellion against rules and the establishment.

The Dean knocked gently on the door before entering the class. A look of excited expectation came over the girls that some announcement might pre-empt the balance of this political science class. A few whispered words were exchanged between the Dean and the teacher who then looked, with a warm smile, directly at Sarah.

"Could you join me in the hall a minute?"

Sarah felt her face go hot. She made a comment trying to get a laugh and cover her embarrassment.

"More consulting on world affairs, Madame Dean?"

Her classmates chuckled. The dean did not.

Her mother and Catherine had both been exemplary students, setting expectations that Sarah was unlikely to fulfill. It was more likely that she would be the shadowy dancer on the wall and not the observer her mother had once been. Her long, slim carriage and cocky attitude ensured that everyone noticed her presence. To her mother's dismay, she had dyed her blonde hair every color imaginable over the past few years.

When she stood, she pulled the edge of her sweater down to cover a tattoo on her upper hip of a dolphin jumping over a crescent moon and two stars. She pushed her hair back behind her ears, exposing several piercings.

News spread quickly amongst the staff after the telephone message that Sarah's father had been in a serious accident. The outward responses were ones of shock and concern, but privately some had other agendas. The Douglases, after all, were major financial contributors to the college. Many years prior an astute dean convinced Peter Douglas to make a living bequest that would flow to the school upon his death. The current dean knew that a windfall of that sort would place the college on sound financial footing for many years to come. The Dean of Residence was a warm, caring woman who knew the boarders better than most. She regarded Sarah like a diamond in the rough and spent many hours holding her hand while she cried over things that all little girls cry about. She would deliver the news to Sarah.

Sarah brashly saluted her class as though she were reporting for duty. "I'm off to serve my country," she said bravely to them.

The door closed gently behind her muffling the chuckle of her unknowing fellow students.

The dean put her arm around Sarah's waist whose skin pebbled with a sudden chill. She seemed to know that adults only did that when something bad was about to happen.

"Sarah, dear, it's your father. There's been an accident."

"What do you mean a fucking accident? What do you mean?"

"I'm sorry; I don't have much detail…"

"Bullshit – what's going - what's happened?"

"I'm sorry - there's been a terrible accident."

"What kind of accident..?"

"Your father is in the hospital in critical condition."

"What do you mean critical condition...?"

"Sarah, I'm sorry – there is a car waiting."

Sarah ripped the dean's grip from her waist then bolted the length of the hall, bursting through the doors into the court-yard. A black Cadillac stood waiting with its back door open.

Following the pack she had just heaved into the car she leaped headlong on to the black leather seat with face buried in her arms.

"Fucking drive."

- Chapter 10 -

The uniformed officer pressed the talk button on his radio, "This is 4-7. I'm at the Douglas residence. No sign of anyone yet."

"Ten four, 4-7. Check it out on your next round."

In the setting light of forest dusk, Charlotte Douglas smiled to herself when she picked up the fat paper from the step and saw her husband's face smiling at her. It was not unusual that Peter should be on the cover; however she had no idea of the colossal effort required to get his story in place for the evening edition which had been delivered forty-five minutes late.

Charlotte had just returned home from a weekend at Martha's Vineyard. A small gathering of female friends, enjoying the fading weather of fall at a friend's cabin, had kept her busy and out of contact with her husband; cell phones were a prohibited accessory at this particular girls-only getaway.

It was customary for her to be home before Peter on most evenings. Usually he had Schebb with him.

The sound of her friend's car leaving the laneway was the only noise that permeated the chilly fall evening. Fortunately for Charlotte, she'd been at a service center when her car had failed on the return trip and she was able to call one of her traveling companions who circled back and picked her up. Her cell battery was long dead from a week-end in her purse so she had also called Peter at home and on his cell phone, but since there was no answer she had to leave messages.

Being from a rural town she still loved the country but at times like this, alone on the step with no one around and hardly a sound in the air, she felt vulnerable. She felt her chest tighten a bit while she fidgeted with the lock. The intrusive beeping of the alarm when she entered the darkened house was actually a welcome sign that her home was secure.

She quickly punched in her 5 digit code.

The door locked behind her.

Charlotte paused and took a long easy breath.

She kicked off her shoes, flexing her delicate feet and firm, slim calves.

Her long cashmere coat slipped to the floor when she walked. She was exquisitely yet casually dressed, avoiding the crisp and stuffy look of so many of the Boston women to whom she was exposed. She stayed fit and took pride in keeping up with woman ten years her junior. At 39, Charlotte could pass for late twenties or forties, depending on the occasion.

Charlotte met Peter at a gala hosted by the Douglas Corporation, six years earlier, where her ability to mix with any crowd served her well. For Peter, it was love at first sight. For Charlotte, marrying Peter Douglas made great sense. Practicality was the foundation of the union, but she grew to love him and the romance actually improved as time went on.

Peter often complained about Charlotte's downtown activities, where she shopped and lunched with the best of them, but Charlotte was a devoted wife who kept the credibility of the Douglas name uppermost in her mind. She continually reminded Peter that she was his most valuable asset, that he was settled in his ways and that he should get a little zip in his life - especially his love life.

The trick was to get him in the mood and tonight would be perfect.

Charlotte's calf-length fall skirt flowed around her legs when she made her way to the kitchen. The fat paper landed on the center island with a thud. Two Siamese cats appeared at her ankles and purred with affection, watching her pull open the fridge door and scan for an open bottle of wine.

The wine shelf was empty.

"How about some candlelight, guys?"

High pitched meows were the only response. They seemed focused on dinner while she selected a can to feed her two hungry pets.

Charlotte lit several candles then scooped the gourmet cat food into two dishes.

"Nothing but the best for the Douglas cats. And look, no Schebb to steal your food."

Schebb loved cat food, but always seemed to let his conscience get the better of him. Whenever he ate the cats' food, he would come to her or Peter with a guilty look, waiting for an inquisition. The penalty was a soft scolding for Schebb and a smelly house for Peter and Charlotte. Cat food apparently tasted good going down, but didn't sit right when it got there.

Charlotte moved across the kitchen and opened another cabinet. The upper half was refrigerated and housed a selection of fine white wines, the lower the reds.

"Red or white, my Lord?" Charlotte addressed the newspaper on the counter. She pulled one of each and opened the white.

The pleasure of being home again, the quiet house and the candlelight all heightened her sensual awareness.

The freshly poured glass of wine smelled delicious. The first sip went down with eyes closed. The alcohol sent a current of electricity through her when she tipped her head back and swallowed. The corners of her smile turned up, stimulated by the wine. She leaned against the wooden island and felt a pleasant pressure against her tummy.

"I'm ready dear, are you?"

She spotted a red numeral on the telephone blinking at her. She dialed her home voice mail but the messages sounded almost evil when the system strained to play them. One of the few setbacks of living in the country was intermittent phone and cell services. She hoped Peter had received her message and would be home soon.

"Jimmy's."

"Hi, Jimmy, it's Charlotte Douglas. Can you deliver two number nines at about nine o'clock, and add two of those delicious strawberry things you did last time? … Thanks, you're a dear… Jimmy, flattery can get you killed in this town, but thank you anyway… That's none of your business, Jimmy."

Charlotte blew out all but one candle. Smiling to herself she moved through the house toward her bedroom, the flicker of this single candle guiding her. Jimmy was tall and handsome. Charlotte had fantasized, but was never tempted. She knew he had a great body from the time he peeled down to his Calvin's and took a dip in the pool at one of her neighbors' wilder summer parties. The woman talked about him for weeks. Jimmy's business boomed.

She flicked the remote control. The house filled with music. Although her home looked rustic from the outside, the interior had every modern convenience. Its single-level front belied a two-level spread built into the natural shape of the land. Charlotte and Peter shared a beautiful master bedroom. A king-sized, four-posted pine bed with white fluffy everything begged to be frolicked in. The adjoining bathroom featured the beautiful whirlpool tub which was to be her next stop.

Charlotte poured in a capful of bubble bath and started the water. Her first experience with bubble bath in the whirlpool tub covered the bathroom and part of the bedroom floor with heaps of white foam. The amplifying affect of the water jets was amazing. She and Peter had laughed heartily while they cleaned it up, and what started out as a foam-throwing match turned into an evening of passionate love-making. Peter claimed it was the scent of the bubbles that did it. Charlotte had since kept that little tradition alive by always adding the magic liquid to her baths.

She lit two bedside candles.

Her skirt slipped to the floor, exposing long, toned legs topped with a delicate pair of underwear; Peter's favorite on her. Her firm bottom and thighs reflected the fact that she had yet to bear any children.

Charlotte carefully undid each button of her white silk blouse looking at herself in the mirror.

"Not bad, Mrs. Douglas – not bad."

She looked closely at her somewhat plain but mysterious face with smoky chocolate-brown eyes and heavy, dark eyebrows. She bunched up her full lips and crinkled her delicately thin nose.

"Hhumm."

She placed the blouse strategically near the bedroom door.

"A bit of cheese for the trap."

She let her long brown hair tumble around her shoulders and frame medium-sized breasts held in perfect posture by a matching bra. She pushed the under-support and half-cup bra from below and gave herself a deceptively voluptuous appearance.

"I wish."

She traced her nipples that showed through the thin material, then carefully placed this final piece of attire to set the appropriate tone if Peter arrived while she was bathing.

Charlotte lit one more candle and turned off the light. She set her wine glass on the tub's edge while she admired the perfectly measured foam layer bubbling on the water's surface.

She slipped in until the water touched her earlobes. The sound of the frothy bubbles coupled with the firm water jets from every angle felt very good.

The patrolman eased his cruiser into the driveway of the Douglas home. The scene appeared the same as it had on his prior visits. The first few times the officer had walked around the house; knocked loudly at the door and pressed the door chime many times. This time he simply checked the garage, which still housed only one tarp-covered vehicle. The house was still in darkness.

"This is 4-7 to base...nothing yet..."

- Chapter 11 -

A sole light was his only companion.

Brian's eyes were closed.

His head rested against the high sofa back.

He had arranged to have the hospital lounge booked for as long as it was required. It would be the gathering place for the Douglas clan and friends when they arrived.

Brian's PDA, cell phone and laptop computer were at their ready. A television, fax machine and daybed had also been brought in.

The main Douglas offices had been notified of this arrangement and protocol for communication was in place. A security guard stood outside the door with instructions on who should and shouldn't get in. The hospital had a rigidly enforced policy forbidding media. Many continued to try anything they had to for a scoop on an important person at their worst, so long as it was legal.

So far, Brian had only seen his father through the glass windows of the trauma unit. The activity around Peter was impressive. Brian knew that the world's best were being consulted on his condition. The head of the team was a long-time associate of his father's and the family. He promised a full update the moment the information was available.

Brian's thoughts ran the gamut of family life as a Douglas. Peter was Brian's rock of stability, the person he went to for all his intellectual and moral support. As a father-and-son team they worked and played together with extraordinary camaraderie. Yet Brian still felt that he'd always come up short on the emotional connection with his dad, particularly when he was a young boy.

Was he going to lose his father?

Tears stung his eyes and his brain ached with the fear.

I'm not ready to let go. Not yet.

"Hey, bro!"

Matt's voice snapped Brian out of his wanderings. He stood quickly to face him, giving Matt a quick once up and down with his eyes.

"You could've at least changed Matt…you look and smell like a cocktail party… look at your eyes."

"Fuck off."

"Dad's dying in there, and you walk in, half in the bag, looking like you just stepped off a yacht."

"Brian, I had a few drinks on the plane and I skipped going home to come right here. I was in Bermuda. Now get off my fucking case and tell me what's up."

"Bermuda? That's nice. I'm working my tail off here Matt, and you're up to shit in Bermuda."

"Hey, you got what you wanted. You're the big man now, deal with it. I'm just doing my own thing."

"Yeah, one lucky investment and you think you're a golden boy."

"Lucky: no. Successful: quite, thank you very much."

"Boys."

Both men snapped to attention, glancing at each other while turning toward the sharp crisp voice.

"Some things never change, do they?"

"Hey, Mom."

"Hello, Mother. I was just giving your youngest son some guidance."

"Perhaps you should give him a breath mint."

Matt gave Brian a sidelong stare. They all smiled. Both brothers gave Marion a long, family hug.

She wiped tears from her eyes and composed herself.

"How is your father?"

- Chapter 12 -

Two black cars came to a halt nose to nose in the hospital's circular entrance way. Two horns honked when the drivers tried to stake out turf on behalf of their valued and important passengers. Two black rear doors flew open. Out of each jumped a woman who rushed for the hospital door.

A wheelchair made its exit in front of them. Both women paused, their eyes met, then moved on before snapping back.

"Sarah!"

"Catherine!"

The names rang out in simultaneous chorus when the sisters nearly tumbled over the wheelchair in their efforts to reach out and finally embrace in the doorway. Emotions brimmed while Catherine stroked her younger sister's hair.

"What's happened to him?" Sarah's voice was choked.

"I don't know yet, sweetheart. Let's go and see who's here. I've just flown in from Paris."

"Paris?" Sarah leaned back in her sister's arms and looked at her through reddened eyes. "Was it fun?... Was it beautiful?... You promised you'd take me sometime. I have to go there with you."

"Yes to all the above. Now let's go in. Did you just get down from school?"

"Yeah, what an 'effing' dump. I wanted to come straight here, but Brian wouldn't let me. He said there was nothing to do and that I couldn't see Peter anyway. He sent me to pick up Marion at the airport. I just dropped her here and I went to get some flowers."

Sarah held up the huge plastic-wrapped bouquet for Catherine to smell while they marched through the corridor. One Douglas girl turned some heads. Two Douglas girls together turned all the heads. Neither noticed.

Sarah clutched her sister's arm. The blond hair around her blotchy face was wet and matted. She had changed in the car from her school uniform into ripped blue jeans, heavy-soled black shoes and a T-shirt covered by an oversized white cotton sweater.

Catherine was groomed and dressed impeccably, but she could feel that her face was taut. Her spine tingled while she listened to Sarah. The swearing and calling her mother and father by first name were ongoing forms of rebellion that had started a few months earlier.

"I want to be treated like a person, not a daughter or sister," she had invoked to her tolerant but somewhat annoyed siblings.

Catherine bit her lip. This was not the time.

"You okay sweetie?"

"Sure."

"Sure?"

"Sure."

They smiled a bit.

"Okay."

"Okay."

Was this what their mother went through raising four children? Then a divorce? Goodness.

Sarah's silver bangles jingled while the two women made their way to the elevator. The sisters rode in silence. Catherine continued to stroke her sister's hair. She noticed the pink braid and two new piercings in her ear. She smiled to herself and hoped that the piercing would be confined to Sarah's ears.

The elevator doors slid open.

Sarah and Catherine looked directly at the man waiting to get on. They simultaneously gave each other a tight squeeze, acknowledging the handsome apparition. He appeared to be in his early thirties. He had short brown hair, blue eyes, smooth skin and a square chin with a small dimple in the middle. He wore loafers, faded blue jeans, a white T-shirt and a fine brown wool blazer.

They watched him give them both a warm smile when he stepped in beside them.

"Hello."

He smelled terrific and radiated something very attractive: not really sex appeal…just a calmness and poise that was obvious. Both girls nodded politely but stayed silent. The air in the elevator took on an electric feel. The man was just about to speak when the noise of the elevator signaled another floor and the door whisked open.

Catherine and Sarah exited.

"Goodbye."

Sarah snapped a quick glimpse over her shoulder to catch his gaze while the door was closing.

The sisters made their way down the dim, quiet corridor of the Intensive Care wing, passing a security guard on the way without acknowledgement.

Their focus had returned.

Catherine gave her name to the nurse at the reception area.

"Hello, Catherine."

The nurse looked past her.

Catherine turned when she felt a light hand on her shoulder.

For the second time in a few minutes she faced another handsome man.

"I'm Jim Brandon, the Doctor in charge of the team caring for your father. I'm just on my way to see the rest of your family. If you would follow me, I'll take you to them and give you all a briefing."

Sarah made eye contact with her sister and raised her eyebrows. Catherine gave her a nudge, code for "don't be so naughty."

Both had been distracted again for a few moments from the crisis they were facing.

"You must be Sarah. I've known your dad and mother for years." Dr. Brandon reached across Catherine and shook Sarah's hand. Catherine felt the light press of his arm against her front. It was subtle and she presumed unintentional.

"I'm sorry we have to meet under these circumstances."

Sarah nodded, eyeing him suspiciously.

Dr. Brandon smiled at her, un-phased by this young one's outward disdain for him.

When the three arrived at the door with the security guard, it dawned on Catherine that this man was there for their family's protection. It took continual reminders for her to accept how prominent their family was. They could hear voices behind the door.

"Matthew!" Sarah bolted for the arms of her brother.

Catherine hugged her mother, then gave a big smile to Brian, who walked over and held out his arms.

"It's great to see you, Cath. Sorry it has to be like this."

"I know. I came as quickly as I could."

Sarah left the clutches of her one brother to greet her other brother Brian but with slightly less affection. Catherine gave Matt a knowing look, then kissed him lightly.

"Eau de Vodka?"

Matt smiled stiffly and sat down.

Catherine gave her mother another warm hug.

"Hello, Marion."

Sarah flicked her mother a look that only a daughter can give a mother who is being blamed for all the current grief in her daughter's life.

The tension in the room had risen dramatically. All the relationships had crystallized into their historic patterns.

"Where's Charlotte?"

Quick looks were exchanged amongst the group. They looked back at Catherine.

"Oh no. Did anyone call her?"

The room erupted in questions, speculation and accusations. Brian held up his arms. "Quiet, everyone…We haven't been able to locate her. At first there was some concern that she might have been with dad in the car, but we've ruled that out after speaking to the air ambulance crew. It turns out that she was in Martha's for the weekend with some friends."

Marion scowled at these words.

"We've got full co-operation from the highway patrol and a trooper is stopping by the house every thirty minutes. We've emailed, called and left messages. I have Marjorie working the phone from the office trying to track her down. As soon as we find her she'll be here. In the meantime we have to focus on what's best for Father."

"Where's Schebb?" asked Matt. "Dad doesn't drive anywhere without him."

Dr. Brandon broke in.

"I don't want to rush you or interrupt you, but if you will take a seat, I'd like to give you a briefing on Mr. Douglas."

Marion sat on the couch between Catherine and Brian. She clutched their hands. Sarah squeezed into an oversized chair with Matt and looped her arm through his. They were all staring at Dr. Brandon when the door opened behind him. The man was almost in the room before he realized it was occupied. Catherine and Sarah recognized him from the elevator, but before they could acknowledge him, Matt was on his feet.

"Excuse me! Can't you see we're busy here? Brian, I thought you had security outside."

"I did, but...."

"Geez Brian...can you not..."

"Gentlemen, gentlemen, calm down," Dr. Brandon tried to take charge of the unwieldy group. "Come in Michael."

Michael's face was red. "Sorry Dr. Brandon I was..."

Dr. Brandon continued, "it's okay. Folks, this is Michael Phillips, a friend of the hospital and friend of yours, if you wish. He's our ... Michael, what do they call you... spiritual touchstone?"

He continued to flush under the gaze of the Douglas family.

"Sorry about that...I just thought...anyway..." He extended his hand, "Matt Douglas."

"I understand. My apologies for intruding. I was just looking to..."

Catherine and Sarah exchanged a glance.

"Perhaps you could join us...Catherine Douglas." Michael shook Matt's hand first then Catherine's. "We're just about to get our first update on the condition of our father. He's had a serious accident."

"Catherine...we don't want to burden this young man with our personal business."

"Mother...it's okay."

"I understand." Michael moved toward the door.

"No, no, please stay. We may need someone with your..." Catherine paused.

"Yes, please stay," agreed Brian. "We Douglases aren't the most religious people in the world, but hey, at a time like this we could use any support you'll offer."

"Sit over here." Sarah patted the chair next to hers and looked at Catherine.

"Thank you. I'll join you for a bit, but let me say that I'm not very religious either. I have found a way of life, though, that I guess you'd have to call spiritual. It has helped me grow and deal with life's misfortunes in a more balanced way. I'd be happy to talk to any of you any time, if you feel the need."

"All right, now." Dr. Brandon took the floor and commenced his briefing. "First of all and most importantly, Mr. Douglas..." He looked at Marion, then he scanned the Douglas children whose eyes were riveted to him. "...your father is alive."

Together the Douglases took a deep breath and prepared for more.

"But he's been in a serious automobile accident which plunged him and his car over an embankment into icy water. Someone, and we are not sure who yet, risked his life to help Mr. Douglas and see that he arrived here."

Dr. Brandon held up his hands to quell the Douglas' urge to speak.

"Let me continue. We have determined that it was not the automobile accident that caused his injuries, but an incident while he was driving. It appears that an aneurysm in his brain ruptured, causing a general short circuiting of his bodily functions. His body was completely traumatized and we believe that the physical injuries he sustained were a result of this trauma. His body and bones however are in remarkably good condition, all things considered."

The Douglases held tightly to each other.

Dr. Brandon took a breath of his own.

He saw tears dripping down Catherine and Sarah's faces.

He looked at Michael who was observing, presumably, to get some reading on this interesting family.

Brian and his mother went pale hearing this news so bluntly delivered.

Matt had closed his eyes to listen.

"It seems to us that the frigid water played a key role in keeping Mr. Douglas alive. He was out for a long time, and we won't know the effect of this for a while. We have treated all of his bodily injuries and stabilized his vital signs. We are continuing to warm him and he is breathing on his own now. I am pleased to say his body is responding well to our efforts."

Dr. Brandon paused again.

The Douglases noticeably stiffened, bracing themselves for something big to come.

"However, at this time, there is no brain activity that we are able to measure."

"You mean he's a vegetable?" Matt burst out.

"Doctor please what does that mean…?" Brian asked.

"How do you know…?" Matt asked.

Sarah whimpered. Catherine reached across to squeeze her arm. Michael sat in quiet observation.

The pain of those in the room was displayed on their faces and body language.

"Matt, please." Brian put his open hand up to get Matt's attention.

"Shut it, Brian." Brian ignored the comment and urged calmness. "Please, everyone, please…steady… Dr. Brandon, continue."

Dr. Brandon took a deep breath, seemingly relieved that part was over. He spoke in a steady tone.

"His heart, lungs, kidneys … everything seems to be functioning remarkably well, considering what he's been through, but we're baffled as to why we can't get any measurement of brain activity. Mr. Douglas is in some sort of coma.

"We are fortunate however, that some unique and very sophisticated equipment is arriving from Europe on a flight tonight. We had previously agreed with a sister institute to run some trials with it. I think it may be useful in helping us get some readings on his brain activity. We are in the process of performing a battery of traditional tests and brain scans in an effort to exhaust all possibilities. We must get your father's body temperature up to normal before any of the tests are conclusive. It is possible...and I stress *possible*...that his hypothermic condition is responsible for the lack of brain function. Until his temperature is normal, it is impossible to predict with any accuracy what the likely outcome might be."

The room erupted with more questions.

Dr. Brandon concluded by explaining his plan of action.

"For the time being I do not want any friends or family members to have direct contact with Mr. Douglas. The specialized monitoring equipment will be installed overnight. Today we want to run a variety of tests and establish whatever baseline readings we can. When the baseline is established, one family member at a time can visit. My hope is that contact with intimate people might have some effect on the brain's response. Each initial interaction will be set up and monitored carefully for any signs of brain activity to see if he responds differently to different people." He paused for a moment to let that all settle in. For the first time the group was silent and looking at him with expectation.

"I want to stress to you the importance of maintaining a positive attitude amongst yourselves especially when you're in Mr. Douglas's room. I want you to act on the assumption that he is fully aware of his surroundings; that he can hear what we say and feel what we feel. Our job is simply to wake him up."

Despite their protests about having to wait, they all expressed a desire to co-operate in any way they could.

"Dr. Brandon, as CEO I can assure you that the full scope of the Douglas corporate resources is available to assist our father." Brian looked at his family. "Listen, why don't I stay tonight?"

"Okay, thank you Brian," Catherine said. "Mother, Sarah, you come stay with me. I'll also call the school in the morning and get your work sent down."

"Cath.," Matt spoke up quietly to his sister.

"Yes…"

"Ah, nothing…forget it."

"Matt…"

"I'm fine Cath. I'm fine."

"Is it about Susan?"

"What?"

"Sus…never mind."

Matt and Catherine exchanged looks. He wondered what she was thinking or if his fiancée, Susan, had left Catherine a message as well. He didn't ask.

"Thank you for allowing me in tonight. Just so you know, I volunteer my time here at the hospital many evenings from six until ten. I have a little office downstairs." Michael reached in his breast pocket and started to hand out small colorful triangular cards.

"This has my telephone numbers on it. Please call anytime if you feel the need to chat. It's been a pleasure meeting all of you. I hope we'll see each other again. I'll be praying for your family and Mr. Douglas."

It wasn't until Michael was leaving that each person was discovering his card was more than it appeared.

"Hey, what's this?" Sarah held hers up high and looked at it on both sides.

It was several triangles connected together with writing on each side.

"Life's little puzzle." Michael smiled as he spoke. "It's so simple anyone can do it."

"Do what?" asked Sarah. "The puzzle?"

"No…life." Michael looked at them warmly across the room, making eye contact with everyone present, then departed.

Sarah followed shortly after him into the hallway.

Dr. Brandon was grinning widely, watching the Douglas family's reaction. They were all intrigued with the peculiar card Michael had given each of them, smiling together now as they each tried to figure it out.

"Why does he give these out?"

"Well Catherine, he once explained to me that solving life's puzzle brings people together and makes them happier. I think Michael is a gifted man. You should get to know him."

The Douglas family looked at each other. For a few seconds they had forgotten their troubles completely and shared a special moment together.

Michael had already touched their lives. Brian cleared his throat.

"Doctor, you said someone saved dad's life. I'd like to get the details on the accident from you. Catherine, could you keep calling his house and try to find Charlotte? Then I can get Marjorie at the office to start the hunt for Schebb."

An overhead speaker in the lounge startled everyone except Dr. Brandon.

"Dr. Brandon, 169 please. Dr. Brandon, 169."

To all present the page meant nothing. To Dr. Brandon "1" meant a high priority emergency, "6" was the floor number and "9" was a patient identifier.

"I have to go. We'll talk soon."

Dr. Brandon rushed from the room and headed directly for Peter Douglas's bedside. He was surprised to see Sarah in the hallway outside her father's cubicle, staring through the window. The fingers of both hands were pressed against the glass and tears streamed down her face. Passing her, he nearly collided head on with a woman wheeling her cleaning cart along the hallway. Dr. Brandon pulled the curtain, blocking Sarah's view.

"Look at this, Dr. Brandon." Two interns were waiting. They handed him the graph tape from the EEG machine. One intern held it up so the three of them could view it. It showed a long straight line then a stream of spikes followed by another long straight line.

"What's the time line?"

"About 90 seconds."

"Any other indicators of his brain activity?"

"None."

Dr. Brandon put his hand to his face and stared at the tape, alternating glances toward Mr. Douglas. He didn't share his private thoughts but thanked the interns for their quick response. Once they were gone he moved to the bedside. With his right thumb he alternately rolled back each eye lid to expose crystal-blue eyes.

"I know you're in there. I know you're in there, but how am I going to get you out?" Was there more to this than he could see?

Dr. Brandon made several notations on the tape then folded it carefully and slipped it into his lab coat pocket.

In the hallway he saw Sarah walking slowly back to the lounge while she read the writing on Michael's card.

Dr. Brandon smiled to himself, feeling a precious moment of good in the battle against bad.

- Chapter 13 -

"**C**opy that, Bearded One. You are a man's best friend."

The CB radio crackled as Fuzzy Polonski talked to his trucking buddies, heading south on Interstate 95. Fuzzy loved to drive at night. From his perch high up in the cab he felt in command of the vehicle and his destiny. The sky was black, dotted only with the pinpoint lights of stars. The steady blur of headlamps driving north in the other lane were just a white streak of "Nobodies going nowhere," as he liked to call them. He hated the new halogen bulbs that scattered eye piercing beams in his direction when the angle of the north and south lanes was a certain way.

What he did like was the way truckers had taken to decorating their rigs with colored lights. This provided Fuzzy with immense amusement. It had started simply enough with one driver making a cross with lights on his grill, proclaiming his faith and carving out his individuality. Whoever it was had wanted people to perceive him as different from the stereotyped, pot-bellied, unshaven, rough-talking, T-shirt wearing bullies so often portrayed in movies. The "Light Up Your Life" movement just seemed to take off.

Drivers now spent thousands of dollars expressing themselves in lights. Some were subtle, some garish, but all of them gave a glimpse into the head of the man behind the wheel. Drivers flashed their headlamps at passing rigs if they liked what they saw. If they didn't, they would turn off their head lights for a second to indicate their displeasure. From crosses grew other symbols, and from symbols and letters grew an industry made up of, glorifying in lights, the personalities of truckers across America. Some used letters to spell a name or initials. Others used animals like cats, dogs, eagles, horses. Still others used sequencing circuits to make lights blaze in various arrays.

Fuzzy flipped his high beams at the Bird in Flight on a passing rig. He did nothing for crosses any more, they were passé. Fuzzy had not invested in lights for the front of his rig, but he had spent plenty making it his pride and joy. His top-of-the-line rig had everything a man could want on the road. The temperature-controlled cab was beautifully appointed, the sleeping area in the back had an oversized double bed, DVD player and screen, laptop computer, flat panel TV, micro-kitchen and wash up facilities. Fuzzy was self-sufficient. His truck was his home and it seemed to him that he'd stayed in nearly every corner of America. He made good money, but after expenses and taxes there never seemed to be much left over. Still, he always managed to send some home to his parents every month.

Fuzzy stared ahead in disbelief at a massive rig heading north.

He was right but still couldn't believe what he was seeing.

Drivers ahead of him were flashing their lights like crazy, and he could hear the vibrato bass tones when the loud horns of trucks ahead of him trumpeted.

"Hey, Fuzzy, check out the HUMPER headin' north at ten o'clock."

Fuzzy didn't respond. He just stared in disbelief, watching the illuminated version of a porno flick on someone's grill. A male figure outlined in lights was sequenced in mock intercourse with a female figure.

"Hey, Fuzzy, nice fuckin' lights, huh? Get it? *Fuckin'* lights."

The roar of crackling laughter filled his cab. Fuzzy extinguished his headlights for a few seconds to send his disapproval across the median. The HUMPER was obviously ready for this ridicule. No sooner had Fuzzy put his lights back on when the penis and vaginal area of the grilled portrait turned red and flashed. This was followed by a burst of light before the whole grill went dark.

The CB came alive with commentary. By the end of thirty minutes of school-yard chatter, Fuzzy knew that the HUMPER's lights broke all the codes, that he had spent $12,000 on his light show and that it was capable of simulating any number of sex acts. Fuzzy had the last say when he clicked from CB to a news station on satellite radio.

"In late breaking news Peter Douglas, the wealthy founder of the Douglas Corporation, is…"

A bark startled Fuzzy. The dog had been curled up well into the leg cavity of the passenger side.

"Easy, fella…" Fuzzy adjusted the volume.

" …in critical care and rumored to be in a deep coma after a tragic car accident this afternoon. Dr. James Brandon, physician in charge of the Douglas case, would not comment except to say that his patient is alive and under observation. We'll have more news regarding one of the city's most prominent citizens as it happens. In another tragic crash today…"

"Holy shit, boy, that's your man they're talkin' 'bout…he's alive."

Fuzzy turned down the radio as he spoke. His voice was wavering. Delayed anxiety swept over him from the events of the day now racing through his mind. He'd assumed that the man he'd pulled from the car was dead. He'd had no idea that it was Peter Douglas. Taking the dog along with him had seemed the natural thing to do at the time rather than leave him without a master.

Staring out at the stream of lights ahead of him, he pondered his day.

He could smell the rubber from screeching tires.

Gunshots boomed in his head.

Cold water chilled him.

His muscles still ached from exertion.

He felt deeply fatigued.

Fuzzy's eyes blurred. The corners of his mouth sagged beneath his beard. Steering his rig into the approach lane of a trucker's rest stop, his lower lip quivered.

When the hiss from the air brakes subsided, Fuzzy put his hands to his face. His whole body shook with quiet sobs.

The first lick went unnoticed.

The second one placed a long wet tongue right into his ear.

Fuzzy sat back.

He smiled while his face and salty beard got a good clean-up.

Laughing heavily now, he pushed the attacker away and gave him a brisk pat around his head and ears.

"Thanks, boy, I love you too, but you have to do something about that breath of yours!"

The dog whined and licked Fuzzy's hands which were still sticky with tears.

"Are ya hungry, boy? I'm starved. Let's get us some chow."

Fuzzy rolled the rig forward into the overnight parking area then started up the generator before shutting down the massive diesel engine. Spending money on something useful like a super-quiet generator made sense. Fucking lights did not. Fuzzy liked his independence so he had his rig wired to provide power to all his modern conveniences without having to plug in or leave the diesel plant idling all night.

"Stay there a sec, boy…"

The dog whimpered.

"I'll just be a minute..." Fuzzy held up his hand. "Stay... it's okay."

Fuzzy eased out of his captain's chair onto the outboard steps then down to the ground. Behind the cab he opened his toolbox from which he pulled out a small piece of yellow nylon rope.

"This'll have to do."

He walked the long way around the rig, checking while he went for anything unusual. Fuzzy was proud to have one of the best safety records on the interstate list.

When Fuzzy opened the passenger door of the cab the dog leapt into his arms. He held himself steady with one hand and the dog with the other.

"Easy boy, c'mon down. It's okay."

Fuzzy jury-rigged a collar out of the yellow rope, slipped it around the dog's neck and walked toward the truck stop facility.

"Hey, Fuzzy, your girlfriend's a dog," yelled one of his trucking mates.

"Ya, Fuzzy, where'd you get the blonde?"

Fuzzy ignored all the catcalls that came his way. He tied Schebb securely to a post near the window where he would be sitting for dinner. Faces peered through the glass. Several truckers stopped to pet the dog and ask Fuzzy questions about his new comrade. They all knew that Fuzzy was a loner. Most of the men stopped their conversations or looked up from their meals when Fuzzy entered the building. He had been a loner all his life, and although lots of truckers traveled with pets, they never brought them near the building. That was just the rule. It's tough enough on the road managing relationships amongst the truckers without the threat of someone's dog, cat or possum getting in a squabble with another.

Fuzzy had never been to a press conference, but he guessed from watching television that this is what it must be like as dozens of questions were hurled his way.

"A stray. Just a stray," was his only response but Fuzzy was uneasy.

He'll be gone in the morning.

A few more perverse remarks were yelled out, but the laughs and comments finally subsided then the group settled back to their previous activities.

Fuzzy walked the food line, filling a tray for two. He could feel a bead of sweat moving down his back and probably couldn't have told anyone what he'd taken after he finally settled in for his meal.

His companion lay tied to the post, a prisoner of sorts for the second time in his life. The trucker and the dog stared at each other, seeming content with their mutual affection and the secret they now shared.

Swallowing fork after fork of food, barely taking time to chew, Fuzzy glanced up at the television to see a full color photo of Peter Douglas above bold headlines.

He glanced again at the dog, felt his forehead moisten with sweat, then pushed a half full plate of food to the middle of the table and stood up.

- Chapter 14 -

She lay wrapped in a thick white bathrobe, surrounded by white pillows and a fluffy white duvet. The candle by Charlotte's bed had sputtered to its death. The sound of the door bell was a distant tone in her dream, but when it repeated, Charlotte's conscious mind took over and brought her out of a deep, groggy sleep.

The doorbell rang again; she wondered who it could be this late? After she swung her feet onto the floor, she turned on a bedside lamp then shook her damp hair into a semblance of order. She smoothed her face with her hands and tidied her robe while she walked out of her room and down the stairs.

Was Peter not home yet? Where could that man be? So much for romantic plans.

She noticed a light on the telephone blinking as the doorbell rang simultaneously. She answered and made a mental note to check the ringer switch after the call.

"All right, all right, I'm coming... Hello? Catherine! Hi, just a second, I have to answer the door..."

Charlotte dropped the receiver and moved to the foyer.

Jimmy stood outside, waiting and wondering what could be taking Mrs. Douglas so long. He also questioned why she would be ordering up dinner for two when Mr. Douglas was in critical condition at the hospital. Every paper, radio and television had been featuring the story since late afternoon. But it was not

Jimmy's place to worry or ask such questions. His clientele's business was not his own.

The sight of Charlotte Douglas in her white robe sent his mind racing. He felt a slight sexual surge.

Charlotte greeted Jimmy who started into his usual banter. She jousted verbally with him for a few seconds, which distracted her attention from the waiting telephone.

"That food smells delicious, Jimmy."

"So do you, Mrs. Douglas." Jimmy smiled.

Charlotte could feel her skin go taut. She had played this little game before.

"Thank you, Jimmy. I just finished a wonderful bubble bath, and I'm clean from head to toe."

"I'd start with the toes, then."

"In your dreams, Jimmy. In your dreams."

"Sorry I'm a bit late. Is everything…all…I mean are you okay?"

"Yes, why?"

"I dunno, I just thought that…I mean dinner for two?"

Charlotte took the package from him. Their hands brushed.

"Thank you, Jimmy. That will be all for tonight," Charlotte smiled.

"Are you sure? Mrs. Douglas…I just wanted to say…"

"Yes? What is it?"

"Well, I just wanted to say that….I hope everything turns out okay."

"Oh, I'm sure everything will be just great, Jimmy. Thanks for caring so much."

"Yeah, well, ah, it's no problem. I hope you're right."

"Okay, goodnight Jimmy."

Why was the usually smooth Jimmy at a loss for words and looking somewhat perplexed?

She deliberately and admiringly watched him walk through the foyer out toward his car. Charlotte carried her dinner to the kitchen, brushing aside the peculiar exchange.

The cats tangled at her feet while she set the boxes on the counter beside the paper. She opened the refrigerator, uncorked the bottle with a pop and poured another full glass of white wine.

All thoughts of Jimmy vanished. She held the bottle up and realized she had drunk the better part of it. She re-corked the green vessel, tapping the top firmly in place with the heel of her hand before laying it back in the wine rack. A few drops hit the floor which the cats lapped up instantaneously.

"Not tonight, guys. No party for you two,"

Charlotte took a long sip from the newly freshened crystal glass. She reached down to turn over the paper and see what headlines her famous husband was making tonight.

The crystal shattered into a thousand pieces when the glass hit the floor.

The cats scurried.

She felt a fever break out across her entire body.

She stared at the phone handset still waiting for her attention.

"Catherine, Catherine! Oh my God, Oh my God, I'm so sorry, I'm so sorry, what has happened?"

Charlotte rushed around in a panic, grabbing a few things to throw in a bag and dressing quickly for her night time trip to town.

She ran for the garage. "Shit."

She ran back to grab her cell phone from the charger then headed back toward the garage again.

"Fuck."

She stopped dead in her tracks. She was suddenly very scared. Her car was miles away.

To take Peter's vintage Mercedes sports car or a wait for taxi or friend were her only choices.

Biting her lip, she eased the Mercedes gingerly out of the garage.

The smell of burning clutch fouled the air when the engine over-revved.

Tires squealed…then stopped.

The gears ground loudly. The car popped out into the night then she stopped again abruptly.

Charlotte was breathing fast.

She reached above the visor and pressed the button to close the garage door then watched it drop in her rearview mirror. Thoughts of prowlers having their way in her home gave her stomach a sick feeling.

With the door safely down she eased the car into gear and drove into the night.

She lowered the driver's side window to let the evening air flow in replacing the smell of rubber and clutch. She fumbled in her bag to find the cell phone that she hoped now had some charge.

It did.

"Jimmy's, can I help you?"

"Jimmy, it's Charlotte…Charlotte Douglas I mean."

"Hi, Mrs. Douglas, that was quick. Is there a problem with your food?"

"No, Jimmy… it's Peter. Why didn't you say something?"

"Mrs. Douglas, I did, but…."

"Never mind, it's okay. I need a favor, Jimmy. I'm going to be in town, I don't know how long. Could you keep an eye on our house like you did before? You know where our key is. Please feed my cats and water the plants. I could be away for a while. You can stay there if you like."

"Sure, ya …absolutely. It's the least I can do after…listen…"

Her voice trembled. "Jimmy…it's okay. I'll be fine."

"Charlotte… I mean, Mrs. Douglas…"

"It's okay, you can call me Charlotte."

"I'm your knight in shining armor. I'll be on my horse right after work. You can rest assured that everything will be covered."

"Thanks, Jimmy, you're sweet. Pray for Peter."

"You got it."

She sped down the black road, only slowing at the stop signs, making several turns toward the interstate to Boston. She ran red lights, sped through the darkened town, cringed when she blew through the one in front of the town hall and police station.

No one noticed.

Her headlights periodically caught the bright eyes of a raccoon.

She adjusted the radio, impatiently trying to find some music to calm her down. A stiff, chilly, evening wind blew her hair back.

Her headlights illuminated bright orange highway cones ahead of her. She slowed slightly out of reflex and stared at the point where a car had obviously left the road. She wondered if it had been Peter's.

Tears streamed down her face.

She drifted around the curve…then was snapped from her daze when two blinding bright lights appeared directly in front of her; a loud horn jolting her to attention.

She swerved hard to the right and slammed on the brakes.

Tires screeched. The car swayed sideways onto the gravel shoulder. Charlotte's hands gripped the steering wheel; both feet drove the brake and clutch pedals to the floor.

The wind of the passing tractor trailer rocked the car now skidding along the shoulder toward the ditch.

The sound of the air horn faded.

Charlotte's car came to rest a few feet from disaster.

The truck continued on its path without stopping.

Charlotte buried her face in her hands.

Her stalled engine cooled against a backdrop of evening noises. Crickets sang. An owl hooted out a warning. Forest animals stopped to stare at the bright lights piercing the darkness. Lush green smells of the evening forest were masked by the pungent smell of burning brakes and rubber.

Charlotte's sobs were muffled. She sat alone with nature, wrapped in a moment that could have spelled a fate similar to her husband's.

- Chapter 15 -

"Susan, hey it's me...did you see the news?"

The engines of the jet whined just prior to the brakes releasing.

Matt fingered a drink while he filled his fiancée in on all the details he had. "I guess I'll commute...I have some stuff to finish up...so I can stay close to him...yep, I will...promise...they're all at Cath's...call them there...okay...love you...okay...bye."

Matt squeezed the hand set, pressed his lips tightly together, and closed his eyes for a moment. Then there was silence at the end of the phone; another lie.

He took a deep breath then slowly opened his eyes to stare straight ahead while he took a long sip of his drink.

He felt his body press into the leather seat.

The plane lifted off.

For now, Boston, Peter, Susan and all that he detested about himself were left behind.

He smelled her perfume when the door of the jet opened, its fragrance buoyed on a tropical breeze coupled with several drinks en route, temporarily erasing the memories of his long day. He felt his heart pick up and blood pressure rise.

She smiled up at him. Cara looked gorgeous. Her blond hair covered string-like straps on her tanned, bare shoulders. She wore a short cotton summer dress with no evidence of a bra.

Matt strode down the steps, took Cara's hand and slipped into the back of the waiting limo.

"Let's go."

He took Cara in his arms. Her one leg flopped over his. Music from one of her favorite bands filled the car. Her mouth opened wide when he moved in to kiss her. Matt's hand slid down her back, over her bottom and onto her bare thigh. It retraced its path, this time underneath her dress. As his hand wrapped around her, he realized she wasn't wearing any underwear.

"Surprise" was the only word she could get out with Matt's mouth pressed hard against hers.

He felt her fingers dig into his back. His cologne wafted from his body heat.

Matt glimpsed for a moment to ensure the driver's view was obscured. This wouldn't be the first time she had coaxed him into having sex in places which posed greater risks of being caught. For Matt, excitement and potential peril seemed to go hand in hand.

He felt her hand slide around to the front of his pants.

He hoped she'd be impressed.

She smiled while they kissed.

Underneath her dress, he traced her firm cheek until the edge of his little finger discovered the wet answer he was seeking.

Cara unzipped his pants then opened the single button on his boxer shorts.

Matt took one last glimpse and noticed the driver straining to see what was happening.

He slumped into his leather seat and stretched out his legs. Darkness, music and the tropical wind blowing through the car were his cloak.

In a single, deft move Cara was instantly astride and facing him.

Matt closed his eyes and let himself sink deeply into the familiar abyss of lust and passion that was both his shelter and his prison.

- Chapter 16 -

Brian's thick brown hair was tousled. Pillow creases marked his face. He was a younger version of his father, pleasant but plain, with a less than perfect complexion from battling acne when he was a young man. Tall and thin, he was more of an artist than an athlete; a high metabolism rather than vigorous workouts kept the pounds off. His long, slender fingers meshed with each other. His hands rested under his chin in prayer.

Brian lay asleep on a couch in the makeshift family room. He had been fielding and making calls all evening, organizing press releases, putting contingency plans in place for his absence, but ultimately he'd succumbed to sleep while reading a briefing on the Douglas Corporation's latest takeover target.

A few hundred feet away in the new room to which Peter had been moved, a flurry of activity surrounded the patient as half a dozen specialists connected the newly arrived monitoring equipment. Dr. Brandon, head of this team, deferred to two seasoned specialists from Europe who had accompanied the equipment. The gear was experimental and its development still in infancy. He had heard that many in the medical community doubted its reliability, but others were impressed with its capacity for sensing life in apparently lifeless patients.

The smell of burning protein filled the air. The sound of steel on bone filled the room as a surgeon drilled two small holes into shaved patches on Peter's skull. A mixture of blood and fluid from inside Peter's head oozed around his ears and matted his hair. The holes would provide access for the Doctors to embed sensors into his brain.

Dr. Brandon had been fully briefed.

Chemical and electrical activities would be monitored closely, but the unique part of the equipment was a metallic framed structure erected like a camping tent over and around Peter's bed. Within the structure, tens of thousands of highly receptive electronic sensors mapped Peter's global body electromagnetic aura. Chemical reactions were important to observe, but the sub-cellular monitoring of electrical activity, the basis for all functions in the human body, painted a far more detailed and telling picture.

Special precautions were being taken to eliminate possible outside electrical interference by programming the equipment to ignore existing electronic "noise" in the surrounding environment. Anyone who entered the Douglas room was required to walk through a scanning device like those at an airport. Their electronic statistics were logged and automatically ignored from then on. This allowed a flow of authorized visitors in and out of Peter's room without disturbing the precise monitoring.

Once all preparations were complete, a central monitoring station set up in an office adjoining Peter's room would present the Doctors with a full-color, three-dimensional view of Peter Douglas. The eerie computer-generated display showed blood flowing through his veins, the beating of his heart, electrical and chemical activity in his brain and an impressive list of bodily functions. This equipment had been rumored to have recorded unusual activities at the time of death of a number of patients. Proponents pointed to images of electronic interference just prior to expiration and suggested that they indicated the spirit moving out of its host. Researchers had been trying to establish a method of tracking this energy by digitizing patterns of electrons when they appeared and transferring the monitoring over to highly sensitive satellite-based tracking equipment to see if the flow could be followed. Hushed conversations were held over theories of the movement of such electronic patterns from a dying human to another form taking life.

Peter observed all of this activity from within his prison of flesh. His agitation level was extreme. He screamed to the figures around him, but no one heard. He looked left and right, but no one saw his eyes move. He perspired profusely, but nurses merely wiped him dry. If he had been conscious and standing, he would have been screaming and jumping up and down flailing his arms about for all to see, yet in this terrifying state he was a silent captive of his own damaged body.

"Ready for background check."

"We'll map existing noise before calibrating the equipment for monitoring."

"Computer booting up. Logging in."

"Power within tolerance. Monitor a go."

"Commencing primary sequence."

The monitor exploded with color. Sensitive speakers squawked and screeched with an ear-shattering racket.

"Power down," the technicians yelled.

They hovered over the equipment.

"That's right guys I'm alive. I'm in here…in this useless body you silly asses."

Discussions ensued about sources of electronic signals. All unnecessary personnel were ordered out of the room, leaving the technicians on their own. Dr. Brandon went out to do some rounds, asking to be paged when they were ready to go. Hospital engineers were consulted by telephone to determine if any non-specified equipment was being operated within range of the sensors. Programs were designed to take into account all usual hospital gear such as ECG and EKG machines, computers, x-ray equipment, pagers, speakers, televisions, all types of telephones and electronic gadgets.

The most obvious source was being ignored.

"If this guy kicks off soon, we can catch the grand finale and get home."

"Let's re-calibrate with a higher threshold. If there's a big surge when he dies, we'll catch it. It's not like there's anything going on in there now."

"Right, I'll make a threshold adjustment of 400 percent, which will eliminate all the noise. Assuming no brain activity now; if he starts thinking we'll pick it up."

The weary technicians colluded to speed up their jobs. The rest of the crew waited outside.

"Sounds good. Dr. Brandon said electrical activity so far was negligible."

"Commencing primary test for new threshold. I'll try to catch the peak."

"Don't shut me out! I'm here. I'm alive. I'm alive!" Peter screamed.

Peter suddenly realized it was him causing the major volume of electrical interference. What he hadn't realized was that his agitation had actually reduced the likelihood of anyone sensing irregular electrical activity. The technicians were about to set a threshold that assumed levels they were reading were normal. The higher threshold would therefore discount them all together. Peter tried desperately to calm himself. The screen which had been dancing with activity steadied.

The technicians looked at each other and grinned. "Ah, look at this. All is calm now."

"Okay, let's avoid any late-night calls. Scan back, pick the peak activity range and lock it in as a baseline."

"Shouldn't we set it now at this lower level?"

"Yes! Yes! I am in here! Can't you see? I am alive!" Peter shouted.

The screen flashed again into a blaze of color.

"See what I mean? Do you want to take a call every time some joker in the area winds his watch?"

"Threshold set."

The two technicians eyed each other knowingly.

"Fucking Yankees," they'll never know.

Peter felt his jail cell had just been sealed. His agitation level was so intense at first that the technicians had erroneously set a baseline much higher than normal. Peter's body electrical activity would now go unnoticed. Staying calm was an impossible task. He was struggling between reason and panic. Had he been unconscious, the levels would have been set extremely low and thus his first waking would have generated tremendous output on the screen. Now, it would take an immense explosion of energy on Peter's part to generate anything above the locked-in levels. Peter's panic gave way to complete despondency now that he realized the key to his prison might have just been thrown away.

"Let's get some sleep. We can program for three dimensional imaging tomorrow. We're capturing data now. Let's check with Dr. Brandon and the folks outside."

Two tears, one from each eye, rolled down Peter's cheeks.

The monitor registered no activity.

After a short conference, Dr. Brandon told his team to call it a night. Peter Douglas was an important patient, but not the only one in this hospital who needed attention. From this point forward they'd play the waiting game until there was a better understanding of Peter's condition. His wounds needed time to stabilize and start healing before any more treatments were attempted. Dr. Brandon knew it could be weeks, months or longer before any changes might occur. He peered through the glass at Peter's limp body surrounded and connected by the best medical equipment in the world. He muttered aloud, "God have mercy. Whatever is your purpose here? Where are you taking me?"

Dr. Brandon knew that millions of dollars could be spent on this one patient with little hope of recovery, when so many others could be helped, healed and get on with a productive life.

He had faced this moral dilemma many times. Private insurance companies had quietly developed new plans and incentives that forced the issue of maintaining life in apparently hopeless cases onto the shoulders of hospital physicians and administrators. To facilitate the decision to promote termination, insurance companies would donate between 25 and 50 percent of the projected care costs of terminal patients to those who could not afford insurance, or whose benefits had run out. This arrangement put tremendous moral pressure on the hospital administrators when they vetted decisions around termination then discussed the equally delicate task of deciding who should benefit from the available resources.

Turning from the window, Dr. Brandon was startled to see a woman behind him, mop in hand, peering through the glass at Mr. Douglas.

"You startled me, Mrs. Rossi. You got those squeaky wheels fixed."

"Yes, I move quiet like ghost now, Doctor." She looked up at him through ancient eyes. "Mr. Douglas, he special man. God want keep this one."

"Pardon?" Dr. Brandon re-focused.

"This special man. He live. He live." Mrs. Rossi wheeled her bucket away, humming quietly to herself. Dr. Brandon shivered slightly when she passed. He looked once again at Peter Douglas, remembered the EEG tape from the afternoon. He cast a final, curious look at Mrs. Rossi.

He was too tired to put any of this together, but when he left the window a glimmer of promise washed in from somewhere. He closed his eyes, gave his head a shake and left to end another long day. With his hand in his coat pocket, walking away, he fondled the paper tape of the EEG.

Mrs. Rossi entered Peter Douglas's room through the electronic archway. When she did, it scanned her electromagnetic imprint. Her information went directly to the computer monitoring Mr. Douglas. It was automatically screened out of any display analysis, thus avoiding false alarms or readings unrelated to Peter's electrical activity.

When she passed through the archway the computer screen burst alive with flashes of color and graphic waves, indicating massive readings. The computer whirred as data entered and was processed. The cleaning woman's readings exceeded all previously set thresholds, causing the computer automatically to re-calibrate its previous data. Peter Douglas would have to give off extraordinary amounts of electrical energy to cause any readings at these new levels. Mrs. Rossi smiled when she observed the screen. She continued to hum to herself.

Peter was unaware of anyone entering his room. He was in his version of sleep, replaying the day's events over and over, dwelling on Sarah's face while she peered at him through the glass. More tears leaked from the corners of his eyes. He became aware of a beautiful melody. Every other sound that day had been registered through his ears, but this music was inside him. It filled him with hope. A wave of joy passed over him.

Abruptly his ears turned on. He heard a bucket bump up against a chair and water slosh about inside it. To the world his eyelids were shut, but he could see the cherubic woman staring at him.

He could feel her smile inside. Her name tag said Mrs. Rosie Rossi.

He smiled back. She nodded and went about her business.

The music started again in his head. He understood that she was humming, but he was hearing her music from within.

"Who are you?" he called. "Can you hear me? Do you know I'm in here? Can you help me?"

There was no response, just her music. She continued her duties.

He could feel her presence; a warm, loving feeling that relaxed him and made him feel hopeful.

She wiped down his bed rails. She cleaned his side table and adjusted a few things that were out of place. Her music continued. She paused and looked down at Peter's face. Through closed eyelids he looked directly into her tired eyes. She smiled a worn smile and touched his arm. Peter could feel her warm flesh against his. Heat and energy poured into him. She eased her grip and turned away.

"Good night, Mr. Douglas."

Peter heard her words inside, not through his ears. He could not see whether her mouth had moved or not.

"Can you hear me? Can you help me?" Peter was desperate for contact with anyone who could help him solve his predicament or at least know that he was more than what he appeared.

His panic rose. The familiar feeling of confinement engulfed him. He tried hopelessly to reach out.

The music started again as she wheeled her bucket out of the room. When she passed under the arch the screen blazed again.

He couldn't see, but Mrs. Rossi smiled to herself.

Peter was desolate.

The music was gone.

Chapter 17

Every thirty minutes throughout the night a rotation of nurses came to Peter's bedside to perform a variety of checks. They made notes on a clipboard and went about their business with dispatch. Four different nurses passed through the archway, and none registered more than a flicker on the computer screen. Peter was calm for now and slept intermittently between visits.

To the nurses this was just the evening routine. Peter quickly realized it held little excitement for them. When each nurse approached his bedside, he struggled to communicate or make some bodily movement to let them know he was alive and trapped inside. Nothing worked. His efforts seemed to be for his distraction alone. Each nurse checked his pulse and blood pressure, and then compared them to readings constantly playing on green screens beside him. They would then pull back his sheets, exposing his body to check for soiling in his diaper. They adjusted the balloon catheter on the end of his penis to ensure an easy flow of urine into the clear plastic bag hanging from his bed.

Peter squirmed thinking about being seen in this condition. His fit body was badly bruised. His genitals felt like they had shriveled and dropped off. His vanity overwhelmed him. He laughed bitterly at himself and his predicament, the laughter a product of fear and fatigue.

Nurses took temperature readings at various points on his body. They inserted an electronic probe in his armpit and gently adjusted his scrotum to slip it against his upper groin for a second reading. They checked the intravenous supply, the controls and the puncture points on his arm. Each nurse rolled his eyelids back to check for response to light.

During all of these checks, each nurse displayed her own idiosyncrasies. Two were quiet and businesslike, one hummed out loud or talked to herself about things she had to do next, but it was the last nurse who Peter found himself waiting for. She was quite a bit younger than the previous three, and when she entered Peter's room she had teenage buoyancy in her stride and friendly warmth about her. Her blond hair was pulled up under her nurse's cap and her white uniform was crisp with a tight tailored fit. She had a well-proportioned body and when she bent over the bed it was obvious through the thin fabric that her undergarments weren't standard hospital issue. She went about her work happily. At one point early in her visits she spoke out loud.

"So you're the wealthy Mr. Douglas? Well, I'll be taking good care of you, even if you don't know it. Do you mind if I call you Peter?"

Her temperature-taking technique was different from the rest. Instead of pulling Peter's sheets back, she merely exposed the appropriate region and inserted the probe. When it came time to do his groin temperature, she slid her hands under his sheets and made the necessary adjustments without looking. She also looked directly at him as though she expected him to open his eyes and say something.

Peter was mystified.

First Mrs. Rossi stared at him.

Now a beautiful young nurse stared right at him too as she adjusted his privates.

Her name-tag said Terri Queen.

She smoothed her hand across his forehead before leaving his bedside.

"We'll take good care of you, Peter."

Before leaving, Terri walked into the bathroom across from Peter's bed. She proceeded to hoist up her uniform, exposing one half of her non-standard issue undergarments. She slid her white satin briefs to her ankles and sat down.

Peter was embarrassed yet curious at the sound of water tinkling in the toilet. His field of vision was not like normal eyes: he realized he could see in 360 degrees, directly on plane or a few feet above or below his usual plane of vision. This skill had been with him all day, but it only dawned on him now when he strained a little to observe Terri.

Ironically, the situation was frightening. He was living a new life, feeling childlike in his discovery of this new power, yet his body lay damaged and paralyzed.

Terri stood up, reorganized her clothing and rinsed her hands. She smoothed her hair in the mirror and dabbed on lipstick. She undid several top buttons of her uniform and adjusted her bra so that everything was sitting just so. Redoing all but two buttons, she turned and looked at Peter once more.

"You're not watching this, are you? Embarrassed, Peter turned his eyes to look in another direction.

"Terri? You in there?"

Terri started at the sound of a man's voice. She turned off the bathroom light.

"Right here, just checking supplies."

"Are you on break now?"

"As soon as I finish with Mr. Douglas here."

"The guy in the papers today?"

"Yeah, the billionaire. He's pretty good-looking too, for an older man." Terri seemed to be working to get a rise out of her male caller.

"Yeah, too bad he's a vegetable. C'mon, let's get a coffee."

Terri returned to Peter's bedside and made a few notes on her clipboard. She looked at Peter. "He didn't mean what he said. He doesn't know you. I don't think that way at all, Peter. We'll fix you up, don't worry."

She turned and left the room.

Peter was stunned by what was happening. He was hearing and seeing things not meant to be shared. He felt uncomfortable, yet curious. He wanted to take comfort from her words, but assumed they were just the musings of a hopeful young nurse.

What did this predicament mean? Where was it all leading?

His mind was full of questions.

Quiet blanketed his room once again; Peter fell into a troubled sleep.

- Chapter 18 -

Two fluffy white cats played at Charlotte's feet while she made her way through the unfamiliar geography. She tiptoed around the spacious Beacon Hill townhouse, trying not to wake anyone. From the outside the flat had appeared like two separate addresses, but Catherine owned both units. Her fashion sense was evident in the furnishings and finishes. Although Charlotte had only slept a few hours the previous night, she still admired the high ceilings, hardwood floors and ornate trim.

Charlotte knew that Marion had chosen to stay with a friend once she'd heard that Charlotte would be staying with Catherine. Charlotte and Marion knew each other, but usually met only in social settings when each was wearing her feminine armor. Neither Charlotte nor, presumably, Marion had a longing to shed tears together over Peter or see each other in a disturbed state, with their guard down.

Catherine and Sarah had received Charlotte warmly when she arrived badly shaken. Catherine made her take another hot bath and drink a glass of warmed red wine. She and Sarah listened to Charlotte's story of waiting at home for their father to arrive and then surviving near-catastrophe on the highway.

Catherine gave Charlotte all the details she knew about Peter. Some tears were shed. Sarah listened quietly at first while Catherine and Charlotte chatted, eventually joining in with them, and several hours disappeared in a broad range of discussion. Tension eased and shared laughter made the three feel close.

Charlotte was welcome to stay for as long as she liked, Catherine said. She mentioned the interesting man, Michael Phillips, whom she and Sarah had first met in the elevator. She paid particular attention when describing Dr. Brandon. Charlotte learned more about the girls in those few hours than she had in all the time she'd known them.

Catherine's fast lifestyle took her in and out of many adventures and men's arms. It also turned out that Sarah was not far behind Catherine in the hell-raising department. Drugs, alcohol and boys weren't on the official curriculum at Hélène Marie College, but apparently they got more than enough of Sarah's focus. Charlotte was tempted at times to be motherly, but stopped short, thinking that Sarah was more likely relating to her as an equal or a friend.

They had taken a call from Matt's fiancée Susan, whom they talked to together over the speakerphone. Susan had declined their invitation to come by but expressed appreciation for their sharing of news and concern. They all adored Susan, who seemed to set the bar high with everything she did. When asked by her if they knew what work Matt was up to in Bermuda they deftly avoided any speculation.

"You know, I really love Matthew but sometimes he is just so distant," she'd expressed.

Thirty minutes later all of the ladies had exchanged boyfriend stories that seemed to share a common theme: nice girl chases bad boy and loses nice guys along the way.

"I wish I knew where this was all going," she'd said. "I can't wait forever."

At the end of the conversation Susan shared the secret that she had lost a baby that prior year, which seemed to have been a negative turning point in their relationship.

The ladies had chuckled at Sarah who had offered to see what she could do to get her brother Matt to "man up", as she called it, and commit.

"I know how he thinks."

- Chapter 19 -

Edward instinctively hit the snooze button at the first chirp out of his radio, cutting off the morning news. A bell rang in the distance, somewhere deep in his next dream. It continued to ring while Edward's dreams rolled on.

When his arm swung out a second time to hit the snooze button it was intercepted by a solid grip on his forearm.

Edward jolted upright in his bed to hear deep laughter filling his room.

He cleared his head and focused on the face of his book editor, Frank Miles, who had arrived for their scheduled seven a.m. breakfast meeting.

"What the heck are you doing here?"

"Good morning sleepy. I'm here to review your research, remember?"

"What the... how'd you get in here?"

Edward was presented with a set of keys.

"These were in your door. Were you expecting company?"

"My goodness no, no, it's just that I was so tired when I got in from Europe last night that I must have left them there. It was a late flight...we got delayed on both ends while they loaded and unloaded some medical gear. All hush hush, ya know?"

"Terrible thing about your boss. You must be pretty shook up."

"My boss? What are you talking about?"

"Where have you been, Mars? It's the top story on every radio, television and newspaper. It's all over the Net. Check this out."

Edward covered his mouth as he stared at Peter Douglas's picture on the cover of his morning paper. The bold headline screamed out at him: **MEDIA MAGNATE NEAR DEATH IN COMA.**

Blood flow filled Edward's ears. Beads of perspiration stung his forehead while thoughts of his life long friend raced through his mind.

"I am such an idiot. I got a glimpse of the cover from a distance when we exited the plane but Peter on the cover is no big deal…I mean…"

"Whoa, heel down there boy, heel down. Not your fault. He's not dead, just…never mind. Go take five and rinse off. We'll get some coffee, and I can tell you what I know."

While Edward showered, his mind retraced his path from the day before.

How could I be so dumb?

"Damn, damn!"

He scrubbed down quickly taking a few extra seconds to massage his leg which ached from the long flight. He turned off the water, quickly toweled down, grabbed his cane and electric razor.

"You go ahead; I'll just be a few minutes."

While he dressed he did his best to read a few words of the paper that was strewn across his bed. He felt sick.

"Aren't you forgetting something?"

"Huh…"

Frank, now double-parked in front of Edward's Massachusetts Avenue brownstone, dangled Edward's set of keys in his face.

"Damn, damn keys." He grabbed the ring and hurried back to the door which he had left unlocked again. He fumbled with the balky cylinder until it finally submitted.

He turned toward the car just when the telephone began ringing inside his house. He hesitated.

Did I miss that too last night?

"Let's go Frank."

- Chapter 20 -

The traffic in Peter's room was already heavy as the team from the previous night reviewed the collected data, made adjustments and relocated the monitoring station to the adjacent room.

"Nothing unusual to report last night, Dr. Brandon."

"Bullshit!" Peter yelled.

He listened in disbelief while these so called experts made their views known.

"We had one enormous pulse right…there." One technician pointed to the screen where a colorful display rolled past.

"Probably an anomaly, something in the electrical fields in the building."

"When did it occur?"

The technician replayed another view of the screen. "Right there, when this person entered the room Doctor."

"Who is it?"

"Let me run the profile and create an image."

The screen came to life, showing a life-like picture of a heavy-set woman pushing a mop and pail.

"I'd say it's your night cleaner."

"Mrs. Rossi? What would cause the spike in the readings?"

"Could be her metal bucket, a pager or cell phone going off, interference from a hearing aid or heart pacer. Something like that."

"Yeah, could be her gold teeth bringing in a late night FM radio show," chipped in another technician.

Everyone cast a silent gaze his way…then a light chuckle rippled amongst the group.

"It doesn't matter. The system has now screened her readings out so the next time she comes in she could be in direct contact with aliens and we won't get any interference."

"It wouldn't surprise me with her."

"Pardon?"

"Oh nothing," Dr. Brandon replied.

He'd always gotten weird vibes from Mrs. Rossi. His feelings now were no different. He parked those thoughts in the back of his mind and headed to the Douglas's waiting room.

"Good morning, Brian. How was your evening?"

The elder Douglas son's back was to Dr. Brandon when he entered the room.

"I slept on the day bed and caught a shower down the hall in the staff lounge. I hope that was okay."

"So long as you're not showering with any of my nurses, make yourself at home." Both men chuckled then sat down.

"Doctor, we're having a family meeting here at about nine. I'd appreciate it if you could give them a briefing, but I'd like a quick update before then. How's my dad?"

"There's really been no change since last night. His vitals have stabilized. His temperature reading is normal. We've set up the monitoring equipment I referred to yesterday. It was flown in last night. With this in place we should be able to determine the slightest activity in your dad's brain as well as carefully monitoring all other functions in his body. It has unique technology that monitors the sub-cellular electrical activities."

Brian's brow furrowed. He listened intently.

"I won't leave anything to chance, Brian. If your dad has any hope, we'll find it. But it's up to Peter now. We'll have to wait a while and see what happens. I can't make any promises or predictions. We are dealing with a realm that is very unpredictable. Your father could snap to consciousness, or he could linger in this state for a long time. At this point his life is really in our hands and…"

Brian put up his hand to cut him short.

"We'll be doing everything possible to keep my dad alive, Dr. Brandon," Brian said in a strained voice. "Let's not even broach other possibilities."

Dr. Brandon nodded. "Yes, yes, of course. What I meant was we'll be monitoring his progress in minute detail so that we can take the appropriate steps for his well-being."

Brian knew from his vast experience in negotiation that both of them had just staked out their respective turf.

"I think it's important that you and your family try to get back to your daily routines as soon as possible. There is very little any of us can do at this early stage but wait."

"Thank you for your guidance, Doctor, but this family will set its own agenda. My father needs us nearby, and that's where we'll be for now."

Dr. Brandon prepared to leave. "That's your prerogative, of course. Please have me paged when your family arrives."

"Fine, thank you."

Brian could see the tension on Dr. Brandon's face and feel it on his own.

They shook hands and parted.

The telephone rang. It was Brian's assistant Marjorie asking how he was and letting him know that all of his meetings for the day have been covered or rescheduled."

"Thanks Marj."

Brian brought her up to date on his father's condition, trying not to telecast his feelings to Marjorie. He was surprised by her exceptional warmth when she said, "If there's anything that I can do, I'm there for you, of course."

Brian felt a pang of loneliness sweep through him.

"Thank you, Marjorie. I really appreciate your thoughtfulness."

Both hung up at the same time.

He stared for a few moments at the telephone and wondered if she may be doing the same.

Brian headed down the hall towards his father's room. He stopped to speak with his security personnel to ensure that no media or other unwanted people got near the lounge or his father.

"Are you new, George?" Brian looked at the rent-a-cop's name-tag. "I haven't seen you around Douglas before. I'm Brian Douglas."

George jumped to his feet. "Yes Sir, I've just been hired, but I assure you I won't let you down, Sir."

"Okay, fine, sit down. Welcome aboard. I'm counting on you and your other guys to ensure our privacy."

Brian noticed that George seemed a bit twitchy but assumed it was just nerves from the first day on the job.

"Yes, Sir!"

When George sat down he could feel the lump in his hind pocket created by the fifty ten dollar bills he had counted earlier and put there.

If only Brian knew that his real employer, *The City Star*, had paid him a bonus for getting this job he wouldn't be so friendly.

George fiddled with the mini-recorder and micro-camera he could feel in his other pockets.

Now, where am I going to put these so I can get some nice juicy scoops and make some cash for myself? Then I'll get a job with a decent paper.

Two carts loaded with flowers had accumulated outside the Douglas lounge. Brian stopped at the nursing station and asked the attendant on duty if she could see that the flowers were distributed to as many rooms on the floor as there were bouquets. He knew that this would just be the start of the well wishing. Everyone else might as well enjoy some of these gifts since his father could not.

Brian stopped outside his father's room. He peered through a large glass window overlooking the bed.

He closed his eyes.

The sight had made his insides tighten.

Anxiety rippled through his body.

His brain flashed a million images of him and his father.

This is unbelievable. I can't take this.

He opened his eyes and gazed through a blur at this man who, only days earlier, was the vibrant hero Brian looked up to and emulated. He now lay lifeless and pale, with wires and tubes connected all over his body.

Brian stared at the heart rate monitor and watched each spike registering on the tiny screen. The digital read-out of Peter's blood pressure was another small sign of life to him. Two clear plastic tubes poured precious oxygen into his father's nose, replacing, as Dr. Brandon had told him, the ventilator that had been used initially. A long, pale arm lay uncovered. An intravenous needle was covered with white tape to protect where it punctured his skin.

The room was dimly lit, with outside blinds blocking any natural light. Brian traced the electronic framework that encased the bed and followed the tangle of wires that passed along the floor and attached to the archway positioned inside the door.

So this was the special equipment to which Dr. Brandon referred.

The bundle of wires ran out of the door and under his feet leading down the hall to enter another room.

Brian's curiosity drew him along the trail of plastic-coated strands to the closed doorway. He listened but could only hear the hum of a cooling fan inside. Gently, he turned the handle and eased the door open. His first vision was that of a large computer screen with a digital clock in the bottom right-hand corner and a small computer image of his father in the upper right-hand corner. A straight white horizontal line flickered across the middle of the screen. When he eased the door open further, he saw a pair of white shoes on the table that supported the equipment. A pair of legs led up to a white lab coat and finally to the back of a man's head with very short cropped hair. The man was reading a book and leaning back in his chair.

"Hi."

The man nearly fell backwards. "What? Oh, hi there." The white-coated man turned with a start to acknowledge Brian. In doing so, he balanced precariously on the rear legs of the chair. He pulled against his feet and got the chair re-positioned on four legs.

"Can I help you?" He was clearly annoyed.

Brian recoiled. "No, ah, wrong room. Sorry. What is all this anyway?"

"This? Oh, we're monitoring the old man next door for any brain activity."

"How's it going?"

"Boring, that's how. You think I'd be reading a book otherwise? We haven't had a blip since we started."

The tech looked past Brian to ensure his next words weren't heard by anyone else. He lowered his voice.

"That guy's dead as a pickle. You couldn't wake him up with a bomb." The technician chuckled. "Oh well, that's what I get paid for. That's what I went to school for ten years for: to sit and watch a TV for hours with nothing on it."

A flash of heat burned across Brian's entire body. Instant sweat broke out on his skin. He felt his blood pressure spike.

He wanted to kill this man. His fist turned white as he squeezed the steel door handle.

"Sorry." He pulled the door closed firmly.

"Hey, it's okay, drop in anytime. I'll be here."

Asshole.

Brian was back at the glass staring at his father. The insensitive words of an uncaring imbecile rang in his ears. His hands cupped his face.

Peter could feel the presence of his son and looked over to see him standing in the window. He could see that Brian was upset, but could not sense any feelings from him. He found this odd and wondered why. Even the perception of him was weak, although it was real.

"Brian, can you hear me? It's your dad, son. Can you hear me?" Peter called out hopefully, fighting the temptation to panic.

Peter saw Brian look up and stare directly at him.

Peter felt momentarily hopeful, but then saw Brian's eyes wander about the room while he wiped some tears from his face.

Peter felt an enormous rush of energy. A warm bright light beat down upon him. He felt a sudden force against his body like he was rising in an accelerating elevator.

In the adjacent room an alarm barked out a signal, a red light flashed on the screen, the technician sat up abruptly in time to catch the faintest wave of activity displayed on the screen. There was a small spike slightly above the horizontal line which indicated Peter's energy threshold. The screen immediately reverted to its original display. The alarm did not signal any further unusual readings.

The technician had picked up the telephone to dial his supervisor, but now placed it gently back on the cradle. He stared at the screen, then leaned back in his chair and reopened his book.

Peter was sitting beside his young son Brian in the small sailboat they used to have at their summer home on Cape Cod. It was a brilliant sunny day. A breeze rocked the boat and filled the sail. In the distance he could see their house on the shore. A woman, a young girl and a young boy played on the lawn. Marion, Catherine and Matt waved to them from the shore. Brian and Peter waved back. Peter could smell the air, hear the ripple of waves against the boat and feel the wetness of the water when he hung his hand over the side.

How did I get here? Am I dreaming?

"Dad? Dad?"

Brian's young voice hung in his ear. It was real and yet it was surreal at the same time.

"Yes, son?" He felt real words come out of his mouth. He could feel his face and his tongue when he spoke.

"Are you having fun, Dad? Aren't you glad you came?"

Peter instantly recognized this time, thirty years earlier.

He remembered it vividly.

Brian had begged him not to go to work that day. He'd pleaded for Peter to stay and spend the day sailing with him. It was only after Marion threatened him with domestic misery that he reluctantly called the office and canceled his meetings so he could stay an extra day on the cape. He had done so grudgingly, and his mind really wasn't with his son on the boat. It was at that moment in the day; right after Brian's question went unanswered, that a son accused his father of not loving him or any of the family and yelled that he should have gone to work.

A small scuffle had ensued and the boat capsized. Brian swore at Peter and swam to shore, leaving his father to right the boat and sail back to the dock. The day was a write-off. Brian was upset, Marion and Catherine treated him with disdain, and even young Matt refused to co-operate when Peter suggested they do something together later in the day. To Peter it was like

Matt knew that he was trying to make up for his bad behavior. Everyone recovered, but a chasm had been cut in his relationship with Brian that never fully healed.

Peter felt conscious and yet not. He was there, and yet he felt he would not be staying. Everything was real, yet it lacked a feeling of permanence. Suddenly he heard two voices, both the same, but coming from different places.

"Well, Dad, are you?" The words sounded and then repeated.

Looking back at his son, Peter was startled to see a boat, identical to his, sailing directly at his stern on a collision course. Peter saw himself and his son Brian in duplicate. The second little sailboat bore down upon them. He felt his legs to feel if they were really there. He looked ahead into the sun and back again, directly into the eyes of his double who was staring through him, oblivious to his son or his surroundings. The double looked like a zombie out of place in this sunlit setting.

Wait, that was me then. I'm replaying that time. I've been given another chance.

The twin boat was within feet of his stern. He could see that the other Brian was agitated. The event was about to replay exactly as it had some thirty years earlier. Little Brian stood up to yell at his father and the second boat started to rock. When it did, Peter's boat began rocking in unison. Brian stood up, about to speak. His face was wrinkled with anxiety. Peter grabbed his hand and the boy tried to pull away. The boat rocked violently. Peter seized the chance he'd been given.

"Son, I'm very glad I'm here. Especially with you. Thank you for inviting me. I love you very much."

Little Brian's grip softened and a big smile came over his face. He fell into Peter's arms. "I love you too, Dad. I'm glad you stayed."

The boat stopped rocking as a puff of air billowed the sail. Peter held his son in his arms and opened his eyes to see where the other boat was. When he did, he winced as it sailed right into them and merged into one. There was no noise, no wood splintering, no impact at all; the second boat just seemed to evaporate around them when it made contact.

Peter watched while he drifted above; him and his son of earlier years. Both beaming from ear to ear, as they sailed on pleasantly.

The feeling of extreme gravity returned and Peter felt like mist being sucked down a colorful pipe. He experienced a high speed spinning sensation, bright light swirled about him. He had no sense of body or mind, just a presence. And then there was nothing.

He looked over to where Brian was wiping his eyes. The wires and tubes were all still in place. The heart rate, blood pressure and brain activity monitors eerily displayed their readings like a heartbeat had not been missed. The straight line of the EEG display indicated no brain activity.

Peter was back in his body-bound jail pondering what had just occurred. He felt different inside, like he had eaten something delicious. He had a warm, full feeling like after a great turkey dinner. It was like he had regained something he had lost.

Brian's hand had barely moved. Peter surmised that although it seemed he had been gone for some time, no time had passed in the hospital. He wondered if the monitors had detected anything but realized if they had that people would be arriving to inspect the cause.

Peter focused his thoughts.

He could see the technician next door.

He was able to replay the event and see that the guy hadn't moved when the alarm had beeped a second time just an instant after the first. The timing of the two alarms was so close and the signal itself was so brief that he hadn't noticed there were two signals, one from Peter's energy when he left on his journey and another a worldly instant later when he returned. Peter quickly came to the realization that no worldly time had passed while he was away.

Yet to him it felt like he'd been gone an hour or more.

Brian started and spun around, feeling a firm hand resting on his shoulder.

"Uncle Edward! It's so good to see you." Edward and Brian embraced in silence. While Edward held Brian, he looked over his shoulder at the body of his employer and best friend. He closed his eyes at the sight.

Edward wasn't really an uncle, but ever since the Douglas kids could talk they were always introduced to him as Uncle Edward.

Edward wore his usual well-pressed gray suit, crisp white shirt and black tie. His balding head supported a dark gray felt hat with a black band that held two pheasant feathers. The hat had been a gift from Peter, as had all the hats that had come before this one.

"A hat like this gives a stylish man like you style," Peter said each time he presented him with a new one, which was about every two years.

Edward stepped back and placed his hand on Brian's shoulder. "Look at you. You look like shit. How are you holding up?"

"Thanks for the compliment."

"You know what I mean."

"I stayed here last night, down the hall. I slept on a day bed and grabbed a shower this morning."

"Living in style, are you?"

"Not exactly. But I wanted to be nearby in case anything happened. But nothing happened. I guess maybe I was expecting a miracle."

"And?"

"You know the answer to that one, don't you? Nothing but a long night happened here. But as you've said before, miracles take time. God's a busy person, right?"

"Right."

"You don't seem too upset, Edward. Aren't you shocked?"

"Brian, I've had my share of trauma in life. I am surprised and upset, but I've learned to live by God since I was a young man. And I'll die by God. He's never disappointed me yet. Trouble is, he works on his timetable and not mine and that can be a real pisser sometimes. One has to accept the hand we're dealt and play the best game we can. Your dad has had a fulfilling and wonderful life so far, and whatever the purpose of this tragedy, we will all in the end be stronger because of it. Have faith that life for all of us will play out as it should."

"It's hard Edward. It's very hard."

"Yes, Brian, but we've discussed before, it's the difficulties we meet in life and how we handle them that are our true measure of character. Face it, life has many more challenges than rewards. That's why we have to live in the now. Feel everything and appreciate our ability to feel pain or joy, for both are truly a gift."

"Oh you are so wise, Mr. Barkley," Brian said mockingly. Edward knew it was his way of expressing appreciation.

The two smiled at each other.

Brian nodded his approval to this man he had known all his life.

"Brian! Uncle Edward!" Sarah was running toward them in full stride down the hall, blonde hair streaming behind. They cringed at the sight of an elderly person ambling out of their room and nearly being steam-rolled.

Following her were Catherine and Charlotte. Both waved and smiled. Catherine pointed to the lounge. Brian nodded.

Edward took Brian's arm and pulled him away from the window. He didn't want this reunion with Sarah to take place in full view of Peter's limp and wired body. Edward stepped ahead of Brian and Sarah literally leapt into his arms. They did a half turn before Edward grunted and put her down, steadying himself with his cane.

"Heavens, child, what have they been feeding you up at that sinful school? You must have gained twenty pounds. I think you've thrown my back out."

"Oh...ya, sorry about that, Uncle."

Sarah knew that he was joking since he was one of the few people in her life she didn't pull attitude on. He wouldn't have let her get away with it anyway. For some reason she seemed to identify with him better than anyone in her family.

"Remember, no man wants a skinny girl. Gotta have some meat on them bones for cold winters."

"I know. Look at this fat ass." She spun around, exposing a perfectly shaped behind packed into skin tight, ripped blue jeans. She wore an un-tucked white cotton shirt, black shoes and black leather jacket. Her skin was flawless even without make-up at this early morning hour.

"I bet there wasn't anyone quite like me back when you and dad were hustling girls at boarding school."

"We never..." Edward tried to change subjects by grabbing her ear. "Is this new?"

"Oh, yes, you did, Mother told me. And yes, it is. Do you like it?"

"Well, I'll tell you there were plenty of beauties, and lots better than you," he lied, then he rubbed her hair and motioned Brian down the hall. "C'mon, let's have a sit down."

Edward watched Sarah circle back and grab Brian's arm. Her bravado had evaporated. "How is he?"

"Dr. Brandon is about to tell us."

"Good morning, Mother." Brian kissed her cheek. "You look terrific."

"Marion."

"Sarah."

The mother and daughter exchanged challenging looks but evidently decided to let well enough alone for the moment.

"Why, hello, Edward."

"Marion. Good to see you."

"Really?"

Marion gave Edward a cool look when he and Sarah entered the lounge. She'd never really liked Edward. It was really a jealousy thing and she knew it.

How did those two ever get along anyhow, she wondered? They're black and white literally and figuratively. What an odd pairing, Marion repeated that often thought puzzle to herself.

"That's exactly why we get along so well," Peter would always say.

Peter also told her that Edward was one of the wisest men he knew. Not the smartest, but the wisest. That distinction was lost on Marion. Peter and Edward eventually concluded that she was indeed jealous, particularly when she accused Edward of being instrumental in their marriage breakup.

"Mom." Brian pulled her close for another kiss on the cheek, but whispered to her, "Charlotte's here."

"I know, darling. Why do you think I'm dressed like this?"

Brian grinned and shook his head. "You amaze me."

"Good morning." Dr. Brandon was standing a few feet away from the mother and son.

"Good morning, Marion."

"Good morning, Jim."

"Sorry," Brian said, "but have you two met other than here?"

"Yes, we've met at several hospital functions. You're lucky to have such a wonderful mother."

"Smooth Doctor, very smooth," Brian smiled.

Although he was quite a bit younger, Marion had always had a girlish crush on him and after a few glasses of wine didn't hesitate to share her feelings. It seemed harmless enough. She was married to Peter Douglas, after all. It wasn't as though this Doctor could do anything about her flirtations, and although it made him feel uncomfortable he often played the game just to keep her happy.

Dr. Brandon smiled back at both of them and opened the door to the lounge. Marion let her son go first so she could move closer to the Doctor when they entered.

Sarah sat beside her brother and held his arm tightly. Charlotte, sitting beside Catherine, didn't notice Marion at first.

"Hello Charlotte." Marion was now standing in front of Charlotte, her hand extended. So close, in fact, that Charlotte could not get up.

"Oh, Marion." Charlotte wore jeans and a sweater over a cotton shirt, her hair, still damp from the shower, pulled up under a baseball cap. She couldn't rise without planting her face in Marion's waist. She reached up from her submissive position and took Marion's hand.

"It's unfortunate that we have to see each other under such strained circumstances." Charlotte tried to stay on neutral turf.

"Aren't they always?"

Brian spoke up. "Dr. Brandon, shall we start?"

- Chapter 21 -

All eyes looked past Dr. Brandon when the door swung gently open again. Michael Phillips stuck his head in, looking a bit surprised by the size of the group. "Am I interrupting?"

Sarah and Catherine spoke in unison inviting him in to meet the rest of the family.

Dr. Brandon looked at his watch. "Please, folks, I do have other patients. Perhaps Mr. Phillips could do his introductions after my briefing."

"Of course." Michael took a seat near the door.

Marion and Edward looked at each other, back to Michael, then shrugged.

Sarah squeezed Catherine's arm which nudged her back as if to tell her to calm down.

"Let me be brief, because there isn't much to tell," Dr. Brandon began. He had a smooth movie star accent, a mixture of British and Caribbean.

"As you're aware, we've brought in special monitoring equipment to ensure that if there is any activity at all in Mr. Douglas's brain we will know about it. We'll be watching around the clock. He needs time now for his wounds to heal and for his body to stabilize. Let me remind you again that it is a miracle we are even here talking about this. By all rights Mr. Douglas should not have survived this accident."

Dr. Brandon was used to the sort of stare he was receiving from his audience while they listened and processed information that was foreign to them.

"I can give you no assurances regarding his prognosis for revival. I don't want to give you false hope. Mr. Douglas is stable. His body temperature is normal. He's breathing on his own, but still in very, very serious condition. I'm sorry to be blunt, but it is important for all of you to realize that he could slip away on us very easily or he could come back. At this stage I couldn't even give you odds."

Dr. Brandon scanned the silent room. Brian, Marion and Edward seemed to take his words in stride. Sarah's eyes and nose were wet. Charlotte and Catherine remained stoic.

"You can visit Mr. Douglas, but I have to ask that only one person at a time go into the room. Please don't touch any of the equipment. It is on loan and very delicate. It will scan you when you enter the first time. After each of you has entered once, then you can go in together if you please, but only one person should walk through the electronic doorway at a time. Talk to him, sing to him, read to him and touch him. Do anything that might trigger a familiar note somewhere inside. We really don't understand why some people bounce back, so we'll try anything positive."

"I think I was on the plane that the equipment you are using came from Europe on."

The group looked at Edward.

"I am working on a coffee table book about castles and wealth of Europe. A charity fund raiser book sponsored by Peter. I was away doing research."

"How could he possibly hear or feel anything?" Marion broke in.

"Please, I will update again tomorrow. Be patient."

"Where's Schebb?" Edward asked. "He's got the best connection to Peter of all of us."

Dr. Brandon watched a collective acknowledgment pass over the group.

"Who's Schebb?"

Brian explained the close bond between the dog and their father and his certainty that Schebb was in the car when the accident occurred. "No one knows if Schebb was killed in the crash, drowned or just got scared and ran off."

"Schebb wouldn't leave Peter. No way," Edward added with certainty.

"We'll put out a press release to help us find him if he's alive," said Brian.

"You realize, of course, that even if you find him, no animals are allowed into the hospital," Dr. Brandon said.

Edward smiled and looked across at Brian with a wink. "Of course. We would just like to know where he is. Right, Brian?"

"Right." Brian winked back.

Dr. Brandon made a quick exit, avoiding a hail of queries for which all of his answers would be pure speculation. Michael Phillips seemed to know the drill and stood up, extending his hand to Marion.

"Mrs. Douglas, nice to see you again."

He smiled warmly but Marion returned a calculating gaze. When he introduced himself to Edward and Charlotte, Michael explained again his role as a counselor. Handing out more of his unique cards, he reminded everyone of his availability.

"I thought you were only here at night," Sarah asked slyly.

Michael blushed. Her youthful attention was not lost on him.

He quickly explained that, given the unpredictable nature of patients and medicine, he found it best to keep his schedule flexible. He avoided explaining that most of the unpredictability was with friends and family.

By the time he slipped out the door, Edward was spinning a pyramid shape between his fingers and smiling.

"What's that?" asked Sarah.

"That's life's little puzzle, and it's for you to figure out. Did he give you one of these?"

"Not you too," Sarah objected. "I'll figure it out on my own."

Edward smiled. "We all do, sooner or later."

- Chapter 22 -

To reach the telephone, Matt had to move a silver ice bucket containing two upside down green bottles. Untangling himself from Cara, who was still sleeping soundly, he looked at himself in the mirror while dialing. He wasn't very impressed. Lines from wrinkled sheets were pressed into his face. His eyes hung a little heavier than normal. It was a familiar look that he knew he could shake off, but also realized that each late night took its toll.

His sheet was pulled down to his waist. He admired his abdominal muscles and did a few half sit ups, flexing them while he waited for an answer, mind drifting.

I'd better get back to the gym if I want to keep this up.

Matt yawned a wide, eye-watering yawn.

He looked back to see Cara's beautiful, naked back with blonde hair splayed across her shoulders. He smiled to himself.

For now, everything is a-okay.

"Douglas Corporation, how may I help you?"

"Hi, it's Matt. Can you connect me to the hospital lounge?"

"Right away, Mr. Douglas."

Matt liked that.

"Where the hell are you?" Brian's tone shocked the room.

Brian motioned to the group and waved his hand toward the door. The room emptied without hesitation.

"Let's get a coffee," Edward suggested tactfully. He gave Brian an open palm signal to stay calm.

Matt's head started to pound.

"I'm on the Island. Why, is anything going on?"

"No, nothing at all, you asshole. Our father is lying here in the hospital near death and all you can worry about is getting your rocks off?"

"I resent that."

"I resent you, Matt, and your cavalier attitude about this and just about anything else in life that might have a bit of responsibility attached to it. Everyone's here this morning except you."

"Well, that's good. If the hospital blows up, at least there will be one of us left to tell the story of the fabulous Douglas family. We can't all be fucking heroes like you Brian, can we?"

There was a long pause on the line while both brothers caught their breath. Matt broke the silence. Another sibling tiff had passed.

"Well, how is he?"

"No change. It could be a while. Are you coming back today?"

"I can."

"Why don't we meet for a drink at the little bar next to the hospital at five?"

"Fine, I'll be there. I'm going to need a little stabilizer before I see him. How does he look?"

"Not pretty, Matt." Brian's voice cracked a bit. "It's not a pretty sight."

"Okay, I'll be there. Okay? I'll see you at five."

Both brothers hung up without saying good-bye.

Matt replaced the receiver and fell back on the pillows. He watched the fan spin around while listening to Cara's soft breathing.

He closed his eyes.

He stroked her soft skin.

He took in her scent.

What was Brian doing now? And Susan? Why didn't this son and father spend much time together anyway?

You're a good guy – no, you're an asshole like your brother says. Fuck I'm tired.

Matt knew inside that he was a good guy. He was driven, though, to chase something. To prove something to himself and the world.

Why was he so unhappy with himself?

Brian took a short breath, closed his eyes and gently shook his head from side to side, thinking about his situation and Matt. He was feeling a tremendous amount of strain and the exchange with Matt just added to the pressure inside him. Matt was his baby brother. Brian had been his protector and provider all his life, seeing him through one difficulty after another.

He knew that the divorce and the business succession had both been very hard on Matt. He also realized that Matt seemed to be the one who got the least attention from their father when they were growing up. Brian was sure that was more about timing than anything else, although he seemed to have picked up where his father left off in the rearing of his younger brother. He loved Matt and felt a deep sense of obligation for his well-being. Perhaps it was one way of making up for the fact that he didn't have a family of his own.

When he opened his eyes it took a few moments to realize that Cara was no longer in bed with him. The sound of her shower blended with the tropical breeze and waves on the shore below. Groggy, he wiped some salty stains from his cheeks.

He felt weak and nauseous.

His head hurt.

His body was wet and clammy.

He could still feel alcohol in his system. His hangover made him disgusted with himself.

I've got...no I am going to get my shit together.

"Good morning."

Matt focused.

Cara was radiant. Her face was slightly flushed from being freshly scrubbed. She stood at the foot of the bed wearing a thin white silk night shirt just long enough to leave any details to the imagination. Cara smoothed the material over her upper thighs with the backs of her hands.

"How do you like it? You bought it for me while you were away."

Matt smiled and nodded his approval. The silk stuck to her where her skin was still moist in places. She toweled her hair, causing more drops of moisture to fall onto the silk. They painted dark, expanding polka-dots. Her nipples pushed against the delicate material. Two drops of water fell perfectly on her left breast and a pale brown quarter-sized sphere showed through.

Cara sprayed several puffs of her perfume in the air near her body, then moved to let each one to land on her skin. She bent her right leg up behind her to catch the falling molecules before they fell to the ground. More perfume rained down from a squirt over her other shoulder. The overhead fan spread her scent around the room. It tingled deliciously in Matt's nose while he watched her little show. He was completely focused. His headache had abated, his hangover was on hold. He felt that familiar surge.

"I'm still a little tired. Do you feel like a nap?" She looked coyly at him.

Matt nodded. How'd she guess?

"Why don't you wash the cobwebs off and join me back here?"

Cara began to crawl from one corner of the oversized bed towards its head. As she crept, her damp hair hung down around her shoulders. Her shirt fell open, revealing a beautiful view of her small breasts which hung gently. She looked like something out of a movie as she feigned an evil look and continued her trek. Her shirt no longer covered her hips, and when she crawled Matt watched the muscles in her thighs and buttocks flex and relax. He reached out, but Cara had angled her trip toward the farthest corner, laughing as she scurried to neutral territory.

While she crawled she reached over and pulled the sheet off of Matt's body. He lay flat, fully outstretched. She cast her eyes from his chin down over his chest and onto his stomach which was nicely displaying half a dozen muscles in tidy order.

"Not bad," she murmured to herself.

She knew exactly how to tease him and he loved her doing it.

She'd told him she loved that he wasn't as immature and excitable as guys her age. She also loved the fact that he seemed to really appreciate her and wasn't distracted with a lot of young bullshit.

Her eyes continued their tour down his legs.

"Your best feature," she often told him.

She started to tickle his feet, making him crazy.

"Go freshen up," she smiled, "I'm not going anywhere."

"Okay, if you say so."

Matt rolled out of bed and walked toward the bathroom. He didn't see that Cara had a full side-view in the mirror across the room.

"Wow. That's pretty nice…and big."

Matt looked back over his shoulder to see that Cara wasn't looking directly at him, but somewhere on the other side of the room. He scanned to meet her eyes reflected in the mirror and looked down at himself.

"Hey, that's not fair." Matt grabbed himself and quickened his pace doing a couple of little dance steps.

"Dance for me, baby!" she called. "Hurry back."

A shot of modesty pierced him and Matt felt his flesh weaken.

After he stepped into the shower his feelings of guilt returned. His arousal had abated. His mind was working on him again. He felt the depressive effects of his hangover drop over him like a veil. Self doubt and anxiety invaded his brain. He cranked the shower on full pressure, but left the tap on cold.

He hoped the water would rinse away these feelings.

If not, his dark side told him that getting back in bed with Cara would.

The water hosed his naked body and rinsed some of his bad feelings down the drain. He heard music coming from the suite and presumed Cara was feeling pretty chipper.

He remembered a quote: "Youth is wasted on the young."

The fog in his head lifted again.

Perhaps he should order up champagne and orange juice. Yes, that would do the trick, champagne and orange juice.

His spirits rose.

He reached out of the shower and dialed the wall telephone.

"Concierge desk. This is Sandy Dugas. May I help you?"

"Oh, uh Sandy, I mean…uh sorry I was dialing room service." Matt quickly turned off the shower, putting on his best morning voice and placed his request.

"No problem Mr. Douglas. Everything okay up there?"

Matt sensed a sort of light, jealous, sarcastic tone.

"Yep…ah…just great." He grabbed a towel and feigned professionalism.

"Any chance you could send up a bottle of Veuve?"

"Sure, one glass or two?"

Matt was about to play the game but stopped short. She already knew too much. Always best to keep the staff happy.

"Two please. Thank you."

"You're welcome…anytime." Her voice hit a higher note which he noticed.

You never know, Miss Dugas. You never know.

"Perfect. Thanks."

Matt paused after hanging up the phone.

He toweled his hair but left his body wet.

- Chapter 23 -

After showering and eating, Fuzzy fed the dog, fueled his rig and did a walk around his vehicle. They'd been up since dawn.

Fuzzy kept a meticulous log on his truck. He knew that was one of the big differences between someone who owned his own rig and someone who jobbed out and drove other people's equipment. Fuzzy had a perfect driving record and he was very proud of that, considering more than half the trucks pulled over on the interstate were banned from further mileage for one infraction or another. Corruption was rampant amongst the drivers. Forged logs and payoffs to inspectors were commonplace. Everyone blamed the tough economy and high taxes for forcing honest men to become criminals.

Fuzzy didn't buy the credo by which dishonest truckers lived. He knew that the bad ones were gamblers and drinkers and that much of the money that should have been spent on their rigs went to support their bad habits. Drugs and prostitution were also a way of life for many men who rarely saw their homes or families. Dope would help them work long hours to make extra money. Unfortunately, extra money ended up being spent on vices to comfort the lonely driver who had been out on the road so long he'd forgotten what the loving comforts of home were like. After he'd spent all his money, he'd have to work long hours again to make up for it. Most men on the road had to send money home at least twice a month. It was a vicious circle. Some of the drivers ended up in jail or losing their licenses from highway accidents. Many innocent people had been killed by driver negligence. Others were lucky and got matters sorted out.

Fuzzy really admired the couples that worked together as a team, driving together and sharing their duties. They were able to work long hours and make a good living with time and money left over to enjoy life. Many would leave their kids with grandparents for two weeks a month and then have two weeks at home as a family before heading back out on the road. Fuzzy hoped to find himself a partner one day. He was very independent and set in his ways, but figured there must be someone out there for him. His mother had always told him that the right girl would come along some day.

The diesel engine had roared to life and Fuzzy nudged the big rig into gear and eased out of the service center. Chatter on the CB was typical for the early morning hours. Talk of hangovers, hookers and poker games usually got everyone revved up for another day. Normally, Fuzzy would put in a CD of one of his favorite country artists to ease him into the morning, but today for some reason he decided to catch the early news. The breaking story early that morning was targeted at him.

"…And this morning, media magnate Peter Douglas shows no signs of progress, according to the limited information available from the Douglas spokesperson. The family is asking if anyone is aware of a mature blonde Labrador Retriever that may have been seen wandering in the vicinity of Needham, that they please report any information to this station. Mr. Douglas's family is offering a $1,000 reward to any information leading to the recovery of Mr. Douglas's pet plus a $5,000 reward for the return of his dog, which goes by the name Schebb. In other news today…"

"Well, I guess our gig is up, boy … I mean, Schebb. Too bad, I kinda like you fella."

Schebb's ears perked up when he heard his name. He let out a slight whimper. Fuzzy felt sadness set in with Schebb's sigh.

"C'mere boy…c'mon up Schebb. I know, I know. You must be missing your master huh?"

Schebb jumped onto Fuzzy's lap but slid off to the side. Fuzzy rubbed his head vigorously, making Schebb open a drooly mouth as though to smile.

"For now it's just you and me pal…just you and me."

Thoughts of getting Schebb back to his owner had consumed him since the first news that morning. Fuzzy knew it wouldn't be long before his fellow truckers started asking questions. He didn't want any publicity and contemplated how he would anonymously return Schebb to Peter Douglas's family. For now though, Schebb could continue to ride with him and Fuzzy would come up with a plan.

He decided first that he would dodge his usual truck stops to avoid being questioned by other drivers. He rolled down his window and let the damp morning highway air clear his mind. A wet tongue painted the right side of his face as Schebb clambered up high for a taste of the breeze. His ears flapped in Fuzzy's face as he strained to get his head out the window. The warm weight felt comforting on his lap so the bearded trucker let the dog share his vantage.

"Enjoy it while you can. You'll be home soon enough, and your trucking career will be over."

Schebb leaned back and gave Fuzzy a lick, then yawned widely before he let out a whimper and settled in for some more trucking.

"Breaker, breaker 19…this is the bearded one…"

- Chapter 24 -

Leaving the others over coffee, Marion made her way back to the floor where Peter's room was. She could hear Brian on the telephone when she passed the lounge door, so she continued on her way to his room. She felt her stomach knot. She paused at Peter's window and gasped.

Tears streamed down her face.

Her hands shook.

She stared at Peter and the science-fiction complexity of equipment surrounding his bed.

Peter's face was ashen and gaunt. His body lay completely limp. She put her hand to her chest and took several deep breaths.

Stay calm Marion, stay calm, she encouraged herself.

She felt powerful feelings stir within her at the sight of this man for whom she had born and raised four children

He was her first lover. A man to whom she had committed her life and stood by through the ups and downs of his business career before being unceremoniously dropped at middle age when he entered some new phase of his existence that she had yet to understand.

This was a man to whom she gave the best years of her life before he left her to fend for herself. He had been generous enough during the divorce; Marion would never want for anything material. What he couldn't give her was enough independence and confidence to face the world like an individual, rather than Mrs. Peter Douglas. She had fallen victim to a situation she had observed many times in her social circles, one she swore would never happen to her when middle-aged men left their lifetime partners in search of something. It appeared they always seemed to find it in the arms of a younger woman.

Marion and her friends never really understood, although they eventually all concluded, that their husbands and men like them were hunters, gatherers, builders and conquerors who had found cerebral happiness in the business world and satisfied their procreative drives through family. However, they seemed to reach a stage at which they desired to find something deeper and more meaningful. Some primal urge beckoned them to reach inside and discover their true purpose for being. This was a spiritual journey that so many men like Peter were driven to take: filling a longing, empty space inside.

Some men changed careers, or took up interests for which they had never previously shown any enthusiasm. Quiet men became outgoing. Passive men took up athletic pursuits or participated in endurance sports. Men who had never shown any artistic inclination suddenly began painting or writing beautiful pieces inspired from somewhere within. Most of these men in their renaissance disrupted their family and business lives in a dramatic way.

And yes, many ended up with younger women, but contrary to what their ex-wives or peers may have believed this usually turned out to be coincidental. In the telling the sudden change of life or lifestyle had exposed them to new and different social crowds. The new vibes that these enlightened men gave off seemed to attract a younger flower to their garden of renewal.

Some men rejected this calling and, to everyone's detriment, committed suicide after suffering in emotional darkness and silence for years without anyone knowing. Others lumbered along; carrying the weight of their lives like a beast of burden wears a yoke until it crushed them with a heart attack or nervous breakdown. In reflection, the theme was common.

The ex-wives were always shocked and bewildered when they discovered what their husbands had known all along: that they didn't really know their partners at all. Their man was a lover, a provider and a father. He didn't take chances and open up his spirit in his younger years because he was afraid that it would show his weaknesses in a time when he needed real and perceived strength to care for and provide for his family.

Once he was secure that his bloodline would live on, he felt free to release and discover himself. Marion and her friends talked about men in this regard at length, but their emotionally selfish blinders kept them from discovering an answer that very few couples seemed to find.

Marion, periodically, would see an older couple walking hand in hand, obviously very much in love. She wondered what their secret was and hoped it would be like that with her and Peter in their later years. If she had taken the time to ask, she might have learned what simple wisdom the elder woman could have passed on.

"What's your secret to a lifetime of happiness together?" she could have asked.

The elder woman might have gripped her husband's hand and looked piercingly into Marion's eyes and said, "It's simple, my dear. Everyday that I have been with this man I forced him, in the morning and before we would go to sleep, to tell me how he was truly feeling. At first it was difficult, with him not wanting to tell me what he was thinking, but after a while, with some coaching, he caught on and began to share his innermost feelings with me. Sometimes I didn't like what I heard, but I never judged or criticized, I just listened. After all, these were his feelings and thus could not be right or wrong. I never again mentioned the information he had so lovingly confided, I just let it be. Eventually he realized the value of this safe haven, this emotional playground into which he could cart his most personal feelings and kick them around without fearing anyone's opinion. When he spoke his feelings aloud, he was able to hear them and judge them and use that which was his truth to guide his life. It was only in the airing of his words that he could hear his truth."

It may have all seemed so simple coming from someone else.

"He grew to look forward each day to sharing his feelings, and he came to share mine similarly. We deemed them to be even more important than our thoughts, for it was these feelings, we concluded, that governed our thinking and thus our actions. As years went on we grew closer rather than more distant. We carried an emotional road-map about each other to guide us through our lives together. That has been our bond."

Marion's fist slammed down on Peter's chest with a dull thud. His lifeless body absorbed the blow bouncing on the bed.

"I hate you. I wish you were dead."

Her fist slammed down again and again, jarring the body and shaking the equipment attached to the bed.

Her face reddened.

She folded herself limply across Peter's chest and sobbed.

"Why have you done this to me? I've given you my life, and now I'm alone. You promised you'd love me forever, and you lied! I hate you! I hate you! I took care of you. I raised our children. Now I'm living with my mother. I'm living with my mother, Peter! You bastard."

She was helplessly in the control of her rampant emotions. Words flooded forth without pause. A release of subconscious anguish had been triggered for which Marion was merely a conduit.

Peter was stunned at first by the outburst. Marion's words cut him with their truthful edge. He had no physical sensation, but he could feel the anguish she continued to share. He brushed her hair with his hand and could sense the smooth strands in his fingers.

Marion felt nothing when she lay weeping on his chest. Her words subsided to a fatigued mumble. Peter was aware of an aura of negative energy surrounding her. He could actually sense it, a thick heavy coating weighing her down. He still held a deep love for this woman with whom he had spent so many years. When thoughts of his love for her filled him, he could feel the layers that pressed down on Marion start to dissipate. He was absorbing or somehow dispersing the dark veil that hung over her and his feelings of love were filling a space from which her hurt was leaving.

"Marion, are you alright?"

She stood abruptly when she felt two hands on her shoulders.

Edward had broken Dr. Brandon's rule about one person being in the room at a time, but felt that Marion's needs warranted the exception.

Marion turned and wrapped her arms around him. He felt her press gently into the shoulder of his jacket and hold him tight. As Edward returned her embrace, he stared over her shoulder at Peter lying in bed.

Marion felt a warm, loving glow come over her. She had not experienced such a sensation in many years. Feeling light and surprisingly peaceful, she stepped back and looked at Edward.

"Thank you, Edward, I'm fine. Thank you. Everything is going to be alright." She smiled and smoothed her dress, then kissed Peter's forehead.

"Goodbye."

She smiled, then stepped past Edward to make her way out of the room.

Edward could feel her positive energy.

He looked down at his friend.

"You're in there, you son of a bitch. You're in there, aren't you?"

- Chapter 25 -

The butter was soaking through and the toast barely radiated any heat. Sarah handed her brother a bottle of orange juice and some toast in a wax paper bag. Brian received the gesture graciously, but couldn't resist a dig. "Very healthy, sis." He held up the butter-soaked bag. "Is this what they feed you at school?"

"Hey, what do you expect in a hospital, health food?"

"How's baby brother?" Catherine ventured.

Brian covered for Matt. "Oh, he's okay. He's working on another project and won't be here until the end of the day. I brought him up to speed."

"What's her name?"

"Catherine!" Brian frowned.

"You've been covering for him all his life. Why should I expect anything different now? Maybe he'll grow up one day and take charge of his own life for a change."

"That's right. Everyone has to carry their share of responsibility," Sarah added with a bravely serious tone.

Brian and Catherine both looked across at her inquisitively.

Sarah blushed, but said nothing else. She plunked herself down on a couch and took a keen interest in a six-month-old fashion magazine.

Charlotte met Marion halfway between Peter's room and the lounge. She felt herself stiffen when she approached the usually bristly Marion. She was surprised when Marion stopped to greet her. Smiling, she took both of Charlotte's hands in hers.

The contrast of their hands spoke volumes. Marion's hands showed the wrinkles of age; of a woman who came from a farm, who worked hard all her life to make something of herself, who raised four children on her own, who had been a tireless supporter of her husband, who kept a beautiful home and grounds without the assistance of maids or gardeners. The lines of time and liver spots told her story while they held the unblemished, delicate and manicured hands of Charlotte.

Marion's hands were warm and soft.

"Go to him, Charlotte. Go to him now. He needs us. He needs our love."

Charlotte felt a powerful radiance. It was like someone else was speaking to her from a distant place. The words rang with an honesty and love she had never witnessed from Marion.

Charlotte felt Marion's hands give hers a firm squeeze and, with a friendly motion, led her in Peter's direction. She held Charlotte's hands until the last possible second before releasing her and continuing on her way.

Charlotte walked slowly, letting the exchange sink in. She stared down at her hands until her eyes stopped on a pair of black shoes.

Edward stood silent, smiling.

He and Charlotte made eye contact, but no words were spoken.

Edward's eyebrows rose as though to say, "Well, what do you make of that?"

Charlotte returned his gesture. She smiled softly and nodded. Edward moved forward to pass and placed a hand on her shoulder. She felt his hand linger; the two silent friends going in opposite directions, until his reach was fully extended and his arm returned to his side.

Outside Peter's room Charlotte raised her hand to the glass in a mute attempt to reach out to him. She stood for a few moments in silent meditation.

Peter's attention was distracted and it wasn't until she was at his bedside that he noticed her. He watched while she held his hand and rubbed it gently. He could feel the warmth of her skin against his and could faintly make out her scent. She wore his favorite perfume.

Peter tried to reach out to her. "Charlotte, can you hear me? Can you hear me? I'm alive, Charlotte, please let them know I'm alive!"

Peter fought to contain his panic.

Charlotte, as with each visitor, was a new opportunity to attempt to make contact but he continued to fail; laying there as a passive recipient of their words and feelings without the visitors knowing that they were being heard and felt.

Her words overlapped his. "Peter, this is awful. I'm so sorry I wasn't here sooner. I had prepared a wonderfully romantic evening for us. I had taken a beautiful bath in your favorite oil. I wanted everything to be so perfect. I was ready for you…ready for us. It was the right time. I couldn't think of anything…"

Peter pictured the scene, the smells, the lighting, and the bedroom, Charlotte emerging from the bath wrapped in something beautiful and sexy. He could feel and see it all with great clarity.

Charlotte sank into a chair beside the bed. She held his hand to her face. Peter listened.

"I couldn't think of anything I wanted more than for us to make a baby together. And now this and I didn't know, and when I found out I had to drive in and I was scared and nearly killed myself. Oh, Peter, everything is ruined. I should have been with you."

Peter was back in his house, watching her enter in darkness and pick up the paper. He traced her movements while she prepared the evening. He saw the cats, the kitchen, the candles. He watched her disrobe for her bath, saw her sleeping, answering the door, heard Catherine's voice on the telephone. He watched Jimmy flirting with his wife, but could tell that there was no substance to the exchange. Charlotte's heart belonged to only one man.

He saw her panic when she quickly got ready to leave. He rode above her as she drove in the darkness and watched the truck approaching. He could tell instinctively that death was not in the air. This was a close call and that was all. He wondered what death would look like.

"Please come back, Peter, please come back."

He was again with Charlotte. He tried to reach out and take her pain away the way he had with Marion's, but although he could sense it, he could not feel it the same way he had before. Marion's energy had been vivid and easy to grip. Charlotte's was mixed and confused, harder to attach to.

He listened.

She spoke quietly.

She was beautiful.

She sat beside him and poured out her love. Peter could feel a swelling inside as he received her affections for him. For a change he lingered in the blanket of emotion rather than close it out and try to escape the way he had all his life.

I can do this, I can change, please give me the chance.

- Chapter 26 -

The computer continued to record high levels of electrical activity emanating from Mr. Douglas. Its monitoring screen, however, displayed only a horizontal line which to any observer would mean no activity. The technician on duty read his book, oblivious to the information pouring into the micro circuits under his feet. Each person who had entered Peter Douglas's room had elicited unique electrical responses from themselves. Some were extraordinary and others were nondescript. All were recorded.

The movement of Peter's entire energy field had happened twice now: once when he revisited his son on their sailboat and now a second time when he connected with Charlotte's mind and traveled back to his home to retrace her voyage. Each event, although it was played out in real time to Peter, lasted only a nano-second of earth time, but each had been captured on the sophisticated equipment monitoring Peter. Had the thresholds not been set so high, alarms would be ringing and technicians would be working feverishly to analyze the data. Dr. Brandon's hunch would be supported empirically and scientific news would be in the making.

But for now, Peter was a mystery to everyone but himself.

Marion and Edward had said good-bye to the group in the lounge. Marion said she needed time alone and wanted to call her mother in Florida. Edward planned to come back that evening when things were quieter. He would drop by the Douglas offices later to catch up on his mail and messages.

Brian thanked Edward for being there; he knew it meant a great deal to his father, he said. They exchanged hopes that the press release might bring some leads on Schebb. Edward said he'd be more than willing to check any serious leads out, that he'd probably give Carl at GBC a call while he was at the office to brief him on Peter's condition.

"If anyone is going to get first-hand news, it should be Carl, Brian. He and your dad have been lifelong friends."

When Charlotte returned to the lounge, her face was blotchy from crying but composed. "Where's Marion?"

Everyone looked at her with surprise. Charlotte and Marion, they knew, did not get on very well.

"What? It's okay. It's all under control. Okay?"

"She left, but I have a number for her if you want it," Catherine offered.

"Thanks, I'd like to contact her later."

The room was silent.

Charlotte smiled and settled onto a sofa where she ignored the stares, picked up a magazine and started to read.

"Well...I guess it's my turn." Sarah stood stoically.

"Are you all right?" Brian asked softly.

"Yeah, I saw him through the glass last night. The shock is kind of over." Sarah felt her knees quiver a bit. Her stomach had tightened with tension.

Brian, Charlotte and Catherine all offered to escort her.

"I'm okay...really," she lied. Out the door she went.

"I don't think she is feeling as brave as she makes out," offered Brian.

"She looks so innocent and fragile; no young woman should have to face this," responded Charlotte.

"Poor little dear. I hope her soft side catches up to the tough girl act and takes over. In a weird way, maybe this will help." Catherine looked at Brian and Charlotte who nodded agreement.

Sarah walked gingerly down the hall. She visualized what she was about to see so it wouldn't be as much of a surprise. She passed the window without looking in, but paused at the doorway before entering the electronic archway.

"Sarah?"

She started and looked back over her shoulder to see Michael Phillips, just two feet from her.

"Michael…what are you still doing here?"

He told a white lie. "I forgot my briefcase in the lounge, and then I saw you walking down the hall. This must be pretty scary for you. Would you like me to go in with you?"

"No, I'm fine, really. I don't need anybody with me."

She moved toward the door, and then paused. "Well, I'm sure I would be okay, but now that you're here, well, yes, join me if you wish, but there is only supposed to be one visitor at a time."

He smiled and pulled back the one side of his sports coat, displaying a badge with his picture clipped to his belt. "Hospital staff, remember? I'm your official escort. After you."

Sarah felt her lip quiver when she smiled back.

The monitoring computer registered more readings when these two people passed through the archway one after the other, but not high enough to exceed the threshold. The computer imaged and stored the readings, and the software instantly adjusted the programs to screen these additional two people out of the future monitoring profile.

The technician was oblivious to the activity on the screen. The images were quickly generated, logged and stored. A pattern was beginning to develop that would go unnoticed unless the thresholds were lowered and historical data re-run at the lower sensitivity levels.

Peter had watched his daughter come in. Sarah stood silent and motionless at her father's bedside, peering down at his lifeless body. Of all his visitors, this was the one for whom he felt the most heartache.

That's my baby. So tender and young. So innocent of life. Why should she be without a father? How will it affect her?

Peter ached to reach out and hold her. He looked at the young man beside her whose eyes made direct contact with his. He emitted a bright field of energy. Peter read his name but didn't know who he was, although he liked him immediately. He was glad that someone like him was with his daughter.

"Do you think he's in there, Michael? Do you think he knows we're here? Is he even alive?" Sarah bit her lip on these last words. Her shoulders shook with quiet sobs.

"Father, it's me, Sarah, I'm here. Can you hear me? I miss you, Daddy. They told me at school, I came right down, but Brian wouldn't let me come in at first and then the Doctor wanted us to wait. Your whole family is here, Uncle Edward too. I love you. We all love you."

Peter focused his energy toward his crying daughter, trying to get through to her. There was no connection. He spoke to the young man. "Michael ... it's Michael, right? ... Can you hear me? Take care of my daughter. I know you're a good young man. I can tell."

Sarah felt Michael gently, almost timidly, place his arm around her shoulder. Any other time with any other man, Sarah would have recoiled in her coy fashion and commenced the mating game that she had already perfected. At this instant though, Michael's gesture was just what she needed. The comfort of his strong arm eased her pain. Her tears subsided. She allowed herself to relax into his compassionate embrace.

They stood for several minutes in silence. Mesmerized, Sarah rested her head on his shoulder, her blond hair falling against his jacket. The quiet hum of a fan and the near silent beep of the heart monitor gave the mood a hypnotic feel.

Peter could see Michael's aura surround his daughter. He could sense her comfort. He felt relieved.

I remember when I was that young. Would it be so?

He smiled.

- Chapter 27 -

Choy Lee peppered her conversation with animated gestures, switching between perfect English and Chinese. She was seated at a large round table in the Ambassador Dining Room of the Hong Kong Presidential Hotel. Her photo assistant and editor flanking her, she outlined the nature of her latest project to a potential publisher and financier.

Choy's reputation as a first-class photojournalist preceded her, but she still felt pressure each time she launched a new project. This time she was proposing to do an educational piece based upon seismic activities on the Asian continent. It was certainly a credit to her name that the well-known American Douglas Foundation had sponsored two of her early projects, which became internationally acclaimed. The link between Peter and Choy was known only to themselves. Choy quoted from the preface of her draft document:

"The project will be a historically and geologically correct essay wrapped around hundreds of photos of the devastation caused by recent earthquakes and tropical storms in the region. The premise for the project is that better land use planning and architectural integrity, coupled with an appropriate disaster plan with adequate funding, could save tens of thousands of lives. It is intended to be a thoroughly researched and graphically presented critique of the current state of affairs in the region."

The project's contention was that many of the natural disasters that occurred recently with abundant loss of life had been predicted by experts well in advance. The information had been ignored by administrations in favor of continued economic development. Current leaders were coming under severe scrutiny for receiving illegal payments resulting from fast-tracking permits for billions of dollars in commercial development. It had become clear that these monetary gains were made by risking the lives of the citizens for whom the administration was responsible.

In Choy's opinion, the deaths of thousands of people rested in the hands of such greedy and negligent leaders.

Needless to say, her project would not be received favorably by anyone associated with the current government, and that is why Choy's new associates were known to be staunch opponents of the leaders of the day. They liked the notion of anything that would cast a bad light on their adversaries and were willing to pay handsomely for such efforts.

The meeting was going well.

Choy continued to present her project but her eyes were periodically drawn to the space between the two gentlemen's shoulders. Through the gap and out beyond the etched glass separating the dining room from the grand lobby, she could see the colorful images of GBC International News flickering on a large television. She stopped breathing and speaking when a close-up of Peter Douglas stared at her. Clips of an air ambulance and car wreckage being hauled from a river followed closely after. The Chinese sub-titles which scrolled across the bottom of the screen were illegible from Choy's distance.

"Miss Lee. Miss Lee, are you all right?"

The English-speaking financier broke Choy's trance. She refocused on her table guests.

"Oh yes, yes, I'm sorry. I just had an awful thought about the thousands of people killed and injured in the last quake." Her tragic expression was perfect for the comment, although motivated by a different topic. It was an excellent recovery though, and caught her backers appropriately. Both nodded and shook their heads solemnly.

"Miss Lee, we are behind you one hundred percent. We have reviewed your budget and are prepared to advance you twice what you are asking to ensure the quick commencement and successful conclusion of this most needed effort."

Choy's eyebrows rose.

Was that all it was going to take to get these guys on board?

"We can see that you are deeply concerned and committed to this project. We admire and support these sentiments."

Choy was unnerved by what she had seen on television.

The now daunting task of getting the project done was squarely before her, although the immediate source of her concern was her friend and former lover. In an ironic way Peter had once again helped her finance another project. She recalled a saying he often quoted, which helped guide her wishes and desires: "Be careful what you wish for, because it just might come true."

Choy hoped now that, in aggressively seeking these partners, she wouldn't later regret her wishes. Her new partners stood up and handed her an innocuous package.

"Here is your advance Miss Lee. Hold it safely."

Choy realized then that her "partners" were fair-weather friends. If anything went wrong, there would be no way to trace funds to them thus any consequences for stepping on the wrong toes would be hers alone to bear. The men shook her hand, bowed respectfully, and then turned to leave.

"How will I contact you?"

"We'll be in touch, Miss Choy."

"But…"

The men departed, leaving Choy standing speechless holding an envelope stuffed with cash. She was beginning to feel that she had just signed a deal with the devil, dropping the package, unceremoniously, into her leather backpack. When her two associates jumped up and congratulated her, Choy feigned enthusiasm. "We will celebrate officially when the money is somewhere safe," she promised. "You will each get one thousand dollars tomorrow at breakfast. Let's quickly review the path forward from here. These people do not hand out cash and then wait for results."

After a brief review Choy excused herself and walked to the lobby. Shutting herself into a beautifully crafted mahogany business booth, she dialed her long time friend Terrance Sing at the GBC office in Hong Kong.

After the call, he went to work on the GBC computers to pull up the latest information on Peter Douglas.

Choy knew of everyone in the Douglas clan, but had never met any of them. Peter and Choy kept the details of their trip and ongoing communication to themselves. She knew there would be a lot of explaining to do if she wanted to communicate directly with any of the family or somehow arrange a personal visit.

When Choy arrived at GBC headquarters, she had to call Terrance from the security desk for authorization to enter his building. News was treated like gold at GBC. He had told her that their Hong Kong enclave was under continual security scrutiny to avoid having any news or file information stolen or leaked. Periodically one of the competing networks would scoop a story through bribery, planted snoops or electronic surveillance. Competition to get a story out first was brutal, and the competition's technology for sniffing stories right out of the air was more sophisticated than anything available on the planet. He'd said it wasn't unusual for governments in and out of favor to pay substantial amounts of money for news information about topics or people of interest. News media were as much in the espionage business as any spy agency on the globe.

Encased in a glass cubicle in front of a computer terminal, Terrance's fingers flew over the keys. Choy tapped her finger on the glass and gave a small wave. Terrance pressed a white button under his desk to buzz her into the secured area.

"I'm just scanning our world wide data bases for up-to-the-minute information on the Douglas story."

A small stack of paper lay in the out tray of the laser printer beside him. Single sheets fell gently out of its rotating jaws and settled onto the pile. To Choy, the operation was impressive to behold. The energy was palpable with people scurrying about, presumably chasing assignments or late-breaking reports. Dozens of television monitors projected pictures from all over the world. She was watching the non-stop process of monitoring, manipulating and sometimes generating the news, incessantly marching onward.

"This Douglas fellow of yours is hot stuff. I've got reports from everywhere. People are very interested in whether this man lives or dies. I've got governments, charitable foundations, corporations and financial institutions all on the system panning for information. One of my contacts in the States has a quiet lead on a story about the possibility of a mole inside the hospital."

"Peter is a highly respected and influential man, Terrance. But my interest, as you know, is much more personal. I need to know his medical condition and not just what's being reported to the press. I want to know his real condition. Can you find that out?"

Terrance looked into Choy's eyes. "Choy, you and I go way back and we have resorted to many, shall we say, unorthodox methods for getting or verifying information. If the Boston Trauma Center is on line..."

Terrance paused and looked around in case someone might be listening. "All of their information is accessible...for a price."

"How much, Terrance? I don't need the details."

She knew that Terrance had more contacts than most in the news business; all of them made one conversation at a time, slowly building trust through mutual exchanges, sometimes money, at other times information. He'd told her that in the dirty world of news gathering he and his network were clean players. Sure, they broke the law of the land, but they never used tactics such as violence, blackmail or intimidation to get what they wanted. Some cash here, some electronic surveillance or an insider there. It was all clean and quiet, yet very effective.

Terrance used contractors that were a global chain of unseen hackers; computer whiz kids who, for a few dollars, would stay up days on end cracking codes and entering the systems of unknowing organizations. Every week or so they would leave a trail or two to be found by inside security people, who would invariably go public with their latest catch and brag that their security systems had foiled another attempted hack. Little did they know that this was exactly what the hackers wanted to keep the sniffers off their real trails which, by virtue of their track record, were untraceable.

Terrance employed these keyboard wizards through his connection with one man who was respected and idolized throughout the clandestine world of surreptitious computing. He knew that this man was the lord of the networks, who doled out sub-contracts to agents all over the world. He apparently used technology that wouldn't be seen on the market for years, or perhaps ever; rumored to have been provided by the very people who made the systems they claimed were impenetrable.

To the global giants of computer hardware and software, it was just test marketing; a place to check out the most advanced developments from their laboratories. To him, it was keeping Big Brother on his toes, all part of a system of unwritten checks and balances. Terrance had never met him. All meetings were conducted via computer. He simply went by the code name Sammy, reached through a network address that changed every four hours. Sammy's few direct clients had to apply an alpha-numeric formula to determine how to contact him. The address, when accessed, routed communications through an around-the-world tour of hundreds of linked networks which had been calculated to be untraceable within four hours. This kept Sammy's whereabouts and activities a mystery to all.

"My contact is the best in the business. His keyboard is like a divining rod. He's not cheap, though. Twenty-five hundred to get to the door and then a hundred a minute while he's on their system mining information."

Without blinking, Choy undid the top two buttons of her blouse. Terrance watched curiously when she withdrew a number of pre-wrapped stacks of U.S. one hundred dollar bills then placed ten of the stacks beside Terrance's keyboard.

"This should help him find out if Peter's heart is beating or not, don't you think?"

A hint of perspiration had formed on Terrance's forehead. "You're serious about this guy, aren't you?" He checked to see they weren't being watched.

"Matters of the heart are always serious, Terry."

Terrance nodded, thumbed one stack to get a rough count then slipped the bills out of view. "Apparently they are. I'll be in touch soon."

"Thanks, Terrance. I owe you one."

He smiled. "I'll add it to the list."

"Just friends, right?"

"That's right Choy, just friends."

Choy disappeared out the glass door with a wave.

Terrance made several keystrokes, entered a password and quickly reviewed a playback of their meeting which had been recorded in full color, with sound, through a pencil-size camera mounted in a hanging plant in the corner of the cubicle. After quickly burning the file to a DVD, he deleted the original then quickly connected to the public network where he entered the complex code to reach Sammy.

Terrance would add the DVD of their meeting to a collection of "insurance policies" he kept in a safety deposit box.

Peter Douglas was hot property.

Terrance Sing was a cautious man.

Choy had another "associate" whom she would contact. Madame Wong had been a friend and psychic advisor to Choy for many years. She was also involved in networking of sorts. Her skills as a meditation coach, medium and cosmic traveler were extraordinary. She had helped guide Choy through many crises and decisions. Choy hoped that with her help she might be able to reach Peter in a manner a little less grounded in copper, fiber optics and computer chips.

Choy had been to Madame's home many times and the routine had never changed. Madame always wore flowing robes, greeted Choy in silence and led her through a fog of incense and fragrances of essential oils. They would sit opposite each other on embroidered satin pillows. Madame, who said very little to Choy over the years that wasn't prompted by the spirit world, would look upon her through crystal eyes set in a wrinkled and weathered face. She spoke the same kind words each time.

"What is it that Choy seeks of Madame?"

- Chapter 28 -

Catherine had taken a sudden interest in the specialized equipment being used on her father and, surprisingly, Dr. Brandon had time available to talk to her about it. Walking toward Peter's room, they met Michael and Sarah coming down the hall together. Both Michael and Sarah flushed red at the sight of Catherine and paused only long enough to exchange pleasantries. Sarah and Catherine exchanged looks that only sisters can.

At the entrance to Peter's room, Dr. Brandon took Catherine's hand in both of his. "Catherine, we're doing everything we can to help your father, but like I said before, it could be a long wait. You need to carry on. We'll keep you and your family up to date with any changes. Being here too much can become a real strain on all of you. Besides, you're distracting me from my rounds."

With a quick smile and squeeze of her arm he turned and left her alone to visit with her father.

"Hi, Daddy. It's me, Catherine."

Peter watched his daughter Catherine hold his limp hand in hers. He sensed the warmth of her touch. "I'm here, sweetie. I doubt that you can hear me, but I'm here." He was feeling tired and discouraged that his daughters could not hear him.

Catherine sat in the chair beside the bed and started to talk. She rambled from one topic to another.

"This is awful, and I'm so tired," she said dejectedly. "I must still have jet lag and last night I was up late with Charlotte and

Sarah catching up. In some ways I wish you had…" She couldn't actually bring herself to say it. "…I don't mean I want you to, but this, this is terrible for everyone. Including you, I suppose. Or maybe not, because you don't even know. Matt is off in Bermuda spending your money on booze and women. He hasn't even been to see you, though I guess he's coming tonight. He and Brian had a fight on the telephone. I'm so glad you gave the business to Brian; he's the only sane one in the bunch. Uncle Edward was here, but I think he's trying to find your dog. Schebb is missing. He probably died in the accident. I hope we don't find him dead somewhere."

A wave of sadness washed over Peter. He called out Schebb's name.

Catherine talked on obliviously. "Mother and Charlotte have always hated each other, and now Charlotte thinks they are friends. That's so weird. Mother wouldn't even stay at my house because Charlotte was going to be there. Why did you leave her anyway? Couldn't you have just had an affair? She had little in her life but you, and now she's miserable living in Florida with Grandma."

His daughter was making no sense at all. Just a random flow of babble. He tried not to fault her for it, but couldn't help wondering if the strain was too much for her.

"It was pretty weird when mother called. I was in bed with Albert. Yes that's right, Albert. Your daughter actually has sex. In fact, your daughter likes sex and has it regularly. It's about the only thing in my life that is going well. I can't seem to find a man I want to keep, so I keep just finding men I want. I'm sure you'd be surprised at your little angel saying this, but it's true."

She was right. Peter did not want to hear this outpouring. He preferred to see Catherine like the little girl that would never grow up. He tried but could not shut out her words.

"That's nothing, though. Sarah's worse than I ever was, but that's another story." How much of this personal disclosure was he going to have to endure?

"I hate this business I'm in. Everyone is so shallow and self-centered. I had to leave everything to my assistant in Paris to finish. She's probably screwing her way around the town trying to get on someone's good side. Oh well, I'm here and you're here and it looks like you'll be here for a while, so we'll try to have a few laughs, right?" Catherine's voice cracked with her attempt at humor.

"At least you've got a handsome Doctor…Mom has always had a crush on him, but I get the feeling he likes me. She'll be so pissed off. You're all over the news, too. You're even more famous. Isn't that always the way? We never acknowledge our heroes until they're gone. More famous dead than alive."

Peter agreed with her on that final point, but was not interested in that sort of fame.

Catherine sat in silence with her head down and fingers folded in her lap. Salty droplets splashed on her hands.

A feeling of relief came over her. Suddenly, Dr. Brandon's words replayed in her head. "I want you to act on the assumption that he's fully aware of his surroundings. That he can hear what we say and feel what we feel." Catherine composed herself. She flushed when she recounted her ramblings. "Father? You can't hear me…can you father? No, no, I know Dr. Brandon just wants us to keep our spirits up by thinking you can. Of course you can't hear me."

Catherine raised her head to acknowledge a tap at the window. It was Brian, motioning that there was a call for her. He smiled and indicated that he would wait for her. She kissed her father's forehead, then they walked back together to the lounge where she took the cell phone from Brian's hand.

Peter was stunned by the soliloquy he had just heard. It was a side of Catherine he hadn't known. It was honest and raw. He found that strangely comforting.

When he returned to his father's room, Brian found two nurses hovering just inside making notes on a chart. The technician, with whom Brian had the exchange earlier in the morning, was checking the equipment surrounding Peter. The nurses stopped talking and quickly excused themselves. Brian found it odd that people often responded that way.

Was it him? Why are people seemingly so intimidated by him? Was it the money thing?

He tried to be friendly and relate to people on a common level, but when they found out who he was, he noticed that things changed. A distance immediately opened between them which rarely closed. He hoped he'd have a friend like Edward one day.

The technician looked blankly at Brian, then did a double-take when he recognized him. "Oh, you still around? I haven't had a damn thing come through on my screen all morning. I'm just checking to make sure everything is hooked up right."

The technician stood up from his work and extended his hand. "Ralph Koontz, technician. Not that I expect much outta this fella, but I guess you never know. My wife seems to think that the flowers in her garden talk to her, so who knows? Maybe Mr. Douglas here will sing us a song before the day's out."

Brian gripped Ralph's hand and was tempted to punch him in the face. He could feel his blood pressure rise and his pulse elevate when he faced this blunt and insensitive man. He chose a direct approach.

"Brian Douglas, son." He stared icily into Ralph's pale blue eyes and watched the color drain from Ralph's face while the significance of the introduction sunk in. Brian held on firmly to Ralph's hand. It moistened with sweat.

Five or six seconds passed in steely silence. A full sweat had broken out on Ralph's forehead and the color came rushing back to his face. His cheeks went red. He hung his head and covered his face with his free hand. Brian's pressure released so Ralph could ease his other hand free.

"Sorry, I'm really sorry," he mumbled, edging past Brian and out of the room.

Staring across at his father, a big smile broke out on Brian's face. He knew his dad would have loved that and he was right.

"What are you smiling at?"

"Edward! You startled me. What have you got there?"

Edward held up a fistful of papers clipped together at the top. "These, young man, are all warm leads on Schebb."

Peter listened intently while they spoke of Schebb. "We've had hundreds of calls and emails over at Carl's office. Lots of crackpots and gold diggers, but we think we've eliminated most of them. Reward money sure brings out the kooks. I've reviewed these with the security chief at Douglas, and he's working on a theory. We still aren't sure who the man was who helped save your father's life. We've had enough information come in that we now have a description. Security is putting together a composite drawing and a profile. Sounds like quite a hero...I'd say he risked his life to save your father's. We'll cross-check the composite with the pilots of the air ambulance and see if we can find him. My bet is that if we find him, we find Schebb."

"That's great news Edward, but let's not get ahead of ourselves. So far my father doesn't have a life."

"That's not the point. Someone risked his neck for your dad's, and in my book, that's a hero."

"Sorry, you're right. It's hard to see the roses on the thorn bush sometimes. I'm going to call Marjorie and get some coffee. Do you want anything?"

"No thanks, I'll sit here awhile with your dad. Then I have to leave, but I'll be back tonight."

"*Edward?*"

"Yes?" Edward looked toward the door.

"*Edward, can you hear me?*"

"Hear who? Jesus, I'm hearing things."

"*It's me, Peter. I'm alive. I can hear and see you.*"

Edward flexed his eyes open and shut.

I'm going crazy. I need to get out of here and get some sleep.

"*Edward, wait, it's me Peter. Don't go. I'm alive. Just listen to me.*"

Damn hospitals, this place is crazy.

"Peter, old pal, I gotta get some rest. I'm hallucinating, buddy. I'll see you tonight."

Peter wanted to scream in frustration. Panicking, he struggled pointlessly against his confines but quickly gave up. Edward left the room but for the first time Peter felt buoyed with hope. He now had to figure out some way to get Edward to hear him without scaring him off.

- Chapter 29 -

The champagne and orange juice had done the trick. Matt's headache was gone and the extra few hours of sleep after a delicious breakfast in bed with Cara had revitalized him. Matt had finished his second shower of the day and was dressed for his trip to the hospital. While he prepared for his departure to the mainland, Cara grilled him a little more than normal about his return schedule. Matt played it vague but had that sinking feeling that Cara might have an alternate agenda.

"Cara, I'm well known around here, and the fact that you are my guest is also well known, whether we like to admit it or not. I want you to have a good time while I'm gone but... well let's just say we are getting enough press already because of dad. This is a very small island."

Cara stepped forward and put her arms around Matt's neck. "Matthew, you know it's no fun around here without you. Just hurry back. I'll probably just do some shopping and hang out by the pool. I'll stay out of trouble, you don't have to worry."

"Do you still have my credit card, or are the numbers worn off it?"

"Matt, I haven't spent that much. And besides, everything I buy is for you in a way, isn't it?"

I am such a sucker.

Was that the price he had to pay to keep someone like Cara around? Ah, but it was worth it for feminine youth; the most natural aphrodisiac on earth.

Matt pressed his lips against Cara's, letting his hands slide down her back and onto her firm cheeks. A gossamer layer of silk separated his skin from hers. Her mouth was wet and sweet. Her smell invigorated him when its vapor surrounded his head.

He felt that familiar surge.

He stepped back, slightly dizzy. "I have to go. Bob is probably already at the airport." He took one last kiss, smiling at Cara, who melted him with a soft pout.

"I'll miss you. Hurry back and maybe there'll be another surprise for you like the last one in the limo!"

"I like surprises. Hold that thought."

Matt stopped in the lobby to speak with Sandy Dugas at the concierge desk. "Sandy, will you let Stephen know that I'm off the island for a few days, and that my guest will be staying."

"Oh, you mean Cara?"

"You know her?"

"Well, yes. It was a bit of a coincidence, but we were both shopping in the same store and bumped into each other trying on some..." Sandy paused. "Some, you know, women's items. She has very good taste."

Matt blushed when he realized that Sandy had one on him, but came back quickly. "Yes, especially in men. Wouldn't you agree?"

Sandy's professional persona couldn't hide her blush. "Mr. Douglas?"

"Please, Sandy, it's Matt, you know that."

"Okay...Matt. Anthony Houston is having a big party out at his estate tonight. Everyone will be there. I was going to go myself. I could invite Cara if you thought she'd enjoy it."

Matt was cornered. He quickly did the math. The last place he wanted to send Cara on her own was to a high-profile party where every good-looking young man on the island would be salivating over her. But since Cara and Sandy were acquaintances, if he suggested that he didn't want Cara invited, it would only be a matter of time before Cara found out. Matt did a quick time calculation and figured if the evening went well on shore, he could be back for a late bedtime. That should keep Cara in check if she went to the party. He would call her later.

"Sure, Sandy, that would be really nice of you. I'm sure you both will be the center of attention."

"I'm planning on looking for a new dress when I get off work. Maybe I'll ask Cara if she'd like to join me when I go shopping. Oh, your taxi is here."

Matt smiled at Sandy. He didn't like this but what choice did he have? "You two have fun...but not too much fun."

This could be interesting, thought Matt. I better get my butt back here ASAP before this comes undone.

He knew that the maintenance requirement on this relationship had just moved up a notch. Once Cara was exposed to the island social scene, she would be bombarded with invitations to all sorts of activities. Matt figured that she wouldn't be satisfied any longer with sitting by the pool waiting for him to come and go the way he pleased. He also knew from experience that the situation would come to a head soon. Cara would either want some further commitments, or she'd be gone.

The jets were spinning when Matt's car pulled up on the tarmac. Bob looked at his watch when Matt stepped out.

"Hey, Cap, sorry to keep you waiting."

"We're going to have to hustle if you're meeting your brother at five."

"I know, I had some business to take care of." Matt changed the topic. "How's Eden?

"Nice switch," Bob grinned, acknowledging Matt's control of the agenda. "She's great. Leaves tonight for three more weeks of flying. I'll see her next month, I hope."

"Hey, you're not getting serious on me, are you?"

Captain Bob smiled. "C'mon let's go. I'm not getting any younger."

A package had arrived from the Douglas offices outlining his schedule for the next few weeks. Matt was basically a professional board member. He sat with the directors of numerous corporations and foundations. He also played an observer's role on the boards of a number of Douglas subsidiaries. Brian, however, made sure that Matt had no real authority and that all decisions of consequence were vetted through him. The various boards liked having Matt around. Despite his bachelor lifestyle, he was intelligent, articulate and funny. He livened up any occasion and he gave people access to the sizable Douglas Empire. Matt had an open timetable and he liked it that way. He also lived within his budget which, according to his brother, was bigger than that of most small towns in the country.

Matt had made an investment in a penny gold stock a few years earlier that went through the roof, earning himself and the Douglas Corporation tens of millions of dollars. To date that had been his only significant financial contribution to the organization, but it had purchased him some temporary credibility as a business man.

While he looked over his schedule, he overlaid it with his personal itinerary with Cara. Bob had set out a bottle of Perrier for him, but he flipped open a wooden panel covering a cabinet on the outboard side of his seat and removed several small bottles of vodka.

The jet taxied to its takeoff position while Matt stirred the vodka, Perrier and lime with his finger. He knew the meeting with Brian would probably be intense and that visiting his father would certainly be stressful. A couple of drinks would take the edge off.

His eyes wandered around the empty jet, admiring the craftsmanship. He'd seen it hundreds of times but was always amazed at how good it felt to be surrounded by the trappings of success. The Douglas Corporation had several planes and although this one was not specifically Matt's, no one other than Brian had the authority, let alone the nerve, to bump him.

The rich carpet and fat leather seats gave the interior of the plane the feeling of a cozy living room. The cabin was full-sized and he could just stand upright without his head touching the ceiling. Captain Bob and his co-pilot were sequestered in their own cabin. At the rear was a full washroom with shower. Every modern electronic device was on board. A work area sported the latest in computer and communications technology featuring full multi-media conferencing and internet capabilities. Satellite-based telephones allowed direct dial communication with the entire world. A small galley was outfitted for complete meal service. The plane could comfortably sit eight, but could take twelve if necessary.

The aircraft's acceleration pressed Matt into his seat. He gingerly sipped the top quarter-inch out of the glass to avoid spilling it. The vodka went straight to his head.

He gained altitude; the world mellowed.

- Chapter 30 -

The burp caught George's attention so he looked up at the half-bald, greasy little fellow who was walking toward him in the reception room of the City Star.

"Whaddaya say there, Georgie boy?" Harvey Kirkland was apparently ready to see him. "Hope I didn't keep my new star waiting." He wheezed a bit, laughing at his own humor. The smell of cigarette smoke was nearly overwhelming.

"Sugar, hold my calls and get us a coupla coffees will ya? How do ya like yours there George? Black? Yes, black, that's what we drink here at the Star. Keeps the eyes open and the costs down."

George half smiled at the woman Kirkland called Sugar. She, with her sweet face and pouty red lips, smiled back, he was certain.

George hated the guy. He hated the way Harvey looked and smelled, and he hated the way Harvey treated him like some insignificant peasant. But he had to admit that work at the Star was never dull and his assignments always needed some ingenuity to pull off. George justified his interference in people's private lives by telling himself that if he wasn't doing it, someone else would be.

"Pour enough booze into anyone, follow them with a camera long enough and you're bound to get something embarrassing on them," was the first lesson that Kirkland had passed on to George.

"The best defense to anything is a file full of pictures or recorded conversations," was the second. "Besides," he further justified, "If you're in the public eye you have to expect to be harassed anyway."

"So George, my man, sit down." Kirkland smacked him in the back, "How's the Douglas project going?"

George assumed everything he said was being recorded.

What the fuck, I'm in over my head anyway.

"Here's what I've got so far." He opened a manila envelope and pulled out a sheath of 8x10s.

"I just printed these. I've got a couple of old man Douglas, that's him there all wired for sound. The equipment has been brought in from Europe. I've gotten to know the technician running it, bought him a few coffees and such. He's bored as fuck up there. Says Douglas is a total vegetable, that they are wasting their time. Now, these are all the family members and the ex-wife. That guy is some old friend of Douglas's. His name is Edward something. And check these out!" George's voice squeaked with excitement.

"There was a ton of action the first day, everyone going in and out. I was able to put the micro-camera in a fire hose case right across from the room. These are all taken through the glass, so they're not perfectly clear. There's some real juice here, boss. I got a view straight down the hall so I can fire the remote whenever someone is in the room."

George laid the pictures out on Kirkland's desk. He dealt them with pride, like a winning poker hand. "This is the ex-wife. Look, she's hitting him! Here's his daughter all lovey-dovey with some guy from the hospital. And look at this, that Edward guy hugging the ex-wife... and this. This guy in the suit has been in and out of the office with the technicians a few times. He looks familiar but I'm not sure why. His badge said Zalkow something."

George thought he noticed that Kirkland had taken a keen interest in that bit of information.

"The technician guy is a real talker. He says they've tracked energy waves leaving bodies and coming back or being transplanted into something else. He's a real crackpot, though. I wouldn't put anything on that. Oh and I also bugged their lounge telephone with the chip you gave me. Not much going on there except an argument between the brothers."

George watched Kirkland continue to scan the array of photos.

"Mr. Kirkland, the City Star hired me to get hired as a security officer for Douglas Corporation so I could photograph and bug them at the hospital. Here's my first report. Pictures, recordings and a head full of information. How am I doing?"

Kirkland continued to survey the array of photos. He was dreaming of the major headline stories that were in the near future of *The City Star*. Kirkland paused. He was actually stunned by what George had accomplished. He could see the exclusive exposé in his head. Circulation would skyrocket. He'd be contacted by Douglas and paid off; thousands...no, hundreds of thousands for this stuff.

People like the Douglases wanted their privacy and were willing to pay.

Kirkand composed himself.

"George, this is fine work. It is a good start. Not the best I've seen, but for a rookie you've done a fine job here. I'm going to cancel those other two guys who were trying to get on board. I want you working overtime at the hospital. Keep this up, and you'll be in for a good chunk of change."

"Mr. Kirkland, you do remember that you and The City Star hired me on a project basis for this one?"

"I guess so, yes."

"I've got my ass hung out there real good, and these photos of the Douglas family and the recordings and the bug, that's what you want, right?"

"What's your point?"

"You're paying for it, and you're asking me to break the law for you, right?"

"There're loopholes, but yes, we'll pay you."

"I know that you'll extort handsome profits from this, so I want to be compensated as we go. In cash."

George could feel his testicles tighten. His face was beet red. He was in a full sweat, but he knew he had the goods and figured if he didn't go for it now, he might never get another chance. He could quit now and be off Scott free, but if he were going to continue, he wanted cash.

"How much?"

George felt his stomach drop.

They are going to make a killing with this stuff. Now's my chance...now or never.

He swallowed hard. "Five thousand for each drop like this and a thousand a day while I'm inside." Sweat rolled down his back. He squeezed back some flatulence, but stared straight at Kirkland and didn't say another word. He had learned one thing about negotiating from his father, who was a crack car salesman: "Put your best offer on the table, then shut the fuck up and wait for the other guy to blink."

Kirkland stared back at George and watched the sweat run down his fat cheeks. He knew he'd make twenty, maybe fifty times what George was asking. Kirkland was much better at this game than George, but he knew that the young man was explosive. He also knew that the Star's profits were way down from competition at every turn.

"Done."

George released a noisy fart, feeling like he had moved his bowels right there in Kirkland's office. He realized immediately that he'd bid too low, but he was relieved to still be employed. He smiled at Kirkland.

"Jesus, couldn't you hold that till you're outside?"

"In some countries that's considered a compliment."

"Get outta here. You disgust me."

"One more thing I forgot to mention in my offer and this isn't negotiable." George was full of himself now.

"Everything's negotiable. What is it?"

"I, ah, want ah, Sugar out there to be assigned to me as my assistant while I'm on this project."

Will Kirkland actually buy this shit? Unbelievable if he does.

"You know, printing, errands; you want me working overtime, I'll need someone to help me out."

Kirkland was laughing now, listening to George ramble. "You're pathetic, you know that? You've already been in this business too long." Kirkland pressed a button on his intercom.

Pathetic am I? You have no idea Kirkland...you slimy prick. You've taught me well and now I'm your enemy.

"Roxanne, honey, come in here for a minute."

George quickly mopped the sweat from his face, smoothed his matted hair and tucked his wrinkled shirt into his rumpled pants. Kirkland winked at him while they waited for the door to open. "I've had her. She ain't that great."

Roxanne and her voluptuous body entered the office and stood beside George. Her bosom and bottom were packed into a tight blouse and matching skirt. She stood five foot five in heels. George could make out the pattern of her bra through her shirt. He was sure it would be a three-hooker and he played with his fingers while imagining undoing it with one hand and fondling her with the other. She smelled like a flower garden in bloom. George liked that cheap, sweet perfume.

"Sweetheart, you've been doing such a good job for us that I'm putting you on a very important assignment. You're going to work with George here for a while. You'll report to him. There'll be some overtime involved and if there're any problems, you know you can always come to old Harvey. Make sure you cover for yourself here at the office. George will give you the details. Any questions?"

George's mind raced. He'd hit the mother lode.

Did I bid too low? Doesn't matter. My next move will be money for sure.

Plus, he had Roxanne at his mercy. Or so he hoped.

"Just one, sir." Roxanne curled up her nose and looked at Kirkland. "What's that smell?"

- Chapter 31 -

The Douglas family had dispersed for the afternoon. Edward followed up with Douglas security on the leads they had for Schebb and the man who had saved Peter. Marion gathered with some of her lifelong female friends for comfort over a few games of bridge and several gin and tonics. The conversation quickly moved from Peter's condition to juicier subjects like who was having an affair with whom and which ex-husband was dating which new bimbo. After each round was poured, the conversation dipped to a new level of lewdness. Eight middle-aged women, mostly intoxicated, sharpening their claws on the backs of those not present to defend themselves.

Catherine went to her office to track down her assistant in Paris and catch up on dozens of voice messages and emails.

Sarah, at the insistence of Catherine, had returned to her flat to do some school work. She studied; fiddling unconsciously with her precious stuffed rabbit, her mind drifted. Bunny was always with Sarah; she slept with him, traveled with him, studied with him. She even took him on dates, usually stuffing him in the bottom of her bag. Sometimes that had meant being penned up with a mickey or a baggy of pot. The little stuffed friend gave Sarah comfort and love. After the make-up was off, the fancy dress was hung and the lacy under garments were stowed for laundry, Sarah would slip into her pajamas and squeeze bunny up to her face to help put her to sleep.

Her usual alternative for handling pressure would be to venture off and get drunk or high and perhaps sleep with someone in the process. She didn't like that part of herself, but it gave her short-term comfort in times of need. She read from her textbook; her mind refusing to focus. She kept having to go back and re-read pages she had just reviewed and highlighted. Michael's card acted as a bookmark. Besides his name, address and telephone number, the unusually shaped card had single words on each triangular section. One triangle read BODY. She liked that. It had such a sensual flavor to it. Another read MIND. She didn't like that. It sounded too much like effort. A third read SPIRIT. This word rolled smoothly off her tongue and lips when she repeated it to herself.

"Sssspirit. Ssssspirit."

Very mystical. I'm not sure what it all means but I like the feel of it just the same.

The final section had the word HARMONY. She breathed it: "Hhhhharmony." It felt smooth and comfortable. Not a word she used in her day-to-day speech, but a nice word nonetheless.

"Body, Mind, Spirit, Harmony. Spirit, Body, Mind, Harmony. Harmony, Spirit, Body, Mind." She played with the words in her mind, speaking them in different sequences.

Interesting; they feel good. What was Michael up to right now?

She was used to guys always coming on to her, but Michael was different. Maybe because he was older, probably ten years or more, she hadn't asked. He sure wasn't in the same awe of her looks that seemed to stun most guys senseless. He had a confidence and calmness about him that she found very attractive. He spoke from his heart about living life in a loving manner and seeing the good in everything and everyone. He was not judgmental. He spoke of how he always tried to avoid "the first thought."

He'd said, "The mind tends to offer us our initial impression of everyone and everything we see. Typically, that first thought is judgmental and often negative. The second thought is always the best one to listen to. It comes from the spirit or heart and therefore takes a bit longer to surface since it is more about how we feel about something than how we think. The second thought, if we take time to listen to it, is always kinder and more sensitive to the deeper meaning of a person or situation. The first thought is great for saving a life, but not living one."

Sarah would ponder that philosophy for a while.

Michael also said that he wasn't easily swayed by people's opinions, nor was he tempted by quick routes to personal satisfaction. He talked about how everyone has their own struggles and challenges. Everyone has their own story that you couldn't see from first appearances. "You just have to know that, inside, everyone is doing the best they can with the hand they've been dealt. Treating people the way you hope they will be, instead of how they appear to be, is a much better way to live and understand the people and world around you."

Maybe there was more to a man than preppy banter and uncontrollable hormones. Sarah reached over to her night table and picked up Michael's card. She turned the card toward her window for illumination and drank in each word, trying to figure out the odd shape. She held it in her two hands folding it to her chest. Moments later she was sleeping peacefully.

Brian went home to shower in his own bathroom, shave and change his clothes. He felt remarkably refreshed when he crossed back through the Boston Common and walked the ten minutes from his downtown flat to the Douglas offices. Brian lived in the penthouse of Bridge House at the corner of Arlington Street and Commonwealth Avenue. It was one of only six units in the historic corner building and boasted a three hundred and sixty degree view of Boston. Its subtle exterior, well-worn steps and pleasing wrought iron and brass trimmings belied the most stringent and modern security available.

Brian avoided several news types. They stood off to the side where they smoked and drank coffee in boredom. There they waited for someone of substance to emerge from the Douglas office tower. Marjorie greeted him with a surprisingly warm hug. He chalked it up to the circumstances; she however, took a slight advantage of the opportunity. Flowers, email messages, cards and couriered letters from all over the world had been pouring into the office. Marjorie had brought in temporary help just to keep up with the standard responses. All requests by the press had been denied, but they persisted with new ones every few hours.

After discussing several business items, Marjorie organized a conference call with a dozen key Douglas people in meetings, cars and hotels around the country. Brian wanted a message of certainty regarding the health and affairs of the company to be circulated through every office. He hoped that hearing from him was the best way to start. Brian was an adept business leader who delegated the day to day operating of the company with mastery. He would continue to maintain a significant presence even during this crisis. An official internal release by voice mail under his title would follow. That way every employee with a telephone would hear from Brian Douglas in person. The Douglas system had a unique feature which could be programmed to erase a message after it was listened to. This avoided any leaks to the media since the message would come unannounced and only once.

Marjorie and Brian discussed the issue of media coverage at length. Brian thumbed through a sheath of news clippings and pictures regarding the accident and the life of Peter Douglas and his family. It would only be a matter of time before speculative articles were running about the odds for Peter's survival.

Paparazzi photos of Brian and his family were already running in the papers. The photos indicated that news people were staking out the hospital entrances and snapping pictures of the Douglases as they came and went. He expressed his confidence in the tight security inside the hospital and decided that he would only allow exclusive access and coverage to his father's friend Carl at GBC. There was nothing he could do about the photos taken in public.

The activity in Peter's room had abated. The floor staff were now accustomed to his presence and a routine for his care had been established. Dr. Brandon stopped in periodically, but knew at this stage that patience was the best medicine. Nurses bathed Douglas's body, changed dressings and verified readings with a manual thermometer and blood pressure cuff. A physiotherapist had been in to measure Peter for electro-physiotherapy contacts and these would be attached each day, allowing an electrical impulse to stimulate his muscles as a form of artificial exercise. This would ensure that if Peter did recover mentally he would have a body to use. Otherwise after a very short period his muscles would atrophy. Without this stimulation, if and when he did wake up, he could be months getting his strength back. He was also getting a complete body massage every four hours to keep his muscles limber and promote circulation.

Peter was continuing to discover the unique gift he had been given in his condition. He was realizing that different people had different levels of ability to communicate telepathically, but he could easily get trapped exploring their thoughts. The process was fatiguing since most gave off very little mental energy. So far Mrs. Rossi had been the most radiant. He had now realized that his friend Edward had the same ability but hadn't yet developed it. He was beginning to understand that this flow of energy had to be managed. The way it had happened with his son Brian, people could inadvertently pull him into their thought processes. The more intense the thoughts, the more realistic the encounter could be. In Brian's case, a very intense mental process when he reflected on a painful childhood experience combined with Peter's innate empathy for his son created a journey of vivid proportions.

When people entered and left Peter's room, he had in some cases found himself immersed in their thoughts. He was witnessing parts of the lives of complete strangers. It was intimidating and scary to see what people had on their minds. Sex, family, relationships, jobs and recreation were primary topics when they came and went from his room. Although they were there to care for him, most did their work on some sort of auto-pilot, never really letting it enter into their consciousness. He wondered how these people might react in an emergency and hoped that it wouldn't be his.

At first Peter had been bounced in and out of people's thoughts unwillingly. He had now begun to understand that when he started to feel the force pulling himself toward someone or into the bright light that he had experienced earlier, he could resist by focusing on his own thoughts. He could tell during this voyage of discovery that there was much more to the process than the little sample he had encountered. He felt that he was entering a dimension of life he had occasionally wondered about but never given much credence to.

Where did this new dimension end? Or was it infinite?

Scary but invigorating.

Maybe there was hope after all.

I can figure this out if only I could communicate somehow. Hopefully Mrs. Rossi can help.

- Chapter 32 -

The sun shone low over a fleet of private business and personal aircraft. Matt slipped the balance of his third vodka tonic down his throat as the jet taxied to the hangar at Gate 2 of Norwood Municipal Airport. Forty minutes later Matt walked through the doors of the Eye See You Tavern & Eatery (a.k.a. ICU) at a few minutes to five. Even he was impressed with his punctuality. The bar was aptly named considering its proximity to the hospital and the fact that its client base was primarily hospital staff and visitors of patients. On numerous occasions the board of the hospital had lobbied to buy the place or have it shut down, but that effort was for public consumption. The truth was that virtually every male staff member crossed the threshold of the popular strip bar and watering hole regularly. Females were welcome, and some dared enter during times when the dancers were on break.

The menu featured drinks like Vodka IV, Transfusion, Tonsillectomy and a Bloody Enema. It had food selections like Cardiac Salad with Heart of Palm, Cesarean Sections of Beef and Freshly Amputated Leg of Lamb. The daily special was always the Surgery Du Jour.

Music pulsed through the smelly air while neon lights flickered between the mirrored walls. The entire layout was focused toward a brass-floored stage, complete with mirror ball and twin brass poles. The place was packed with men in lab coats and suits. Some had stethoscopes dangling from their pockets; others had their hospital ID badges hanging from their shirts, or numerous pens protruding from a vinyl shirt-pocket liner, emblazoned with the name of some pharmaceutical company. Considering that these seventy-five or so men were supposedly health care professionals, the action at the bar and smokers outside suggested, instead, a gathering of rock and rollers.

The atmosphere was definitely not a healthy one.

Matt could not spot one woman amongst the crowd of men. He felt awkward.

What if Dr. Brandon showed up? He'd kick my ass out of here and tell me to get back up and see to father's needs. He'd never come here…I hope.

Awkwardness quickly turned to curiosity when he looked toward the stage at six naked female dancers posed in freeze frame with artificial smoke billowing around their legs. They had slipped onstage in the darkness and now stood under the spotlights, posed like three couples frozen in nude embraces. Matt stared for several moments before he realized each couple was locked in an open-mouthed kiss. In only a few seconds the entire crowd was focused upon the stage. The room went silent except for the low whispers with men exchanging suggestive comments.

"CODE 888! EMERGENCY IN ICU! PALPITATING HEART, ELEVATED BP, GROINAL INFLAMMATION! HELP! IS THERE A DOCTOR IN THE HOUSE?"

The room exploded with howls and cat-calls. Volunteers yelled out that their services were available. The music volume escalated with a pounding base and seductive rhythm. The strippers pulled apart and broke into an erotic choreography of dance moves and body contortions that made a full medical examination possible from thirty feet. The crowd of men was mesmerized.

"Here it is, Doctors, your five o'clock whistle."

A loud steam whistle blew over the noise and music. The announcer whipped the crowd into a frenzy.

"Time to blow off some steam. For the next ten minutes it's two for one at the bar."

The sea of bodies surged in the direction of the bar when several extra topless bartenders appeared to meet the demand.

"Remember, nine out of ten Doctors recommend table dancing as a non-drug remedy for post hospital stress disorder."

The room howled again.

The dancers gyrated.

The men watched them maul and lick each other in places that they couldn't reach on their own. This otherwise respectable crowd had wives, families and mortgages. They languished in a haze of booze and fantasy while each seemed to forget the world outside ICU for a while. Every wife or girlfriend of a hospital male eventually figured out that being "stuck in ICU" as an excuse for coming home late was an inside hospital joke, but new guys would "use it 'till you lose it," as they were told during their orientation rounds.

Matt felt a tug at each sleeve of his linen sports coat and gave in when two men in suits pulled him down into an empty chair. Matt twisted his head to see if he could spot Brian. His eyes made contact with a heavy-set young man in a security guard uniform who was staring at him, but the crowd pulsed, blocking his view. Brian wasn't in sight. Matt went with the theory that if someone is looking for you, you should stay in one place and eventually you'll be found.

A round of frosty martinis (a.k.a. Vodka IVs) landed on the table. Matt felt a damp, boozy breeze in his one ear.

"You're Matthew Douglas," the man yelled over the racket.

No, I'm the fucking Prince of Darkness, you drunken idiot.

"That's correct," he yelled back. A bony hand shot out in front of him.

"Joe Zalkow…. Dr. Zalkow. I'm on the board with your dad. Terrible accident, terrible."

Matt strained to be heard and definitely didn't want to be engaged in a conversation with this man. "Yes, well, we'll keep our hopes up." Matt put a hand patronizingly on Zalkow's shoulder. "He's getting the best care in the world that money can buy, right?"

Zalkow nodded solemnly. "Absolutely, you can count on it."

Matt noticed the gold band on Zalkow's left hand. "How's your wife and family, Dr. Zalkow?"

Zalkow feigned deafness and changed topics. "Guys, Guys!" he yelled at the table of men. "Matthew Douglas." Zalkow raised his eyebrows in an effort to add some weight to his pronouncement. A round of inaudible introductions took place before Matt gestured to the stage in an attempt to say "Cut the small talk, let's watch the girls."

Zalkow made short work of his martini, looked at his watch and expressed surprise at the time. "Supper time, gotta get home," he spat in Matt's ear. "All the best for your dad."

Matt nodded, smiling inwardly when the good Doctor made his exodus. The three other men sat with their chairs turned to face the stage. Matt picked up his martini and focused his attention similarly.

"Hey, buddy, no pictures allowed. One more and I'll have to take that camera and stick it where the sun don't shine."

George looked up, startled by the monster that stood over him. Fear cut through his chest and he wondered if the bouncer was about to beat him up and heave him out the door. He mustered up all his humility. "Sorry, pal, I didn't know. I just wanted a souvenir. I'm from out of town." The bouncer took in his story. "My brother, he's in the hospital next door. I thought these might cheer him up. Car accident on the freeway."

"Yeah, okay, it's all right. Pussy like that'd cheer anybody up."

Both men bonded at the basest level. George grinned, turned away and sucked back the rest of his beer. He had dodged another bullet and figured he'd better leave before something else happened. He had stopped in for a few pints to calm his nerves and voila, Matthew Douglas rolled in. He couldn't believe his luck.

He could see the headline now: DOUGLAS SON WATCHES STRIP SHOW WHILE FATHER DYING.

"Thanks, man." George extended his chubby little hand to the bouncer who swallowed it in his grip. "My brother will appreciate these."

George exited the first door into the dark foyer. The sounds of the club were a loud hum in the background. Instinctively he quickened his pace, departing the scene of the crime. When he pushed opened the exterior door and burst into the late afternoon sunlight, he slammed, face first, into a raised forearm. George crumpled to his knees. The camera bounced onto the grass and blood poured from his nose into his cupped hands.

"Whoa, are you okay?"

Neither recognized the other at first. George's face was buried in his hands to contain the blood flow, and Brian was so close he hadn't recognized the insignia of the Douglas Security uniform.

"You came out so fast I thought you were going to run me down. Let me get you a towel."

"It's okay, I'm okay," George protested in a muffled voice.

"No, stay here. I'll be right back." Brian hurried into the foyer of the bar and pulled open the entrance door to face a blast of music, sweaty air, and a 290-pound bouncer. He was virtually blind since his eyes had not adjusted to the dimness.

On the sidewalk, George gathered his thoughts and got to his feet. He wiped the blood from his nose onto the sleeve of his uniform. Looking around, he realized he was alone. He was about to break into his overweight version of a sprint when he realized that he didn't have his camera. He patted his pockets in confusion.

Where's my fucking camera? No. Not him. Shit me.

His rising blood pressure caused his nose to bleed again. He scanned the sidewalk and area several times before he lunged for the little silver square nestled in the thick grass.

Fuck me. Thank you.

He kissed the camera and bolted down the sidewalk, leaving a path of bloody droplets behind him.

The bouncer couldn't have cared if Brian's mother was having a baby outside. After five it was ten bucks for all comers. He'd heard every excuse in the compendium and wasn't about to learn a new one. When Brian was finally back on the sidewalk the only sign of his encounter was a small pool of red liquid and a telling trail. Brian looked into the distance but could not see the man.

George's eyes widened when he recognized his boss while watching him from behind the hedge while he was circling the parking lot. Blood dripping onto his hand, he gingerly raised his camera and snapped a few shots of Brian Douglas standing under the Eye See You Tavern & Eatery sign.

He could see the headline: DOUGLAS BROTHERS DROWN SORROWS IN PUSSY PALACE.

Sweat and blood dripped down his face.

He smiled, still watching Brian pace the length of the sidewalk.

George's smile froze, then melted when Brian moved in his direction to a point at the edge of the parking lot, just ten feet from where George crouched, shaking. Fortunately for

George, the color of the Douglas Corporation uniform blended perfectly with the shrubs. Brian paused for another moment, scanned the area, then turned and made his way back to ICU.

George thought no further about the Douglas boys meeting in a strip club. He wasn't paid to think; that was Harvey Kirkland's job. Once the door closed behind Brian, George waited a couple of additional minutes. His first stop was a bus shelter where he dialed the Star and issued Roxanne her first assignment.

"It's George. I've been injured while under cover." George gave Roxanne directions to pick him up. "It could be a long night and you may be needed into the wee hours," he said in his most dramatic tone. Still dabbing the blood from his nose, smiling an awkward smile, he hung up.

This might not be so bad after all.

- Chapter 33 -

The steam from the shower rolled out the open door of the bathroom and into the motel room. Fuzzy hummed to himself, washing another day on the highway down the drain. Schebb lifted his head and sniffed the air filled with the fragrance of soap that wafted near him. He then buried his face in the bowl of food that Fuzzy had put out for him. He paused after every two or three gulps to swill down water from an adjacent bowl. Both were set on one of the motel's white towels at the foot of the queen-size bed.

He usually stayed at the truckers' center just over the Florida border, but felt that the attention he had drawn when he showed up at the previous night's stop would only escalate the number of questions being asked. He was sure at least some of his fellow truckers had heard the news. There was a good chance someone might have figured out that the blond Lab Fuzzy was traveling with and the one being advertised as missing were one and the same. He hoped that their distance from Boston mitigated the import of the news being received by people in this area. He needed time to think and his remote motel room would provide him with some much-needed privacy.

Besides, he did enjoy a good hot shower and the clean sheets of a bed someone else would have to make in the morning. Schebb gave him an appreciative look while licking his lips to clean the final drops of dinner off his furry chin. Fuzzy walked toward him with one bath towel wrapped around his ample waist, using a second to dry his hair and beard.

"How was that, boy? Did you save me some?"

Schebb raised his head. He whined when Fuzzy's hand stroked his fur. From a small suitcase Fuzzy took out a fresh pair of green work pants, a clean black T-shirt emblazoned with the Harley Davidson logo, a pair of clean XXL white under-wear, a pressed denim shirt with imitation pearl buttons, and a pair of fresh gray wool socks with three red stripes around the top. He liked the feel of putting on clean clothes. It reminded him of being at home where his mother made him wear clean clothes every day, which she had laboriously washed and ironed.

Fuzzy moved a medium sized cooler beside the only arm-chair in the room then settled in with a sigh. Schebb strolled over and nuzzled himself into the space between Fuzzy's legs and the base of the chair. Fuzzy pulled two bottles of icy beer from the cooler and slipped a long submarine sandwich from its clear cocoon. He placed the beer on the lamp table beside him, spread a small white towel on his lap then unwrapped his dinner. His mouth watered when the smell of the still warm double roast beef drifted up to his nose. Schebb twitched at the scent, but didn't bother to look up.

Fuzzy twisted the cap off one of the bottles. He tilted his head back. He felt the frosty liquid bath his parched mouth and throat. With a great sigh and a belch, Fuzzy continued un-wrapping the sub.

"This is the life, isn't it?"

He opened his mouth wide and with both hands inserted the end into the waiting cavern. His teeth severed the first chunk from the whole, juices from beef, pickles, tomatoes, onions, olives, horse radish and mustard dribbled onto his beard. He placed the paper-wrapped sub back on the towel and picked up the half empty beer with one hand and the television remote with the other. The remaining contents of beer number one soaked the doughy bun and mixed with its contents in his mouth. Chewing, he pressed the on button of the remote. The screen came to life.

His throat constricted

Fuzzy stopped chewing.

Schebb lifted his head and stared at the screen where in the top right hand corner was a photograph of Schebb. In the top left hand corner was a pretty good composite drawing of Fuzzy.

The announcer sat at his desk, flanked overhead on the screen by two photos. "This is a GBC Channel Five News Bulletin. The well-known Douglas family, owners of the communications giant Douglas Corporation, continue to seek any information which may lead to the return of this dog that goes by the name Schebb. He was last seen with this man who is believed to have been instrumental in the rescue of Peter Douglas. Anyone with information regarding the dog or the man pictured above should contact us at one of the numbers on the screen. Generous rewards are being offered."

Fuzzy turned off the television and recommenced chewing the large bite followed by two more of similar proportion. He twisted the top from beers number two and three and drained each in long swallows. He let a long quiet belch drift up and escape his mouth. Schebb was moving about under his feet then took up an adjusted position.

A drip from the shower and the dog's breathing were the only noises in the room. Fuzzy's head sank back into soft cushions, his eyes closed.

Schebb's bark happened at the exact instant the knocking at the door began. Fuzzy awoke instantly.

"Mr. Polonski, are you in there?"

He just knew it was a couple of State troopers, hiding behind black aviator glasses, flanking the door with pistols drawn. There were at least ten highway patrol cars strategically positioned around the motel with more ready on back-up. The officers had all pulled the sawed-off shotguns from the dash mounts in their cars and were ready to deal with whatever resistance Fuzzy might put up.

Schebb barked in rhythm with the sharp knocking at the door. It was obviously the butt end of a pistol making the clean crisp sound against the wood.

"Mr. Polonski, it's the front desk clerk."

The troopers must think I'm stupid. I've seen this trick in every cop movie I've ever seen. Was it over for him? Was there no way out?

"Yeah, I'm here. What do you want?"

"I have something for you. You'll have to open the door."

Handcuffs, most likely. I'll have to surrender or be shot running.

"I'll be right there." He tried to buy a little time while he got a story straight in his head as to why he was in possession of the Douglas dog…in Florida! He reached into the cooler and pulled out bottle number four. Tipping his head back, he closed his eyes and didn't open them until the last drop drained from the bottle.

"Mr. Polonski, are you coming?"

"Well, Schebb, this is it. It's been fun while it lasted." Fuzzy eased himself out of the armchair. On his way to the door he paused at the wall mirror and inspected his appearance; assuming he'd be photographed, he might as well look tidy.

Without undoing the chain, he eased open the door, expecting to see the barrel of a pistol in his nose. He looked straight through the crack across the parking lot to a shopping plaza on the other side of the street, then adjusted his view downward until the figure of the diminutive front desk clerk was clearly in his vision.

At five foot zero he was a full eighteen inches shorter than Fuzzy. "Hi, Mr. Polonski. Sorry to disturb you, but you left your change and receipt in the office. I figured you'd need it before tomorrow."

Fuzzy undid the chain and took the cash from the clerk. He poked his head out the door and scanned from left to right.

"Looking for someone?"

"Ah, no I was just...just seeing if a friend of mine had arrived."

There were no state troopers, no highway patrol cars with shotgun-toting Smokey's and no handcuffs. He was a hunted man, but for now he was still a free man.

"I can direct him...or her.... to your room when they arrive." The clerk smiled.

Fuzzy gave the clerk a bewildered look.

"Well, uh, if there's anything you need, anything at all, just let me know."

"No, no, it's okay. If they aren't here by now, then they're probably not coming. Thanks a lot. Goodnight, now."

Fuzzy closed the door and slipped the chain back in place. He went into the bathroom, ran cold water and doused his face three or four times. He grabbed one last dry towel from the rack and soaked up the moisture.

The armchair made a whooshing sound when his frame compressed the foam. He reached his hand into the icy cooler and pulled beers number five and six onto his lap. The sweat on the bottles soaked into his pants. Two twists and four gulps later, five and six were dead. Fuzzy reached for his sub and tore off a mouthful with his teeth. While he chewed, his arm swung down beside the arm chair and into the cooler. His fat fingers entwined around the necks of seven and eight.

Fuzzy let out another audible belch then pressed the "on" button of the remote to surf some channels.

His head was buzzed from consuming nearly three times as many beers as normal.

Meaningless pictures flickered in his eyes.

He needed a plan.

- Chapter 34 -

The distraction of pulsing lights, stage fog and gyrating naked bodies did not aid Brian's quest. Approaching a table of well-dressed men, a tall, naked brunette raised her head and torso quickly to full attention from a position that had previously allowed her short hair to touch the ground. She stood on a mirrored box with her feet wide apart. In her upright position her long legs created an inverted V through which Brian could now see his brother's smiling face. They made eye contact for an instant, then the woman swung her head between her legs and stared back at Matt whose face was now inches away from her buff behind.

Brian continued his approach; the tall dancer performed this demonstration of flexibility several times, to the delight of the men at Matt's circular table. Each time she threw her head alternately skyward then back down between her calves, the men applauded with increasing vigor and rained five, ten and twenty dollar bills around her red high-heeled shoes. Four or five times Matt appeared between the woman's legs.

Brian could now tell from his glazed eyes and puffy face that Matt was well on his way to inebriation. The litter of over-sized martini glasses on the chrome table was further testimony to the men's aggressive consumption.

Matt was standing up, peeling several crisp bills from his money clip when Brian made it to his side. The woman continued her dancing oblivious to the changing audience. No words were exchanged. Brian was unimpressed with his brother's actions.

Brian tapped his watch, shooting Matt a scorning look and motioned with his head toward a door. Matt slipped a small wad of bills into the red and black lace garter on the woman's thigh. The indentation of Matt's vinyl seat had barely recovered before one of the other patrons at the table shifted from an observer's position to front and center for the continuing performance.

Another tall, heavy set bouncer swung the solid door open. The sound of clicking balls and soft rock music was a dramatic change from the entertainment lounge.

"This is where I meant, not out front."

Brian and Matt walked into the adjoining billiards room.

"I've never been in here."

"Really? What a surprise."

"Fuck off."

Twelve tables were busy with men plying their pool skills over crisply lit green felt. Some were in business attire while others wore operating greens. The outside walls of the room were lined with four seat booths. Brian and Matt walked past the bar toward a quiet booth in a back corner.

"Black coffee and a pint of Coors please."

"Who's the coffee for?"

Brian just looked at Matt and kept walking.

"You're late." Matt made an attempt at offense.

"You're disgusting. How can you sit down here, half bombed, staring at those sluts while your father is up there in a fucking coma?"

"Exactly. He doesn't know I'm down here."

"Don't be too sure."

"What do you mean?" Matt stared at the waitress's cleavage when she bent down to serve them. His eyes followed her when she walked away. "Hey, don't knock it till you've tried it," he taunted his brother with a grin. "So what's up?"

"There's some weird shit happening up there." Brian motioned with his head in the direction of the hospital. "First of all, I had a daydream while I was staring through the window at dad. It seemed to last forever, and I swear it was a life-like hallucination, but it only took a second. It was a time way back when dad and I got into a fight at the cottage. I swear to you I relived it right there in the hospital, and now I feel completely different about it, like it never happened. I held a grudge all my life, and now I can barely remember why."

"Then Mom came out of there acting all weird and friendly toward Charlotte, and Edward says she actually hugged him. We've got rumors of leaks to the press and our IT manager has reported two attempted break-ins to our systems by unauthorized and unknown users."

Brian took a long draw on his draft. Matt sipped at his coffee.

"Then, when I came in the other door to see you, I ran right into some fat guy who was leaving. I think I busted his nose, but when I came back out with a towel he was gone. It was very strange. I have a feeling I should know who he is."

"Is there any good news?"

"Yeah, some. Edward and security are tracking down the quality leads we have on Schebb and the guy who helped pull dad out of the river."

"So, how's he doing?"

"Why don't you go up and see for yourself? He won't bite you."

"I know. I will. I just want to be prepared."

"Nothing's changed. He's all wired up. He looks like death. They've got this big framework over the bed that monitors electrical current from his brain and when you go in the room you get scanned to avoid interference. Dr. Brandon says it's a wait and see game, but the guy running the monitoring gear says we're wasting our time."

"He said that to you?"

"That's another story. He didn't even know who I was, but he does now. How's business on the island?"

"More work required. It's brutal over there, but someone has to take on the tough jobs, right?" Matt said with a tone of mock exasperation.

"Right. Nice try." Brian placed twenty dollars on the table while they caught up. He couldn't deny that in a way he envied his brother's lust for life and he did enjoy a vicarious taste of it now and again.

The brothers left from the rear of the building and followed a gravel pathway around to where it connected with a sidewalk leading to the parking lot.

"See, right there, that red stuff. That's blood from the guy. Now follow these drops down the sidewalk. See how they get farther apart? He was running away. Now why would a guy run away if I was trying to help him?"

"Did you recognize him?"

"No. He was overweight and wore a uniform of some sort. I was too stunned to take notice. Besides, I figured he'd be blaming me for bashing into him."

Matt elbowed his brother. "Picking on short fat guys in uniforms now, are you?"

"It was an accident. He came bursting out that door."

"Yeah, yeah, sure buddy. Tell it to the Judge." Both laughed, walking across the parking lot into the hospital.

"Do you know some guy named Zalkow? Dr. Joe Zalkow?"

"Yes, why?"

"He was in the club, all over me about dad. A real treat of a guy. Claims he's on a board with dad."

"He is. The hospital board. He also happens to be Chief of Staff and he's currently battling a major suit launched against the hospital and him. Dad has a real distaste for the guy. Goes all the way back to boy's school. Don't put anything past him. He's always been pro-choice if it meant the hospital could save some money. Believe me; the two do not get along. Dad's been working quietly for years to get him removed and Zalkow knows it. Also, the guys in Douglas security have hard information that he's the money behind the City Star. He's dirty as they come, but he knows the politics game and how to get what he wants…whatever the price. Dad thinks that's how he has protected his position for so long."

"That rag?"

"Yep."

"He looked the part. He was right up front with the pussy too."

"So were you."

"That's different. I'm single."

"Single?"

"Well…ya… sort of."

"You're also Matthew Douglas. Whether you like it or not, that's the kind of shit that ends up in the Star."

"Good point."

The elevator opened several floors below Peter's. Three nurses stood in the open door looking at Brian and Matt.

Matt smiled scanning them. "Going up? Furniture, hardware, men's wear, underwear and lingerie."

Matt made eye contact with the nurse in the middle. They ignored his commentary and stepped in. She stood in front of Matt and turned her back to him. Brian stared at the illuminated numbers over the doors. Matt stared at the nurse's hair, then roamed her length with his eyes. The elevator continued on its ascent.

"Are you in again tonight, Terri?"

"All night."

"Is that intern friend of yours working?"

"I have no idea."

The three giggled a bit. The door opened and six more people came aboard. Matt had slipped into a fantasy. A wave of intoxication brought on from being motionless in such close quarters rose over him. More stops were made and with each additional passenger Terri was forced back toward Matt until her behind was pressed lightly against him. She seemed to let each movement of the elevator translate through her and gently into Matt, who stood motionless, enjoying the moment.

The original five left the elevator last when it stopped at Peter's floor. When Terri was about to leave, she turned her head, raised her eyebrows slightly, and disappeared from view.

Brian held the Open button a minute longer. "How was that?"

"How was what?"

"She was pressed right up against you. How is it always you? That never happens to me."

Matt smiled drunkenly. "Just lucky, I guess. Besides, you've got a corporation to run. Can't have you being distracted."

"Great."

The buzzer sounded. Brian released the button. They escaped through closing doors and walked toward their father.

At the door of the lounge, Brian paused. "I'll be in here. Dad's down there."

Matt felt his stomach tighten. He looked at Brian, who put his hand on Matt's shoulder and gave it a squeeze. Matt could feel his emotions well up.

This was a real moment, a moment when one does an instant inventory of life and comes up with a value score. It was as though he could instantly measure his life's activities and accomplishments against some greater moral purpose from a third party's viewpoint. Matt was very tough on himself in such circumstances and drew on an ever-present plan to mend his ways and become a pillar of virtue. He did not score well.

"I'll be right here." Brian's words were soothing, but Matt knew the task at hand was his alone.

He turned quickly from his brother and walked away. Brian was Matt's touchstone, his grounding that helped keep what was important in life in perspective. Right now it was his family and his father. "Thanks. Thanks," Matt said quietly and kept walking down the hall.

"Excuse me, Mr. Douglas, sir."

Brian composed himself and turned to face a tall, skinny, young black man in a wrinkled Douglas Security uniform. It hung from his bony frame like wet toilet paper on a seat.

"Yes?" Brian looked at the kid and made a mental note to speak to his security chief about recruiting and uniform policies.

"I just came on duty, sir. I guess this is my spot. Is everything okay? Can I help you with anything?"

"Who are you replacing? Didn't he hand off a detail report?"

"No Sir. I got called in early. A guy who was supposed to be here is sick."

"So where's George, our regular man?"

"I don't know, sir. He must have left already."

Brian made another mental note. "I'm fine. You have your assignment, right?"

"Yes Sir. No unauthorized personnel near Mr. Douglas Senior. Especially no newspaper types."

"Exactly. Especially no newspaper types."

Matt stared at his father. His feet were frozen to the ground. His fingers pressed against the glass. He was deeply moved by feelings for his father he had rarely acknowledged.

Peter saw his son at the window and tried to reach out to him. He could feel nothing. He pressed his mental energy outward but sensed no response. He wondered again how it was that he could read the mind of total strangers but not that of his own son. Peter's words echoed hollowly inside his cavern. He could see the pain on Matt's face but could do nothing about it but watch.

Matt stopped in the electronic archway. He looked at it suspiciously but realized he had no choice but to proceed if he wanted to enter. When he did, the scan produced normal readings which went unceremoniously into the computer data bank.

Matt paced the room like a caged cat. He pulled back the curtains to catch a view of the parking lot and freeway in the distance. He could see the entrance to Eye See You below and watched a few patrons make their way in and out of the doors. He wondered about their lives and imagined the activities from a distance.

He wasn't like them, was he?

The steady beep of the equipment and the sound of oxygen flowing through a clear plastic tube into his father paced his thoughts. The lights were low. The room smelled like hospitals do: a non-smell that has no description yet everyone seems to identify and dislike.

Matt walked to his father's bedside and stared down at him.

"I could have done it, Dad. I could have done it. I was young, and I'd made some mistakes, but you didn't have to leave me out altogether."

Peter listened.

"You always liked him better than me. Of course when the girls came along, well, it was like I didn't exist. It was me against the world then. I'd show all of you. But I guess I haven't shown anyone anything, have I? I'm just a Douglas and that's it. Without that, what would I be? Probably unemployed. Who'd hire me? Who could afford to? I'm really pissed off at you, you know. I've felt this way since you left Mom. I should have told you then, but I didn't have enough courage. I guess I still don't; here I am telling this stuff to a dead man. You know you've never told me that you loved me? You always told the girls. I heard you say it. Did you love me too, Dad?" Matt gripped the chrome railing of his father's bed, his knuckles white.

Peter felt the pain of his son's secrets cut him deeply. He wished it would end. If he could die then he could somehow be free of receiving the burdens he seemingly had placed upon all those around him.

Was I really such a bad person? Had I made everyone's life so miserable? Was building financial security for my family selfish or selfless? Was I not doing the right thing? I've been a good employer. A good father and friend. A valued member of his community. What about the praise and the awards? The honorary degrees and titles? Did that not mean anything in the face of such raw judgment?

Matt continued , "I loved you, I just never knew how to tell you, and now it's too late. It's too late. You'll be gone and you'll never know and I'll be here always wishing you did." He raised his arm to his face and wiped it. His lips were strained, sticky with the force of his feelings. "I'm very angry." He raised his voice forcefully and then went silent, taking a breath to compose himself.

Again he paced. "You know it's pretty lonely being me. Trying to live up to the Douglas name and all the expectations that go with it. Trying to wear a shoe that doesn't fit that well. You know Dad; we've never really talked, just you and me, man to man. It was always your way, wasn't it? You always thought you knew what was best for me. Maybe you should have asked my opinion just one time what was best in my opinion. Now it looks like we'll never have a chance."

Peter was stunned at his son's words.

How could he not know that I loved him? Of course I did. Did I really never tell him? I must have.

Peter felt his body sob gently. A single drop of water slipped out of the corner of his eye and trickled down his cheek. He still could not feel any of the emotions that he was hearing expressed by his son. He longed to reach out and hold him and tell him that he did love him.

Why did I wait? What was I afraid of? I should have told him. I should have told all of them more.

Peter felt the claustrophobia of his containment rising. He had to keep control and use his new skills carefully. He felt torn between energy explosion and containment. He breathed slowly in and out, again and again. He focused on his son, who paced the room.

Matt walked back to stare down at his father again. He noticed the trail of moisture on Peter's cheek. He reached out and ever so lightly tracked the path of the tear. He looked at the moisture on his fingertip.

Peter could feel the warmth of his son's touch on his cheek.

Matt had never touched his father so gently in his life. The skin felt rubbery and lifeless. Matt shuddered and made a fist around the dampened index finger locking the tear away forever.

He walked away. He was drunk. Emotional turmoil combined with alcohol clouded his brain. Through the window, the last crimson of a fading sunset still showed. The freeway was a steady stream of white and red lights, like colored ants crawling unwaveringly to some distant destination. He reached down and pivoted his body until it settled into the vinyl lounge chair facing his father's bed. Resting his head against its high back, he closed his eyes. The vinyl piping at the top of the chair cut into his head.

Off balance, spinning slowly like a top that is wobbling to an end before it falls on its side, Matt was released from consciousness and fell into a deep sleep.

"Your mommy's pregnant and we're going to have another baby. You'll have a new little brother or sister. I want you to know that no matter what, whether it's a boy or a girl, I love you and I'll always love you. I'll be spending time with the new baby and I'll be telling the baby that I love it too. Do you understand?"

It was Christmas in the old Douglas home and a young Matt sat on his father's lap in front of the decorated tree. Brian busily shook presents. A very pregnant Marion prepared supper in the kitchen.

Peter was awake. He was really there. This was his house and his family. This was the evening he had missed while having one too many drinks in an airport waiting for a flight. He remembered the call to Marion. He remembered her disappointment. He remembered lashing out in anger at her lack of understanding. He remembered hearing his boys crying into the telephone when they heard their father wasn't going to be home that night. He remembered his next few drinks and another lonely hotel room with another nameless, faceless body. Just a lost soul caught in the glamour of the exciting world of business travel for the sake of making money at any cost.

It had happened again. He had been granted another chance to make a difference to the souls of his family.

Matt stood on his father's lap and wrapped his arms around Peter's neck. Peter could feel the warmth of his son's body and his sharp little ribs when he hugged him.

"I love you, Daddy."

"Me too, me too." Brian clamored to get in on the action and Peter's two boys entwined themselves around their father. Peter looked between their heads and saw his pregnant wife standing in the doorway, smiling, watching her three men with happy tears in her eyes.

Bright lights and sudden acceleration shocked Peter when the gravity of movement seemed to elongate his body down an iridescent corridor. Flashes of color appeared, at first without form. He accelerated toward an unknown end. He could feel the unhappiness of this experience. Then, like a multi-projector slide show, he saw images all around him; birthday parties, Christmas and holiday celebrations, children crying at night, babies awake in the darkness, hospital rooms, and always Marion. The images flashed in sequence like a fireworks display. Accompanying sound effects reverberated in his head. Sadness prevailed like a single theme that wove its way through this high-speed show. It was his absence from each picture.

Proceeding, Peter tried desperately to stop the motion and reach out to his family, but each time an image evaporated to be replaced by another. Frustration at his inability to change what had happened overwhelmed him.

"Why? Why? Give me a chance like before. I was wrong. I didn't know. I've changed. You'll see, I've changed." Peter cried out in vain to an empty audience. He was the only attendee at this exclusive performance.

As suddenly as it had started, all lights went out, all noise stopped and the images were gone.

Peter's journey was over, but he had made a small connection with his son. He hoped for more.

"Are you all right?"

Matt opened his eyes but couldn't focus at first. His eyes stung and were dry. He was aware of a subtle familiar fragrance and he realized that a woman stood over him with her hand on his shoulder. She nudged him gently.

"Can I get you a drink?"

Matt's eyes cleared. The pretty face of a friendly nurse in her white uniform was inches from his. She backed away. Matt focused on her plastic name tag: TERRI.

Once Matt realized that he was in the presence of an attractive young woman his instincts kicked in. "Vodka martini would be nice," he grinned foggily and straightened up. He ran his fingers through his hair.

"From the smell of you I'd say you've already had your share."
Terri reached in her pocket and handed Matt a package of gum.

"Is it that bad?"

"I'm a nurse, remember? I'm used to objectionable sights and odors."

Matt already liked her. She was feisty. He liked the challenge.

"Well, I'm one for two. Should I ask?"

Terri smiled, turning to walk into the bathroom.

Matt admired her model-like walk.

"No."

Matt was conscious enough now to appreciate her tight-fitting uniform and remember their encounter in the elevator. Terri returned with a glass of water and a wet towel.

"It looks like you've been crying." Terri gave Matt a look that said she was baiting him.

"No, no, just allergies. There's something about these hospitals." Matt wiped his face with the offered towel.

They both knew he was lying. A silent truce was made.

"You're supposed to be taking care of him, not me." Matt pointed to his father.

"I'm taking good care of him. How do you know him?"

"I don't, I just walk around hospitals and wander into strange men's rooms and fall asleep. He's my father, Peter Douglas. I'm Matt." He stood up and extended his hand.

"I'm Terri."

"I know. We were on the elevator together earlier." Matt raised his eyebrows.

"Oh, really? Sorry, I don't remember. I see so many people in a day."

Was she lying, he wondered? He couldn't tell, but if she was she was good.

"I better keep on my rounds. If there's anything you need…" Terri paused.

Matt's nature told him to move in for a kill, but when he reached down for some of the bravado he used for seducing women, he couldn't find any. Normally he'd be booking at least a telephone number, if not a date. Something was missing.

"No, that's great. Thank you for taking good care of my father. I love him, you know."

Whoa, was that me who said that? What's going on?

"Okay, I'm on evenings from six until six."

Matt walked over to his father's bedside and ran his hand gently across Peter's forehead. He gingerly touched the points at which the wires entered his skull.

Peter could feel the warmth of his son's hand, and for a few seconds he felt Matt's emotions. The connection wasn't strong, but it was more than he had before. Peter longed to get back into Matt's life and touch him the way he should have years ago.

"I'll see you soon, Dad." Matt bent down and kissed his father's forehead.

Another first. I feel dizzy. I guess I'm sobering up.

He left his father's room with memories of the strange dream lingering in his mind.

- Chapter 35 -

Edward and Brian were in the lounge talking when Matt returned. He appeared worn out when they looked at him, but neither said anything other than to greet him warmly. They had been chatting about how tough this was on everyone and how each person would handle this trauma in his or her own way.

"Situations of tremendous stress induce various reactions. It is impossible to predict how anyone would react to a given situation, even when someone knows them well," Edward was sharing with Brian. "Some explode with emotion quickly and let pressure release freely and publicly. Others show little or no reaction. They would add this or that new situation to an emotional stew that was no doubt simmering inside them. Some people go a lifetime and never show their true emotions about anything. Then when cancer, a heart attack or a nervous breakdown happens, people are surprised. Meanwhile, the burning has been going on inside for years."

Brian had observed that Edward seemed to be able to strike a balance between emotional outbursts and silent stewing. He seemed to communicate easily yet forcefully with people about how he was feeling and didn't exhibit any embarrassment around discussing his emotions with others. He always said that he was simply being selfish. Perhaps this ease of sharing was rooted in his difficult beginnings.

"Why should I be the only one to know how rotten I'm feeling," he would joke if he was having a bad day. He had told

Brian that the very act of exposing himself in such a manner put him and others at ease and got him on a better emotional track. He always liked to say, "Act the way you want to feel and soon you will, or treat someone the way you want them to be and so they shall be."

This time was no different than many others he experienced in his life, he said. While he sat and spoke with Brian and Matt, he expressed openly the pain he felt for Peter's situation and how much he loved their father and the Douglas family.

When he spoke, his voice quivered and his eyes moistened.

Both Douglas boys were moved deeply to hear such an honest expression of feelings. Listening to Edward, they felt a new closeness. They both admired his strength and courage and felt growing esteem for him.

Brian was learning a valuable lesson while he listened to Edward. He had always been concerned that an open expression of emotion was a sign of weakness and yet here he was admiring Edward's strength. Right then Brian made a pact with himself: he would no longer be weighed down by carrying a sack over his shoulder filled with emotional hurt from the past.

Edward consistently referred to faith he had in the natural order of the world and the greater universe. He expressed confidence that life had and would continue to lead him where he needed to be. "I try to learn something from every experience," he said. "I ask myself why I might be facing any difficult circumstance and what I might gain or learn from it. The process doesn't remove the pain, but it adds a broader context in which to measure it."

He reflected with the Douglas boys on times of great sorrow, like his school days as an outcast and how, as painful as those times were, he now realized that learning to deal with the taunts and name calling of insensitive school boys helped him build strength of character and confidence that served him well.

Matt interrupted; "Listen guys, I have to make a call. I'll be back."

"Use the phone here."

"I don't want to disturb you and Edward. I'll step outside."

"Matt, Mom has invited all of us to have dinner together tonight. I hope you'll come," Brian urged his brother. He felt what Matt needed was to be surrounded by people who cared about him, people who would support his emotionally fragile state even though Matt probably wasn't aware or prepared to acknowledge that there was anything fragile about him. Brian knew that Matt's habit, like many people, was to avoid confronting emotional issues by suppressing them or denying they existed. He also knew that different people used different methods to deny how they truly felt. People rarely reach for help when they need it most. They would often overdo one area of their life to suppress another. In Matt's case it was exercise and sex in copious quantities. His good looks, money, penchant for young women and fast lifestyle were a volatile combination. Brian worried about his younger brother constantly.

"Okay, I'll let you know." Matt headed for the door.

Brian and Edward exchanged a knowing look.

When the telephone rang for the fifth then sixth time, Matt began to wonder what Cara was up to. Since there was a telephone in the bathroom he assumed that she was not in the suite. When the voice message service came on the line Matt pressed zero and asked to be transferred to the concierge, hoping that Sandy might know where Cara was.

His mind started to work on him since fear of the unknown now left a place for negative thoughts to dwell. The electronic message reported that Miss Dugas was unavailable to take a call. Matt pressed zero again. His palm was sweating and sticking to the phone. His annoyance increased rapidly. Matt was a man of action and did not like when things didn't go his way. He asked to speak with Stephen Merck, but got his secretary who was working late.

"Good evening, Mr. Douglas."

Matt asked the whereabouts of Steven.

"I think everyone on the Island except me is out at Anthony Houston's big shindig tonight, Mr. Douglas."

Matt could envision the whole scene, having been to many such "shindigs." Every beautiful and moneyed man and woman worth inviting would be at Houston's enormous estate on the secluded tip of Spanish Point. People would be arriving by taxi, yacht and speedboat with many high rollers coming in by private jet and helicopter from the mainland. It was definitely not the place Matt wanted Cara to be without him even though he had supported the idea.

"Did you happen to see my guest and Miss Dugas together?"

"Yes I did, and they both looked stunning. Those two were a striking pair."

Merck's secretary had no idea that every word was like a dagger in Matt's stomach. He was getting totally rattled.

"In fact they went with a group from here in the Sands' limousine."

"Okay, thanks. You should be out there having fun too, not working." Matt feigned a bit of humor and sympathy.

"Thanks, Mr. Douglas. It's nice to know that someone thinks so. We hope to see you soon."

"Oh, you will, you will," Matt said firmly, pressing the button to end the call. He quickly dialed Cara's cell phone while trying to stop himself from reeling inside. He felt like he had just been hit with several body punches. His mind scanned a series of images: his father, his family…but kept coming back to his beautiful Cara being harassed by dozens of drunk and horny men at Houston's party. He envisioned her in a skimpy little dress like one she wore the other night when she picked him up at the airport. He knew she liked to play the seduction game, but it drove him crazy to think of her playing it with anyone but him.

Cara's voicemail picked up.

Matt called Bob next and barked a detailed message into the handset that they were heading back to Bermuda ASAP.

Edward had agreed to meet Brian and whoever else made it for dinner that evening at the chosen restaurant. For now though, he wanted to spend some quiet time with his friend Peter.

Brian left the lounge and paused to check in with the security guard. He made another trip to the nursing station to request the distribution of more flowers that had arrived and confirm that he wanted no non-family members other than Edward to be allowed in to see Peter.

He knew that Marjorie was getting a continual stream of requests for visiting privileges. For now she was taking names and promising that their best wishes would be passed along. They would be notified when the family was ready to allow visitors. Brian knew that sooner or later he would have to deal with those requests.

For now it would be later.

- Chapter 36 -

The hospital floor was quiet now that evening had settled in. The mood along the corridors was muted, with lights now dimmed and the evening staff going quietly about their duties. Most of the Doctors and interns that scurried around all day doing their rounds were gone. The overhead announcements were down to a trickle. Meal carts were gone, as were patients touring each wing in wheel chairs or lying about on gurneys waiting to be taken for X-rays, tests or surgery.

On his way to Peter's room, Edward passed only one man. He was wearing a suit and seemed to be coming from the area where the technician sat monitoring readouts from Peter.

Normal enough. Except that the guy stunk of alcohol.

"Well, old man, here we are." Edward took a seat beside Peter's bed. The room was in semi-darkness, giving the equipment and framework around the bed an eerie feel. Each monitor either displayed numerical or graphical data or beeped out its own sound.

"There are so many things I want to say to you. Things that I should have said before, but never took the time or had the courage. Where can I possibly start except with one undeniable fact, and that is that I love you? You are the most important friend in my life and I love you for that." Edward drew a handkerchief from his pocket and blew his nose.

"I know and I love you also," responded Peter gently, trying not to scare away this chance for outside communication.

Edward heard the words in his head. They seemed like a normal response. For the first time. The words didn't register for Edward at first.

Was he just imagining the words or hoping what Peter might say?

Peter had finally made a mental connection with someone. It was so much different than all the times he had yelled out into oblivious space. He hoped Edward would acknowledge him.

"What?" It clicked now that he was hearing a voice. He looked around the room and then at Peter's lifeless body. He squinted and gave his head a shake. "Damn place. This place is too spooky." Edward continued. "You were the only person at school who took a chance on me and became my friend. I would have been a real outcast except for you. I don't know if you ever knew how important that was to me, but it changed my life."

"It changed my life too, Edward. Now it's time for you to help change my life again."

"What's going on? I can hear a voice that sounds like yours, but I sure as hell know it isn't, because you're right here and your lips aren't moving."

"It is me, Edward. It's Peter. I can see you and hear your words and thoughts. You have to believe that it is me."

Was he going a bit crazy in there? Just hearing what he wanted to hear?

I want my friend back so badly that I'm hearing him in my head. I don't believe in ghosts.

"I'm not a ghost. I'm me. I'm trapped inside my body, but my mind is working perfectly. In fact, better than before. I can see things and hear things and..." Peter made himself slow down. He wanted to share all of this with Edward, but knew he had to figure out a way of convincing him that it was okay to believe him.

Edward put his hands to his ears. "Quiet, be quiet, I can't think."

Peter went silent, realizing that he was overwhelming his friend. Peter felt frustrated, but did not want to lose his friend. Perhaps there was a less obtrusive way of communicating without invading someone's head like a bad hangover.

Edward's head went silent too. He took his hands from his ears and listened.

That's better, he thought. I'm just tired and upset.

All he could hear now was the hum of the equipment. Edward stood and started walking around the room. He paced, reminiscing aloud about days at school, watching Peter grow and prosper, the opportunities that Peter had provided for him, the many adventures they had together but most importantly the enduring fact that Peter had made him part of the Douglas family. Truly, Edward was the 3rd son even though he and Peter were the same age. For Edward this was the most important thing in his life and for that he struggled with words to express his gratitude and love.

When Peter listened quietly, he could feel his thoughts connecting with Edward's. The connection amplified when Peter realized that he was no longer hearing words; he was feeling and becoming part of Edward's mind. While Edward made reference to specific incidents that they had experienced together, Peter could feel the familiar pull. It was the force that allowed him to be transported to that particular time, the way he had been with Brian and Matt.

But now, instead of being involuntarily ripped from the present into the past, Peter found that if he focused on the present he could hold himself in place, even though the other person's mind was moving about. Loud sounds in his head and white spinning lights intensified with the pull but eased off if he stayed focused on the current.

He was beginning to feel a sense of balance between now and wherever it was he was being drawn. He was learning a basic skill in a new version of existence. He could stay in the present or he could allow himself to slip into another person's thoughts, world and life, current and past. He wondered what would happen between two people who were equally gifted or between a group of people so skilled. Perhaps there was a neutral place at which they gathered mentally before taking these telepathic tours of mind and spirit. For now, he was a novice and had only one not so advanced fellow-traveler to worry about.

Peter practiced his new skill while Edward talked. Edward would make reference to a specific incident that his mind focused upon and Peter could allow the feeling of his friend's thoughts to transport him to the past.

Each time he arrived at a historical point, he was stunned by the realness of everything. He was fully aware that he was a visitor from the future who had traveled back in time, yet everything was exactly the way it was when he experienced it originally. Each time he was able to participate, or not participate and merely observe. On each occasion, time seemed to catch up with him the way it had when he was with his son on the boat that day at the cottage.

He instinctively knew that he could not stay beyond that moment of contact with himself. He wasn't sure why or how, but he sensed that he had to allow himself to be released back to the present.

Each time he returned to the hospital room it was like nothing had happened except that Edward's mind had changed and he moved on to a new topic.

Mastering this ability to travel mentally or telepathically was surprisingly like learning to ride a bicycle. At first there are only two apparent axes, upright and rolling along or flat on the ground, with no evident ability to control either. With experience, the novice rider begins to feel a new axis: a third one, which is balance or harmony with the bicycle, gravity and the hard ground. The rider effectively harnesses the forces to move forward, turn and travel.

Peter realized that he was learning to harness the forces of his mind that were allowing him to move through time and space. It was like many of the great dreams he'd had in his life while he slept, except now his eyes were open.

Peter stayed focused on the present and tuned out Edward's ramblings asking himself what the purpose of this new gift was. What would happen if he made a material change when he was in the past? Could he influence Edward's or anyone else's thoughts and be transported to a place of his own choosing? Could he go without the influence of another? Could he see the future?

He waited for an answer. Nothing came.

His mind was clear for now. He had disconnected from Edward's.

How had that happened?

He recalled a proverb about the teacher arriving when the student was ready. He realized that in his life he had been provided all the answers to questions which he had. It was true that the answer didn't always come when he wanted it. It wasn't always the desired answer but most often the answer to any dilemma he was facing came when he least expected it.

He would be patient for now and thankful for the knowledge he was gaining. He now had some confidence that there was a purpose in this circumstance and in time he would understand.

Thoughts of being trapped or trying to escape his predicament had faded. He felt peaceful, comfortable that something good would come of this. He hoped he was not fooling himself.

"…We've got lots of leads on Schebb, and I bet we'll find the man who helped you. I know you'd want to reward him." A clear picture of Wilton Polonski appeared in Edward's mind the way it had been sketched and posted. At first he ignored it and continued speaking, but the picture grew more intense.

Edward stopped pacing and sat.

"*This is the man, Edward.*" The image of the sketch was brighter and clearer now. "*This is him.*"

Edward put his face in his hands.

Projected in full color against the blackness of his mind, he could see the picture of Wilton Polonski and knew innately that this was the man they wanted to find. He pulled a folded piece of paper from his jacket pocket and opened the current composite sketch that they were using to find this man. He withdrew a fine black marker from another pocket and started altering the sketch. He added more beard and heavier eyebrows, drew crows-feet around the eyes and a vertical line on each cheek where the face wrinkled from when he smiled. He added some width to the face and widened his eyes a bit. Then, like his hand was being guided by an unknown force, he wrote five letters at the bottom of the page:

F U Z ZY.

Edward looked across the room at Peter.

"Did you do that?"

"*Yes.*" Edward heard the answer he wanted to hear, but could not bring himself to believe it. He had to call GBC, update the composite drawing and try to determine just what FUZZY meant.

He rose to leave then caught a view in the darkened window of an elderly woman. She smiled and turned away. Edward could feel her warmth even at a distance.

"Good night, old friend. I'll be back tomorrow. This has been quite an evening."

"*Goodbye, Eddie.*"

Edward just smiled to himself and wiggled a finger in his ear. Eddie. I haven't heard that name in a long time.

When he left the room he bumped into a Wet Floors sign, skidding it across the floor. He bent to move it back into place and noticed the woman from the window working a damp mop back and forth across the hallway floor. Edward smiled apologetically. "Sorry, I didn't see it."

"That is okay. It's hard to see everything that's going on around us. Even when we can, it's hard to believe all we see."

Edward gave her a perplexed look, and then nodded politely. "Goodnight."

"Goodnight," Mrs. Rossi responded.

Edward couldn't be sure. He had heard her words in his head, but he could have sworn that her lips hadn't moved. When he looked again her back was to him. She continued the rhythmic sway of her mop.

That also struck Edward as odd.

Why would someone be using a mop when the hospital was well equipped with power equipment for such jobs? Noise reduction I guess. Was that actually the reason?

"Damn place. Damn strange place. I hate hospitals," Edward mumbled to himself, starting down the corridor. He passed the Douglas security guard and walked to the waiting elevators.

- Chapter 37 -

She hummed, working her mop back and forth across the halls, mop strings silently stroking the vinyl leaving a shiny film that dried minutes after she passed. Mrs. Rossi was one of the first employees hired at the hospital, and her retirement age had come and gone.

Although she was a union member out of necessity, not choice, being the member with the greatest seniority gave her certain privileges. For decades, at each contract negotiation, her union boss would come to her on the eve of the final negotiation and seek her input on the contract. For years she had always offered advice that proved crucial to achieving an amicable settlement.

No one understood or questioned her and no one really knew how the tradition started. Everyone including the hospital board knew that until Mrs. Rossi said there was a deal, there was no deal. It was like she had them all under a spell.

Sometime in the early years of contract renewal, as a special thanks to her for the good advice, one of the union bosses asked if there was anything they could add to the contract that might help her out personally. Her first request was that she would never have to work Sundays. Her reason was that, on occasions when she was forced to work Sundays, she couldn't have local homeless children, winos and derelicts into her home for a Sunday meal and prayer session. The "Rossi Clause," as it was called from then on, always received unanimous approval.

Not one person ever questioned this unusual insertion in the union contract.

Every few years or so, the contract got fatter and Mrs. Rossi would make another request. The premise was always for the benefit of others. One year it was the establishment of a Help Fund, another year a donation to restore an orphanage and so it went. The contract grew with each new Rossi Clause.

In her entire history, Mrs. Rossi asked only once that something be inserted for her benefit, which was that she would never have to operate one of the mechanized floor scrubbers and polishers.

She was a perfectionist whose work was superior at all times to that of the younger cleaners being dragged along behind the modern, noisy equipment. She baked her own bread, grew her own vegetables, made her own preserves and still did laundry by hand before hanging it in the sun to dry.

She felt that machines distanced people from nature and took away their pride and creativity. She loved the harmony she felt with her hand tools and reveled in the natural rhythm they took on when she worked with them.

The Rossi Clause was thus amended without question and another contract received her blessing.

Peter could feel her presence before he saw her quietly wheel her bucket through the archway into his room.

"Good evening, Mr. Peter Douglas." He could hear her words inside his head. She spoke with a slow cadence, heavy with an accent. Her words felt purposeful and distinct.

"You have been busy, I can tell. You learn much in one day."

Peter could see her clearly now. Her eyes sparkled when she looked at him, and he realized that even though she spoke to him, her mouth was not moving.

"Who are you? Why is this happening? Am I going to live? How do I get out of here?" Peter quickly lost his peaceful composure

peppering this woman with questions. He felt certain she knew the answers.

"*Very good Mr. Douglas, you have learned your new skills well. Be calm, my friend. Be calm.*"

Peter now realized he was communicating telepathically. More mysteries unfolded. He took nothing for granted now. She continued, her English slightly broken.

"*So many questions you have, and I will help you find some answers. You have been given gift in order that you may complete some tasks.*"

"What tasks? Why am I here? Why am I trapped like this? Am I going to die?"

"*So many questions. I do not know any of that. Only you will know when you know.*"

"How will I know? What will I know?"

"*You will know. You will understand. We all come to understand our purpose in time.*"

"How can you talk to me like this? You do it without effort, but you are not trapped in your body like me."

"*I have been this way always. I have met many people like you in many different circumstances. I have concluded after many years that my gift is to help people like you find their purpose.*"

"When your friends…these people that you helped… when they found their purpose…did they live? Or die?"

"*What does that matter? Once person fulfils purpose on earth, life and death as we know them are not so important. Then we move to next journey.*"

"What journey? Where do we go? What do we do?"

"*I do not know. I am still here too.*"

"I've been traveling. I mean, I've been back in time and it was real. Do you do that?"

"*I have heard from those who have done so. I never have.*"

"So how can you help me?"

"*Do you feel better knowing that there is someone who can hear you?*"

"Yes, much."

"Then I have already helped you. Continue to work with your gift. Be careful when you travel. Do not disturb that which should go undisturbed."

"How will I know?"

"Hi, Mrs. Rossi. How's Mr. Douglas doing?"

"Good evening, Theresa."

Mrs. Rossi and her mother were the only two people who called her Theresa. Terri loved the way she spoke with broken English although she had always suspected that there was more to Mrs. Rossi than met the eye. Her thick Italian accent made the name Theresa sound so rich and wonderful…There-ay-sa. There-ay-sa.

"He still sleeping. Take good care of him. He special man."

"I'm sure he is. He also has a very special son," Terri smiled at Mrs. Rossi.

"Be careful what you wish, Theresa." Mrs. Rossi looked at the young nurse shrewdly. "You might receive it…goodnight."

"What? Receive what?" Her words were lost on Terri.

Mrs. Rossi quietly rolled her bucket out the door.

"Goodnight, Peter."

Her words filled his mind. His thoughts were fully engaged contemplating another remarkable experience.

A bright, smiling face replaced Mrs. Rossi's. "Hello, Mr. Douglas." Terri looked around. "Peter, it's me, Terri. Back to take care of you for another night."

Peter relaxed. He felt a great weight had been lifted from him. He had someone to communicate with; that gave him hope. He now understood the role Mrs. Rossi must be playing. His faith had been restored. With that intact, he could continue with some sense of purpose; without panic.

He appreciated the beauty of this young woman. Terri placed a stainless steel bowl on the bedside table and rinsed a sponge thoroughly in the water. She washed his face and shoulders. He could feel the warmth against his skin. She moved under the sheets and bathed his chest and sides each time rinsing the sponge. She moved to the foot of the bed and washed his feet before working her hands up and down his legs. After undoing his diaper, her sponge made its way to his groin. She stopped. She pulled back the sheet to expose Peter's fully erect penis.

"Hmm, what have we here? I wonder what you're dreaming about in there."

Peter was oblivious to the fact that his body was having this reaction.

Terri removed the condom catheter and washed the end of his penis thoroughly.

Peter strained unsuccessfully to see what she was doing. Then, as though he had been uprooted, he tore free of his body. With a single upward surge he found himself floating above Terri and his bed. This was new as every other occasion he had been free of his bed ridden body he had traveled to some other place. He watched Terri now washing his erection with the sponge and rubbing in and around his scrotum.

A fog of euphoria overcame him. The room blurred. His mind leapt a thousand light years into space. Pleasure so intense that every nerve in his body felt stimulated at once washed over him. It was reminiscent of the experience of smoking opium when he had been overseas, but many times more powerful.

He no longer cared what happened.

The room refocused, and he slammed back down onto his bed. On Terri's face he could see a look of total surprise.

"Oh, shit. Why me?" She grabbed a dry towel and slipped it under Peter's erection, catching the creamy white ejaculate pouring out. Peter could no longer see her hands but he could imagine what she must be dealing with.

"You obviously have some life in you, Peter!" she said, frowning. "Now, if we can just wake you up."

She finished her duties quickly and noted the events on her chart. Peter slipped into his first deep rest since the accident. His entire being felt discharged.

Peter slept, dreaming the most vivid and real dreams of his life. He met with old friends and relatives who had passed away. He moved freely back through time and viewed events of his life while floating over them.

This perspective was different from when he was linked with someone else's thoughts. He realized he was still attached to himself in the hospital room and could not directly participate in the events. He was, however, conscious within himself and fully aware of his circumstances. His state was a true out-of-body experience.

He moved effortlessly from event to event and country to country. He witnessed some of the great geographical wonders of the world from a perspective high above the earth. He determined it was his mind that controlled the destination and the pace at which he moved. He had only to will himself to move faster, slower or focus on being at a place or event and he was instantly transported there. When he moved he could feel the fabric of this new dimension, and although he couldn't see or hear any but those he chose to visit, he came to understand that he was not alone. He allowed himself to believe that hundreds, thousands, even millions of people were traveling in this manner, each separated by a membrane of consciousness that kept them apart.

Peter was doing what many have only dreamed of: flying freely through time, viewing the world and its goings-on from God's perspective.

He had truly been given a gift. The euphoria he felt was unlike any earthly pleasure. He was one with the universe. His heart and spirit soared.

"Peter." At first he barely heard his name being called in the distance.

"Peter." The word was louder.

He paused to focus on what he was hearing. Perhaps it was just in his head.

"Peter, are you there? Can you hear me?"

He knew now that someone was trying to contact him.

He focused on the hospital and was instantly hovering above his bed. All was quiet. He looked down at his limp body and scanned the room and corridor for anyone who might have called. He was alone.

He realized that although his real body was lying lifeless and unresponsive, his traveling body was the body he had when he was a younger man. He was in peak physical condition and all of his senses were highly aware of the stimuli they were receiving. He had created himself in the image of which he thought most positively.

He heard his name called again.

With only a thought he was soaring high above the globe yet still within the atmosphere of Earth. He could see the great continent of North America bracketed by the Atlantic and Pacific Oceans. He willed himself toward Europe and instantly he floated above the cluster of countries which he had visited throughout his life. He felt suspended on a warm, humid wind that cradled him like a soft glove. Losing contact with the voice, he traveled west to North America. The voice grew stronger.

"Peter, can you hear me? Peter, it's Choy."

"Choy." Peter was elated. "I can hear you. Where are you?"

"Focus on me, Peter. Bring your thoughts, your energy, your love together and focus on me."

Peter closed his eyes and breathed. He pictured how Choy looked the last time he had seen her. His mind scrolled memories of their trip together. He could see her beautiful face, her olive skin, her jet black hair and rich brown eyes. Choy's features became clearer. She smiled a warm smile that filled him with love.

"Peter."

Peter opened his eyes to see the image of Choy suspended before him. *"Choy! I don't understand, but it's wonderful to see you —"*

Choy placed her fingers on Peter's lips. She closed her eyes and placed both hands gently over his. Peter's mind filled with images of the time they had spent together. He could feel her love flowing through him. Her thoughts became his.

He learned that the image of her he was seeing was an image he had created and attached to her traveling consciousness. He immediately knew of Madame Wong and how she had helped put Choy into a meditative state to travel freely in search of him. He understood now that he existed on a different plane. It seemed she had also been granted the gift of out-of-body traveling, but in a much more limited sense than him.

For now her place was on Earth. Choy was pleased to understand that Peter had not passed on, although she felt urgency in their connection. She sensed a torment within him. A pull between good and evil. She felt that he was to face a struggle, but could not give him any insight into what it might be. She and Peter drifted together, sharing a profound spiritual connection. Their thoughts and feelings intertwined, the images of their bodies revolved together in an intimate celestial intercourse.

"Miss Choy, Miss Choy." Madame Wong wiped Choy's forehead with a damp cloth.

Choy was unconscious on the cotton mat. Madame shook her gently. From a tasseled silk purse on her hip she removed a short stick of incense and lit it on a nearby candle, waving the smoking stick under Choy's nose.

On the second breath of the potent smoke Choy's eyes sprang open. She coughed violently while Madame wiped her brow again with the cloth.

Choy placed her hand on Madame's and smiled a dazed smile. "Thank you," she whispered. "Thank you." Tears of exhaustion slipped down her smooth cheeks.

Peter felt her being torn from his mind. A wretched pain ripped through his body. His head felt wounded. His temples pulsed.

When Peter opened his eyes, Terri was wiping his forehead. Dr. Brandon shone a bright light into his pupils. Several men in lab coats stood over the bed with clipboards and took notes while Dr. Brandon read vital statistics from the equipment and gave his verbal commentary.

Peter felt ice cold.

Terri toweled moisture from his body, now oozing sweat from every pore. The pungent smell of the powerful incense used to awaken Choy lingered in the hospital room.

The technician from the monitoring center ducked through the archway. "The readings are back to normal. I've run a print-out. The electro-magnetics are right off the scale. There were two bursts. One here...see that spike? That's when I called in to report the alarm. And then this one here...only a few seconds between them, but whatever happened was created by some-thing powerful. We're dubbing the recording right now and should have it for viewing in a minute."

"What about outside interference?"

"It's always a possibility, but we've been here long enough now that I think we've screened out just about every potential source that could cause a spike like that."

Dr. Brandon drove home slower than usual. The Douglas case was weighing heavily on him and now with the first seem-ingly verifiable readings it had just gotten more complicated. He was not looking forward to the call he would have to make to Dr. Zalkow.

- Chapter 38 -

The ride to the airport had seemed endless due to an accident on the freeway. Matt had worked himself into a panic over Cara. Despite his desire to snap his fingers and be in Bermuda, he had no choice but to bide his time while Bob readied the plane.

His head fell back against rich leather, his eyes rolled shut, and he was asleep.

The jet was refueled and prepped for flight.

A long wait for take-off, combined with the previous delays, meant they were several hours later than expected arriving in Bermuda.

Matt immediately called and reached Stephen Merck on his personal cell phone. "You bet. Sandy's here too."

"Stephen, would you do me a favor and try to find her? I'd like to speak to her before I head out there. You know, to make sure we don't cross paths." Matt attempted to hide his anxiety.

"Sure, Matt, anything. I'll call you back the moment I find her."

Matt's attempt at calmness didn't work, but Stephen understood his concern.

The hand-built Italian Riva speed boat sliced through the dark waters of Bermuda's Great Sound at forty miles per hour. It raced through Two Rock Passage to short-cut the distance from the party to town. The roar of the powerful engine mixed with music that rumbled through the speakers. Sandy stood flanked by two young men on each side; all were sons

251

of prominent families on the island. The driver on the far left gripped the leather-wrapped steering wheel, peering into the darkness in a wasted effort to spot any obstacles protruding from the black water.

Sandy clinched both hands to the windshield in front of her. She had two of the young men, one on each side, with opposite arms wrapped around her. She could feel the squeeze of their hands through the thin material of her summer dress. She saw them exchange drunken grins and listened to these comrades who howled in windswept harmony with the stereo. She could feel the wind and friction of their grip pulling up her dress and exposing her thong underwear and bare behind but she didn't seem to care.

Salt spray peppered them from the boat's polished mahogany hull slicing through the choppy water. Wind tears streamed horizontally across Sandy's face. A drunken grin stretched across her cheeks; her hair blew straight back. The wind forced its way into her nose. The cocaine heightened her senses. Every nerve was alive.

The pilot swerved the stolen boat perilously close to the rocks off Long Island. He howled, gunning the engine, with each powerful sway of the three-ton hull leading them toward the faint, distant lights of Hamilton Harbor.

A fourth boy, Jason, on Sandy's far right gripped the chrome rim of the slanted glass that ran along the gunwales. He glanced left across at his friends, to the driver and then back over his left shoulder to Cara who was slumped on her side across a leather bench seat in the stern of the boat. The aft light radiated off her face and golden hair.

The boat bounced through the waves creating streams of light that illuminated her breasts which shook with the motion. The wind licked at her thin-strapped mini dress and flapped the loose fabric.

Jason continued to stare over his shoulder at Cara. He was being treated to alternating views of her white panties and bare breasts. He looked forward to see that his friends and Sandy were oblivious to him and Cara. He looked back again; her breasts were now in full view with the wind holding the top of her dress at bay. He felt his erection growing. His mind raced with erotic thoughts. He could already hear himself justifying his actions later.

She was a little drunk, that's all. She wouldn't have dressed like that if she hadn't wanted the attention.

He sat down to get a reprieve from the wind. The music played above the engine noise. One of his favorite songs roared out from beneath the dash, buoying his spirits. He could feel the base from the speaker directly in front of him pulsing in his abdomen. He reached into his pocket to remove a small glass vial topped with a clear plastic stopper. He shook it upside down once to fill a small cavity in the stopper with the white powder held in the vial. He removed the stopper and placed the open end against his nostril. He snorted stiffly.

The cocaine blasted up his nose. The heat and moisture melted it on contact. Instantly the thin nasal membrane allowed the chemical to enter his bloodstream. A deep breath of air through his nose enhanced the rush to his head: he prepared another hit. His second snort similarly lightened his head and heightened his senses. His bravado escalated. He slipped the vial into his pocket and climbed carefully over the back of his seat and made his way toward the stern of the speeding boat.

"Jason, where ya going?" yelled the driver. He leaned behind his passengers so his friend could hear him over the blast of noise and wind.

Jason made eye contact and ducked his head toward Cara. He and his buddy exchanged wide, drunken grins. So far Jason's plan was working well.

Suddenly, Sandy screamed.

The driver turned back just in time to gun the engine and swerve to avoid a huge, well-marked reef.

"Yee ya hoo!" The boys in front howled peering into the darkness, oblivious to the potential perils ahead.

When the boat swerved Jason landed squarely on Cara, forcing the air from her lungs. She gasped twice. He righted himself and settled onto the seat beside her. Pushing her upright against the side of the boat, he noticed a big bruise over her right eye and blood on her knee. He recalled her stumbling with two of the boys from the dock onto the boat.

With Cara propped in the corner, Jason got up on his knees then reached back to unscrew the stern light. Darkness fell upon them. His friends in the front remained illuminated in the red hue of the dash lights.

Jason buried his head in Cara's bare neck and breathed in the smell of her skin. He kissed her there and whispered into her ear. "Are you awake? Cara, are you with us?"

She muttered briefly so he wrapped his arm around her neck and rubbed her bare shoulder. The thin strap of her dress slipped off. He pressed his face into her hair. Her smell added to his intoxication. He massaged the inside of her thigh with his right hand, causing her legs to splay limply.

The sound of his own breathing rasped in his ears. He took a deep sniff through his nose to get another charge from the cocaine lingering there. It combined quickly with the adrenaline surging inside him. He quivered with nervousness. He felt the firm pressure of his arousal pressing outward.

The wind pulled at the free side of Cara's dress, completely exposing her breast. Jason dropped his head, taking the firm white sphere in his mouth. At the same time he gently pried her legs wider and slid his hand into her crotch. He stroked the soft cotton a few times before he pulled it aside. He sucked harder on her breast and bit down on her erect nipple. Cara groaned but didn't resist. He removed his hand momentarily and wet his fingers with saliva before plunging them back between her legs, probing for an opening. He moved his mouth to her neck and started sucking hard.

Cara groaned when his fingers penetrated her. Jason gasped for air, his excitement level overwhelming him. His mind was awash with eroticism.

He held her neck tight against his mouth forcing him to breath through is nose with wet snorts; his body hungry for oxygen. Jason was frantic now working his hand in and out, pressing himself firmly against her knee and thigh.

He could feel the rising tide of orgasm and he quickened his manual thrusts while grinding against her. Cara's legs were now wide apart, her dress bunched around her waist. The wind whipped her hair, snapping at the onslaught.

The driver turned his head to observe the activity in the aft of his boat. He did not need night vision to sense that something sexual was going on in the back. He tried to get the attention of his buddies without alerting Sandy. When the moon suddenly broke through the clouds, he could clearly see Cara's bare breast and white legs spread wide. He watched while Jason humped, forcing himself upon her.

His passengers in front screamed when the dark shape of another boat loomed squarely in their path. The unlit craft bobbed quietly on the dark water, oblivious to the approaching speedboat. The driver steered hard to port, narrowly missing the anchored vessel. Sandy and the boys gripped the windscreen but were tossed sideways.

Jason and Cara were thrown to the floor.

Sounds of tearing wood and flight seemed to happen simultaneously when the speedboat launched off a solid coral head protruding several feet out of the water. The tachometer pressed hard against its retaining pin with the engine revving wildly. The boat went airborne for 150 feet.

A gash had been sliced at its water line.

The passengers were weightless in this projectile of wood and engine arcing through the night air. The boat descended to carve the surface again, water pouring in through the rip in its hull.

The revelers had steered themselves into a mooring area where boats of all sizes and shapes floated peacefully.

Although the incoming rush of water was beginning to weigh the hull down, the boat had lost little speed. The driver knew instinctively that he had to keep moving or they would sink. He wove his boat through the maze of stationary hazards, steering aggressively. The stainless steel propeller of the inboard engine severed mooring lines, leaving boats free to float with the outgoing tide.

The lights of shore highlighted a deserted area of beach.

The boat was sinking.

Its engine moaned under the load of the extra weight.

The driver pressed the throttle to its full open position, pouring gas into the straining machine.

The boat sped toward shore.

Sandy and the boys in the front threw themselves onto the bench seat and braced against the dash. Jason wrapped himself around Cara.

The engine stopped with a thud as the propeller cut into the sand. The hull commenced its slide up the beach. With its lost flotation, the hard rail of the v-bottom cut sharply into the sand. The boat decelerated rapidly, throwing its passengers in the front against the dash. Heads and faces crunched on contact with solid surfaces. Jason and Cara slid along the floor and slammed into the back of the bench seat where their friends were slumped.

The boat stopped moving.

Water sloshed in the bilge, steam rose through the engine hatch.

The stereo blasted music into the quiet evening.

The driver sat up.

"Fuck me…"

He looked around the grounded boat.

"My fucking head hurts. Everyone okay?" The driver took control.

It took two solid kicks before the source of the music was obliterated.

The others gathered themselves and assessed the damage.

Jason sat up with a groan and lifted Cara's limp body into an upright position. Blood streamed from a gash in her forehead. He pulled her shoulder straps up, covering her breasts and quickly reefed her skirt toward her knees.

The area was deserted except for a drunken night security guard several hundred yards from where they'd landed.

"Hopefully that guard is passed out or something."

Sandy began to cry. "Is she okay? We're in deep shit. Do you know who she is? This was just supposed to be a little hazing joke… not a date rape." She had the boys' attention now. "I don't want to lose my job or go to jail. She's with Matthew Douglas. He's only from one of the richest families in the States. He'd rather have you killed than spit on you." Sandy was in near hysterics.

"Shut the fuck up, bitch. It's not our fucking problem that your friend's a slut. You were in on it too."

"Yeah, she's just a partier like the rest of us. If she can't handle her stuff, that's her problem."

Jason held a towel to Cara's head to stop her bleeding. "She's out cold. We can take her home and let her sleep it off, but we have to get the fuck out of here."

"I'll call my brother. Let's start walking," one of the other boys offered.

Jason and another boy slung their arms around Cara and pulled her along. Her bare feet moved with every third or fourth step. She grunted occasionally.

When Matt called Stephen back he was able to relay that a boat had been stolen, that several young men were suspected and that neither Sandy nor Cara were at the party. He added that both young women were seen to be having a very good time earlier, but their whereabouts were unknown.

Perspiration stung Matt's pores while he listened.

This can't be good.

He went on that Anthony Houston's security people had reported the stolen boat to the police and harbor patrol who were in the process of preparing a helicopter search team. The party was buzzing with rumors about the missing boys but nothing about Sandy and Cara.

"Matt, they probably jumped a cab and headed into town to one of the clubs. The group here is a bit aged for them anyway. I'll keep ya posted if I hear anything else…promise."

Matt called the Sands from his taxi which was speeding toward the hotel. He rang his room for Cara, praying that she would answer.

Was she asleep with the ringer off? Was she out for a walk? Nope, this isn't good.

There was no point in going to the party or calling her cell again. Cara was either at home, out somewhere or in trouble. In either case the place for him to be was in his hotel room waiting.

The boat's driver and one other boy had gotten spooked and left before their ride came, saying they would take their chances on their own. Sandy, Jason and the remaining boy eased Cara into the back of the brother's car and headed for the Sands. Sandy directed the driver to a back lot and told them to wait by the fire exit. She tidied herself up, walked to the main entrance and whisked through the lobby to the rear of the building without being spotted.

Great security, she thought.

They carried Cara up the stairwell stopping at every floor to look for the security patrol. She searched Cara's purse, which she had grabbed from the boat, and found the plastic key card for the security lock on her door. A tiny light flashed green, the door chirped and the electronic lock opened; they were in.

The room was dark except for the reflection of the perimeter floodlights. By the time they flopped Cara on the bed, Sandy was in a complete panic.

"We have to get out of here. This is so crazy. We're dead if we get caught." Sandy's mind reeled with potential consequences.

Matt's taxi screeched to a halt under the portico of the Sands. He threw the driver a wad of bills and dashed into the lobby. Several guests returning from Houston's party lingered, chatting through an inebriated haze.

"Mr. Douglas. Missed you at the party."

"We certainly did." The man's wife gave Matt a blurry smile.

Matt nodded and kept moving toward the elevator.

"I'm leaving." Sandy pulled at Jason's arm while he straightened Cara on the king-sized bed. "C'mon, Jason, let's split."

"I just want to make it look like she stumbled home and crashed…and I don't want her to die in her puke."

"You just want to fuck her. I saw you on the boat." Sandy stood holding the door until fear overcame her. When it swung shut, she bolted to the fire stairs, beckoning the remaining accomplice to follow her.

Jason was alone in the darkened room with Cara.

Only the sound of the ocean against the rocks below broke the silence. He knelt over her and paused; thinking fast now. He could never get a girl like this.

Her dress was high above her waist. Her panties were still pulled to one side. Blonde hair spread across the white pillow.

Fuck, you are so fucking hot. Even passed out.

He looked over at the closed hotel door and glanced over each shoulder to take in the room.

Nice fucking digs, Douglas, whoever you are.

He reached his arm under her back into her dress and lifted her up. With his other hand he pulled the dress over her head and dropped it to the floor beside the bed. Jason was breathing heavily, his heart pumped wildly.

His hands were wet from handling her. Beads of sweat formed on his forehead. Cara's head bobbed sideways, draping her hair across her bare chest. Jason slid both his hands under her bottom. Her legs flopped helplessly apart. He pulled her toward him.

Cara's body tensed.

Then with one immense convulsion, she projected the contents of her stomach toward Jason. Her body contracted again and heaved; she gagged and coughed. Vomit dripped down Jason's face, shirt and shorts.

"Fuck me! You bitch." He pushed himself away from her. "Ah, shit." Jason felt the fetid mess dripping onto his legs. He reached for the sheet to wipe his clothes and skin. The smell sickened him.

Her head bounced off the pillow shaking her to semi-consciousness. "Matthew! Matthew!" She cried out.

The click of the lock didn't register, but the sound of a door knob turning did. Jason snapped his head around to see the widening shaft of light spread across the carpeted floor.

"Cara? Cara? You in here?"

The light blinded Jason temporarily. For Matt, the beam illuminated his worst nightmare. Jason was kneeling over Cara, naked except for her underwear. She looked beat up.

"What the…who the fuck are you? What's going on?" Matt was instantly in a rage.

Jason raised his hands defensively as Matt lunged.

"Matthew!" Cara wailed.

"Wait! I can explain!" Jason jumped up, dripping with vomit. He sprang from the bed through the air toward the open patio doors. The screen vanished in front of him; his feet hitting the concrete balcony.

"I'll fucking kill you!"

Jason's momentum carried him stumbling forward. He lifted his leading foot to catch the back of a heavy, cushioned patio chair in an attempt to stop his forward motion. His foot landed squarely in the middle, compressing the pillowed back cushion and buckling his knee. Stumbling, the chair tipped toward the railing, endorsing his forward motion. His trailing foot caught the seat edge of the falling chair and caused his body to elongate fully in the air.

Matt took off after him.

When Jason landed, his chest crushed against the railing and knocked the wind from his lungs. The forward motion of his fall placed more weight over the railing than on the balcony side and Jason commenced a slow-motion forward roll with his body falling head first.

He instinctively grabbed the barrier railing.

His feet went high into the air, his body twisted like a gymnast on a high bar. Jason desperately tried to swing around and reverse his grip on the railing.

Successful, though not rewarding, he managed to get turned around but came slamming back face first into the balcony barrier.

The sound of tearing muscle and tendon ripped the air; he clung to the bar with both shoulders dislocated. Jason hung on for his life, feet stretched toward the ocean.

His shriek of pain pierced Matt's ears.

Cara responded with a loud scream of her own.

Matt looked back at her, wrecked and assaulted on the bed. His rage exploded.

Jason's feet dangled beneath him. His shoulders and back torqued unnaturally. Pain shot up his right arm causing his grip to slip loose from railing.

He screamed for help, suspended by one arm several stories above the rocks.

"You fucker," Matt screamed, slamming his fist down on Jason's remaining hand. "Die, you fucking punk!"

"No, don't, please don't, I'm sorry, I'm sorry," Jason begged for mercy.

Matt struck again at Jason's hand and leaned down to lash at his head. Matt was an animal. Every instinct said to kill this person.

Jason stared up at him.

Jason was the enemy. He must die.

Jason screamed, "No, Mr. Douglas, please no."

Matt's soul was screaming with all the pain he had ever felt in his life. He saw Jason's sweaty grip loosen and give way, gravity pulled him toward the rocks below.

The sound of his name was like a gunshot in Matt's head.

It must have only taken a thousandth of a second, although it seemed like an eternity. The world slowed to a complete crawl. Matt's head was suddenly filled with visions of his comatose father. He felt the sorrow of his whole family. He felt the sorrow that would be if this young man perished. He saw his father's silent image.

Matt lunged forward and grabbed the collar of Jason's shirt as he fell.

The world was back to full speed.

The force of breaking Jason's fall wrenched Matt's shoulder; Jason now hung suspended in mid air.

"Help me, man. Please help me," Jason sobbed. His face was crimson and covered in sweat. Veins bulged in his neck and forehead. Mucus bubbled from his nose and mouth.

Matt grabbed Jason's shirt collar with his other hand. He groaned heaving against the boy's weight.

The shirt tightened around Jason's torso and slid upward. His limp arms were flung skyward until they met over his head. His body started to slip down through the shirt.

Jason was falling and Matt could no longer stop him.

Jason's nails clawed the fabric, tearing them back from his fingertips and exposing bloody raw tissue. His fall slowed then stopped; his ten fingers had caught just enough material to grip.

Matt's shoulders strained against the full stopping weight of the falling body. For a quiet, breeze-swept moment, all forces were frozen in a steady state while these two adversaries stared into each other's bulging eyes.

Matt's index fingernail pierced the material first. It started to rip.

Jason heard the sound and made a futile attempt to climb up the shirt. His struggle only served to accelerate the tearing of the fabric. An instant later Matt was looking past the white vomit-soaked shirt to Jason's falling body.

"No!" he screamed above the terrified Jason. He released his grip. Jason's shirt fell after him.

The world and time seemed suddenly to slow.

"*Noooo...*"

Matt put his hands to his temples, peering in horror at the rocks below.

Seemingly from nowhere, a soft illumination cast a warm cushion of light over the place where Jason would land. In the hazy glow below, Matt saw the voluminous froth of a large sea-born wave crash to its resting place, creating a deep albeit temporary tidal pool on the surface of the rocks.

Jason's body made impact at the moment of highest tide and settled solidly on the rocks when the wave retreated. His shirt fluttered down beside him. He lay gasping, half submerged on the hard surface, while salt spray rained down on upon him.

Matt watched, the light dissipated, he couldn't believe the outcome.

He felt a warmth of love and calmness flow over him.

He whispered the only word that came to mind: "Father?"

The world and time reverted to normal.

Cara's coughing pulled Matt's attention back.

He rushed through the darkened room, sweeping her into his arms. She coughed and cried softly while he held her. Matt brushed the soiled sheet to the side. He yanked a pillow from its case and wiped her face. The smell of vomit permeated the air. Matt didn't care.

"Matthew, Matthew, I'm so sorry. I love you."

Tears welling in his eyes, Matt stroked Cara's hair and kissed her head. "I love you," he murmured through trembling lips. He reached for the telephone, removed the receiver from its cradle and set it on the table. He dialed the operator and brought the telephone to his ear.

"This is Matthew Douglas. There's been an accident in my room."

- Chapter 39 -

The constant tone of the television and Schebb's claws scratching at the door had been the catalyst for numerous dreams that were a fabrication of the real and the imagined. It took a few seconds when he woke for Fuzzy to realize that the sounds he was hearing were not in his mind. Fuzzy clicked off the TV set and twisted the knob of the small lamp on the table beside him. His mouth was dry, his eyes were sticky. He wiped them, remembering that in one of his dreams he had been crying.

Schebb whimpered at the door then looked back at Fuzzy. "I have to go too, boy. C'mon, we'll take a walk."

Schebb and Fuzzy walked into a beautiful cool night. The sky was alive with stars. Fuzzy and Schebb exhaled their visible breath into the crisp air.

Schebb ran silently across the parking lot, onto the grass and over to the hedge. He squatted gracefully and did his business before scratching the ground with his hind feet to cover his trail. While Schebb ran and marked a perimeter around the property, Fuzzy stepped behind a shrub and relieved himself with a lengthy drain and some potent flatulence. He looked around instinctively but there was no one to hear. He let a long, windy belch rise up from his stomach and felt his belt loosen with the escaping gas.

Crossing the pavement toward Schebb, he admired the way his rig sparkled in the lights of the parking area. The rig looked completely different at night than during the day. Fuzzy and Schebb strolled along the darkened sidewalk enjoying the quiet. Schebb paused every few dozen yards to extend his perimeter.

The strip of pavement that ran past the motel was a secondary highway that saw little traffic that night. Fuzzy stopped and stared down the long black ribbon. He figured most people preferred the interstate, where services and assistance were readily available. Schebb looked up at him while Fuzzy thought. The plan he needed had gelled in his mind.

"C'mon, fella, we're hittin' the road."

Fuzzy was about twelve hours from his destination.

He figured if he took the secondary roads at night his speed would be slower, but the likelihood of being spotted would be reduced dramatically if he drove from after midnight until dawn. If his papers were all in order he could drop his trailer at the shipping depot and head back north in his cab. By staying off the main roads and avoiding his usual stopping places, he felt he could make it all the way home unchecked.

Fuzzy re-packed his few items and tidied the room. He didn't want to draw any attention to himself. Schebb watched, unused to so much activity at night, but followed the quiet commands of his new master obediently.

The click of the motel door behind them was like the starting gun of a new adventure. Fuzzy did a quick walk around the rig then loaded Schebb in through his door. A belch of black smoke erupted into the air when the giant diesel mill fired up. The noise reverberated across the parking lot and Fuzzy prayed that no lights would come on. He eased the lengthy beast back and out onto the road. He turned his head, scanned the motel and breathed a sigh of relief; all windows were still dark.

"Here we go. I sure wish you could talk."

Instantly, Fuzzy's heart began to pound and his dry throat constricted when the flashing blue roof lamps and bright headlights of a police cruiser appeared on the bluff in the distance and closed on him.

He shifted his rig to neutral and eased off on the accelerator pedal. The truck rolled along quietly while the cruiser approached at high speed.

Fuzzy looked in his rear view mirror to see if he was being boxed in by another car, but only blackness filled the glass. He would surrender without resistance and tell his whole story. It would be a relief to get this burden off his mind.

The cruiser flashed its high beams on and off several times blowing by Fuzzy's truck. He watched in his mirror while the red taillights faded into the distance.

Am I getting paranoid or what?

He gave his head a little shake, then eased the gear lever forward and pressed hard on the accelerator.

Schebb curled up on the floor on the passenger's side, sighed loudly, then closed his eyes.

- Chapter 40 -

He watched the sun rise over the city through the tinted floor-to-ceiling glass. Brian had been up all night working in the Douglas Corporation's boardroom.

The previous evening, after an enjoyable dinner with his family, Matt woke him with a call from Bermuda to recount his incredible story.

They had a long discussion about whether Matt should leave the island immediately and return to the mainland, letting his legal counsel sort through the mess, or whether he should stay and let his good reputation and the circumstances surrounding the evening speak for themselves.

After a decision to choose the latter, Brian roused two of Douglas's top lawyers and dispatched them by private jet to assist Matt in what would be an all-night de-briefing. Several calls were exchanged between Brian and Matt through the night. Fortunately, thus far his brother had not been implicated in any crime.

Jason was alive, but he had suffered a spinal injury amongst others. It was not conclusive what the consequences of that injury would be.

Matt knew Jason's family, who, like the families of all the other boys, were very well off and very well known. The other three boys were in custody. No other names had been mentioned. Cara had recovered from the drugs in her drink and claimed to remember nothing of the boat ride or accident. She underwent a complete physical exam to determine whether or not she had been raped. She suffered two cracked ribs and numerous cuts and bruises. The Doctor had given her a small bottle of pills to dull the pain of her hangover and reduce the discomfort of her injuries.

With his original suite sealed off like a crime scene, Matt had also watched the sun rise from the balcony of his new suite while Cara rested quietly under the clean sheets of a new bed. He was tired and broody.

Where was all this going? Why were so many things seemingly going against him? What if he was now sitting in jail charged with murder? Things need to change, Matt. Things need to change.

When Marjorie arrived at the office, her attention was immediately drawn to Brian's open door. She could see that his entrance to the boardroom was also open. She called security and alerted them that if they didn't hear from her in two minutes there was a problem in the boardroom.

Peering stealthily through the crack of the door, she saw Brian, sound asleep, face down in his arms. When she slipped into the room, she could hear his breath, see his chest expand and contract. She felt a warmth come over her, stealing this personal moment with him. She knew that Brian always had his armor on and although Marjorie longed to be closer he never gave her the opening.

She stood beside him and listened to him breathe, admiring him. He was dressed in jeans, a buttoned-down shirt and loafers without socks. She could smell the faint fragrance of his cologne.

Marjorie's mind drifted.

Without thinking, she placed her right hand, ever so lightly, on his head and ran her fingers gently through his hair.

She felt excited by this intimacy.

She let her hand slide off his head and onto his shoulder, then gently massaged his tight muscles. She could feel the firmness through his shirt.

Marjorie faded into a euphoric haze, picturing where this might lead if he awoke that very second. She imagined him turning and, without speaking, wrapping his arms around her to ease her down on the table, smashing the boundaries of person and profession with regard only for the passion between them.

"SECURITY, don't move!"

Both entrances to the boardroom burst open without notice and several armed Douglas security guards appeared, each with their guns drawn and pointed at Marjorie.

Brian sprang up, pushing back his chair, throwing Marjorie to the floor. He spun around to see her sitting on her backside with her legs wide apart. His first view was directly into her dress at her bare legs and satin underwear. He stared for an instant too long, stunned by what was going on, then focused on her flushed face.

"Marjorie, what's going on? Guys, guys … it's me, Brian. I came in early. Sorry, I didn't tell anyone."

"Sorry Mr. Douglas, but Marjorie called to say there was a problem."

"I didn't say there was a problem. I said there might be one and I'd call you back."

"That was seven minutes ago. We had to assume there was trouble, but I can see you have everything well in hand." He smiled at her. The other guards could barely hold back a snicker as they holstered their guns and retreated.

"Okay guys, okay. That's good for now. Thanks." Brian was still oblivious to the facts.

The senior officer looked at Brian and then directly at Marjorie.

"Would you like a full report, sir, from the time I got the call to my observations when I arrived?"

"No, I think it's obvious. I was asleep at the table and Marjorie was about to wake me. Is that right, Marjorie?"

"Yes, yes, that's right. At first I thought there was an intruder, then when I realized it was you I didn't want to wake you right away. I was just about to tap you on the shoulder when the commandos arrived. I had gotten lost in thought, taking in the view of this beautiful morning." Marjorie motioned to the window, trying to change topics.

Brian noticed, but didn't press any further. "Not a great place to sleep. It's a wonder I can move my neck. Well, let's get on with our day. Thanks for your quick response. No report needed. Marjorie, let's have a coffee and review the day's agenda."

Brian took a few minutes to shower and shave in his personal bathroom. He kept fresh clothes at the office for such occasions. When he and Marjorie met back in the boardroom he was in full business mode. Brian sipped a fresh coffee while Marjorie gave him a rundown on activities throughout the company. Brian dictated quick responses and issued directives which Marjorie would send out. He was due to send another electronic update but was not in the mood for that yet. He wanted to be well rested and energetic when he addressed his employees. The illusion of omnipotence must be maintained.

A buzzer sounded in the distance and Marjorie excused herself. She slipped through Brian's office to her reception area. The young man from the mailroom handed her a special express package to sign for. It was marked: TO THE ATTENTION OF BRIAN DOUGLAS – TO BE OPENED IMMEDIATELY. The envelope bore the markings of the law firm Wilfred, Barney, Smith and Klaxton. Marjorie was not familiar with the firm, but brought the package directly to Brian.

"That's dad's personal firm, Marjorie. We'd better open this one now."

"Would you like me to leave?"

"Why? You know just about everything about me. Why stop now?"

"Fine." She smiled at Brian; her mind spoke to her about knowing even more. "I'm here for you."

"I know. I appreciate it." Brian tore open the padded envelope and removed a DVD disc. He handed it to Marjorie. "Shall we make some popcorn?"

Marjorie closed the doors and raised an electronic panel from the surface of the desk. With several flicks of switches the blinds on the full-length glass closed and a screen dropped from the ceiling. Marjorie inserted the disc into the recessed player. "Ready?"

"Do I have a choice?"

Marjorie pressed the remote; the screen came to life. Both audio and video played the same message: "This material is the private property of Mr. Peter Wilson Douglas and the Law Firm of Wilfred, Barney, Smith and Klaxton. Any use or copying of this material without the express written consent of the above named parties is an offense punishable at law. THIS IS THE LIVING WILL OF PETER WILSON DOUGLAS AND THE LAST WILL AND TESTAMENT OF PETER WILSON DOUGLAS."

Brian's stomach felt hollow at the words. Both he and Marjorie sat up in their chairs. Peter's regular will would see to the orderly disposition of his estate once he died, of course. Brian didn't know his father had also prepared a Living Will which gave Peter the opportunity to express his wishes and have them carried out in the event that he became incapacitated.

"Are you sure you want me here?"

Brian placed his hand on top of Marjorie's with a gentle squeeze for a second before releasing. "Yes, I'm sure."

Marjorie felt a shiver run up the length of her arm and tiny goose bumps instantly formed.

The screen came alive with a full view of Peter Douglas.

"Goodness." Brian put his hand to his chin and squeezed.

Peter looked vibrant and healthy. He was dressed in a handsome brown three-piece suit. His hair was full and stylishly cut. His eyes twinkled when he spoke. He held his hands folded in front of him, sitting at a board table. The lines on his face and around his eyes looked like lines of living, not of aging. His skin was taut and tanned. He seemed quite relaxed and happy. He was presumably under the assumption, reinforced by those involved, that no one would see this recording for years. He smiled when he spoke. His teeth were large and straight, showing only the wear and staining of over six decades of use. He was a man in command of his circumstances and his life.

Brian admired and envied his father's confidence and easy nature, something Brian continued to struggle with at times in his role as captain of the Douglas ship.

"I hereby swear under oath, in the presence of my attorneys, that my name is Peter Wilson Douglas. My Social Security number is 565-09-8762. I am of sound mind and body and this is my Living Will and Last Will and Testament."

The camera panned back to show two men in suits, one on each side of Peter. They introduced themselves and made similar sworn statements to verify the accuracy of the material being presented.

"My attorneys have a valid copy of both my wills in writing, signed and sealed by myself. They have been appointed as my agents to undertake my request under the terms of my Living Will and as my executors under my Last Will and Testament. I presume that if you are watching this recording, that one of two things has happened..."

Brian and Marjorie sat in complete silence, staring at the screen. Brian could feel the pressure build behind his eyes. He glanced at Marjorie, whose cheeks puckered with sympathy. Their hands moved closer on the table but stopped before touching.

"… Either I have passed away or I have become incapacitated. If the former is true, I instruct the executors of my estate to proceed with the directions of my Last Will and Testament. If the latter is true, then I have been rendered helpless and am being kept alive by artificial means. If there is no evidence of brain activity satisfactory to conclude that I will recover, or if my wounds are such that I cannot live without the support of artificial means, then I request that all such artificial means of life support be removed. Please allow me the dignity to die a natural death. This herewith is my Will and my Request. My lawyers, who are attending with me here today, have the documentation and therefore legal right and duty to fulfill this request."

The screen went black then flickered white. The words "EDITED COPY" and the certification of the law firm were projected onto the white background.

Brian and Marjorie sat for a while before she pressed the STOP button on the remote. The screen quietly retreated into the ceiling.

For a few minutes she left the lights off and blinds drawn.

The silence continued.

Her eyes had adjusted to the lack of light and she could see him wiping his eyes. He sniffled a bit in the darkness.

Marjorie wiped her eyes with a tissue and blew her nose. "You okay?"

He sighed. "Yeah, I'm okay. It's been quite a night and it's going to be a long day. You haven't even heard about Matt yet. You better get those guys on the telephone and set up a meeting."

Brian's mind was in overdrive. He respected his father and his wishes, but he did not want to lose him.

Especially not that easily.

– Chapter 41 –

Peter watched Marion give Dr. Brandon a chilly look then, without speaking, walk to his bedside. She was the first to arrive at the hospital and entered Peter's room just as Dr. Brandon and his crew of interns and technicians were leaving. If tension could be measured on Peter's machine, the spike would be off its scale.

"I'll see you in a bit when we meet in the lounge, Marion."

Peter had watched the Doctors and technicians fuss over him for nearly thirty minutes and realized that the likelihood of their figuring out his potential was about nil. The only person that he was able to get any readings on was Dr. Brandon, and even he seemed to have a healthy dose of skepticism surrounding the case. It was a welcome relief to see the mother of his children arrive for a visit.

Marion kissed him on the forehead and took his hand. He could feel the warmth of her skin against his and could sense strong feelings coming from her.

"Hello, my love. I guess I can say that. I mean, I'm sure you don't mind. It's not like you can hear me, is it?"

Peter had not seen this side of Marion in many years. She exuded warmth.

He listened to her soliloquy of regret and self doubt about why their marriage had failed.

"…I shouldn't have let myself be so dependent on you for my happiness. But I guess it's a little too late for that, isn't it? And now we have four children who are afraid to get married. We didn't set a very good example."

While Marion spoke, Peter allowed himself to enter her mind and visit many times they had shared over their years. They had been good years, but not necessarily happy ones. When he visited the past again, it confirmed how often he had been absent from family events. Marion's mind was full of family memories that didn't include him. He kept getting an image of an old business acquaintance of his. His image was present in many of Marion's thoughts. Peter pressed for details.

"Peter, I never told you this, but I think it is about time that I got it off my conscience." Marion could hardly believe what she was saying, but she felt compelled to come clean. "For many years I had an ongoing affair with your friend Carl."

"Carl!" The sheer force of the energy of Peter's surprise rang out. Marion heard it in her mind but assumed it was her own thought.

A technician appeared in the doorway. "Excuse me," he said, "Has anything unusual happened with Mr. Douglas?"

Marion was startled. "No, he hasn't moved."

"I've picked up an atypical reading on his screen. Nothing to be alarmed about."

Marian assured him that everything was the way it appeared, and the technician withdrew. She looked at Peter sadly. "I know you can't hear me, darling." She smoothed the sleeve of his pajamas and returned to her confession.

"Carl and I had been in love for a number of years before you left me. I was lonely, Peter. You were never there and he was. He spent more time with your children than you did."

Marion was getting more upset while she continued to justify her actions. Peter was stunned that his good friend Carl was seducing his wife behind his back. It was so painful to lie helpless and listen to Marion unload her baggage and think that he really had been an absentee father and husband.

"He came by our house regularly after his divorce. It started out innocently enough, and then one afternoon while we were upstairs… you and I hadn't made love in months. I needed to feel the love of a man, Peter. Can you understand?"

Months? It couldn't have been months. Could it?

"He was kind and caring and very passionate…in the end, you left and Carl stayed."

Marion stayed with Peter for another half hour, reminiscing aloud about their lives together. For the first time in her life she was truly letting her feelings out and telling Peter exactly how she felt.

Peter soaked all of this in while listening to her speak. He could feel her anxiety releasing and flowing into him. He was happy for the fact that she was able to finally let go of this burden, but his friend Carl and Marion?

Peter felt the sorrow of the years come over him.

He shut her out and wallowed in pity for himself. For the first time since he had been in the hospital he found himself dipping down into a state of depression. A dark hole awaited him and he was slipping into it. Marion's image faded. He could no longer hear her voice. Everything went black and cold.

Perhaps death is upon me.

His mind seemingly closed in around him.

The fact that Peter could no longer hear was unknown and irrelevant to Marion. The more she let out, the more that came out. It was a tremendous relief that continued until she heard Brian tapping at the glass. He pointed to his watch and motioned toward the lounge.

Sarah, Charlotte, Catherine and Edward had already made their way to the lounge for Dr. Brandon's briefing. When Brian and Marion arrived at the door, Michael appeared in the hallway.

"Michael, good morning."

"Good morning, Brian, Mrs. Douglas. May I join you?"

"Certainly," said Brian, squeezing his mother's arm.

Marion smiled coolly. She knew the look and figured that this fellow had designs on her daughter. "Your schedule seems to be quite flexible these days, Michael."

"Any opportunity to visit with your family, Mrs. Douglas, is time well spent."

Marion smiled graciously at Michael's overt attempt at flattery.

Brian ushered his mother and Michael through the door.

Very smooth, Michael, Brian thought.

"Good morning, all."

"Michael!" Sarah sat up.

"It's nice to see you, Michael." Catherine broke the tension. "Sit beside me, you handsome devil." She was teasing her little sister and Sarah could do nothing about it. The atmosphere in the room lightened slightly.

Brian smiled a tired smile at his family. "I've had quite a night; I should bring all of you up to date before Dr. Brandon gets here. Michael, you've become a friend of the family but I have to ask for your assurances again that anything we discuss in here will remain strictly confidential."

"Brian," Sarah protested.

"No, Brian's right, Sarah," Edward spoke up. "I've had the privilege of being a friend to this family for many years, Michael. It's not always fun watching them do their laundry, but the love I've developed for everyone in this room has made it all worthwhile. If you stay, you may never get out of their clutches."

Everyone laughed. Michael briefly made eye contact with each person, stopping at Sarah. "It is a privilege to know all of you and an honor which I would not sacrifice by breaching the trust you have placed in me."

The room was silent. Michael's eloquent words hung there. Everyone nodded approval.

Brian took charge. "Excellent. Let's continue shall we? I have some news about Matt who was involved in a bizarre series of events last night in Bermuda." Brian did his best to explain what had happened without making it look like Matt was involved in a dirty little affair with a college girl. He could let out needed information later to the appropriate family members later. He stressed that Matt was unharmed and that the Douglas lawyers were with him now, ensuring his safety and the preservation of the Douglas name.

"That's the minor news. Now for the big story. I was at the office with Marjorie very early this morning when a courier package arrived from dad's personal lawyers."

All eyes were now glued to Brian.

"It was a DVD recording. I decided I should review it before coming here this morning. You're all welcome to come back to the office and see it for yourselves." Brian paused. He could feel everyone hanging on his words. He was not enjoying being the elder Douglas.

"Marjorie and I watched it. It was definitely made by Dad." Questions flew and Brian held his hands up. "It was an introduction to his last Will and Testament and, unbeknownst to me, Dad has also prepared a Living Will." He paused to gather himself and let this new information sink in for a moment. "It states that if he were incapacitated and on artificial life support that he wished to be...terminated..."

Brian choked hard on this last word and paused again to compose himself. The strain on every face was evident. They sat in stunned silence, waiting for more.

"...Unless there was conclusive evidence that he would recover. The way I see it, Dad wants to die with pride and not be kept alive for the sake of doing so."

Catherine was the first to speak. "Can we see this recording? He can't be serious. Dad would want to do everything possible to stay alive."

"Maybe it's a fake, Brian. We have to be certain." Charlotte's face was drawn. A flood of questions erupted. Most didn't understand the nature of a Living Will. Speculation was rampant with each wondering aloud what had motivated Peter to make such a request. This was typical Peter Douglas style: to make major decisions in absence of family consultation. His family continued to be the beneficiaries and victims of his independent nature.

"I thought so too, Cath, and yes, everyone can see the video and make their own interpretation. Dad is alive and healthy on the screen and has two lawyers present. It's for real. I expect to meet with the law firm today and learn all I can. I'll set up another meeting for all of us when I have more details."

"Did you see his will?"

"No, Mother, it was just an edited version. As we all know, Dad's estate is sizable. Many people outside this room gain to benefit from his death. It's crucial that no discussions take place around this issue. I'm prepared to say right now that I plan to do what I can to block any attempt to ah...well let's just say we need to be absolutely certain about the situation before any other steps are taken."

"I agree, Brian."

"Me too. He's our father." Catherine and Sarah staked out their positions.

"Children, Peter's a strong man. We have to be careful to respect his wishes."

"Mother! How could you?" Catherine protested.

"She's right," Charlotte said quietly. "Peter always knew what he wanted and how to get it. He's directing his life from a coma. That's so like him." Charlotte had said little in the meetings; now her tone was even and slightly bitter.

Brian realized that of all the people in the room, Marion and Charlotte knew him best. Their bond seemed to have strengthened another degree.

Edward cleared his throat. "Let's let Brian gather more information before we come to conclusions. Lots can happen in a day around these places. For all we know, Peter might wake up tomorrow and be home by the weekend. We have to keep our cool and stick together."

The door swung open. Dr. Brandon sailed in but stopped in his tracks when he saw the faces of everyone present. "Sorry, am I interrupting?"

"Not at all. You're next on the agenda. Right, Brian?" Edward kept things ordered.

"I wish I were here to report some new conclusive evidence of Peter's recovery, but I am not. His body is healing well. We are giving him electrical physiotherapy twice daily to keep his muscles toned. He is getting massage and manipulation to stimulate his circulation. He's on around-the-clock care, but there is no new outward evidence of brain activity. He continues to be in a deep coma."

"Doctor, with all that fancy equipment, are you saying you can't find any signs of brain activity?" Edward queried.

"No…I'm saying there is no obvious or conclusive brain activity. I wasn't going to mention this yet because we haven't determined the cause, but we did have some powerful readings early this morning. The technician called me to report two major spikes on his screen. We can't explain them yet, but we are testing now to rule out the possibility of outside interference. Even if we determine that Peter was the source of the energy, we may not have enough information to conclude anything."

"But it's a good sign, isn't it?" Sarah asked hopefully.

"I wish I could say yes, but I can't. I could form an argument that it's a bad sign, so let's wait until we have more information. It is very important, though, that if any of you notice anything unusual when you are visiting Mr. Douglas that you tell me. Even the most insignificant detail could be helpful."

"What sort of details?" asked Edward.

The overhead speaker crackled to life startling the group.

"Code 169 blue, Code 169 blue."

Dr. Brandon instinctively looked up at the speaker and then to his audience to see if they recognized the code. They did not.

"Excuse me; I have to attend to something. I'll be back." He withdrew swiftly but tried to avoid creating any concern in the room. The emergency was in Peter Douglas's room again. The blue code meant that something life-threatening was happening. Down the hall he saw a team of staff rolling emergency equipment into Peter's room. He broke into a sprint, hoping that none of the Douglases were following.

"What's happening?" he shouted.

"We have total life sign failure. All monitors went into full alarm twenty seconds ago."

Peter could feel himself sinking deeper into the blackness. He was now completely unaware of any activity around him. His thoughts were empty, his mind blank. Complete silence surrounded him.

A nurse ripped the covers from Peter's body. While one intern prepared an imposing syringe of clear liquid, another team member wiped a conductive paste on both sides of his chest. With a sharp downward thrust the intern drove the long needle through Peter's chest and into his heart, squeezing a sizable dosage of epinephrine directly into the heart muscle. Another intern held the handles of the two defibrillator paddles, placing them on Peter's chest.

"Clear!"

The intern discharged a sharp burst of electrical current directly into Peter. His body stiffened abruptly on the bed.

"Nothing!" the intern yelled, her eyes staring at the straight green line of the heart monitor.

"Hit him again," Dr. Brandon commanded.

The machine whined to a high pitch as the electrical charge built up. The discharge was repeated.

Again Peter's body stiffened and bounced on the bed.

Peter felt a force begin to pull at him, like being sucked into a vacuum cleaner. He felt himself pulled free of the blackness and launched forward into a burst of bright light.

Then he stopped.

The picture focused and he was hovering over his bed, looking down at his body and the team working on him.

"Let me go, just let me go."

The intern drove a second needle through his chest with a sound like puncturing a watermelon. She squeezed the syringe until it was empty.

Peter could see the monitors beside his bed. The brain monitor showed a flat line. The heart monitor showed a flat line and a reading of 00 heart beats. His blood pressure readings were OO/OO.

Peter was dead.

Dr. Brandon looked at the window at the same time as Peter to see Sarah and Catherine staring in, horror in their eyes, faces white. Dr. Brandon waved them off and barked at an intern to pull the curtain closed.

Peter felt their pain and tried to reach out to them.

I must survive.

Reluctantly, he summoned all of his energy and focused on his body and the people around him.

"One more time," Dr. Brandon shouted. "We're not losing him, people!"

He grabbed the paddles from the technician and held them himself.

"Clear!" He pressed hard against Peter's chest then was thrown back when Peter's body jolted.

"Nothing. No life signs."

The room went eerily silent.

Peter could feel the darkness settling in over him again, and despite his will to stay conscious he could feel a strange pull against him. His vision went blurry and all sounds were blocked out.

"Bastard," Dr. Brandon cursed loudly. He peeled Peter's eye lids back and shone his flashlight into them. "We've fucking lost him."

The emergency crew backed up a step at this statement from the Doctor.

He put his hand to his face and squeezed the bridge of his nose with his thumb and forefinger. His eyes were closed.

He would now have to face the entire Douglas family and tell them that he had failed, that their father was dead.

Opening his eyes, he stared down at Peter's lifeless form. Slowly, he pulled the white sheet toward Peter's face. He fought a wave of nausea. The emergency crew retreated out of the room, leaving Dr. Brandon and a nurse beside the bed.

Peter's arm had slipped out from under the sheet so Dr. Brandon reached down and picked up the lifeless hand to place it under the cover.

When touched, the hand constricted around his like a vice. Dr. Brandon screamed with pain; his fingers were being crushed together.

The nurse screamed in response to the scare he gave her. It took a moment to realize what was happening. He tried to pry the grip free with his other hand, but Peter's grasp held firm.

Dr. Brandon could feel a fire race up his arm.

Fighting fiercely against the grip; the blood drained from his face and the breath rushed from his lungs.

The nurse tried to pry his hand free, then reached for the call button to summon help. In her panic, she pulled it from the wall plug and pressed the button several times before realizing the futility of her efforts.

Dr. Brandon's eyes shut. He felt Peter's darkness and the terrifying depth of sorrow he was witnessing. He could feel Peter's struggle to free himself from the dark hole into which he had fallen. It seemed like Peter was draining life from Dr. Brandon to save his own.

Dr. Brandon could feel the grim pull of death.

Just then, Peter's hand relaxed, Dr. Brandon collapsed on the floor.

Through a hazy white light, Catherine Douglas's beautiful face filled his vision as he regained consciousness. Several Doctors stood over him while the world refocused. He realized that he was in one of the recovery rooms near Peter Douglas. His first instinct was to raise his hand to ensure that it was still there. He wiggled his fingers to see that everything worked and was surprised to find that nothing was broken.

Catherine put her hand on his forehead. "How are you feeling?"

"Weak. I'm so sorry about Peter."

"What about him?"

"He... he's..."

One of the interns spoke up. "Dr. Brandon, he's back. Mr. Douglas is alive. According to the nurse, his vitals returned to their previous readings just after you hit the ground. She says his hand responded to your touch in a delayed electro-convulsive reaction. It scared the wits out of both of you. You must have gone into some sort of shock and passed out."

Dr. Brandon knew it was more than a convulsion, but said nothing in front of his colleagues. He was just pleased to hear that Peter was back, even though it almost killed him. He sat up and smiled weakly at Catherine. "It's been a long time since I've fainted in a hospital. I'm a little over tired. I didn't get much sleep last night worrying about this Douglas family." He smiled.

"How about a quiet dinner on me tonight Doctor? I assume you don't cook at home."

He knew the risks of getting involved with patients or their families.

"Sure. That's just what a good Doctor would prescribe."

Screw it, he thought. I almost died today.

Peter was surprised and exhausted. Staring at the ceiling of his hospital room, he felt completely drained by his ordeal. So, death was not the welcome relief for which he had hoped.

He remembered seeing his daughters and calling upon a tremendous desire to live. He had found himself back in his body, yet still slipping down into the deep black hole he had come from. A voice or chorus of voices had urged him to reach out and grab life before it was too late. He remembered a vague and elongated image of Dr. Brandon before everything went black. He felt his body on fire, pulling himself from the hole, then light returned to his life.

His final recollection, before realizing that he was still alive, was the faces of his children flashing before him while they grew up.

Damn it, I can beat this thing, whatever it is.

"You had a close one today. We almost lost you."

Peter stayed silent while Edward talked. He had to reach him the way he had the previous day, but he had to go slowly so that Edward would accept that the communication was real.

"We heard about your Living Will today. That's going to cause some serious tension if we don't wake you up real soon."

"*Edward.*"

Edward spun around to see who had called him.

"*Edward, it's me, Peter. Don't leave.*"

"Peter?" Edward whispered. He looked to see that no one was watching him.

"Where are you? How can this be? I must be crazy, hearing a man in a coma."

"No, Edward, it is me, Peter."

"Prove it." Edward stared.

"Edward, I've been awake and trapped in my body since I was brought in. I've seen all of you come and go. I can communicate with some people but not others. I don't know why. Edward, you don't even have to talk and I can hear your thoughts."

"Hear my thoughts? Cripes, what am I thinking now?"

"It's not like that. If you are about to ask me something or say something to me, I can hear you before you speak. If you are thinking about me or something we've done, I can feel and see those thoughts. Go ahead. Try it."

Edward formed some questions in his mind. Peter answered them before he could even ask.

"Schebb. Sarah. Right 47, one and a half left 24, right 16. There, now I can rob you blind."

Edward sat in silence knowing that he had never given his home safe combination to anyone.

Son of a bitch. How is he doing that?

"I don't know. I'm trying to figure that out." Peter had just answered Edward's question the instant he'd formulated it.

Edward smiled nervously and shook his head in confusion. "How can I help? I can't tell anyone I'm talking to you. They'll just think I'm crazy."

"I know. I'm just happy I've finally connected with someone and, Edward, I'm so happy it's you. By the way, I love you too."

"You heard all that stuff? I didn't mean any of it. It was just an old man talking about old times."

"I understand. Edward. By the way there is one other person I think has the ability to hear me. Do you remember the cleaning lady last night?

Mrs. Rossi is her name. She understands. She says I have something to do and that's why I've been given this gift."

"Gift? It seems more like a curse to me. They used to burn people at the stake for stuff like this. What went on with Dr. Brandon? You scared the life out of him."

"He saved my life. I can't explain it."

"Seems like there's a whole lot of explaining to do around here. Peter, I have to think some about all of this. You aren't going to follow me when I leave, are you? Can you read my mind when I'm out of here?"

"No, but I have been traveling."

"Traveling? Peter, this is crazy. Stay with us, my friend. I'll be back soon."

"Edward? Thank you for...for everything. Pray for me."

Brian noticed the chair, usually occupied by the security guard, was empty when he left the lounge on his way to the Douglas offices, so he went back in and called Douglas security who confirmed that a fellow named George was on duty and should be there.

When he re-entered the hall he bumped squarely into a uniformed guard standing just outside the door. The rotund guard raised his arms to protect himself and Brian stopped short of knocking him backward. A red-faced young man with white tape across his nose apologized profusely.

Brian knew immediately that it was the same person he had run down outside the bar. Obviously he had injured him. Brian went on the offensive, hoping that he wouldn't be recognized. "Where have you been? You are supposed to be on duty, protecting our privacy."

He lied. "I have been here Mr. Douglas. I just went to take a leak...I mean, use the men's room. I checked everywhere before I left, and all was clear."

"Okay, okay. Just be quick if you have to leave the area." Brian walked towards the elevator, still hoping George hadn't recognized him.

George dropped his head in mock humility and nearly choked when he recognized the loafers that Brian Douglas was wearing. The same pair he had seen outside the strip bar. He prayed that Brian would not recognize him. George took a breath and wiped his brow. He unconsciously patted the pocket that contained the digital pictures. So far he had gathered dozens of pictures and recordings of private Douglas family discussions. His remote recorder, which he had been busy fiddling with when Brian first came out, had a limited range so he had to sit very close to the door to receive a clear signal. That positioning, he'd just found out, carried a heavy risk of discovery.

What will Harvey Kirkland think when he see these beauties? He'll kill for them and pay me handsomely in return or maybe I will sell them on the Net.

No. Then he'd kill me.

- Chapter 42 -

Marjorie was shocked to learn that Peter had nearly died, and that Peter's hold on life was tenuous. She greeted Brian warmly, had scheduled a meeting with his father's lawyers where the recording would be reviewed in front of Brian's counsel.

"Options would certainly be discussed," Brian had stated.

He hoped to get some indication of where the bulk of his father's estate was headed. He knew that none of it was for him. His father had made that clear when the business transition was concluded. Brian hoped to learn who, if anyone, might be motivated financially to see his father's life end.

Brian took a call from Matt, who sounded a little calmer.

He was not being charged with any crime.

The boys were being charged for their escapades, and Cara was still considering her options. He confided in Brian that her tests had shown that she had not been raped. There were indications of sexual assault, but the evidence would be hard to prove.

Cara had no recollection of the incident and the boys in jail claimed they knew nothing about Jason's actions. He was in bad shape in the hospital and was professing innocence about any assault on Cara.

Matt would let Cara make her own decision after hearing the procedure for bringing charges and getting to trial. He hoped she would choose not to proceed. He told that to Brian, and that he felt Jason had been dealt a severe enough punishment for whatever he had done.

Each of the boys was being represented by expensive legal counsel. The families hoped a deal for restitution could be worked out with the local authorities to avoid a lengthy trial with an uncertain outcome.

The brothers agreed to meet on the billiard side of Eye See You the next night at five.

Marjorie reviewed the growing list of people wishing to visit Mr. Douglas. Brian, now more adamant than ever that his father's privacy and security be protected, asked her to see that the security at the hospital was doubled. He dictated an update to be sent out over electronic voicemail on his behalf. Brian left it up to Marjorie to explain the reason why she, and not he, was delivering the message. "Be creative," he said, looking and feeling very tired.

"You should go home for the afternoon and rest after the meeting with the lawyers," Marjorie suggested. Brian agreed it would be a good idea.

Wouldn't it be great if she came along? She is a beautiful woman and she obviously likes me...

"Brian? Brian?" Marjorie realized she was losing him.

"Sorry I was just thinking...I was just thinking how good your idea was. I'm very tired. What time are the lawyers due?"

"Any minute."

"Call downstairs and get my guys up here. I'll freshen up and see you back here in fifteen."

"I'll have some coffee waiting for you."

"Marjorie." Brian looked directly into her eyes. "I really appreciate all you're doing. I know this is not an easy time."

"I'll put it on your tab," she smiled. Brian went for a shower.

The lawyers were all assembled when Brian re-entered the boardroom, crisp in a fresh shirt and tie. The smell of hot coffee filled the room. Peter's three lawyers, two of whom were his executors, sat on one side of the long table. Marjorie sat to the side of Brian's two lawyers who had left an empty seat between them for their boss. The men all stood when Brian walked in. He waved off the round of perfunctory handshakes and commenced.

"Gentlemen…excuse me, Marjorie, we're all friends here. We are here to see that the wishes of my father are carried out most appropriately. Let's play the recording so we can all start from the same point. Marjorie?"

Brian took a seat at the head of the table, hoping to avoid the appearance of having taken sides. The viewing ran through quickly and Marjorie brought the lights back up.

"Gentlemen, if my father dies, I trust that the orderly execution of his wishes will be carried out without delay. I do have a major problem with his request to terminate his life on speculation that he may not recover. My dad is in a coma, but he may wake up tomorrow or he may wake up thirty days from now. So long as there is a shred of hope that he might be revived, I will do everything I can to block his termination. I know he would want to live if he knew there was a chance of doing so."

One of Peter's lawyers, a weathered man with thinning gray hair and a gray mustache, spoke. "Brian, I've known your dad for more years than you have been alive. In many ways I probably know him better than you, no offense intended. Your father made it very clear to me on numerous occasions that he had no desire to be kept alive in a way he saw as inhumane or to end up spending the rest of his life incapacitated or in a nursing home. I appreciate your feelings and can completely understand them, but as your father's friend and one of his executors, I intend to see that his wishes are carried out as instructed. As you know, I fill a seat on the board of the hospital. Peter is getting the best care possible. Consultations with world experts are being carried out daily to ensure that any possible hope is explored.

Every day in these circumstances is a long one. Let's see how things are looking each day, but I'm legally bound to inform the board of your father's request."

"I'd like to see a copy of the asset distribution schedule."

"That's not possible until after his death."

"Gentlemen, we all know that certain individuals and organizations stand to benefit handsomely from my father's demise. I think that, as a matter of security alone, we should be aware of who may be motivated to that end."

"That's just not possible."

"I'm here trying to protect my father's life, and you don't seem to give a shit for anything but your legal papers. Now, whose side are you on?"

"Easy, son. On your father's side. His life to date has been the result of his wishes, his goals and his efforts. We don't intend to deprive him of his final wish for a death with dignity."

Battle lines had been drawn.

Brian rose abruptly.

"Gentlemen, thank you for your time. Let's hope we don't come to blows over this. I don't relish the thought of losing him, but I sure as hell don't want to be fighting over who pulls the plug either. Good day."

Brian rose, exiting briskly into his adjoining private office closing the door firmly behind him.

He flopped down on the couch, his skin flushed with heat, his face reddened, his emotions took over; he put his hands to his face.

"God, why me?"

– Chapter 43 –

"You have to have confidence that events will play out the way they should," Michael said gently to Sarah. He talked of how difficult it often was to understand why we are put through seriously painful events. He spoke of the need to understand that within each of those events was an opportunity to learn and grow.

"Although they often make no sense at the time, all events have a purpose which we will eventually discover."

Sarah had waited with Michael until the news came that both her father and Dr. Brandon were out of danger. He had a way of putting her at ease.

"All growth," he said, "Requires experiencing some difficulty or pain. Studying is hard and exercising is hard, but the rewards are obvious. The rewards for emotional pain are much harder to explain."

He asked her to accept that facing the pain she was feeling for her father now would make her stronger and more able to handle difficulties she would face throughout her life. It was important, he told her, to acknowledge difficulties openly, to accept the emotional pain and not deny that it exists.

Sarah listened carefully.

Most of what he said made sense. By focusing on a bigger picture than this one day at the hospital, she could feel that the events she was enduring were a little easier to handle.

They embraced lightly. Michael kissed Sarah on the cheek and squeezed her hands. "If you need to chat you can call me tonight."

"Be careful, I just might."

Michael stood lead-footed, not sure what to say so he wisely said nothing. He just smiled and walked away.

Sarah walked slowly past her father's window, checking to see if anyone was in the room. It was empty except for her father, which was comforting after witnessing the crisis and realizing she'd nearly lost him that morning.

"Hi, Daddy. It's me, your favorite daughter back to see you." Peter felt her warm kiss on his forehead.

Sarah sat down and began to ramble. "It's strange that we've never really talked. I mean, we've talked, but not really. You know what I mean? I guess you weren't around all that much. I probably talked more to Uncle Carl than I did to you when I was growing up."

That hurt. But, I guess I deserve this.

"I know you thought I was a real little angel, but I've done some bad things. I guess I party too much. I drink and take some drugs. Not crazy stuff, but all the kids do it. I guess I kind of get wasted every weekend if you have to know the truth, but I'm still doing okay in school. I'm not a virgin either."

Peter was delighted to see her but wished he wasn't hearing all this. He knew that if she knew he could hear her, his daughter wouldn't be talking like this. He supposed she came by the partying honestly; he was not exactly a bookworm himself. It seemed that all of his kids except Brian had inherited the party gene. He only hoped that Sarah would not follow in Matt's footsteps.

"It sure wasn't love, I can tell you that. It just sort of happened the first time. I was at a party and got a little drunk and high. Things got a little carried away. I was just kissing this boy at first, but he wanted more and I didn't want to be a prude and the next thing you know, he was getting dressed and my virginity was gone. I always thought it would be different, but I decided right there that I would be the aggressor from then on. Do you know what I mean? I mean I've had sex, so why not have it again, right? Don't worry, I use condoms. I carry some in my purse. If I had my bag here I'd show you…"

Listening to his daughter talk about her escapades was something Peter could definitely do without. He had never talked to Sarah about sex and he was now seeing the results. She was learning on her own.

"It's not like I'm a slut or something."

Peter grimaced.

"All the girls do it. Well, most of them. I've never told Mom, but Catherine and I talk a lot about sex."

That fact gave Peter little comfort. He knew that his eldest daughter was a bit of a man-grinder too.

"But now I've met this Michael guy. Remember, he was here with me the other day? Michael's not like the boys around school. You haven't made much progress, so could you hurry up? We want you back. Today they said there's a video about you wanting…" The words stuck in her throat. "Daddy, it says you want to die if you can't get better."

Sarah laid her head on her father's chest. Peter could feel her tears and hear her heart beating against him. The rhythm gently reverberated. He felt the ache of loneliness and desperately wished he could hold his daughter and tell her it was okay.

He felt the net of confinement tighten around him. The pull of darkness was evident when he drew in his daughter's emotions. He panicked a bit.

Wait, this could be bad. Steady yourself man, steady. No self pity. There is more to this than that. There just has to be.

"I'm not going to die, Sarah. I'll get out of here. I'll find a way."

Sarah's words were strained. "Michael says there's a reason for all of this. That I need to be strong and understand, but I don't understand. It is so hard to see you like this. Why has this happened?"

Peter asked the same question of himself over and over. Even Mrs. Rossi had said there was a purpose. His daughter spoke volumes of wisdom though she didn't realize it.

I guess we do have to accept our lot and make the best of it, knowing that one day the answer will be clear. Is that why we call it faith?

He felt the bath of his daughter's love.

"Sarah?"

At the sound of his voice, Sarah felt relief come over her.

"Have faith, honey, believe in what Michael says."

Sarah felt her father's thoughts forming in her mind, but did not attribute them to him. "I guess I just have to have faith." Her lips spoke words foreign to her, but they felt so natural she didn't notice.

She kissed him again and squeezed his hands. "I'll see you soon. I love you. Don't worry about me…I think I'm turning over a new leaf."

Peter smiled. Perhaps there is a purpose to all of this. But I must be a very slow learner.

- Chapter 44 -

Charlotte's hips showed just the right amount of curve in a pleated, knee-length skirt. Her face was flawless with only a hint of make-up.

Peter could smell her when she bent down to kiss him. He had yet to conclude why he could hear, smell, feel and communicate with some people more than others.

Her hair was beautiful. Her breasts rode un-tethered in a salmon silk blouse.

To him his whole situation was so bizarre that he just accepted what came when it came. He was in awe of how freely people spoke to him in this state and wondered why he had not developed communication even remotely as open with all of these people during his life.

He was anxious to see what surprises his wife had in store for him.

Charlotte walked over to close the blinds, blocking the natural light from coming in. She pulled the curtain across the hall window and pushed the door shut, sealing them in together.

"Well, my dear, we are alone at last."

Peter watched with amused bewilderment when his wife pulled a candle and holder from a bulky hand bag she was carrying. He grimaced when she struck a match, oblivious to the fact the flow of pure oxygen to his nose presented somewhat of an opportunity for catastrophe. She placed a small CD player on the bedside table and pressed a button, filling the room with one of her favorite selections. She took out a glass and small bottle of red wine.

"I thought we could enjoy a glass of your favorite Merlot together. I told the nurses not to bother us. I finally have you all to myself."

She held her finger under the wine when she poured it, then raised the glass. "To your recovery, my sweet. May you come back to me soon."

Charlotte drew her wine-moistened finger across his lips.

Peter could taste it. It was ambrosia. He'd had nothing in his mouth since he'd arrived in the hospital. These few drops were a precious elixir. His taste buds ached with gratitude.

Charlotte tipped her head back and drained her glass. She filled the it for a second time, emptying the contents of the small bottle, then sat beside the bed. Her head warmed with a light buzz. Her lips curled a bit in the corners in an alcohol-induced smile. "So, my love, what shall we talk about?"

Without hesitation Peter put thoughts of the time they met and their early months together into her head.

"Do you remember when we first met?" she asked.

As if by magic she was transported with him through a series of memories; of trips, outings and events in the first year of their relationship. Happy times were those; partying, travelling, dancing and making love in all conceivable locations. He could feel Charlotte like he was there with her. He could smell the aromas and feel the passion of their love. Her voice spoke to him in his dream.

The dream rolled on for a while, then stopped moving to dwell on a time they rented a cabin in a forest near a stream. He and Charlotte had spent the day hiking and returned at sundown. Both were tired, hot and spent from a day of physical exertion. They stopped by the stream to cool off. After removing their hiking boots, they shared a kiss on the lips which was intended to be congratulatory, but the taste of each other sparked a round of spontaneously potent kissing.

Peter started to undress Charlotte and peel away her sweaty clothes. Charlotte returned the favor. Undoing his well-worked shirt, she ran her hands over his solid chest, splaying her fingers in his hair. Charlotte's top now hung from her waist, exposing her breasts in a patterned bra.

Peter licked her neck. The salt stung his tongue. He closed his eyes as she peeled his shirt over his shoulders.

Charlotte held his head while he pressed his face into her cleavage. Her nipples hardened in the forest breeze. She stood back, watching Peter peel off his trousers and underwear, leaving him standing naked in front of her. The sight of her man rugged and ready released a deluge of heat and moisture.

He stepped forward and pressed against her.

She balanced against him, pulling each foot free from her trousers; now naked except for a high-cut pair of cotton briefs.

Peter slid his hand between her legs.

She bit into his neck, panting.

Peter wrapped his other arm around her and gently lifted, walking her into the water. The pressure of her weight on his hand when he carried her made her stomach ache as her muscles tensed in pleasure. The numbing water rose around them when he waded in.

Every muscle tightened.

Her skin went taut; the cold chilled and excited her.

Peter braced himself on a boulder which protruded just out of the water and turned Charlotte around. She eased on top of him, watching his leg muscles flex when he supported her weight.

He felt her breath, hot against his neck.

Charlotte closed her eyes and placed her hands on each of Peter's thighs. She leaned forward slightly, gently rocking.

Peter doused her back with icy water, kissing her neck intensely, then leaned her back and turned her toward him so their mouths could reach.

The rushing stream gushed up and around them, and beneath the forest canopy the natural smells intoxicated this pair who melded with their surroundings.

Now Charlotte and Peter were reliving the moment vividly.

He became aware of her breathing outside of the dream. It mixed in perfect harmony with her breathing in the dream, rising and falling as though both worlds were one. It grew to breathy moans, fading only to rise again. Then, in a powerful crescendo, the entire scene detonated into countless colorful pieces each projecting out, racing from their origin.

An erotic explosion trembled the forest lovers, and they gripped each other frozen in sculptured lust. The dream gently faded. Peter was back in the candle-lit room.

Charlotte sat low in the chair with her head back and eyes closed, her feet resting on the frame of the bed. Her skin was damp. Her skirt was pulled high up on her thighs.

Charlotte opened her eyes slowly. She quickly scanned the room to regain her presence. She let her flush settle, trying to collect her thoughts about what had just taken place. She had been thrust through time and back, yet it seemed so normal. Her mind was caught in a rift between fantasy and reality.

"Wow. That was wonderful. You don't know how much I've wanted that from you. I've been so lonely. You'd think I was crazy if you could hear or see me, but I wanted to be close to you. I just had the most powerful dream. It seemed so real. It was like you were right inside me. Peter, I love you so."

She rested her head on Peter's chest. She could hear his heart beating and feel the rise and fall of his breathing. She ran her hands up and down his chest under the cotton sheets. His body was cool against the warmth of her flesh.

She let her hand roam freely over his body. At first when her hand bumped against him, it didn't dawn on her what she was making contact with. After a few seconds she became aware of the position of her hand and looked down. Outlined beneath the sheet was a definitely familiar shape.

"How is that possible? It's not possible, is it?" Surprised and embarrassed, Charlotte couldn't let herself believe this was anything more than coincidence. She raised the sheet and looked again to confirm that the outline had not disappeared.

There must be an explanation. I'll ask Dr. Brandon…no, I'll ask one of the nurses first.

Charlotte blew out the candle and put the glass, corkscrew, candle and holder in the drawer of the bedside table. She left the CD player where it was. "I think the music was good for you, Peter, so I'm leaving this here. I hope you enjoy it. By the way…" Charlotte looked at Peter and smiled. "Will you call me in the morning? No? It's okay, I know you're shy. I'll call you."

Charlotte kissed his forehead and quietly departed, taking with her a mind full of images and a heart full of hope.

Peter closed his eyes. Tension released, unwinding every muscle. His mind and body were born on the sensation. A stream of white fluid drained from his penis and filled the latex cap.

When Charlotte walked past the nurses' station, she nodded to the duty nurse. She was older, harder and abrupt, but she had a kind look and rosy cheeks. Charlotte decided to take her chances. "Excuse me, nurse?"

The woman strutted out from behind the counter to greet her.

Can I actually ask her? Yes, I must. I need to know.

"Hello, Mrs. Douglas. How can I help you?" She eyed Charlotte's expensive clothes and imagined her privileged life with disdain. "Did you have a good visit with your husband? He's doing well…considering everything."

"Thank you, yes. I, ah, wanted to ask you something medical, but it's very personal." Charlotte blushed.

The bulky nurse stared at her inquisitively. She was well ahead of this inexperienced housewife; she'd seen it all in her thirty years in the hospital business.

She took Charlotte's hand. "Hon, I can tell by your look. If I've seen it once, I've seen it a thousand times. Let me answer before you ask." She was enjoying this now. "Men are men, my dear. You can knock 'em out, cut 'em up or break their bones, but they still get boners. It's just the way it is. Old or young, it doesn't matter. They're always on the lookout to spread their oats. It's nature, I guess. We spend plenty of time hitting them with our pencils or just wiping up after them. You should see the looks on the young girls the first time it happens. They don't know whether to run or lift their skirts." The nurse let out a belly laugh at her own attempt at humor, bringing an awkward and embarrassed smile to Charlotte's face.

She didn't know whether to be offended by this woman who seemed obtuse and insensitive or to report her to someone. She obviously lacked tact. Perhaps she couldn't be faulted for that, but must she be so insensitive with her morbid humor? Charlotte held back her outrage and pressed on. She correctly assumed that the years had dulled her and this warped sense of wit was one of her only releases.

"Is it any good? I mean, is there life?"

"Absolutely; a routine test can tell you if the sperm is alive, and if it is you can be impregnated."

"You know Peter, my husband, and I were planning to…" Charlotte caught herself. Why am I telling her this?

"Hon, talk to me next time you're in. We'll set up the test for you in the meantime. All you'll need is a sign-off from his Doctor... Don't worry; I can handle that for you."

Charlotte stumbled over her words, bewildered by this most unusual woman. "Thank you, thank you very much...and please, if you don't mind..."

The nurse put her crossed fingers to her lips. She smiled a worn and crinkled smile. "Our secret. I promise."

- Chapter 45 -

Brian could faintly hear the thumping music and screams of the already drunken horde on the dancers' side. He was thankful he didn't have to wade through the haze of lights to find his brother. Brian had slipped in the back door of Eye See You to find his brother, with two martini glasses in front of him, seated by himself in a corner booth. Matt stared into space while he gently poured the clear, frigid liquid into his mouth.

The first glass, now emptied, had been pushed to the middle of the table where it sat in disrespectful isolation. To Brian it seemed that the drunk, apparently, had respect only for the beauty and significance of the freshly prepared cocktail. As for the remnants of consumption, like a one-night stand, there was complete disdain and disregard for the dregs of a meaningless affair after it was over.

"Hey, Bro."

"You must think my life is shit."

Brian was taken aback.

"Having a bad hair day, are we?"

Matt spoke with a thick tongue. "I'm fucked. I'm depressed. I've got a bashed-up Cara waiting on the island. I nearly killed someone the other night. I'm totally unproductive. I look and feel like shit and, as usual, big brother is bailing me out. It seems the only other friend I've got these days is right here." Matt lifted his glass, then tipped its base toward the ceiling and drained its contents. With his head tilted back, he rolled his eyes sideways toward the waitress and flashed a peace sign, ordering two more when she wiggled past his table.

"I often get the feeling that I'm just a dead weight you drag around, and yet you've never really said so."

Brian raised his eyebrows and shrugged his shoulders. "Hey, you're my baby brother, right? I mean, my turn may come. Life's a long game, and each of us will play many roles over the duration. I've got no gripes with you, really. I know, some days you piss me off, but that passes quickly. Someone's got to keep an eye on you, right?"

The waitress placed two more martinis on the table and removed the empties. "Can I get you anything else?" She leaned provocatively into Matt's arm.

"Maybe later." Matt threw the poor woman a crumb of hope and smiled at his brother, who just shook his head.

"They all love you, don't they? I could live off your scraps."

"You know what, Bri? I would trade my life in a minute for something settled and sane. You know, a great wife, a couple of kids."

"Spare me. I've heard this before. I think it was just after that model dumped you."

"I was finished with her anyway," Matt protested. "How's dad?"

"No change in him, but get this." Brian went on to explain about the Living Will and his father's request to be terminated. He told his brother he intended to fight it, or at least try to get an extension. "What do you think, Matt?"

"Do you think you should be tampering with dad's final request?"

"What? I can't believe what you're saying. We're talking about whether or not to kill our father here, Matt. Does that not mean anything to you?"

Matt didn't want to mention the experience he'd had looking down on the rocks when Jason fell. Brian would just think he was drunk. "Well, you know, dad's always liked to call his own shots. He wouldn't have made this request unless he meant it. Brian, we've never talked about religion much. You know better than most that I'm not very religious, but I do believe there is a bigger plan than the one we create for ourselves. There may be some things we just should stay out of. Know what I mean?"

Brian looked at Matt and took a long draw on his martini. He didn't like martinis, but he needed something to cool his blood. "Matt, you believe whatever you want. After you go visit dad, you tell me that you're ready to let him die. I'll be fighting it every inch of the way."

The music from the other side rolled into the billiard room as the connecting door swung open. Dr. Zalkow stuck his head in and looked around. He made eye contact with Brian and couldn't retreat.

"Don't look now…Zalkow," Brian mumbled under his breath.

"Great, get your guard up."

"Boys, boys, great to see you. You're missing a great time next door." Zalkow was well on his way and spoke twice as loud as he needed to, a result of having been temporarily deafened by the noise in the next room. He was a tall, thin man whose suit hung on him like a hanger. His slicked-back silver hair sharpened a receding hairline and amplified his wrinkled face. "Mind if I join you?"

Brian rose quickly. He spoke in a solemn tone for effect. "Actually, my brother and I were just leaving to visit our father."

Zalkow retreated. "How is your dad? I hear we almost lost him."

Brian wanted to thump Zalkow right there and drop him to the floor. He took a long breath. "Mr…Dr. Zalkow, if you were a betting man, I'd advise you not to bet against Peter Douglas. And if you did have some money you wanted to lose, I'd be happy to make the book for you. Our father will be with us long into the future, I'm sure of it."

Zalkow put his wiry hand on Brian's shoulder. Brian tensed at his touch. "I'm sure you're right son, I'm sure you're right. My prayers are with him and your family."

Brian's stress level increased in response to the hollow condolences.

"Will either of you be attending the Hospital's Annual Board meeting? There'll be fireworks. Budgets are being cut to pieces. Departments will close and jobs are definitely on the line."

"I think we'll be passing on that one. I'm sure we'll have plenty on the go." Brian and Matt both knew their father's predicament would be a hot topic of debate at the meeting. The brothers eased out of the booth and bid him goodbye without shaking hands.

They made it out into the fresh air where they crossed the lawn. Brian brought Matt up to date on some business matters. He kept it simple in consideration of his brother's languid state.

Riding the elevator, Matt inhaled and exhaled swiftly.

Brian could taste the cloud of alcohol mist in the air but said nothing. He clapped Matt on the shoulder, then he peeled off into the lounge to let Matt continue toward their father's room. "I'll be in here making some calls."

Matt nodded. He hated everything about hospitals and did everything necessary to avoid them. The smell alone made him nauseous, which didn't go well on a stomach full of cocktails.

"Hey, Pop. Number two here to see you again. How's it going?"

Peter could see that Matt had been drinking when he sat down solidly in the chair beside the bed. He couldn't feel any emotion emanating from Matt. He could hear his voice, but could not get at any of his thoughts.

"So…was that you? Did you save that boy's life? I'd be in jail right now. You must think I'm out of control."

He had been resting peacefully when he felt the pain and heard Matt scream. He had only to focus on the sound of his son and he was drawn out to him, just in time to cushion the falling boy. He didn't know the circumstances that led Matt to where he was, but he could feel that what he was doing was right. He tried to communicate with his son, but as quickly as he had saved Jason's life he was snapped back to the hospital room; no sounds or bright lights…just an unceremonious round trip ticket to Bermuda and back.

Peter tried again to reach into his son's mind without success.

"I guess I witnessed a real miracle. I'm going to change, Dad. I have to get my life moving ahead." Matt went and looked out the window at the familiar stream of cars on the freeway.

"I know you wouldn't approve, but I think I might write a book. It's something I've always thought of doing, but since it's not business related I didn't think anyone would approve. Especially you and Brian. It's time I did something I want to do. Something that I can get my teeth into. You know, not chained to an office. I know this may come as a surprise, but I couldn't really give a shit about business."

Matt took a breath. "I've come to realize it's just something I do, it's not who I am. Maybe I'm just partied out. Chasing money and pussy isn't as much fun as it used to be."

He shrugged his shoulders, hoping his father might proffer an answer.

"I know you don't know this, but I've actually been a bit of a writer all my life. I remember getting good grades on my stories in school. I've written lots of poems and stories over the years. I just never bothered to show them to any of my family. I didn't think they'd give a fuck anyway." Matt reflected, then smiled. "There's a few women who know. I've kept the odd one amused over the years with my penmanship."

Matt wrote an imaginary sentence in the air. Practicing a stage part, he broke into an English accent, "Sometimes," he scripted the air, "the pen…is even mightier…" , he grabbed his crotch and gave a short forward thrust, "…than the prick."

He chuckled while he amused himself with a lengthy soliloquy about the virtues of the single life, a lone actor performing for his watching father.

"It's only regrettable that my actions couldn't imitate my poetic words. Perhaps that's the point. I could always be any character I wished when I acted, but I could only ever be myself when I wrote. Maybe there's a message in that." Matt rambled, with booze lubricating his tongue and loosening his mind.

Peter couldn't remember Matt ever mentioning an interest in writing. But, contrary to Matt's thinking, he approved if that's what Matt felt he should be doing. This was refreshing. Here was a son he had failed to know. It troubled him to realize how little he knew of the people around him.

As Matt said, they were all actors playing roles. Peter had just never taken the time to meet them backstage and get to know who they really were.

"I've been thinking about subjects, Dad, and I think I'll write about a wealthy business tycoon who goes into a coma. He's actually alive, but can't get out. I don't know how it will end yet. I'm hoping you might help me out with that. What do you say, Dad? Would you like to be the star in my first novel?"

Matt turned and looked at his father. His face tensed. "I'm hoping for a happy ending, but I'm afraid I'm being optimistic. I'm afraid I'm going to lose you."

Matt sank into the chair by the window and rolled his head back, trying to clear his nose. He composed himself and wiped his face on his sleeve. He clasped his hands and straightened his legs. His eyes closed. He took several long, slow breaths. The alcohol combined with his fatigue and he slept.

Instantly he and Peter were transported to the camping site where they spent their only weekend alone together. It was totally real. Matt was a teenager. Father and son had spent a day canoeing and were sitting in front of their tent cooking fish on an open fire. Matt was drawing shapes in the sand with a stick and asking his father to guess what they were. Peter recognized immediately why he was there. He had forgotten this precious and important moment and now had a chance to relive it. He looked a few feet away and saw their exact duplication. He knew an important opportunity was upon him. Watching the duplicate of himself ignoring Matt's drawings and resisting the boy's attempts to involve him, he couldn't believe how insensitive he'd been. Matt drew in front of him and now he was asking his father to guess what the picture was. Both scenes were now in complete synchronization.

One father ignored his son's questions, lost in thought, and young Matt scuffed his drawings clear with his foot.

Peter took the opportunity to guess and encouraged his son to draw some more. He guessed several times and, as if by the touch of a guiding hand, he knew what he would do.

"Daddy?" his two boys said in harmony. "What would you think if I said I wanted to be an artist or a writer instead of being a businessman like you?"

Peter waited while his other image answered. He remembered exactly what he said back then and recalled the look on his young son's face.

"An artist? That's for sissies. If you want to get anywhere in the world, you have to be in business. You can always buy art."

Peter shuddered at his shallow, insensitive response. He knew this was his chance to make a change in Matt's life forever.

"Art is a present from God, Matthew. If you feel it's something you wish to pursue, then you should. I don't have much artistic ability and I'm not a great writer, but I admire those who have that talent. Anyone can make money, but art is a true gift."

He smiled at his father. The mirrored scene faded.

"Well, what is it?"

Peter looked down at the ground. Matt had drawn a picture of a tent and two people holding hands, smiling. One big person and one little person. "That's us, isn't it?" Peter rubbed his son's hair, leaned over and kissed his head.

The fish smelled delicious.

"Mr. Douglas? Mr. Douglas?"

It was déjà vu when he focused on Terri.

"This is getting to be a habit! I could roll a cot in for you if you'd like."

"Very funny. Don't you have other rooms to check?"

"I like to save the best for the last. Can I get you a face cloth?"

Matt rose and walked into the bathroom. "Allergies. There's something about these hospitals."

Terri peered into the darkness and let the stream of car lights mesmerize her for a moment. One chance meeting was a fluke. Two chance meetings must be a sign.

She could hear the water running in the bathroom and envisioned Matt bent over the sink, splashing cold water on his face. She looked across the room at Peter as if to seek his advice. He offered none.

When Matt stood up from the sink and turned Terri was a few feet away taking him in. She had paused and now stood frozen, spellbound by the thick chemistry in the space between them.

Matt stared into her eyes.

Terri stared back.

Matt was tall and handsome but looked vulnerable.

Terri figured that he was way out of her league. She rationalized, however, that an attempt to get his affections would cost her little.

No words were spoken.

On cue they each took a half step forward and locked into a passionate, wet kiss. Terri dissolved the full length of her body against his. She could feel his arousal.

Matt's saliva was sweet with mouthwash, but Terri could still taste the overriding flavor of alcohol that saturated his system. She didn't care. She had entered that erotic, intoxicating zone where reality gives way to fantasy and everything that leads down the path toward sex tastes and smells wonderful. Her mind was a million light years away, transported by lust to a distant universe.

They rocked slightly off balance.

Matt opened his eyes to regain his orientation and caught a glimpse of his father, lifeless on the bed.

He stepped back from Terri abruptly and looked at her. "Look at us. Look at him." He pointed to his father. "What are we, fucking animals?"

Caught off guard by Matt's sudden shift of mood, Terri floundered slightly trying to regain her composure. "No, it's just that...I thought that you..."

Matt placed his hands on Terri's shoulders and held her gently at arms length.

"I'm sorry. No harm done. I'm not thinking clearly. This is my fault. I feel attracted to you, but this is not the time or place. I've already got more going on than I can handle without dragging you into it."

"Terri, you in there?" a matronly voice called from the doorway. The shuffle of her synthetic uniform could be heard as she walked toward the bathroom.

Matt could see Terri was mortified. He put his finger to his lips, handed Terri the wet face cloth and stepped behind the shower curtain.

Terri gave him a pleading look. Matt shrugged as if to say, "This one's all yours."

Terri flicked off the light switch and stepped directly into the path of her approaching supervisor. She folded the face cloth into a long band.

"There you are. Everything okay with Mr. Douglas?"

Terri regained her composure quickly. "He just seemed to be getting a little heated up and I thought I'd wipe him down with a cool cloth."

"Don't get him all worked up like you did the other night." Her supervisor laughed.

"No, we wouldn't want Mr. Douglas getting excited now would we?" Terri raised her voice just loud enough for Matt to hear.

Matt waited in the shower for both nurses to leave. As Terri walked by the bathroom she lobbed the face cloth in over the curtain. It landed squarely on Matt's head.

Matt couldn't believe what had just transpired, but he did take comfort in the fact that he didn't have Terri's uniform up around her head when the other nurse arrived.

Maybe I <u>have</u> turned over a new leaf. No, probably not.

He stepped into the view of his father. "Well, did you catch any of that, Dad? Is she hot or what? I know, I know. I am going to change. I promise."

Peter had observed the whole play with some distaste and wondered if his son would ever change. He pressed on Matt's thoughts, but could still not make contact. He had to content himself with being an observer for now.

Matt squeezed Peter's hand. "I've got some business to finish up in Bermuda and then I'll be back to see you. It would be nice if you were awake when I got back. Work on that, okay?

"*I will son, I will.*"

- Chapter 46 -

"*Hello, Eddie.*"

Edward jumped with surprise when he entered Peter's room and heard Peter's voice in his head.

"Cripes, Peter, can't you wait until I've at least sat down and got relaxed before you start screwing around with my head? I can't get used to the idea that you can talk to me without moving your lips. I mean, look at you. You're just lying there. I don't know about you, but I'm going to use my mouth to talk whether you like it or not. Besides, what you doin' calling me Eddie anyway?"

"*That's fine, Sir Edward, but people may think you're crazy sitting there talking to yourself.*"

"*Think* I'm crazy? I am crazy. I can't believe this and there's no one I can talk to about it without getting locked up."

"*Don't forget Mrs. Rossi. She'll understand. You can talk to her.*"

"Well, we'll see how this goes. So, how is it going in there? Can you feel anything? Are you in pain? What is it like?"

Edward listened while Peter recounted the many experiences he'd been having, including the feeling that there was a purpose to his current situation. He couldn't explain what the purpose was, he told Edward, but he could feel a void within himself would have to be filled before he moved on. Watching people behave when they didn't realize he was able to hear or see was frustrating and yet enlightening. He explained that he had different levels of connection with different people and did not understand why.

"I've always been a dreamer, Peter. Ever since I was a little boy I believed that there was a lot more to this world than what we could see and touch. I loved to dream at night and I always remembered my dreams. I've always had a good sense for people's feelings and have often been able to know what they were going to say before they said it."

"Yes, I always admired that in you."

"I always seemed to understand that coincidences in life weren't just flukes, that there was an opportunity in every chance event or meeting."

"Like when you and I met?"

"That's right. What an odd pairing you and me. But it was our job then as it is now to figure out what that opportunity is. I also always assumed that everyone was pretty much the same, but I guess that's not true. There are obviously many levels on which we exist, whether we like to believe it or not." Edward paused and stared at Peter for a moment. "It makes one wonder where we are going as a population, and whether ten thousand years from now we'll have actually done something with our brains and the gifts we've been given. So far we haven't done much more than achieved a relatively mature stage of barbarianism. We seem to be squandering ourselves and our planet. I guess I'm babbling, but the point is, I miss our conversations."

"I do too. But we're here for now, so let's enjoy each other's company and see if we can figure out where all of this is taking us. How's your book coming?"

"Good evening, gentlemen. Having a nice visit?"Terri breezed into the room to take a series of readings for Peter's chart.

"We were just talking about the world's problems. I'm Edward, Peter's friend. Care to join in?" He stared at Terri while she worked around Peter.

"Hey Eddie, remember I can read your thoughts, you dirty old man."

"Cripes," Edward's mouth broadened into a smile then to a chuckle.

"Pardon?" Terri looked at him.

"Nothing, I just had a funny thought. It wouldn't mean much to you."

"She's hot after my son, Ed...They were kissing here not more than a couple hours ago."

"What?"

"Pardon? Another funny thought?"

"I guess so. My head is full of them tonight."

Terri finished up and gave Edward a curious look. "Have a good evening."

"You see what I mean, Peter? Now she thinks I'm nuts and I haven't done or said anything. Maybe I am nuts."

"You're not nuts. This is really happening. We're just two normal people caught in a crazy situation."

Edward gave Peter an update on the Boston Red Sox, who were in hot contention for a World Series Championship. He reported on his trip to Europe and told Peter his perceptions of how his family was handling the crisis.

"What's this about your Living Will requesting that you not be kept alive artificially? You really want us to disconnect you?"

"I've been thinking about that, Edward...I can't say. I just hope that things will find clarity on their own. Let's take each day as it comes." It was Peter's turn to change topics. *"Say, do you remember that time you and I went fishing on the Sycamore River? We had that old blue tent and the wooden fishing punt I'd built?"*

He nodded, smiling widely and closing his eyes, remembering the trip many years earlier. Peter focused on Edward's thoughts and was instantly with him there in the little boat. It was a brilliant sunny day. The fish weren't biting, but these college seniors could have cared less. They talked and laughed, recounting stories of the year gone by, sipping on pops from the ice box.

Edward's day dream ended as simply as it had started. "Peter that seemed so clear in my mind I can remember every detail like I was just there yesterday. Very odd Peter. Very odd. I guess I am a believer though."

Peter smiled to himself. He didn't want to overwhelm Edward with more information than he was already trying to absorb so he stayed silent.

"Well pal, hate to say it, but I'm getting hungry. I think I'll go and get some dinner. Can I get you anything?" He grinned.

"A barbecued steak would be nice. With baked potatoes and a glass of red wine."

"Coming right up. I'm not sure how we'll get it down one of these tubes."

"I know. Sad, isn't it? A week ago life was such a breeze and now look at me."

He could sense in Peter's tone that he needed to change topics quickly. He held up three fingers. "Peter, how many fingers?"

"Three."

"Was that a lucky guess? What color is my shirt?"

"White, but your shirt is always white."

"Good point." He reached in his pocket and without looking at it held up a bill.

"How much?"

"Where'd you get that hundred? You never have more than twenty bucks on you."

Edward looked at the hundred dollar bill in his hand and couldn't remember where it had come from. Peter was right; Edward never had more than twenty bucks in his pocket. "Did you do that?"

"Do what?"

"Well, I'm not sure where this came from. You didn't, I mean, you can't, you know…?"

"It came from your pocket. I didn't put it there. I just told you what it was."

"This is getting weirder by the minute." He looked at the hundred and folded it carefully before putting it back in his pocket. "I'll see you soon, pal."

"I'll be here. Unfortunately, I'll be here. See you soon."

"Yeah, soon." What the heck is going on here anyway? He pulled the hundred from his pocket and stared at it. He looked back at Peter's room and slipped the folded bill back into his pocket.

He could hear the sound of voices coming up the elevator shaft when the car approached his floor. Two men were in a heated conversation. No, arguing. Their voices grew louder.

When the elevator bell rang the men went silent.

The doors whisked open.

"Dr. Brandon." Edward was standing two feet in front of him and could see that his face was red and moist with perspiration. He looked seriously stressed.

"Oh, Edward, sorry…ah yes…ah…just reviewing a tough case with colleague. It may not surprise you to know that we Doctors don't always agree." Dr. Brandon forced a chuckle and wide smile upon seeing Edward, who stood trying to assess the situation.

"Understood. I hope it works out. I will see you at the next briefing."

"Yes…yes…very good, the next briefing."

Dr. Brandon slipped by Edward, who entered the elevator. The diminutive, suited man in the back corner stayed focused while tapping out a message on his PDA with his head down.

Edward pivoted toward the closing elevator doors just slowly enough that he could read the name on the ID badge the man was wearing. He made a mental note, Dr. Joseph Zalkow.

- Chapter 47 -

Catherine and Dr. Brandon sat at a corner table. Candle flames licked at the air of the darkened bistro. Dr. Brandon had picked an out-of-the-way restaurant in hope that they wouldn't see anyone either of them knew. So far it was working. They shared a glass of wine and talked about a wide range of topics. He found her charming, witty, warm and approachable now that he was alone with her. Catherine was an independent woman with a career and a busy life. Dr. Brandon was thirteen years her senior, although she seemed to enjoy the fact that he had his head screwed on tight, knew where he was going and what he wanted. She knew many women who would gladly skip the turmoil of spending time with younger men to latch on to someone less likely to play head games, cheat or break up and run after the next cute woman who looked at them sideways.

"Why aren't you married, Jim? You must be one of Boston's most eligible bachelors."

He took her probing as a compliment and simply avoided any discussion around that topic by blaming his work. As though gravity were acting upon their discussion, the topic ultimately worked its way around to her father, his number-one priority patient.

His comfort level dropped when Catherine pressed him for more details about Peter's prognosis and the efforts they were making to revive him. She asked more about the special equipment, its purpose and the people running it. She dwelt for a while on an article she had read. It was about precise chemical injections into the brain, which were used in an effort to restore consciousness. She speculated as to whether her father had any sense of his condition. "All of us who have spent time with dad have felt there's a definite presence in the room," she said.

He listened politely and limited his answers to the smallest amount of content that would suffice. He did have an interest in Catherine's comments about a presence anyone might have felt around Peter. They spent some time talking about that.

With the evening continuing, he could feel the warm attraction he had toward her. It was a feeling he hadn't known in some time, and it made him uneasy. He knew that if he had any intentions, there were many things about himself that he would have to open up to her about. He knew the risks and the results that honesty could bring. He had built and failed numerous relationships on less than full truth in the past. He had promised himself the same thing would not happen again.

He had learned that the truth in any relationship eventually comes out. The lack of truth festers if unaddressed, to a point where, as if by outside intervention, the relationship fails. He had discovered through his years of medicine the amazing resilience of the body and was always amazed when he was painfully reminded that the heart and spirit possessed the same quality. He knew that truth was a very freeing experience and had witnessed that feeling on many occasions when complete honesty about a situation was the final result of a long period of deception. The long deceptive route to truth was always very rocky. Truth, however, as a final destination, no matter what the chosen course, was ultimately worth it.

"Catherine, I will do everything I can to help your dad but…"

"But what?"

"There are factors outside of my control that…"

"What factors? What do you mean?"

"Let's just say that in hospitals there are Doctors who are Doctors like me and there are Doctors who are career politicians like…"

"Jim?"

"Well, what I am trying to say is that I will work on the medical side of this equation, but your family will need to work on the political side. I am sorry if this is confusing, it's just that politics sometimes gets in the way of good medical care and I just wanted you to be aware of that potential in our hospital."

"And I thought you were bringing me here on a date. Instead I am in a political science class."

The two laughed.

"I get it. Thank you. Is there any particular person or people who may not be on your side of the ledger?"

He paused for a while.

If I tell her, the top is off the spider box. If I don't tell her, I am in the spider box. I hate spiders.

"Let me think on that one, Catherine. I assure you, if there is any overt action that may impede my mission to revive your dad, I will let you know in a more direct way."

"Well I hope there is then. I mean…not that I want something bad…I just…"

"Pardon?"

Catherine was blushed red now but continued, "I mean I enjoyed our dinner and that might be a catalyst for another… never mind it all came out wrong" She brushed her red hair behind her ears. Two diamond ear studs glimmered in Dr. Brandon's eyes.

He raised his eyebrows in an inquisitive way.

The best thing to do would be to say nothing, Doctor. Just say "Thank you" and shut up.

"Well, ah…thank you? I guess?"

Critical Care

When they rose, Catherine took his arm. Her eyes were a tiny bit glazed from the red wine. She felt warm. She smelled very good.

"Are you certain there isn't more to this than you are letting on?"

Zalkow, Zalkow, Zalkow, Zalkow, just blurt it out. Invite her home – tell her there …invite her home, you chicken.

"Nope."

- Chapter 48 -

Terrance Sing looked at his screen before dialing the code on his telephone to let Choy into his building. He waited with his door open, nervously looking up and down the hall. He pulled her in and snapped two dead bolts in place.

His agitation rattled Choy. "Terrance, what is it? You're wound like a top."

"We're in deep, Choy. Sammy really hit the mother lode on this one." Terrance pulled a small data storage device from his shirt pocket and slipped it into the computer.

His apartment rode high over the city, a typical bachelor pad. It was an open concept glass cocoon, long on style and short on substance. The main area, presumably the living room, looked like an electronics store. The flat panel television, recording equipment, stereo and computer gear were all symmetrically placed and visually appealing. Terrance was a technophile who loved his toys. He looked at Choy through his designer specs, then sat down at the thick glass table where his computer rested. He was very excited.

"Choy, you're going to be amazed! We've got medical records, legal files, his Will and financial statements, ties to the media, private notes about a mole in the hospital and much more. Choy, not everyone wants your friend to live. Sammy dredged up notes from a recent hospital board meeting that talk about a one-hundred million dollar gift from Peter to the hospital if he dies." Terrance carefully tapped a lengthy combination of letters, numbers and symbols to clear the password protection on the disk.

"This system is totally secure. One false entry and the whole thing evaporates. Here you go. You get one run-through of its contents. They self-delete as you go. You've got one hour before the whole thing is gone."

Choy took Terrace's seat, gingerly pressed a key and started to read as fast as she could. Terrance handed her a pad and pen. "Take notes in code, okay?"

She scanned the hospital record and read a quick summary of the accident and Peter's injuries. His prognosis report was not positive. He was being kept alive because of his profile as opposed to any assumptions that he would be well again. Politics, not ethics, were driving the process. She read the comments about the monitoring equipment and it could easily be interpreted that Peter was being used as a guinea pig by the hospital or government. The Europeans had reported successfully tracking movement of electrical fields in patients like Peter. They were hoping to replicate these results in a respected U.S. hospital. Choy dwelt momentarily on their celestial meeting and wondered what readings might have been generated. She refocused. Clearly, to her at least, Peter's survival was secondary to the experiments.

Confidential government records about Dr. Brandon showed that he nearly lost his license to practice but made some sort of deal, resulting in criminal charges against him being dropped.

Dr. Zalkow was linked to the City Star, whose computers revealed internal memos about Peter Douglas and the information-gathering techniques which were underway. An operative named George was being used for this; his final assignment with the Star. Zalkow's comments at a recent hospital meeting were focused on a major loss from a lawsuit, and the hospital was facing enormous budget cuts. He also raised the topic of planned giving and the resulting financial upside to the hospital.

Sammy had lifted an actual copy of the will from Peter's law firm. Choy read the disposition section carefully. Peter's net worth was in the hundreds of millions and the list of recipients was long, including a very large donation to the Boston Trauma Centre. Her eyes froze when she saw her name well down on the list. Beside it in the right hand column of numbers she read the sum of five million dollars. She felt like she had just violated the privacy of her friend and lover. The thought that she would be rewarded by Peter's death made her ill. His money meant nothing to her. She wanted him to live; the chance to see him again was far more important than any amount of money. She noted the section and page of the will and continued reading.

The hour ticked by.

She wrote feverishly, hoping she would be able to read her own writing when she was done.

The page changed and a headline from The City Star appeared, but with no date.

$60,000,000 TRAUMA @ BOSTON TRAUMA

ZALKOW MISHANDLES LAW SUIT - CANCER VICTIMS CLAIM VICTORY

Zalkow?? $60m, she scrawled quickly.

Choy copied a list of further links that Sammy could follow if desired. It seemed that once entry to the spider web of information was gained at any point, the entire web was accessible. Choy was looking into the dark eyes of Big Brother. She now realized there were no secrets if one was willing to pay. It scared her to think that someone half a world away, locked in a basement somewhere, had pulled down Peter's pants and had a good look.

She felt a layer of goose flesh form on her body.

The screen went blank startling her. Time was up.

The CD drive continued to spin, voiding the disk of its secrets.

Terrance removed the defunct CD from the computer. "You look like you have seen a ghost."

"I hope not, Terry, I really hope not. I need another favor from your pal Sammy." Choy scratched out a note stating the paragraph and line of Peter's will. Beside it she wrote, "change $5,000,000.00 to $5,000.00." Beside another paragraph referring to overseas orphanage projects she wrote, "Change $10,000,000 to $14,995,000.00."

She handed the note to Terrance who read it in carefully. "Are you sure, Choy? That's a lot of money."

"I've never been more sure of anything. Peter would approve." Choy left the apartment with her notes secured in her bag. She was now burdened with information and the dilemma of what to do with it. The consequences of action or inaction weighed upon her. Thoughts of her project were now secondary to helping Peter. She assumed that her backers would not be pleased if there was any undue delay, but felt confident now that with Terrance and Sammy's help she could get information on them that would aid her in any dispute that might arise.

Choy had gently slipped into the underworld and through the magic of electronics she had barely noticed the transition. She was beginning to see that information or lack thereof, whether real or fabricated, could be deadly.

She wondered what people could find out, or worse, might fabricate about her if she were caught.

- Chapter 49 -

Peter could hear the soft sounds of someone singing in a low breath. He had been drifting in and out of sleep for hours. Some of his dreams were conventional; others were real, out-of-body experiences that placed him in the very event he was dreaming about. He was realizing that each time he visited a past experience he was given some opportunity to participate. Since his hospitalization, each time he had traveled out-of-body he would witness a duplication of a prior episode in his life. He was allowed to participate in the event again as the original episode played out visually in close proximity. As the original occurrence caught up to the point in time at which he was participating during his revisit, there would be a significant instant in which he was given a chance to change something. The two events, once synchronized, would merge, and he would be whisked away to a new place.

This duplication of circumstances became a pattern. He could feel each chance for his participation approach as a mirrored replay took place. In most cases it was simply an opportunity to express affection or avoid conflict when he had failed to do so previously; small deeds which, in their sum, could add up to a life of giving rather than avoiding joy. The effort required was subtle, yet powerful in its effect on people.

If Peter was learning anything about his past, it was that he never participated in the moment. His mind and thoughts were rarely focused on the situation he was in, particularly when it related to family or friends. Whenever he viewed his former self, he realized how distracted and detached he appeared; present in body, but absent in mind and spirit. The effect on the people around him was obvious. They lost out or gained, depending on his efforts. He vowed if he ever woke to participate in life again that he would cherish every moment as if it was his last.

The music soothed him and he realized that it was real and not in his dream.

"Hello, Peter. May I call you that?" He saw the stout Mrs. Rossi doing her chores about his room, singing as she went. She was definitely present and enjoying her place in time. *"What have you learned?"*

"Yes, yes, Peter…of course…hello. You really believe I'm caught like this for a reason, don't you? What makes you so sure?"

"You do."

"What does that mean? You don't know anything about me."

"I know you well. You are like many lost souls caught between here and the next place, trying to make peace with themselves before moving on."

"Moving on to where?"

"You know better than I. You have seen other side of judgment and you have been granted special gift."

"It seems more like a curse than a gift. Well, not really. I have been having many wonderful experiences, but most have simply been re-runs of old events. It is as if I've been given a chance to make up for lost opportunities."

"Like you, I also thought my gift was curse in beginning. Since I was young girl I have ability to read souls. I met many like you. Some move to higher levels, like your friend Edward, and some like you are pushed there. I have been friend to many on their journey, but now I feel 'dat my work will soon be done and I can move on."

"What do you mean?"

"I am old woman. My health is bad. I feel I will soon be called."

Peter was saddened to think that this woman was expecting to die. She did look tired. She had obviously given up much of herself in her lifetime.

"I hope that I get the chance to meet you in person and thank you for your friendship."

"I need no thanks." Mrs. Rossi stood and looked at Peter. There was sadness in her eyes.

"Will I ever meet you, Mrs. Rossi?"

A few seconds passed.

"We have already met. I must go now." Mrs. Rossi hurried from the room like someone trying to avoid something.

Peter felt disturbed by her apparent avoidance of the question. Perhaps she knew the future, or perhaps not; she was unprepared to say. He had been buoyed by the hope that this adventure would lead to him waking up and participating in life once again. Now he questioned his optimism. With those thoughts he could feel his energy declining. He recognized the feeling from his previous visit into the blackness after Marion had confessed her affair with Carl.

He fought back his feeling of doom and tried to think of positive things. He imagined his trip to Asia and time spent with Choy. Instantly he was reliving one of their many wonderful lovemaking experiences. The touch of her skin was real. The sounds and smells were ripe in his mind. The heat of her breath on his neck warmed his being. He could feel another opportunity building around them. He could now see a wave of time catching up, mirroring his actions.

Choy leaned away from him and looked deeply into his eyes. *"I love you so very much, Peter."*

He remembered the time clearly. His previous response had been silence, which Choy had taken to mean indifference. His lack of commitment to their act spoiled the mood entirely. He had cast her aside by not allowing his true feelings out.

Peter leaned away from Choy and returned her gaze. *"And I love you more than life."*

Peter smiled at her. They embraced. The mirrored image of the lovers faded and their lives continued, unaltered but slightly warmed.

The hospital corridors were quiet as Terri did her rounds and checked on her roster of patients. She loved the eerie feeling of a hospital at night. A sense of camaraderie and sometimes intimacy developed between people who worked at night while most of the world slept. They were like keepers of a flame that ensured, when the planet awoke the next morning, everything would still be as they had left it.

The Douglas security guard dozed in his chair. Terri eased open the door of their lounge to see if anyone was asleep on the couch. It was dark and empty with only the tiny green and red lights of computers and other devices winking any indication of presence. Flowers had accumulated on the trolley in front of the lounge. Terri paused to smell a bouquet. She picked up one of the vases and took it with her to the nurses' station.

She checked each of her rooms as she went. Every room had a story to tell and all the stories had their cast of characters with whom she interacted on a sporadic basis. None had quite the impact of Peter Douglas and his son Matt. Terri had been approached by many men in her hospital with offers of nocturnal affairs, but she had always resisted. If they were serious, they could contact her off duty. Most didn't and eventually she'd learn that they were merely seeking a tryst to add some excitement to their dull nighttime routines.

Terri loved to play the game, but never let it go too far. Matt was the first man she had ever kissed within the confines of the hospital. And she had made the first move! She was proud and embarrassed at the same time.

She paused at the door of the monitoring room. It was slightly ajar, and she pressed it open further until she could see where a white uniformed technician slept with his feet propped up on a table. A magazine lay limp in his lap. She looked at all his equipment and wondered about Mr. Douglas and his prospects for a future. She caught herself thinking of Matt and what life with him might be like.

Peter's room was dark and quiet. Equipment hummed gently. Terri made notes of Peter's statistics on her clipboard. Looking down on him, she could see his resemblance to his son Matt.

Peter woke to see her standing over him. He touched her thoughts and she began to speak quietly.

"Hi, Peter. How are you tonight? I know that you can't hear me, but I'm talking to you just in case. I once read a book about a man who was trapped in a coma and never woke up, but he was alive inside. The hospital kept him alive and he spent his entire life trying to figure out how to kill himself so he could be free. In the end there was an explosion and he was blown up. What a way to die, don't you think? The book never revealed the source of the explosion so the reader never knew if it was the main character who caused it. So, don't go lighting any matches, okay?"

Terri smiled.

"I know you can't hear me, but just so you know I talk to all my patients whether they can or can't. By the way, you have one terrific son. If you're talking to him, could you put a good word in for me? I really am quite nice. I don't usually talk this much, but something just seems to be pushing the words out of my mouth tonight. I don't usually attack men in hospital bathrooms either. I'm not sure what came over me."

Terri looked around the room and whispered, "You know, between you and me, I could have done it with him right there in the bathroom. I was very turned on. It was all so...so spontaneous. Do you know what I mean?"

Peter listened while Terri talked. He smiled to himself.

"I know exactly what you mean Terri. Girls like you are why my son can't or won't settle down."

"Terri? You in there?" It was the same young intern as before. She smiled at Peter.

"Oh, oh, more spontaneity. That's a word, right? Well, what did you expect? I can't just sit around and wait for your son now can I? If he wants me, he'll have to come and get me."

Terri giggled.

She left Peter's room with a big smile and a warm greeting for her male caller. Peter wondered if she'd end up in a laundry room somewhere, rolling around in the towels.

It must be the late night hours that drive people. Oh well. Visiting hours are done; time to sleep. If that's what it is.

When he awoke, Peter could hear a group of men quietly muttering on one side of his room. He recognized Dr. Brandon and several technicians who had been at his bedside before. They spoke in low tones as they reviewed charts. A man in a suit shifted his stance to face him.

What the hell is he doing here?

"Hey Zalkow, you self serving prick, can you hear me?"

Nothing.

I know damn sure you're not here to help me.

Dr. Brandon dismissed his technicians. He appeared uncomfortable in Zalkow's presence.

Dr. Brandon held back, but then joined Zalkow at Peter's bedside.

"So, give me some odds, Jim. You've seen dozens of these. What is it, fifty-fifty? Seventy-thirty? Is he going to make it?"

A visible sweat appeared on Dr. Brandon's forehead. He wiped his hand across his brow.

Zalkow waited for an answer.

Peter felt his temperature start to rise as he listened.

"Listen, Joe, there's a lot more to this than meets the eye. I can't give you odds on a man's life. He could wake up any day. I have no way of saying."

"Perhaps not, but as lead physician you have the power to determine if hospital resources are justified for prolonging the life of a virtually dead man."

"You're out of line, Joe. You know that's a decision for the committee."

"Yes, but your recommendation will weigh heavily, and if our next board meeting goes as planned I'll be chairing that committee for the upcoming year. That could be very good for you, Jim…or not."

"What you're talking about is murder and I won't play a part in it. You can rot in hell before I support any decision to kill this man."

"No, what I am talking about is a practical approach to a simple problem. Our job here is to save thousands of people a year, not just one. Sometimes one has to go in order to save those thousands, Jim. You of all people should understand that."

"It's not that simple."

"Sure it is." Zalkow peered to the doorway then lowered his voice. "If he is going to die anyway, we would rather know sooner than later. There is no point dragging on the inevitable, squandering resources and giving his family false hope, when you and I both know his life is tenuous at best. It's morally wrong. Besides, let's just say I have a hunch that tells me his timely passing may assist nicely in funding this hospital, including your department and special research grants. The flip side could be that a month from now, you and all your brainy colleagues could be on the fucking breadline."

"What do you know?"

"Nothing in particular, but remember I went to school with Douglas and I know how he thinks. He's a very wealthy man and you can be damn sure that some of that wealth is heading this way. Now please, get onside before the board meeting, and we'll all get along just fine. Okay?"

"Fuck you, Joe."

Zalkow's eyebrows raised and, just as suddenly, his lips tightened and his eyes narrowed.

"No, Jim, sorry…but the only person doing the fucking around here is me and you know exactly what I mean don't you? You'll be onside, I guarantee it." Zalkow flashed a thin grin at Dr. Brandon, took a sideways look at Peter and left the room.

Dr. Brandon collapsed into the chair beside Peter's bed and hung his head in his hands. Dr. Brandon felt cornered. It was sickening to hear someone like Zalkow talk of morals when he showed none of his own. The "moral argument" was now in vogue for justifying any nasty business around the hospital.

How can you argue with a nebulous subject like morals?

Unfortunately, Zalkow now had the power to push his version of virtue down just about anyone's throat.

Peter was stunned by what he had just witnessed. He was overcome by a total sense of panic; a feeling of claustrophobia smothering him again. He began to scream out.

"NO, NO, let me out of here! Someone please help me!"

He struggled against invisible forces that held him constrained within his body. He writhed, feeling anxiety overwhelm him. His brain exploded in a burst of colors and light as though every nerve ending was shorting out at once. He felt a tremendous spinning sensation, his room became a blur.

Every sound hammered in his head.

His heart beat intensely.

His blood pressure rose and his body let loose a torrent of sweat.

Alarms started ringing on Peter's monitoring equipment, snapping Dr. Brandon from his daze. He slammed his hand against the wall, engaging an emergency intercom.

"Code 169 blue, Code 169 blue."

The technician in the monitoring room pulled his feet from the table when alarms from his computer sounded. Spikes of electrical activity spewed across his screen. Information flowed into the micro-processors.

Peter's blood-pressure readings continued to soar.

The ECG needles scraped a jagged landscape, making paper roll onto the floor.

Two nurses ran down the hall pushing a red emergency cart.

They were followed by two interns whose white coats flapped as they ran. Several attendants followed.

Peter could feel himself being torn apart by tremendous forces. He spun faster and faster. Again, events of his life whirled past him as he spiraled into a vicious vortex.

The cart came crashing into Peter's room.

Dr. Brandon placed his hand on Peter's wet forehead. He could feel that Peter's body temperature had dramatically increased. "Give me a temperature reading."

One of the interns quickly slipped an electronic rectal probe into Peter's body. The temperature reading was at one hundred and five degrees.

"We've got total electro-convulsion. Every nerve is firing," Dr. Brandon yelled at the team.

Seven people reacted together as Peter's body tightened and bounced in the air a full foot off his bed. His limbs jerked uncontrollably. Bloody froth poured from his mouth and ran down onto the sheets.

"Strap him down." Dr. Brandon shouted. "Get ice. I need ice, he's burning up."

Two attendants reluctantly grabbed limbs and attached the Velcro and canvas straps that hung from Peter's bed railings.

A gathering of people now stared through the window to watch these bizarre goings-on. Behind the crowd, holding a tiny camera high in the air, George leaned against the wall.

Peter's body continued to convulse uncontrollably, restrained only by loose straps. More attendants came crashing in with a second cart loaded with buckets of ice. Nurses pulled the vinyl bed liner high up on the railings and applied duct tape to create a mini swimming pool.

"Ice! Pour it all over him." Dr. Brandon worked frantically now. "We've got to get his temperature under control."

Ice and water flew everywhere as the buckets were emptied over Peter's body. The chill sent another shock wave through his system as he reacted to the frigid bath.

"Give me twenty cc's of Valium. I want to shut this guy down." A nurse emptied the syringe directly into the intravenous line. Dr. Brandon yelled to prepare a second injection.

Peter felt a lightning bolt of pain when the chemicals dispersed through his veins and raced toward his heart. He screamed as the pain deadened every other sensation.

Then, everything went black.

No sound.

No feeling.

Nothing.

All systems had stopped. Peter was in a silent limbo.

"He's down, he's down." Dr. Brandon was frantic.

"Temperature dropping, Doctor... No BP, no brain activity."

"Where the fuck did you go, Douglas? I'm not losing you. Give me the paddles. Charge to three hundred jewels. Give me epinephrine. Draw twenty cc's, direct shot to the heart on my order."

One nurse ripped open two shiny and sticky conductive pads and slapped them on Peter's chest. Another slipped a long, second needle through his chest wall until she felt the resistance of the heart muscle. She held her thumb on the syringe plunger and awaited Dr. Brandon's order.

"Charged at three hundred jewels, Doctor…"

"Okay nurse, five cc's now. CLEAR!"

With eyes closed, Dr. Brandon pressed the paddles to Peter's chest. He wasn't sure what would happen, but an explosion of flesh and blood was not out of the question. The defibrillator whined as it prepared to release its charge. Dr. Brandon squeezed the triggers. There was a momentary pause then the electricity penetrated Peter's body.

Dr. Brandon felt the room go into slow motion as Peter's body stiffened and pressed up forcefully against his downward pressure.

What happened next was the culmination of a series of unrelated yet connected events.

The mêlée around Douglas's bed had soaked everything in ice water. When the group stiffened in response to Peter's body bouncing off the bed, the technician holding the cart was pushed back, losing his balance. When he steadied himself, his hand accidentally hit the continuous re-charge switch on the defibrillation machine. The confusion masked any sounds that would indicate that the machine was recharging. Dr. Brandon's white lab coat was completely soaked. His sleeve had been pinned between the paddle and the conductive pad when the machine discharged, sending a bolt of electricity up through his arm and into his heart. Dr. Brandon reeled backward from the bed in response to the shock.

He had been knocked semi-conscious and the electrical shock had the effect of locking his grip on the handles, so when he fell back he held onto the paddles.

339

As he fell, the coiled wires of the defibrillator paddles stretched to their full extent. There was a pause, then the force of Dr. Brandon against the strength of the wires ripped them from their attachment. Dr. Brandon fell freely, paddles in hand, smashing his head against the wall below the glass window.

The stunned onlookers jumped back at the grotesque sequence or events they were witnessing.

The wires began to recoil forcefully. They sprang back toward their base on the machine and when they did, the two live ends twisted together in mid air like two snakes intertwining.

The people on the far side of the bed evaded the flying wires. In doing so, an attendant accidentally pushed the cart with the buckets to the side, spilling water on the defibrillator control and the immediate breech into the sensitive electronic equipment shorted out a safety circuit that would have neutralized the bare wires.

When the uncoiled rubber coated wires snapped back across the bed, they looped several times around the chrome railing and landed with a burst of sparks in the pool of ice water surrounding Peter. The pool became immediately electrified, sending an intense current through the full length of Peter's body.

The staff shrieked in response to the sparks, watching Peter convulse over and over with each contact of the wires with the water.

The onlookers were mortified to see a body strapped by all fours bouncing about, spraying everyone with water and sparks.

Peter's mouth continued to spew red foam.

The lights dimmed in the room and the hallways just prior to the explosion, when the defibrillator leapt off its cart in a flash of smoke and flames.

Screams from the spectators echoed through the hall.

The wail of the fire alarm started a chain reaction of events that would take days to report on, but within minutes an emergency crew was on site to stabilize the situation.

The blast was self-extinguishing and only minor injuries had been sustained by those present. Most were in shock and taken to a recovery room to rest, be examined and debriefed.

In the first few minutes of the commotion caused by the emergency crew no one noticed Dr. Brandon sitting against the wall, semi-conscious. As the room came into focus he pushed himself to his feet and leaned over Peter Douglas, who now lay in a pool of frigid water.

His nursing assistant of twelve years reached across the bed with a smoke-stained arm and placed her hand on his shoulder.

Dr. Brandon put the end pieces of his stethoscope into his ears, closed his eyes, and then pressed the fat silver drum against Peter's chest. When he opened his eyes they were blurry with tears.

The nurse saw his reaction and removed the ear pieces from him and placed them in hers.

She smiled when a steady heartbeat filled her head.

Catherine rounded the corner from the elevator and broke into a run when she saw a crowd gathered near her father's room. When she arrived at his door, Dr. Brandon was leaving with his nurse. He had gauze wrapped around his head, holding a pad over a cut in his skull. His coat was soaked. Blood stained his shoulders and back. Still stunned from the electrical shock, he didn't acknowledge Catherine immediately.

"Jim!"

He held her. "He's okay, Catherine, he's okay." Dr. Brandon pulled Catherine into a narrow hall leading to the other side of the wing and did his best to explain what had happened while he steadied himself against her and a wall.

"Let me get patched up and I'll be right back."

Catherine went to her father's room; she was shocked at the sight. Four orderlies had mopped up most of the water. Peter had been cleaned, changed and shifted to a portable gurney with fresh linen while his bed was being refitted. She moved quickly to his side and took his hand. It was ice cold.

"Daddy, what the hell is going on?" Catherine stroked her father's head and looked around at the mess. She spoke quietly. "Don't get any ideas. We need you here. You can't leave us. Or…maybe you want to leave us and get out of this predicament? It's so hard to see you like this yet I don't want to lose you. Is that selfish? I really don't have any control over it, but I am praying for you every day." She rubbed Peter's hand. He felt a bit of warmth returning.

"This is awful. I have to fly to Paris to finish up a job. But I won't be gone long. You had better be here when I get back, okay?"

She shook her father's hand in a business-like manner to seal their imaginary deal. She leaned down to kiss him and heard him speaking to her mind.

"I love you Catherine."

"I love you too."

On her way to the door she looked back, not knowing what to think about their exchange.

That was odd. I suppose I am only hearing what I want to hear.

Peter's body was still reeling from the effects of the catastrophe he had just been through, but he was thankful to still be present. It was a precious gift he had been given.

I have to stay calm. One more of those and I'm a goner.

Dr. Brandon was walking toward Catherine when she left Peter's room. He had a clean, dry lab coat on and the gauze wrapping on his head had been replaced by a single large Band-Aid. He drank from a cup of water, downing two or more pills.

"I hope you're not writing your own prescriptions, Doctor."

"I've now survived two incidents with your father. If I didn't know better, I'd say that man is trying to kill me or protect his daughter from me."

They exchanged smiles.

Two interns gave them a review of Peter's condition. Remarkably, he was no worse off than before his emergency.

"Jim, this is the second time we've almost lost him since he got here and you've saved him both times." She wrapped her arms around his neck. "Thank you," she whispered before giving him a light kiss on the cheek.

Several nurses at the main station had stopped their work to observe this little show of affection. Embarrassed, both turned to walk toward the lounge. "There goes my image."

"You mean there *grows* your image."

"Touché." He now felt that, because of the Douglas family, his life was about to get a whole lot more complicated.

"I'm leaving for Paris this afternoon. I wanted to come and say goodbye."

"Oh? Business or pleasure?"

Detecting an inquisitive tone, Catherine took his arm and responded gently. Like a hungry dog, he ate up the crumb of affection and listened carefully to her answer.

"I have to finish up the collections. My assistant has done most of my work, but there are just a few orders to sign and details to wrap up."

"Well, I'll do everything I can for your dad while you're gone. Catherine?"

She put her index finger in the air to indicate a pause.

"I'll see you when I'm back."

"Business or pleasure?"

She smiled.

Watching her walk away he could not help admiring her and marvel at how little it took from a woman to keep a man wanting.

– Chapter 50 –

"We've already had calls from eight of our top outlets reporting double-digit increases in sales this morning." Harvey Kirkland smiled while staring across his massive wooden desk at Zalkow. "This could be a gold mine if we play it right. We'll tickle them each day, then in a week or two we'll let loose with all the juicy stuff." Harvey leaned back in his overstuffed black vinyl chair and rested his head in a cracked and greasy spot that had worn in over many years. "After your next board meeting Joe, you may have even more gas for this fire that could create some serious consideration to terminating Douglas."

"Really? What do you mean?"

"Are you ready Joe? I have a source that told me his living will has a stipulation that requests termination."

"You shittin' me, Harvey?"

"Nope. It gets better. He's leaving a whack of money to the hospital. My source wouldn't say how much but I bet it's big."

"No shit?"

"No shit Joe. It's gonna cost us a bundle but I am gonna get a legit copy of the will."

"If that's the case, my sleazy little friend, I can share with you that I have a strong hunch that the lead physician on this case will support termination."

Zalkow winked at Harvey and grinned.

"Besides, if I have to, I can make a very good case around the moral issues of maintaining a hopeless life. You know…strain on the family, abuse of the system, re-allocation of resources, that sort of stuff. Not to mention the deal with the insurance company. I can't argue it, but everyone knows it could mean tens of thousands of dollars to other unfunded cases."

"Joe, you're the master. You never get hunches unless you've got a briefcase full of dirt. But couldn't the family just move him somewhere else and pay the tab privately?"

"They could, but what institution in Massachusetts is going to take this case after our prestigious trauma center has set the precedent? It would be all over the news. The Douglases would look pretty pitiful maintaining the man against his wishes for their own selfish reasons. Besides, who would want the liability with the Douglas Empire breathing down your neck every day? When I'm done with this, there will be plenty of expert opinions denying a positive prognosis. That will effectively deter anyone else."

Zalkow smiled at Harvey then cast his gaze out the full-length windows to an adjoining wing of the office tower. He walked to the glass now lit by the morning sun.

"At this point our hospital has care and control. His prognosis is negative; at least I have good reason to believe it will be presented that way. Now you tell me that Douglas himself has stipulated that he doesn't want to be kept on artificial life support and that the hospital may be in for a windfall?"

"I need a copy, Harvey."

"Yes sir, that's the plan."

"If it's true then you, my sleazy little journalist friend, are in for the news ride of your career."

"I'll take that as a compliment coming from you, Joe. If it wasn't so early, I'd offer you a drink to toast our good fortune. How does that saying go? 'One man's curse is another man's blessing?'"

Both men stood in the window, looking across at the adjoining glass tower, shaking hands and exchanging big smiles.

"If all else fails Harvey, I'll pull his fucking plug myself. I can't stand that bastard Douglas. He's blocked me at every turn in this incestuous town. Besides, if we lose this fucking court case I'm up to my nuts in we'll need every Dutch penny we can get our hands on."

Zalkow pulled open the ceiling-high door and strutted out of Harvey's office all puffed with pride over his mastery of these current circumstances.

He finally had one up on Peter Douglas. A *big* one! He always hoped in the end he'd get even with the rotten bastard.

Roxanne shuffled nervously in her seat while placing her purse on the floor. As discussed between herself, Carl Nathan and George she had pressed the button on a small device to signal that the meeting had ended. Her job with the City Star might be on the line but she liked her new employer, Carl Nathan, better.

Zalkow walked across the foyer and leered over her reception desk. She felt him staring down into her cleavage while he chirped a few suggestive words to her. Roxanne stalled him with flirtatious conversation. She knew that George was now in a full sprint toward her from a temporary office on the other side of the building complex that had been rented by Carl Nathan. It just happened to have a perfect view of Kirkland's boardroom.

Roxanne was quick and sensuous and that threw Zalkow off guard. He was confused, being so used to the brush off, and wondered momentarily if she actually had an interest in him.

He thought the better of it, turned and left confident he had just impressed another young woman with his wit and charm but that it would go no further.

Zalkow pressed the elevator button and waited. He looked back again at Roxanne who smiled politely. "Have a nice day Sir."

"It's off to a good start. A good start indeed."

Roxanne giggled and stared Zalkow straight in the eyes.

The elevator door bell rang diverting his attention. When it opened he was face to face with George. The younger man's face was flushed and wet. He breathed heavily, staring at Zalkow. With a big smile he stepped past him.

"Good morning, Dr. Zalkow."

Before it dawned on Zalkow that this stranger had just called him by name, the doors were closed and the elevator was dropping leaving Zalkow wondering about Roxanne and the young man.

That fat fellow probably recognized me from the television or newspaper, he told himself.

Once outside he stopped for a minute at a newsstand on the sidewalk. A warm flush of self-admiration rolled over him when he read that day's bold headline:

PETER DOUGLAS NEAR DEATH
EXCLUSIVE STORY!

Edward had stopped for a coffee and grabbed a paper while his taxi waited. He felt a hot pang of anger when he read the same headline. He did not recognize Zalkow standing beside him. Back in his taxi, slamming the door, he ordered his driver directly to the hospital. The driver wondered what had happened to the cheerful man who had gotten into his cab just ten minutes earlier.

"Bad milk in your coffee?"

Edward thumbed through the paper looking for details, oblivious to the driver's comment.

"Fly in your coffee there?"

"Pardon? Ah, sorry, no, I just got some bad news. Sorry, keep driving."

"From the news guy? Did the news guy give you some bad news?"

"Yes, sort of. It's personal, if you know what I mean."

They drove on in silence. Edward finished thumbing through the paper and quickly realized that there wasn't even a story to go with the headline.

"Those bastards at the City Star are at it again. Look at this." Edward strode into Peter's room holding up the paper for Peter to see, but then quickly lowered it realizing how out of line he was.

"Good morning Edward."

Peter could feel Edward's anxiousness and probed for details.

"Don't worry about those guys. They'll never change."

"I feel like an idiot. I come barging in here all worked up and then it dawns on me what I'm doing. I should be thankful for my good health and a wonderful day. Instead I'm wasting my energy on this crap. What was that saying of yours? 'You should choose your causes carefully?' I guess this is another time when my emotions got the better of me. It's just that I'm so concerned about you and your family and this…well, it just pisses me off Peter, and I don't mind saying so."

"I appreciate your concern. Remember though, when you get upset or angry you are giving a little piece of yourself away."

"I know, I know …I think I taught you that."

"Right so remember you only have so much to give, so try to give it where it counts. Believe me, I spent a life wasting energy on things that really didn't matter in the long game and now I'm paying for it. I've been able to visit my past and re-live incidents where I hurt other people without even knowing it. I did and said things that probably affected my family in a profound way. Each time I've gone back, I've been given an opportunity to avoid those mistakes. Nothing that would alter history or change the world, just little adjustments in my approach with people."

"How'd all that feel?"

"It is amazing, Ed, how a few words, said or not, can change someone's life. Given the chance to do it again, I'm choosing my causes

and my words carefully. Normally you only get one go around. Each moment in life comes and is gone forever. I see no more than ever it's important to make each one count. I had the chance to judge my own life when I thought I was dying. I can tell you I would have condemned myself to hell if there is one."

"What about God's choice for you?"

"If there is a God, I think he lives in all of us and all of us together create a collective soul comprising the spirit of the world. We have the power to judge what is right and wrong before we do it. I think we just stop doing that at a very young age, since it seems no one is looking or will find out. All that poor judgment added together equals the mess we find ourselves in today. It's like the one vote that wins the election. If everyone just did their part a little better, did it the way they know is right, the world could change in a day. Because when it comes down to it, someone is always watching and that someone is you. In the end you will hold yourself accountable for your actions."

Edward sat in silence absorbing this odd conversation.

He looked peaceful and calm.

He set the paper on the floor, stood beside his friend's bed, looking down at his gaunt face and closed eyes.

Edward took Peter's hand in his and nodded. He whispered, "Amen."

"Peter, I've always wanted to ask you about the time you made me drive you and that girl out into the country. Do you remember? We were at a frat party. We were all pretty drunk I know."

Edward let go of Peter's hand and sat down in the chair. "What happened that night, Peter?"

Peter caught Edward's thoughts. They were immediately riding in a car over forty years earlier. A big sedan rumbled along a dusty country road in the darkness. A small overhead light inside the car and two protruding head lamps provided the only illumination in the dark evening.

The radio was turned up loud. Edward drove. Peter sat in the back with Dorothy and sipped from a bottle of liquor. "Eddie, have a swig," Peter yelled over the music, jamming the bottle in Edward's face.

They had been drinking all night. Edward complied, coughing as the straight alcohol seared his throat. He passed it back to Peter, who promptly poured some into Dorothy's mouth. After she swallowed Peter wrapped his arms around her. He kissed her firmly on the lips. She smiled when they kissed. They fell over on their sides with the effects of the booze and the bumpy road impairing their balance.

Edward continued to drive. He could no longer see them in his rear-view mirror.

Peter kissed her passionately. Her response was to pull him further on top of her. She could feel his bulge even through the many layers of her evening dress. Peter pulled her shoulder-strap down far enough to expose the top of her breast, firmly held in place by a lace brassière. He kissed her neck and shoulders and massaged her breasts over the smooth material.

Edward was still feeling the effects of a girl who had necked and petted with him for over an hour before running off like a scared puppy, leaving him with a pair of aching testicles. The sounds from the back seat aroused him again. His mind fantasized what must be happening. His penis bulged in his trousers, making him shift uncomfortably and adjust himself several times. He felt ready to explode at the slightest provocation. The grunts and groans and giggles from the back seat kept his mind busy. His inner head was being twisted with sexual desire. He envisioned himself with the more-than-willing Dorothy after Peter was through with her.

Peter had worked his hand under the complicated layers of Dorothy's dress and found her warm, wet spot which he massaged generously. She had soaked her undergarments and the slippery flesh aroused Peter further. Dorothy had both her hands between Peter's legs, pulling furiously at him stroking him up and down. Fortunately the friction of his underwear against his hard penis was just painful enough that it distracted him from coming in his pants. Peter lightened his touch on Dorothy, hoping he hadn't imposed the same kind of discomfort.

The car jolted to a halt when Edward stopped and turned off the engine. He couldn't stand listening to the scene behind him.

Peter halted his dry humping long enough to pop his head up and make eye contact with Edward. He grinned drunkenly.

The music blared on the radio. Edward looked over the seat to get a first-hand view of what was happening. The top of Dorothy's dress and her brassiere were pulled down far enough that both her breasts were pushed out, exaggerating her cleavage and stretching her nipples which crowned the generous mounds. She had hickeys all over her neck and her face was flushed. Her dress was reefed up around her waist, Peter's arm apparently trapped in its silky pink mystery. Dorothy continued to rub Peter with both hands. She looked at Edward through inebriated eyes and leered at him.

"You're next, Eddie."

Edward felt a contraction in his groin. He bolted from the car, slamming its door and ran toward the nearest tree, unzipping as he ran. He squeezed himself firmly to hold back the inevitable gush of fluid. He made it to the big oak before several bursts of creamy hot semen squeezed past his grip and arced against the base of the tree. Feeling the pressure release he gave several deep groans.

Many seconds passed. His head swam with the unique dizziness that only an orgasm can cause, no matter how it occurs.

His mind refocused and his sensibility returned. He looked back over his shoulder. The car rocked to the music carried on the still air.

Edward pushed himself upright and tidied his trousers. He limped awkwardly to the next tree where he wilted at its base and lit a cigarette. He coughed when he inhaled and turned his head to the right in mock conversation.

"Do you always smoke after sex?"

A muffled scream emanated from the car.

Peter had managed to get Dorothy's dress unzipped and off. He had pulled her undergarments to her ankles where they were blocked by her high heeled shoes, now pressed against the roof of the car. The pointy heels had dug holes in the cushy fabric of the borrowed auto.

Peter didn't care.

He slipped several fingers inside her, making her gasp. At first she clamped her legs around his hand, stopping his movement. She gradually explored Peter's dampened hand with her own then relaxed her grip, allowing his fingers to bury themselves and reappear.

Peter worked with his other hand to get his pants undone. He was oblivious to the fact that his head was jammed against the roof of the car since his lust now ruled all decision-making. He pulled his hand from between Dorothy's legs and started to lean toward her, targeting his entry. With his other hand he directed his penetration, leaning in he pressed her legs back over her head.

Her heels tore long gashes in the roof fabric.

Dorothy screamed out, "No, stop Peter, stop!"

Edward started at the sound of her scream, but dared not interrupt.

Peter knew what he's doing and Dorothy was more than willing.

Peter's hand over Dorothy's mouth muffled her words. Now her grunts couldn't be interpreted for resistance. He felt her body contract when he plunged inside. He pumped furiously, causing the pressure to ejaculate peak. Dorothy could feel his pulsing and yelled out against his hand. Her muffled cries mixed with the music.

Peter started to release, but the sound of exploding glass shattered his concentration when a softball sized rock smashed through the windshield and landed on the front seat.

Peter sprang upright, slamming his head into the roof. His penis ripped violently out of Dorothy, discharging in a flurry of white pulses.

Dorothy shrieked aloud now that Peter's hand was removed from her mouth.

Edward ran toward the car to inspect the damage.

His pulse raced when he caught a full view of Dorothy, heels still dug into the material of the roof.

There was Peter kneeling, bare-assed and semi-erect.

"What the fuck was that?" Peter yelled.

Edward threw his jacket over the glass on the seat and started the car. "I don't know Sunshine, but I ain't hanging around to find out."

He floored the gas pedal, spinning the car around in a cloud of dust. He steered the car in the direction from which they had come. Peter and Dorothy bounced around in the back seat while they tried to get their disheveled appearance in order.

Peter apologized every time they found another wet spot. By the time they were moving along the smooth blacktop, they all agreed on a theory that some farm kids had probably hid in the bushes and thrown the rock to scare them.

Peter took another long swig from the bottle. He sat with one arm wrapped around Dorothy's shoulder. He let his hand slip down onto her breast. "Cut that out," she snapped, pushing it away. She and Edward declined a drink.

The three rode home together in shared silence.

Peter and Edward emerged from the bushes and Peter shook Edward's hand.

"Nice throw. And just in time. We were a couple of assholes, weren't we?" asked Peter.

"We?"

They smiled at each other and shook their heads disdainfully while they watched the tail lights disappear on the dark horizon. They just saved Dorothy and Peter an unwanted pregnancy, an illegal abortion and a reputation Dorothy would never live down.

Suddenly, the experience was over. Edward looked at Peter with bewilderment. Without thinking, he spoke to Peter without using his mouth.

"Am I crazy or did you and I just visit the past again?"

"Both! But then you've always been crazy and yes, that's what I have been doing since I got here. I've had the chance to mend some fences, so to speak. This is the first time that another person was with me. I'm not sure how we did that, but I'm sure glad we did. I wonder where Dorothy is today"

"Peter, this is getting weirder by the day. You're reading my mind again. I'm going to talk with my mouth. I talk, you answer. Okay?"

"Okay."

"The problem is there is no way to convince anyone about what is happening. If I tried to tell them about this, they'd lock me up and throw away the key."

"Edward, there's a hospital board meeting coming up. Joe Zalkow is likely to get elected to the chair of the committee that makes decisions about people in my condition."

"What type of decisions?"

There was silence.

"Oh, shit, not that type of decision?"

"I'm afraid so. To further complicate matters, you know I have a Living Will, requesting that if I end up this way no artificial life support is to be used to keep me alive. If there's no reasonable prospect for

recovery I've already signed my own death warrant. How could I have expected this? I've never been more alive, and yet to the world I'm dead as a cantaloupe. Even those idiots with their monitoring equipment can't seem to figure out that I'm a fucking audience to their antics!"

"How did Joe Zalkow get involved in this? You've had a dislike for that guy for as long as I've known you."

"I tried to like him back in school but he always had a chip. The first time I met him he was throwing a bun at you in the cafeteria."

"No."

"Yes. Then years later when I didn't hire him, well that was the end. You know Edward, it's funny, I know he's a caring dad and looks to be a good husband. He's with his wife and daughter all the time at outings. But when he leaves home something triggers his other side. Strangest thing. He's an astute politician, Ed. Watch out for him."

"Uncle Edward, are you having a good visit?" Brian had entered silently, startling Edward.

"I was just having a chat with your father. I mean, I was just wishing I could have a chat with him."

"I know what you mean. It's eerie Edward, but sometimes in here I could swear he's more alive than he ever was. It's like he can hear and see everything that's going on. I know that's pretty strange. I'm probably just hearing what I want to hear."

Edward wondered for a minute if what Brian was saying was true. Was it possible that everything that he was hearing was all in his head while he tried to somehow bring his best friend back to life?

"Don't worry Edward, I'm in here."

"Edward? Are you okay?"

"Sure, Brian. I'm fine. I know exactly what you mean. It's like we could stand here and talk to him now and he'd hear and understand. Wouldn't that be something…if all the time we think he's not with us, he really he is?"

"But they say there's no brain activity. So I guess for now we have to believe them."

Both men turned sharply when the toilet in the open bathroom flushed. Several articles on the bureau began to vibrate without cause and the curtains against the far wall swayed like they were being blown by a stiff breeze.

Brian looked wide-eyed at Edward, then turned his attention to his father. He stared in silence.

"This place gives me the willies, Edward. I always feel weird when I'm in here."

"I know what you mean, son. I know what you mean. Let's hope that your father wakes up soon so we can all get out of here".

Brian held up his copy of the Star. "Did you see this?"

Edward responded by picking his copy up from the floor.

"I've got more bad news. I met with dad's lawyers. They won't budge on his will. He has that clause. They say it's valid and they are planning to inform the hospital board before their meeting. Edward, he wants us to pull the fucking plug. There's no way I'll do that. I've arranged a hearing next week. Perhaps I can at least get a deferral."

"That was quick."

"Yeah, it's amazing how high people jump for this guy." Brian pointed a finger at his dad. "Now I guess I've got to attempt to get an injunction against the Star from publishing this kind of crap. Knowing them, they'll probably just do it anyway and take the heat later. These slimy bastards have no respect for anyone."

Edward put his arm around Brian's shoulder. "Your father would be proud of you. I think you are doing exactly what he would want you to do."

"You do? How do you know that?"

"I've know your dad for a long time. He always had a tremendous will to live and I'm sure if there was a sliver of hope for him he would want to be around to find out."

"Edward, you've always been a great friend to the family and I appreciate it. I may have to call on you to testify in that spirit on my father's behalf."

"I'll be there." Edward patted Brian on the back, wondering if Peter could see them or if he was off on another journey somewhere.

Brian and Edward walked down the hall bumping into Sarah who came briskly around the corner. She looked radiant. Her fair hair was pulled back into a ponytail that stuck through the back of her black baseball cap. She wore tailored, faded jeans, a white shirt and a black leather bomber jacket, looking markedly more conservative than she had since she first arrived.

She beamed at them. "Hi guys, how's Father today?"

"You mean Peter?" Brian asked. Edward nudged him. He liked what he saw. Brian didn't relent. "Aren't you the happy girl? Your schoolwork must be going very well."

Sarah colored slightly, but didn't snap back. "It's amazing what getting out of that prison for nuns will do for a girl's spirit."

Edward could no longer resist. "Speaking of spirits, how's that fellow Michael doing?"

Sarah's face went a full crimson. "What makes you think I'd know? As a matter of fact, he's fine, thank you very much. Probably the nicest person I've ever met in my life. He's smart, funny and he's a gentleman."

Brian and Edward stared past Sarah listening to her while she elaborated. "He's good looking. He's down to earth. He's a bit old and all that but I actually think he likes me. I am pretty likable, aren't I Uncle?"

Brian cleared his throat, nodded and looked past Sarah with a grin on his face.

Michael was standing behind her. His face was lit up with an enormous grin. He extended his hand outward and held his thumb and forefinger about an inch apart.

"About this much."

Sarah shrieked and punched him on the shoulder with her closed fist. "Oh my God, I'm so embarrassed. Don't ever do that again!"

The three men chuckled.

Sarah bolted to her father's room.

"It's your favorite daughter again. I am still your favorite, aren't I?"

Peter beamed inside when his beautiful baby girl came into his room. She looked luminous. She reminded him of Marion when he first met her. She kissed his forehead and he could feel the warmth of her lips linger on his skin.

She settled into the chair and began to talk.

Michael sat with Edward and Brian in the lounge. "I had a chance to speak with your mother this morning."

"Really? How was it?"

"Actually it was fine. She and I hit it off quite well. She really has had an incredible life. Did you know she miscarried a child before you?"

"What? I didn't know that!" Brian was shocked. He looked at Edward for support, but Edward shrugged.

"Marion wanted to tell all of you at one time or another over the years but she said there never seemed to be enough time or the right time. She told me that since that loss she pledged if she had healthy children, she would dedicate her life to them. It appears that's exactly what she did. That is why she was so shaken when she and your father split up. She gave her whole life to her family and felt she had failed somehow. She asked me to help let that bit of news out and felt you should know first, seeing that you are the eldest."

"Only second eldest in spirit I guess. Wow, that sure explains a lot of things. I couldn't imagine losing a child then losing your husband. Now she has to face his death." Brian went silent letting this news sank in.

"Your mother feels this is actually forcing her to address many issues in her life that she has just bottled up over the years. She is grieving but she also feels some freedom allowing her to put some closure on family issues that have weighed her down. She is very proud of all of her children and now she feels that she can start her own life. I told her that the best day to start is today. It's never too late to start living your life."

Brian heard those words. Had he been withholding in his life too, while he lived in his father's shadow?

"Some of us didn't have the "burden" of family and had no choice but to start our lives early."

"Burden, Edward? What do you mean?"

Edward put his hand on Brian's shoulder and smiled.

"Oh, I get it. We're lucky, right?"

"You have a great family Brian, and a tremendous opportunity to share in each other's lives. This crisis can work to bring all of you closer together if you let it. Or…"

Edward broke in. "No 'or.' Let's make that happen, Brian. You and I, with Michael's help, I think we can accomplish plenty."

Brian nodded. With everything that was happening he could certainly see opportunity for dissension in the family, but now he could see the healing and the closeness that could arise if everyone tried. He would be first. After all, he was the eldest, in age at least.

Edward looked at Michael, "Son you've already been able to touch people…this family included… in a positive way. The challenge of living in a positive, giving and loving way seems like work sometimes but it pays off in all ways possible as I am certain you know. Now on a lighter note, you seemed to have had quite an impact on Sarah…"

Michael straightened, "Brian, about your sister …"

"Daddy, I know you'll say I'm too young, but I think I'm in love. You remember Michael, don't you? I can't believe how I feel about him after such a short time. It's like we were meant to be together. I've never met anyone like him and I think he feels the same way about me. You have to live. You have to wake up so you can meet him. What if I get married one day and you're not there? It can't be that way. You have to give me away, remember?" Sarah's voice cracked.

Peter wished he could reach out and hold her and tell her that everything was okay. He tried to feel her mind but could not make a connection. He focused on sending positive energy and love, hoping it would reach her.

Peter was quickly reunited with reality by Sarah. "Did you have sex with mother before you married her?"

Out of the mouths of babes.

Peter was trying to keep up with his daughter's shifting moods and thoughts.

I'm in a coma and I'm still dealing with close encounters of the hormonal kind!

"Like I told you before, I haven't exactly been an angel in the past. I'd like to do things right this time."

Peter cringed at these words. He'd already heard enough and hoped no more information was forthcoming.

"Sarah?"

Sarah feigned an angry look at Michael and then broke into a smile.

"How are you doing?"

"I would say better now that I've seen you, but I wouldn't want to stroke your ego too hard."

Michael sat down on the padded arm of Sarah's chair.

"He looks so sad and empty, Michael. I'm afraid of what's going to happen."

"Are you afraid for him or for yourself, Sarah?"

"I don't know. I'm just afraid."

Michael put his arm around her shoulder. They sat in silence for a few minutes while Peter watched them.

Michael and Sarah caught up with Edward and Brian and joined them on the elevator just as the door was closing.

"Michael, I'm sure we'll be having another family dinner soon. I hope you can join us."

Michael stared stoically at the flashing numbers above the elevator door. "Thank you Brian. I'd love to, provided that your sister doesn't mind."

Sarah bumped Michael into the corner with her hip, making the four passengers break the tension with laughter.

The elevator door opened and the occupants stood face to face with Marion.

"Mother," Brian said.

"Marion."

"Mrs. Douglas," Michael added.

"Hi mom," Sarah added.

They all looked at each other awkwardly, none moved waiting for someone to speak. When one spoke, so did the others. They paused to look at each other before breaking into full laughter. The elevator door had begun to close in Marion's face, trapping the group on board, before Edward reached out and held it open.

"Thank you Edward. It's nice to see that there is one gentleman present…in three."

The group stepped out of the elevator. Edward held the door open. "Marion, is that a compliment?"

Marion smiled sarcastically. "Don't press your luck so early in the day. How's father doing Brian?"

"About the same. We've all been in to see him and there is no evident change." Brian put his arm around his mother and kissed her cheek. "I'm sure he'll be happy to see you, though. Maybe he'll wake up when you walk in his room."

Marion smiled, said nothing, and boarded the elevator.

"Mother, how about another family dinner soon?" Sarah asked.

Marion scanned the group but elevator door slid shut before she could answer.

"Was that a yes or a no?" Michael asked.

Brian laughed. Edward put his arm around Michael. "Son, you and I need to have a long talk. I've been around these folks for decades and there are some things you ought to know. Although you certainly seemed to get a warm response."

Sarah rushed in and grabbed Michael from Edward, who smiled and gave mock resistance when she pulled him away and walked down the hall.

Sarah looked back. "Uncle Edward, if you keep it up you'll scare this guy off."

"Good point. Carry on Michael; you are doing me a big favor. Good riddance, young lady."

Sarah flicked her tongue out in fake disrespect. Observing the scene, Brian enjoyed a short reprieve from the problems he had to deal with.

"I like him," Edward offered when he returned to Brian's side.

"Me too," added Brian with a smile.

There goes my little sister. I think she's aged five years since she got here.

Marion waited outside Peter's room while the medical staff huddled over her ex-husband. Dr. Brandon was surrounded by several interns and nurses while he reviewed Mr. Douglas's case with them. Marion watched him do his work without his notic- ing. She admired his looks and confident manner and remembered her years when she could attract men like him. Now the best she could do was leverage her position to gain access. She could still get close enough to flirt with men like Dr. Brandon, hoping that she might catch an odd compliment or suggestive gaze. It didn't matter so much now that she was setting to build a new life independent of someone else. Although it still felt nice to be noticed and she wasn't about to give up that.

The sight of her husband's comatose body stirred memories of life gone by. She wondered if she'd ever see him alive again and was surprised by her lack of concern one way or the other. She loved Peter, but it was the love between adults whose lives had once been shared but no longer held a connection. Recognition of mortality had been resisted and finally accepted by her and her peers.

Youthful vigor and looks had faded, giving way to the appearance of maturity and contentment. Marion harbored simmering disdain for the fact that her husband had left her. She resisted though, feeling that his circumstance was somehow justified. It could have just as easily been herself or anyone else she knew.

She brightened when Dr. Brandon looked up and caught her gaze. He flashed a warm smile and held up five fingers, then motioned her to meet him in the lounge. Marion's heart picked up several beats as she returned his smile and nodded back. It was very rare that she spent time in lone proximity with Dr. Brandon. Usually their encounters were in very public places.

Perhaps, old girl, he has some interest after all.

This new life wasn't going to be easy. Old habits die hard. Marion quickly found a ladies room. Its fluorescent lights exacerbated all of her flaws when she looked with some disappointment in the mirror. She emptied her purse on the counter and did the best makeover she could, given the time and tools available. She then applied a heavy dose of her favorite perfume.

She smiled at the security guard who sat outside the lounge. When the door closed behind her she failed to connect his two quick sneezes to anything remotely related to her. She turned off the overhead lights and let two table lamps cast a light that would give her the best possible showing. She placed her purse on one chair, threw some magazines on the other two and positioned herself at the far end of the long sofa. She practiced a quick greeting and seating suggestion, hoping to get him to at least sit on the couch with her.

The door opened, catching her off guard while she concluded her second dress rehearsal. Dr. Brandon flicked on the overhead lights and made a final note on his clipboard. His nostrils stung from the pungent perfume, but he contained himself.

"Hello, Marion." He extended his hand a full arm's length to avoid having to kiss her and moved the magazines before taking a seat across from the sofa.

Marion's spirits went flat.

"Marion, I have two topics I wish to discuss with you, and there really is never a good time to talk about either. One is your husband. The other is your daughter."

"What is it? Is it Sarah? What's wrong with my baby?"

"No, no Marion, it has nothing to do with Sarah. It's about Catherine."

"Catherine?"

"Yes, about Catherine and..."

"What, what is it?"

"It's about Catherine and...and me. It's about Catherine and me, Marion."

Marion rose abruptly and with a quick step forward smacked him firmly across the face. "You bastard. How dare you take advantage of my daughter at a time like this? Have you no morals? I should report you and have you fired."

Marion turned and stared at the wall. She was shaking. She knew now that there was nothing between herself and this man except her imagination. Her greatest disappointment lay within herself, not with him. She couldn't bring herself to accept this without some reservation. Her commitment to an independent life firmed dramatically. Another old habit died.

"Marion, this isn't a moral issue. This is a human issue. Besides, nothing has happened between us. I just wanted to explain in case you heard; we had a social dinner together, that's all. Normally I wouldn't spend time with a family member. It's just that I have known you for…"

Marion waved her hand like she was wafting smoke out of her presence. She'd heard enough.

"It's okay…it's okay." Marion turned to face him, dabbing her eyes with her handkerchief. "I'm sorry, you're both adults, I'm just a bit on edge these days with everything."

"Honestly Marion…"

Another hand wave.

"Marion, I've always had the utmost respect and admiration for you." Dr. Brandon rose.

"Then let's stop there, shall we?" Marion responded. She leaned in to give him a full embrace, which he gingerly returned before stepping back a respectful distance.

"Now we must talk about your husband."

"My ex-husband."

"Yes, well, Peter then. Please, let's sit back down." Dr. Brandon joined Marion on the couch this time, relieved to have the first topic off his chest. Should he tell her about Zalkow? No.

"We've been unable to detect any signs of brain activity in Peter even though we are using the most sophisticated equipment available. We are keeping his body stimulated and fed, but with each day that goes by the likelihood of his waking up gets substantially lower. In my opinion we are already below a fifty-fifty chance."

"But you said just the other day that you felt quite good about his prospects. Why has your position changed so quickly?"

Dr. Brandon had to move the conversation beyond that point quickly if he wanted to get at least one person onside with the notion that Peter's termination was inevitable, if not imminent.

"Marion, Peter is getting the best possible care, I assure you, but at some point this turns from humane to inhumane. This is also about respect for Peter and his dignity. He was a proud man. I'm sure that's how he wants to be remembered, not like some dribbling invalid who has to have his diapers changed every four hours."

Marion looked at him inquisitively.

She tried to determine whether this was a real change of attitude or something she was imagining. "Yes, he was a proud man. I have to agree with you. Even when he was sick with the flu he would insist on bathing and dressing daily in case someone dropped by. He was so independent. That's what I admired most about him when we first met. That and his good looks of course. He was the best-looking man at school and he was all mine," Marion bragged.

"And a lucky man he was, Marion," Dr. Brandon said. "He's still lucky to have a family who loves him and cares for him. I know you all want to do the right thing." Dr. Brandon stood up and shook Marion's hand. He turned off the overhead light and looked back at her. In the dimmer light he could catch a glimpse of her former beauty. He could see Catherine in her face.

"Thank you, Marion. If there is anything, anything at all, please call me."

Marion was silent.

Dr. Brandon left the room. The door closed.

He felt like he was walking a bit lighter, with a huge weight having been raised from his shoulders. His mind was processing all the new information.

Perhaps there is some potential with Catherine. For Peter Douglas though, this is going to get worse before it gets better. Maybe it isn't the hospital's duty to prolong death. Besides, Douglas's money would help hundreds of others, and he would be proud of that. His family would get on with their lives...Dr. Brandon stopped at Peter's window and placed his hand against the glass.

"God forgive me."

Marion collected her thoughts before leaving the lounge. On her way down the hall she took time to glimpse into the other rooms she passed by. Each one housed a person in need of care and love, each with their own story to tell. They were each as important to someone as Peter was to her. She peered through Peter's window for a while before entering his room.

"Hello Peter." She took his hand in hers, held it, then caressed his forehead.

"It seems that your time here may be more limited than we'd hoped. Or maybe you've been gone since the beginning and we are all just too foolish or selfish to let you go. It's funny how much more one appreciates something or someone in their absence. You know, I can't think of a single thing about you that I didn't adore and I can't recall any time spent with you that I wasn't completely in love with you. Isn't the mind a wonderful thing? The way it holds onto the good and discards the bad? It's good to remember that. I'm sure that thought will help me through many difficult situations in my future."

Peter watched Marion while she spoke. He didn't try to connect with her for fear that he would capture her and fly off again the way he had with Edward.

That would be a disaster. Marion would not be able to handle such an experience.

"Peter, I want you to know that I still love you, and what I am about to tell you doesn't change that. I also want to remind you that it was you who left me and not the other way around. Peter, Carl is a wonderful man and I know you think so too. He will take good care of me and you know that he loves our children. He has lots of money of his own. I know money isn't an issue the way it might be with some stranger. Peter, Carl has asked me to be his wife and I've accepted. We're not planning to tell anyone until after… until later. We made beautiful love last night, Peter. Remember when we used to do that? It was the first time since you left me. It was wonderful."

Peter felt his insides churn while he listened to his ex-wife speak to him about one of his best friends. His first instinct was to be angry or hurt; he overcame it. He also worried that a fit of emotion could have grave medical consequences the way it had before. He knew that if he had any hope of overcoming his circumstances he would need all of his remaining faculties.

"I'm glad I've told you. I have no idea why, but it does feel good to confront you, even in this condition. Maybe that was my problem before. I was always afraid to tell you what was on my mind. Peter, it would have been so much simpler if life between us had worked out. Who knows where we'd be now? I doubt that you'd be lying here and I certainly wouldn't be in love with one of your best friends."

Marion drifted for a few moments. "Life is funny, isn't it? I guess we end up where we are as a result of our own actions and no one else's. In a sense, we are nowhere we didn't plan to be with every decision we made or failed to make. We truly are masters of our own destiny."

The speaker behind Peter's bed crackled to life. "Mrs. Douglas? Are you there?"

Startled at the sound of her name, Marion hesitated, trying to determine the source of the voice. She looked at the tiny speaker.

"Mrs. Douglas, this is the nursing station. Are you there?"

"Yes. Yes, this is Mrs. Douglas."

"This is the head nurse, Mrs. Douglas. I'm sorry to disturb you, but there's an emergency long-distance call for you. Are you able to take it?"

Who could be calling?

"Yes, of course. Can you transfer it here?"

"Right away."

A stream of rapid broken English came hurling down the telephone line from Emily's housekeeper in Florida, speaking hysterically about Marion's mother.

"Juanita, JUANITA," Marion cried. "Be calm. Please be calm. Speak slowly. I c a n n o t u n d e r s t a n d y o u."

Marion could hear crying on the other end of the telephone. Juanita stopped talking and took several, sobbing, breaths.

"That's good. Now speak slowly."

"Yes, Miss Douglas, Miss Ssemily, she drinking last few day berry sad missingg her daughter. She get big head that no go way then fall sleep on floor. I call dee 911 right away and they come take her to hospital dis morning. They say she stroke. I try all time to call you, but I confuse and scared, Miss Douglas. What I to do?"

Peter watched, seeing Marion's eyes get very glossy and tears roll down her face. In a quiet voice she spoke slowly to Juanita.

"Juanita, you did the right thing. I will come to Florida right away and see you and mother. Please go to the hospital and stay with her. Tell her that I am coming today."

Marion listened for a few seconds.

"Thank you Juanita. I know, it's not your fault. No, thank you, I will see you very soon."

Juanita wouldn't stop talking and finally Marion placed the telephone on the cradle. She looked at Peter and put her hand to her face.

The instant Peter connected with her thoughts he was whisked away to the day of their wedding. He stood at the front of the church, looking around to see all of his friends. He could see the beaming face of Marion's mother. Everyone looked so young and happy in anticipation of their wedding.

The groom's mind, as usual, was elsewhere. Like so many times in his life he had already anticipated and responded emotionally in advance to this day. He was already thinking about his next business deal and just wanted to get the formality concluded.

One of his great strengths was the ability to see the direction various events might take him and plan well ahead for any contingencies. This strength, however, robbed him of the momentary joy of being present, of feeling and participating in a real way in each moment in life.

When he stood now and looked around the church, he felt a new appreciation for its interior. He admired the huge bouquets of gladioli on the altar and the decorations on the pews. He absorbed the faces of the guests who were all there to share the occasion with him and Marion. He remembered how he met Marion and concentrated on how much he really did love her.

He felt happiness.

He felt present.

Once again he became the groom and released thoughts of the future to focus on being married to Marion. He made eye contact with one of his best friends. Carl looked back at him and tapped the face of his watch and smiled. It reminded Peter that he had once again created a circumstance that would deplete his ability to be present.

He and Carl had been working on one of their first deals together. He had been attempting to arrange a meeting with several future partners. Carl was to give Peter that signal if the meeting was confirmed. If it was, Peter had promised he would cut his honeymoon short and focus on the deal. This was typical behavior at that time, when Peter continually disappointed friends and associates with what was commonly referred to as his "alternate agenda." Peter already knew the outcome of the day. Their wedding would soon be over. The reception would go the way it was expected. Driving away from the reception hall, Peter would break the news to Marion that something had come up that would force him to shorten their honeymoon.

Marion would commence her new life of stoicism. She would accept Peter's decision and take the short end of the stick. Stains on her dress from the tears that quietly streamed down her face would mark her wedding day.

"After all," he would say, "I'm doing this for our future, Marion." It would be the first in a lifetime of well-worn excuses for not being there.

The wedding march commenced and the rear doors to the church swung open, Peter left the altar and walked over to Carl. The church buzzed with people craning to see what was happening and speculated amongst themselves. Peter leaned down and whispered, then returned to the altar to watch his beautiful bride start her walk down the aisle on her father's arm.

Peter relived that whole day with new appreciation.

People seemed more sincere. The speeches meant more to him. The food and wine tasted better than he ever remembered. His love for Marion seemed boundless. The reception was in full swing when the master of ceremonies informed the crowd that the car was waiting. The newly-weds would be leaving. Marion appeared in a beautiful new departure outfit. Peter had traded his tuxedo for a casual suit and tie.

Driving away in a hail of rice and cheers, Peter looked across at his beaming bride; he was about to disclose the shortening of their honeymoon.

"Marion?"

She looked at him with crystal eyes.

"You know that I've been working on something big with Carl, don't you?"

"Yes."

"Well, some very important people are in town. They want to meet with me right away to conclude a deal."

Marion went silent. She had many of their plans canceled in the past and knew the tone.

"I've spoken to Carl and asked him if he could handle it, seeing as you are the most important person in town in my opinion. I've also told him that I might take an extra week on my honeymoon…if you think you can tolerate me that long, of course."

Marion squealed and lunged across the seat to hug her husband. "And I thought you were trying to cancel on me. I'm sorry for thinking that and, yes, I can tolerate you forever, my love. You know that."

Marion kissed Peter while he drove. He could smell her perfume and taste her mouth like never before. He felt a rush of excitement and knew that THIS would be an excellent honeymoon.

"Well." Marion stood, wiping her face, oblivious to any change. She had been speaking to Peter about her mother continually. The effects of Peter's wedding-day change would wait poised inside, until one day she would recall what a wonderful honeymoon they had. Carl was capable and concluded the deal in Peter's absence, eliminating any potential changes in history resulting from Peter's tampering with former events.

"I'd better pack a few things and leave for Florida. Perhaps I can get Mother brought up here so I can keep an eye on both of you." Marion's face was reddened from crying. She took Peter's hand.

"I just had the strangest thought while I was standing here. It was like time had stood still forever and we were just married. It's a wonderful thought, isn't it? My love, I hope to see you again soon."

Marion left his room.

Peter smiled.

I need to live.

- Chapter 51 -

A white dusting of snow had covered the city. Peter's celestial travels and learning continued. Time ticked by. This day had been the quietest yet since his admission to the hospital. Conversations about snarled traffic and frozen toes preoccupied the staff while they worked in and out of his room, often speaking to him like he had some control over the weather.

He was amazed how quickly his celebrity status had worn off, now that hospital staff had adjusted to his presence and to his case.

Dr. Brandon now just came and went with his interns.

Peter detected a definite change of tone when he discussed the case with them. He made numerous references to the fact that, even though all the best technology was being used and the best minds were being consulted, "This patient," as he now referred to him, did not show signs of progress. Prognosis for recovery was not good. It was like he had begun a quiet lobbying campaign to see Peter's life ended. He seemed to be laying the groundwork to gain grass-roots support for termination. After all, everyone would be surprised if a patient, who had good prospects for recovery according to the lead Doctor on the case, was suddenly terminated.

Peter was shocked at this new callous attitude.

Zalkow was the name that kept popping into his head.

He knew that Dr. Brandon was definitely not in Zalkow's camp.

Was he being forced somehow into this position?

The day slipped by.

Peter anxiously awaited Mrs. Rossi's arrival and immediately started questioning her about what she might know of the plans regarding his case. She listened carefully and spoke slowly.

"You ask me questions I know nothing about. I told you, I feel you are here for reason. Nothing mortal will keep you from that purpose, whatever it is. Peter, you must understand that everything happening like it should. It will lead you to where you are to be...capisca?"

"Capito...I guess."

"Peter of this, I am certain. Of anything else, I know nothing. People talk in halls 'bout you and big meetings, but none of this talk means anything. Only actions count. Have you been traveling?"

"Yes."

"What have you learned?"

"That I am...that I was...a son of a bitch with no care for anyone but myself."

"And...you have done what about that?"

"I wouldn't exactly call it traveling. It is not like I choose the destination. It's more like I'm catapulted into a situation and I usually have only a couple minutes to figure it out. Each time I've been given an opportunity to make a small correction that I feel had a big impact on a relationship."

"You are doing what you are supposed to do. You have no control over the plan. You must participate not anticipate. That is your role. You were taker all your life, and now you have been granted chance to be giver. Embrace that chance ... and you will be embraced."

"Mrs. Rossi, do you know my future? Will you tell me?"

"Your future is like my future, Peter. It is there for us, waiting for us to arrive at proper time and no sooner. Your desire to know before or get there sooner than is planned will only hurt your progress while you live here each day."

"I think I've learned that lesson already."

"Perhaps. You keep asking same question in different words, but is still same question."

"I guess I'm a slow learner."

"Peter, who is Choy?"

"Choy? How do you know her? Have you seen her? Is she here?"

"She needs speak with you. I have had contact with her, but not of this world. You must go to her this evening."

"How? The last time I had no idea how it happened."

"You have learned much. Use what you have learned. Be where you want to be and you will find her."

"Why do you speak to me in riddles?"

"I act merely like messenger, not teacher. You must learn these lessons I bring to you."

"I'm sorry. I'm scared and frustrated. You are my only friend. You and Edward."

"Remember, you are not alone." Mrs. Rossi slipped her mop into the bucket and wheeled it out of the room. Peter's head swirled with questions. He had to somehow reach Choy. Mrs. Rossi believed it was fully within his new skills to do so.

He would try.

Abruptly, Peter was interrupted by the sound of laughter at his doorway.

"You can't come in here!"

"He's a vegetable. He'll never know."

"I said no. Last night was a mistake. I shouldn't have let you."

There were more muffled noises, then a burst of angry comments from the woman and the sound of a hand slapping someone's face.

"Stop!"

"C'mere, you bitch!"

Two people burst into Peter's room. The first was Terri being backed up by the force of someone pushing her. The second was a tall, strong young intern. His hands firmly locked on her shoulders, he pushed her across the room and against the window sill. The door to Peter's room swung shut. The man forced his face against Terri's. She tried to push him off but he kept his lips planted on her face, tongue in her mouth. He forced his knee between her legs. He massaged her breasts roughly. Terri tried to yell, but his mouth muffled her sounds.

Peter struggled within himself, realizing his helplessness. His anger intensified and his vision became very focused on the man attacking Terri. Everything around the incident went hazy and seemed to move in slow motion. The figure of the man was crystal-clear. Peter locked onto his thoughts and spoke directly into his mind.

The sound of Peter's voice startled Terri's assailant. He stopped for an instant and looked directly at Peter. A look of fear came over his face when he felt Peter's grip around him, invisible yet real, being enveloped in an energy coming directly from Peter. A sound unlike any he had heard before started to build in the intern's head; a low buzzing rose like the sound of a camera flash charging except many times louder. He could feel the energy increasing around him, then instantly there was a tremendous release.

The man's body slammed back against the wall. He slumped to the floor in a daze. Feeling the energy build around him again, he was yanked to his feet and thrust toward the closed door. He caught himself against the frame, jerked the door open and without looking back at Terri burst out into the hall. He looked back through the glass, his wobbly legs propelling him away from Terri and her invisible protector.

Peter's look chilled him.

It took Terri several seconds to realize that the incident was over. Peter's defense had left her unharmed. The speed with which it all happened left her wondering what had really taken place. She wiped her face and straightened her uniform. This wasn't the first time she had fended off an overly eager pursuer.

She looked suspiciously at Peter. His face was covered in sweat and his sheets were soaked through.

"Did you do that?" She looked around to see that no one was watching.

"Hi, there."

Terri swirled around with fists raised. The technician rocked back at Terri's aggressive response. He had slipped in quietly from the monitoring room and was pleasantly surprised with his discovery. His thoughts and Terri's couldn't have been farther apart.

"What the fuck do you want?"

"Whoa…easy there…I'm just next door." He gestured through the wall. "I have to admit I was sound asleep, but the alarm on the computer monitor woke me up. I hit the reset right away. You know we've had so many damn problems with it."

"Get to the point."

"Well, it is my job so I thought that I'd better pop in and see for myself. Has anything unusual happened in the last few minutes? I mean, he hasn't moved or talked or anything like that has he?" The technician smirked.

Terri, although still shaken, couldn't resist the opportunity to pull this guy's chain. She took Peter's hand in hers.

"He and I…just had a wonderful moment together. Nothing unusual about that, is there?"

The tech's face went red as Terri stared directly at him, then lowered her eyes to his waist. She smoothed her hair and slowly drew a visual line back up to his face. The technician looked at Peter, then back to Terri and fled the room.

"I guess we told him." Terri replaced Peter's hand. "I'll get you some clean linen, sweetie. Don't go away." She smiled.

"And by the way…" she paused, looked at Peter and raising her eyes to the ceiling. "Thanks for the help…whoever helped me."

From years of working nights in the hospital the unexplained seemed all too normal. She liked the fact there was a lot more going on around people than most cared to admit or accept. She felt privileged to be part of the "Other dimension," as she liked to think of it.

Peter's room was silent again. Only the hum of equipment eased the stillness. He considered the technician and the futile effort being made with the monitoring equipment.

How did he do that with Terri's attacker? Can he do that again?

He could not recall any specific method he had used to project his energy other than the intensity of his anger and his focused will. This could be a dangerous thing if he was unable to control it. He now had two bad habits to contend with: the unpredictable effect of locking onto someone's thoughts, and now this powerful projection of energy with such remarkable results.

It made moving curtains and flushing toilets seem like amateur illusions.

He wondered too for a few minutes how he might get Edward or Mrs. Rossi to discuss changing the settings in an attempt to capture the energy readings that were being missed. He knew it would have to be done surreptitiously. He had a lifetime dealing with "experts" in various fields and knew they had no time for well-intended ideas coming from lay people.

Besides, how could either of them reveal their source of information without being considered crackpots?

His reflecting ended suddenly when his attention sharply refocused on Mrs. Rossi's direction that he must meet with Choy. Again, he wasn't exactly sure how the first meeting had occurred or how to do it again.

Peter tried to clear his mind of everything but images of Choy. He focused on her face and her voice. He could hear her words in his head. The image of her soft skin painted fantasies in his mind.

Peter relaxed.

The equipment beside the bed signaled a slower heart rate and lighter blood pressure.

He began to lighten, feeling a hundred hands slip under his body and raise him high above his bed.

He hovered there momentarily.

Then, like before, he was sucked out like vapor through a fan and projected high above the world.

When he emerged into consciousness, he found the sensations familiar. His voice seemed to echo around the world when he called out.

"CHOY, Choy, Choy. CHOY, are you there, there, there?"

He glided over the oceans and across the continents calling to her. He felt the wind of the upper atmosphere on his face. The brilliant sun warmed his soul. He circled the globe, seeing the Earth like an astronaut.

The perspective was magical, his comprehension total, his love for life and nature complete. His understanding of the connectedness of all living creatures intensified seeing his world as a single sphere providing sustenance for every inhabitant.

He could see how the waters of one nation flowed to another.

He watched while the air above each continent shifted and replaced the air of another.

No one action, anywhere on Earth, went unfelt somewhere else.

He could feel how the ripples of his positive existence fanned out into space in a warm and loving pattern. He could see how the jagged chop of his negative actions disrupted their pleasing symmetry. He realized that one day he would again ride over those waves of self, rolling out into space forever.

Suddenly he was yanked downward to find himself kneeling before Choy in the meditation room of Madame Wong. Her body was motionless in a cross-legged position. Peter appeared in a haze of his image, fully conscious of his presence. The former lovers embraced soundlessly. Once again the spirits of Peter and Choy intertwined.

In another part of the house Madame Wong was completing a reading for a regular client when she felt overwhelmed by the powerful energy generated by Peter's presence.

"I am blocked. I cannot continue. I'm afraid you must leave now and return tomorrow." Her client was puzzled but didn't ask for an explanation. The client stood up, hands in front of her in the image of prayer and bowed her head to Madame before silently exiting the room.

Madame stayed seated. She carefully shuffled her deck of Tarot cards. She turned six cards over for Peter and studied them.

The first card was the Star. It indicates courage, hope and inspiration. It tells of great love being given and received.

The second card was the Two of Cups which balances man and woman. Cups are cards of love. They show the serpents of good and evil twined around a staff, a phallic symbol of life's positive and negative energies. A pair of young lovers and winged lions.

The third card was the Three of Cups. Three young maidens hold high their cups, which contain the wine of life. They represent good fortune in love.

The fourth card a warning sign of danger. The Four of Swords. The knight lays in defeat upon his tomb. Four: the number of poverty and misery. The knight perhaps shorn of his glory by forces of logic and reason.

The fifth card was the II High Priestess: the helper, unraveler of mysteries. A warning to not speak of that which should be secret. The Priestess to a man is the perfect woman of whom all men dream.

The final card was number 13…Death, the card of renewal and transformation. New possibilities follow this card since it represents the destruction of the old and the birth of the new.

Madame studied the cards.

She took a sip of herbal tea before rising then walked purposefully from her reading room, the beaded curtain swinging behind her. She silently moved along the hall to where Choy was meditating. She could feel the energy and was cautious not to inject any of herself into the aura she sensed.

When she moved closer to Choy she could feel the power around her like a thick liquid. She waved her hand gently in front of herself. She could feel the substance on her hand, warm and soft, moving about her like a dense fog. At the open door of Choy's room she was overwhelmed by the feeling of love and joy that engulfed her. Madame stood silently with eyes closed, basking in the warmth around her. She allowed herself to enter a new world.

Peter and Choy looked at her and beckoned her to join them in their rapture. Madame held her hands up in prayer toward Choy and Peter in their intimate encounter. Madame opened her eyes and gently eased away from the door, silently sliding the privacy curtain. When she moved back, a radiation of energy flowed out through the slim vertical openings in the beads and splayed the floor around her feet. She continued to back away until the feeling subsided to an original hint.

She entered another room, illuminated by candles. Incense burned in a brass urn. She made her way to a couch where she let her body collapse. She slipped into a blissful trance, content that the calling she heeded from when she was a young girl continued to fulfill her with wonder and joy.

Choy broke the silence. *"I thought you'd never come. You must have heard from Mrs. Rossi that I was seeking you."*

Nothing surprised Peter now. He would do what Mrs. Rossi suggested and just be in the moment. *"Yes. It is so wonderful to see you. I can't express..."*

Choy put her fingers to his mouth. *"I must speak to you. You are in danger. I believe that you can live, but there are others who do not want that. They are after your money. I know about the donation to the hospital in your will. One of your lawyers has leaked the will. I know about Zalkow and his links to the City Star. Someone named George is feeding information about you to them. The monitoring equipment is being manipulated by Zalkow to fake the readings and Dr. Brandon is being blackmailed by Zalkow somehow."*

Peter listened intently.

He knew some of what Choy was telling him, but she was adding more complex and surprising pieces to the puzzle. Her image began to fade. In the meditation room her body was becoming unsteady and started to waver.

"Choy, you said that I could live. How do you know that? How will it happen?"

"I don't know, Peter; it's the feeling I get when I've been near you. Peter, Matthew is in danger..."

"What? What do you mean?"

Choy's voice faded.

Peter reached out to embrace her. She was gone.

Madame Wong sat upright. Her eyes opened wide, turning on all of her senses and she hurried to the meditation room. Choy lay limp on her side, collapsed in front of a row of candles. Madame rushed to her pantry, taking a small jar from amongst many on her shelves. After she hurried back, she removed the lid and dipped her index finger into the liquid. She knelt beside Choy and smoothed her finger across Choy's dry lips.

Choy's tongue reacted instantly, licking the substance. Her eyes opened. She saw the blurred image of Madame kneeling before her and smiled serenely.

"Am I back?"

"Yes, my child, you are with us again."

"You were there, weren't you? You were there with us."

"Madame is everywhere."

Peter awoke in his room, his head swimming with images. He remembered every detail as if he had just experienced a vivid dream. He replayed it over and over, locking it into his memory.

What had Choy meant by her last statement about Matthew? What danger was he in? How could he warn his son?

Peter was amazed by what Choy seemed to know.

His level of acceptance of his situation and the magic of the world around him had again grown immeasurably.

- Chapter 52 -

Brian entered through the back entrance of Eye See You for another rendezvous with Matt. He sat down in the upholstered booth, looked at his brother and motioned to the waitress.

"I'll have what he's having, except make it a double. What a day. I've been preparing for the hearing and talking with fucking lawyers all day."

"How does it look?"

"No idea. It will all be up to the Judge. We don't even know who's sitting. The court wants to avoid any potential influence either side might attempt to bring prior to the hearing."

"You wouldn't do that, would you Brian?" Matt taunted his older brother.

Brian simply raised his eyebrows.

The waitress placed an icy beverage in front of Brian, who immediately took a long swallow.

"What is this?" Brian had a perplexed look on his face.

"Well, I guess it's a double diet cola." Matt smiled. "I'm off the juice for a while. You know, trying to clean up my act and all that."

"I'm impressed. Are you going to visit Dad?"

Matt sighed. "I guess so. Sooner or later I'll have to face him sober, won't I?"

"Yep, sooner or later."

"By the way, I asked little sister if she wanted to come over to Bermuda with me. You know, a bit of a distraction, break things up."

"What about the business over there?"

"Yeah, I talked to her about that and she's cool. Actually offered some pretty decent advice for a young pup. She's wiser than I thought."

"What about that Michael fellow?"

"Not a chance according to her. She thinks he's cool, that's all. He seems okay to me if that's all it is. Anyway, drink up, I might as well go up there now and see Dad."

"I just got here."

"Oh, did you want to go next door and catch the show?"

"No."

"Well, don't stop me now. I'm on a roll."

Brian nodded, drained his glass, then joined his brother for the walk to the hospital.

Matt walked past his father's window and did a double take when he realized that Terri was bedside, attending to his needs. He waited until her back was toward the door and entered quietly.

Terri shrieked when Matt's fingers tapped her on the shoulder. She raised her hand in the air and spun around.

Matt reacted quickly to fend off the blow.

"Nice to see you too."

"Oh my God, I'm so sorry. I thought you were someone else."

"I'm glad I'm not. Care to explain?"

"It's a long story. I'd rather not. But it is nice to see you." She paused. "And it seems that you're sober for a change."

"Very funny. It didn't seem to bother you before."

"I figured you were harmless then. Now that all your equipment is properly working, I'll have to be more cautious."

"What makes you think I'm interested?"

"Oh, you're interested." Terri scratched her telephone number on the edge of a report sheet and tore it off. "When things calm down in your life, or if you need someone to talk to, give me a call."

She kissed him lightly on the cheek and slipped past him out the door. When she walked by the window they made eye contact as though to say, "I've played my cards so now its your turn to call."

Terri had played her cards.

She hoped Matt would call.

Matt folded the paper and slipped it into his pocket and smiled at her knowing now that he was sober he likely wouldn't use it.

After stopping in the lounge, Brian had caught the kiss when he passed the window on his way in to join Matt. He didn't need all the details to get the drift of what was happening. He smiled at Terri when they passed in the doorway. Her face was slightly flushed.

"Nice." Brian smiled.

"They're all nice, Brian."

"I wouldn't know. You seem to have a corner on that market."

"Yes, but you're a good businessman."

"And you should be thankful for that."

Matt raised his hands in defense. He was.

"I just spoke to Mom. Emily isn't doing too well. She's had a stroke and she's not in very good shape. She's going to stay in Florida. I'll keep her posted on progress here."

Peter watched his two sons. He was saddened by the news of Emily but was pleased to see that, even in difficult times, they were sticking together. He was even more pleasantly surprised that he could now sense Matt's feelings and make a mental connection with him. The only thing new in the equation was that Matt was sober. Peter surmised the alcohol had impeded his ability to make the connection on prior occasions.

Peter hoped there was a chance he could plant the thought that Matt must be cautious, in light of what Choy had said.

There was no way to know what sort of danger Matt might be in, so it was merely a shot in the dark.

"I didn't notice before, but he looks pretty good, doesn't he? You'd think he might just wake up and walk out of here."

"That's my whole point for going to court. You're going to be there, right?"

"Yep, me and Sarah."

"Good. We can't let him slip away by default. If there's any possibility of recovery I want to be sure it's explored."

Matt nodded thoughtfully. "Yes. But Brian...what if we do all this and Dad does wake up? What if he's an incompetent, slobbering invalid, unable to walk, talk, or take a shit without help? He wouldn't want that and neither would we. That would be Dad's greatest fear. I know if I were in his shoes and had lived the life he's lived, I'd rather die. I'd be prepared to take my chances on what's coming next."

Brian was silent. Matt's point sank in.

"All I can say, Matt, is that in my heart I feel I should be taking this course. When I've stood here before in front of dad and when I stand here now, it's like he's telling me that this is the right course of action. I can't explain it. It's just a feeling I have. Besides, after the hearing this discussion may be moot."

– Chapter 53 –

Fuzzy opened the motel door to greet the cool breath of morning. First light was still some time away, thus to any stranger he would just be another businessman getting ready for a long day on the road. He cut a sharp image in his blue suit, white shirt, colorful tie and polished black shoes. His clean face belied the hint of any previous growth. His short, well-combed hair was flipped up in front and tucked neatly behind his ears.

He kept a suit in his rig for rare, special occasions on the road like funerals, weddings and hospital visits. Creases at the knees of his pants told of many months on a hanger. He had met up with a close friend of his, where he spent most of the previous day telling his whole story from start to finish. She was someone he could trust in times of need. He felt enormous relief having shared his burden. She was also someone who could take his mind off work for a while, and did so several times during their visit.

It had been months since Fuzzy had been to see the one and only woman he'd made love to in his life. The stress of his journey seemed to amplify the pleasure of his visit. He had parked his rig in her yard and now backed the car he'd borrowed from her up to the motel door. Fuzzy had prepaid, which was becoming his habit. He shoved his sole duffel bag into the car, then man-handled the wire dog cage in through the rear hatch door.

"I think you've gained weight there, boy. You're going to have to go on a diet." Schebb attempted to bark, but the leather muzzle allowed only muffled grunts to come out. Schebb peered through the wire at Fuzzy and whimpered.

Fuzzy had explained everything to Schebb while he put him into the cage, but the message wasn't clear...yet.

"It's okay, boy, you're goin' home." Fuzzy stuck his fingers through the wire in a conciliatory gesture. Schebb moved his head forward briskly in an attempt to nip him.

"Whoa, boy, it's okay. I understand, and you will soon." Fuzzy draped a blanket over the cage. He placed a cable and lock he had purchased near the cage to facilitate quick removal.

Schebb continued to whimper.

Traffic was light. Fuzzy had no problem reaching the parking area in front of the Douglas Corporation tower. He had driven in reflective silence. He knew that Schebb's arrival would initiate a frenzy of activity, which he hoped he could avoid. He circled the block several times to plan his route out of the city core and away from the building. He wanted to get a feeling for the volume of pedestrians and cars likely to see him come and go. He pulled into the semi-circular pick-up and drop-off area and parked legally between the appropriate signs. He checked his mirrors and did a scan in each direction before leaving the anonymity of his car and stepping into public for the first time in several days.

He played his role well, walking confidently toward the doors like any businessman who had a good reason for arriving at such an early hour. The golden glass tower was impressive. The approach to the building was a broad, well lit stone court-yard, boxed in with granite flower boxes and a waterfall. Fuzzy wove past a massive polished boulder which proclaimed a significant historic event in chiseled letters. A lone clerk prepared for the morning rush in the attached café.

Fuzzy peered through the brass and glass revolving doors. They were locked and the security desk was vacant. He checked his watch; twenty minutes to six. He assumed the guards would be on at six or seven. Schebb would only be alone for that time. He reached into his pocket and removed several toothpicks, jamming one in each of the locks at the base of the doors. He did the same on the two pair of tall swinging doors that flanked the center revolving one.

He returned to the car and opened the rear tailgate. There was no one on the street within shouting distance. The city was quiet. It had that strange feeling, unique to busy places, when the people are gone yet the spirit of the busyness remains long after they have left.

He looped the cable around his arm and slipped the lock into his pocket. When he dragged the cage toward him Schebb whimpered and staggered awkwardly, the motion knocking him off balance. Fuzzy hoisted the cage and shuffled his way to the doors, placing Schebb in front of the only set that had magnetic card access.

Looping the cable through the cage wire and both of the door handles, he snapped the lock to secure Schebb in place.

He looked around and removed an envelope from his jacket pocket.

The lump in his throat nearly gagged him. His body was heating with anxiety. Sweat beads rolled from his forehead.

He slipped the envelope under the doors.

When he pulled the blanket from the cage Schebb had his nose jammed into the wire, trying to make contact with Fuzzy as if to say, "Don't leave me."

Schebb licked Fuzzy's fingers when he knelt briefly to rub his wet nose.

Fuzzy's whole body buzzed with nervousness, but he needed time to say goodbye to a good friend.

"I'm gonna miss you. You're 'bout the best friend I ever had. And you're a darn good truckin' partner. You brought some happiness into my life. I'm gonna miss ya."

"Hey! What are you doing there?"

Fuzzy snapped his head around. The sound of the door being tried jarred him with the fear of being caught. The face of a uniformed guard was pressed against the glass. He was fumbling with his key ring and didn't get a good look at the man kneeling in front of him.

Fuzzy didn't hesitate. He turned his face away and walked quickly to his car, trying not to attract attention. With the locks jammed he knew that the guard couldn't open the door without cutting the cable. By the time he radioed for help, Fuzzy would be long gone.

Fuzzy scanned for observers. There were none. His eyes came to rest on the engraved bronze letters glimmering through the waterfall: WE THE PEOPLE.

Fuzzy'd heard the words before. He couldn't remember from where, but they made him feel good.

He slammed the doors and jumped into his getaway vehicle. In minutes he was on his way out of the city, heading back to pick up his rig.

A passenger jet flew overhead departing Logan International Airport. Fuzzy was envious of its passengers.

En route to somewhere else, I reckon.

He wondered whether he should risk a few minutes visiting with his friend before he left for his parents' place in the country.

It could be some time before I'll be with a woman again.

- Chapter 54 -

"Good morning. What have we here?"

The head of Douglas security was sitting on a cage in the hallway outside the offices of the Douglas Corporation's President and CEO when Marjorie arrived.

"I believe it's Mr. Douglas's dog M'ame. He was dropped off this morning and chained to the building. The morning shift had to cut the cable. They called me right away and I've instructed them to speak with no one about this. So far as I know, you and I are the only two other people aware of this little gift."

Marjorie bent down and looked inside the cage at the dog. He was lying flat on the bottom of the cage. The fur on his back was standing and he was shaking vigorously.

"I wouldn't stick your fingers in there, M'ame."

Marjorie pulled her fingers away quickly and looked at the dog inquisitively, trying to make out a name tag.

"I'll get my guys in security to find out if this is the right dog and if he's healthy."

"I guess it could be a sick joke, right?" She stood up. "I'll call Brian Douglas right away."

"Yes, M'ame. By the way, this was under the door. It's addressed to Mr. Douglas."

Marjorie phoned Brian at the hospital, where he had been for an early morning visit with his father. He had also hoped to spend some time with Dr. Brandon, who would be appearing as a key witness at the hearing. Dr. Brandon had been conspicuously unavailable, despite Brian's numerous attempts to contact him.

"Guess who's in your office?"

"This early? Let's see...the guys from Kyoto Corporation back on their hands and knees?"

"Better than that."

"It doesn't get much better than that, unless it was my father. You'll have to tell me."

"Blonde...in a cage. No guesses? I think it's your father's dog."

"Schebb!"

"I think so. There's a letter with him for you. Should I open it?"

"Absolutely." Brian listened while Marjorie opened the envelope.

"Dear Mr. Douglas, this is your father's dog...."

Marjorie continued to read into a telephone with no one at the other end. Brian was running to the elevator to see the dog and letter first hand.

When he arrived at his office, Marjorie was waiting. "Thanks for saying goodbye." She had closed the office door to avoid any unnecessary attention.

"Sorry, but I wanted to get here as soon as possible." Brian crouched and unclipped the door of the dog cage. Schebb bolted out of the cage and into Brian's lap, knocking him to the floor. His tail wagged wildly, he barked through the leather muzzle.

"Hey boy, hey fella, how ya doin?" Brian scratched Schebb's head and pulled the muzzle off. Schebb started licking him feverishly now that he stood over the blue-suited man lying on his back on the floor. Marjorie had never seen this side of Brian. "Hey, you're fat. Someone's been feeding you well."

Brian got to his feet, smiling from ear to ear. Schebb continued to lavish affection on him. "It's Schebb all right. He looks great. This is fantastic, Marjorie."

Impulsively he put his arms around her and hugged her. She was shocked. She hesitated before hugging him back.

Brian felt elated. Getting Schebb back was a big boost to his spirits. It wasn't his father, but it was still great.

They released their grip on each other and leaned apart. Marjorie felt her knees go weak when his lips made contact with hers. As they did she parted her mouth and received him. The spell had finally been broken. Brian's emotional release had cracked the sexual tension that had been present for years.

When the kiss ended, Brian pulled back from Marjorie and looked at her.

His eyes were wet.

Her body was shaking.

He took a great breath and kissed her on the forehead.

"C'mon, we've got work to do."

"We?"

"That's right. We. Is that okay?"

"That's okay." Marjorie wasn't exactly sure what "we" meant, but it seemed like a big step forward.

"Call that vet friend of Dad's who gave him Schebb and see if he'll come by to check him out. Keep Schebb here, though. We'll have to decide how to let this out. I'm off to meet with the lawyers…again."

Marjorie held up her crossed fingers and mouthed the words "good luck." Still flushed from their encounter, she hated to see him leave.

She'd do her best to keep her feelings in check or risk ruining a potentially good thing.

- Chapter 55 -

Wipers cleared huge flakes of snow from the windshield of the Douglas car as it pulled up to the court house.

"Just keep going," Brian told his driver.

A mob of press people stood on the steps in the cold, like hounds before the hunt. They desperately wanted to get any comment they could on the hearing. Brian couldn't believe the turnout. "Pull around to the rear entrance."

Several news types had staked out the back door but Brian was able to bolt by them with only a curt, "No comment."

Brian made his way into the courtroom where he was met by his lawyers who walked him to the front table. He was pleased to see that Edward, Sarah, Matt and Charlotte would be seated directly behind him. He leaned back over the wooden railing to greet them.

On the opposite side of the court sat Peter's lawyers, Dr. Brandon, Dr. Joseph Zalkow and the Chairman of the Hospital Operations Committee. Other than two uniformed guards and a court stenographer, there were no others present. The court had an eerie feel to it with so few people occupying the grand chamber.

"All rise, this court is now in session, the Honorable Harold Bolstein presiding."

The huge frame of the Judge waddled to the dais and took its seat. He was even bigger than Brian remembered from seeing him at their house when he was a boy. He still had a look Brian would never forget. His head was nearly round, his cheeks red and puffy. He wore a grin that made even the toughest man smile at him. Brian felt an enormous sense of relief that this long-time family friend was presiding.

"You may be seated." The Judge's bass voice rang out through the courtroom over the amplifying speakers. His first look went to the bailiff. "Turn that darn thing off, will you?"

The bailiff jumped at the command and scurried to adjust a volume knob on the wall panel.

"Good morning ladies and gentlemen. It appears that we are all acquainted, but let us not allow that fact to hinder the quality of these proceedings, shall we? This is a closed hearing, not a trial, although by the power vested in me regarding these matters my judgment is binding. Anyone interfering with that judgment after it is made shall be held in contempt of court and subject to punishment under state law."

A chill ran down Brian's spine when the Judge peered at him through bulging eyes. The Judge's brow was already shimmering with his labors.

"Do both parties understand this?"

The lawyers for both sides rose and simultaneously declared, "We do, your Honor."

"Secondly, the nature of these proceedings is confidential. All information disclosed in this courtroom, including my verdict, is confidential until released by my office." This time the looks went to his uniformed officers. "Is that also clear?" They bowed their heads deferentially.

The lawyers jumped up again. "Yes, your Honor."

"I don't want any leaks from my courtroom. I read John Grisham too."

Two of the lawyers snickered, but stopped when Judge Harold's gaze landed on them. "Let us proceed. I have read the

Living Will and The Last Will and Testament of Peter Douglas. I have reviewed the lengthy written submissions of counsel which clearly state the positions of both parties along with the facts supporting those positions. Are there any other pertinent arguments to be made this morning?"

Counsel for Peter Douglas spoke. "Yes, your Honor, we wish to support our written submissions with expert testimony."

"You may proceed, but I warn you gentlemen, let's be brief and to the point."

Brian could feel his skin sticking to the wooden chair through his suit pants. He was normally icily cool under pressure but today sweat poured down his back as he watched Dr. Brandon being sworn in as a witness.

His father's lawyers were very smooth while painting a picture of Peter's life prior to the accident and, now, a coma victim in the hospital with little hope of ever recovering.

"Dr. Brandon, we have submitted your CV in our written brief. The Honorable Judge is aware of your excellent credentials." The Judge nodded when he and Dr. Brandon exchanged glances. "How many coma victims have you cared for during your distinguished career?"

"More than I can remember, but at least fifty."

"Have any of those individuals recovered to lead a healthy and normal life?"

"No."

"None? Not one?"

"No, not one."

"Was there any procedure untried in the care and attempt at recovering these patients?"

"No."

"So you did everything within the power of the medical community to bring the patients back to a normal life?"

"Yes."

"And, Dr. Brandon, are you now doing everything available in modern medicine to attempt to recover or detect some level of brain activity in Mr. Peter Douglas?"

"Objection." Brian's lawyer leapt to his feet, trying to stop the progress of this testimony. The Judge gave him a perplexed look.

"Really? To what?"

Brian's lawyer stumbled for a minute then re-gained his composure. "The witness is being lead down a path to an obvious conclusion, your Honor. He is only one man, with one man's opinion. He doesn't know what's going on inside Mr. Douglas any more than you or I do."

The Judge looked at the lawyer. The courtroom went silent. "One more of those and you'll be waiting in the hall. Please do not waste our time with frivolity. Over-ruled. Continue."

Dr. Brandon went on. "We are doing everything and more with Mr. Douglas. We are utilizing the latest technology to monitor his condition. If there had been any significant signs of electrical activity in the brain, we would have known about it."

Brian glanced back at his row of supporters. All but Sarah had the same neutral look on their faces while they listened; Sarah though, looked distraught.

Brian wondered if having her there was a good idea. His eyes were diverted to the back of the courtroom when the tall wooden door swung open. Michael stuck his head inside and spoke to the guard. The door closed and the guard walked quietly forward to where the Douglas family was seated. He whispered in Edward's ear. Edward nodded without taking his eyes off the lawyers at the front of the court.

Brian watched the guard open the door a sliver and let Michael slip in. He caught Brian's attention and received visual approval for his presence.

Michael had seated himself beside Sarah before she realized he was there. Her face beamed at the sight of him.

Dr. Brandon glanced at Brian occasionally while he testified. He continued to rationalize his course of action to be the proper one, given all the circumstances. He showed no signs of backing away from his obviously rehearsed testimony.

"Given your experience with this case and the dozens of previous cases like this one, Dr. Brandon, do you support the continued use of life support for Mr. Peter Douglas on the assumption that their use will lead to recovery?"

"I object, your Honor!" Brian's lawyer was on his feet, unable to contain himself. "Counsel for Mr. Douglas is essentially asking the witness to commit murder."

The Judge immediately directed the focus of his attention toward the agitated lawyer. The court went deathly silent waiting to hear the next words. His Honor's face shimmered with perspiration, which he mopped while he stared at the only shrinking man in the room.

"This is my second comment to you this morning. It is also my second and last warning." The Judge spoke in measured tones, ensuring that the full import of his authority reverberated throughout the grand room.

"We all know why we are here. This is not a trial. There are no cameras present to capture your grand-standing for broadcast on the six p.m. news with film at eleven. A man's life is at stake, yes, but a man's pride, integrity and Will are the reasons for our presence here today. We are here by request of the patient, not because of his condition. He expects us to make the same good decision on his behalf as he would if he were here making his own. I do not think Peter Douglas would appreciate you interfering in this process with flimsy objections. So I ask you again, if not out of respect for myself and this great court, then out of respect for the man whose wishes we are here to serve and protect, to please put a lid on it. Objection overruled."

The Judge's gavel slammed down, making everyone present rise slightly in their seats. The objecting lawyer shriveled into his chair and whispered something to his partner.

Brian could feel his mood continue to deflate; his mind raced recognizing that one of his father's long-time friends, Judge Bolstein, held the reins of life in his grip.

Youth and wisdom, hmm. Maybe the Judge knows exactly how dad feels about being in the condition he's in. These are proud men who earned their money and respect the hard way. They've seen decades of difficult times; war, the struggles of raising a family and building a career. What do I know about all this? I've been brought up in the lap of luxury. I've known no trauma money couldn't rectify. Now here I sit, fighting the wishes of the man who is responsible for my life. Am I just selfishly clinging to that man? Afraid that when he is gone I will have no pillar to lean on? Afraid that the masked veil of my success will be lifted and leave me exposed? What do I have to show for my life? I have created nothing.

Thoughts of Marjorie suddenly swirled in his head. The need to replace the love of a father sought fulfillment.

"Please answer the question, Doctor…"

Brian's attention refocused.

"Could you repeat the question, please?"

A collective exhalation could be heard.

The observers readied themselves again. The court stenographer re-read the question aloud.

"Given your experience with this case and the dozens of previous cases like this one, Dr. Brandon, do you support the continued use of life support for Mr. Peter Douglas on the assumption that their use will lead to recovery?"

Dr. Brandon paused. His eyes swept across the Douglas family, then crossed the aisle to where Dr. Zalkow was sitting. Their eyes locked before Dr. Brandon turned his head. He responded directly to the Judge, who was looking down on him from his position several feet up.

"No. No I cannot, in good conscience, say that the continued use of life support will in any way ensure the recovery of Mr. Douglas."

The only word the court heard was no, but Dr. Brandon felt he had worded his answer in such a way that he hadn't condoned murder. He could live with the decision of the court.

"No further questions, your Honor."

Brian turned to his family.

They all leaned forward in a huddle.

"This isn't going well."

"That's an understatement." Edward stated quietly. "Your Dad is still running the show."

Or was he? Was it possible that everything he had experienced was in Edward's imagination? It did seem too far-fetched to be true when viewed from the earthly confines of a courtroom. Perhaps he was tampering with God's plan and should just keep out of it. After all, this was between Peter and God, right?

"Counselor, any questions of the witness?"

"Yes, your Honor."

"I thought so. You've been warned."

The counselor stood up and walked around from behind his desk into the middle of the room. He approached Dr. Brandon in the witness stand without saying a word.

The Judge watched him carefully.

Peter Douglas's counsel had stayed behind his desk when questioning the witness. Although there were no rules pertaining to his movements, Brian figured that Judges liked to keep a fair distance between themselves, the witnesses and the lawyers.

Brian was surprised the lawyer hadn't been sent back to his desk.

He walked closer and closer to Dr. Brandon.

The lawyer stopped directly in front of the witness stand. "Dr. Brandon."

Visibly sweating, Dr. Brandon stared back.

The lawyer raised his arm and pointed his finger like a gun directly in his face.

"Have you ever murdered a man, Dr. Brandon?"

The courtroom exploded. Peter's lawyers were on their feet, screaming objections.

"How many people have you killed this year, Dr. Brandon?"

Bolstein's gavel crashed down repeatedly.

"Order. Order I say. Order."

Brian and his second lawyer were on their feet. The rest of the family sat stunned.

"ARE YOU READY TO WEAR THE BLOOD OF PETER DOUGLAS ON YOUR HANDS FOREVER BY MURDERING HIM, DR. BRANDON? ARE YOU? ARE YOU?"

"Objection! Objection!" Peter's lawyers ran to the front of the court screaming their request. Bolstein's gavel continued to bang. The court stenographer had to collect her thoughts and stay focused on recording rather than watching the events unfold.

"Bailiff, bailiff. Remove this man!" The Judge had lifted his huge frame to his feet. He continued to crash the gavel on the hardwood with one hand while motioning the bailiff with the other, yelling over the noise to Dr. Brandon, "Do not answer. Do not answer these questions."

"GO AHEAD, DOCTOR, GO AHEAD AND PULL THE PLUG ON ANOTHER HUMAN LIFE. HOW CAN YOU

SLEEP AT NIGHT? PETER DOUGLAS COULD WAKE UP TOMORROW. HOW WOULD YOU FEEL THEN?"

It took two bailiffs to subdue the lawyer who continued to verbally assault Dr. Brandon.

Brian shot a glance to Zalkow who sat quietly behind the railing, seemingly enjoying this theater.

Judge Bolstein continued standing while the screaming lawyer was dragged, bodily, out the door. The gavel slammed down a final time.

"This court will recess for five minutes." He started to move away from his chair but paused and looked back at the people seated in the courtroom. They were all staring at him.

"None of you are to leave this room. There's water on the table. I'll have some coffee brought in." The Judge's burly figure disappeared into his private chambers.

Dr. Brandon stepped down from the witness stand. He wavered as he made his way to the lawyers' table. Brian could see that he was shaken by the whole ordeal.

The Douglas family huddled with their one remaining lawyer to find out what had happened and discuss the next step.

"That's what he whispered to me," the remaining lawyer said, "I'm going ballistic on him; you'll have to run with it.'"

"All rise. This court is now in session." Judge Bolstein waddled back into the courtroom. His head had shrunk to its former size. He gazed at everyone present - to take attendance presumably - then spoke in a markedly calm tone. "I trust everyone has regained their composure?"

Heads nodded. "Then we may proceed. Dr. Brandon, please take the stand. Remember, you are still under oath."

Judge Bolstein directed his attention to Brian's second lawyer. "May I remind you that you are the only remaining lawyer to represent Brian Douglas? Do you have any questions for the witness?"

The lawyer nodded. He stayed where he was behind his desk. "Dr. Brandon, do you consider the mercy killing of an individual murder?"

The Judge tensed and glanced at Peter's lawyers, but both let the question stand.

"I function under the laws set out by our society through our elected representatives. It is not my position to question those laws, but to abide by them. If I was dissatisfied with the laws governing my practice of medicine, I could work to alter them or leave the profession. The answer is no, I do not. I could argue that keeping someone alive against their will or the will of God and nature is tantamount to torture."

"I'll do the arguing, if you don't mind. So you would have no hesitation disconnecting Mr. Douglas from life support?"

"I will do what this court and my hospital instruct me to do. This will not be my decision alone."

"And if it were your decision alone, Doctor, what would you do?" The question hung in the air. "What would you do, Doctor? Would you remove life support or not?"

"Given the way you've phrased the question, I would have to answer no. No, I would not remove the life support, since it would violate my oath of ethics and eliminate the opportunity, however small, to see the patient recover, but…"

"Thank you. That will be all."

Brian looked at Judge Bolstein, hoping he saw that Dr. Brandon had just changed his position.

"But that's not fair. I have to work within the system."

"That's all, Dr. Brandon. No further questions."

The Judge spoke up. "You may step down, Dr. Brandon."

Dr. Brandon kept speaking even when he stood in the witness stand. "I have no choice but to follow the rules. I have pressures, you know!"

All eyes, including Zalkow's, were riveted.

"Dr. Brandon, I advise you to stop talking and remove yourself from the witness stand immediately."

Brian's lawyer quickly rose. "Your Honor, if the Doctor has more pertinent information that he may wish to volunteer, regarding pressure he may be feeling to perform an act he finds objectionable, then…"

The Judge put his hands up and looked directly at Brian's lawyer who instantly settled into his seat.

"Thank you, Dr. Brandon. Please step down."

The court heard a lengthy discourse on the new fiscal and moral reality within the hospital environment from the Chairman of the Hospital Operations Committee. The Chairman quoted recovery statistics, death rates and pain threshold studies. He talked about the negative impact on families in these circumstances. He gently broached the financial benefits available for re-direction of insurance proceeds. He reminded the court that he was well versed and had very strong feelings on the subjective side of the argument as well. The Judge indicated his appreciation for the latter enlightenment. He assured the man that his presentation of the qualitative information brought a balance to the otherwise subjective nature of the proceedings.

Dr. Joseph Zalkow took the stand as the incoming Chair of the Committee on Merciful Care. He waxed lyrically about the need to direct hospital resources to the areas that could generate the most benefit with the highest likelihood of success. He quoted broad statistics relating to dollars and life expectancy. He talked of the moral breech of interfering when God had taken over. He told the court that his role was a difficult one, given the many close relationships he had in the community with patients and their families. He felt, however, that it was his duty to continue to carry the burden of these difficult decisions and respect the wishes of the patient.

Brian and Matt nearly choked when they heard that statement. Even Bolstein looked like he was having difficulty swallowing this show.

"It is not our role to play God. We must be cautious in our medical approach to any circumstance. We have too often interfered in the natural death of a patient only to prolong the inevitable without tangible benefit to the patient or the family. Our efforts and resources are too often squandered in the service of our own ideals and egos. Given the facts of this case, if it were before my committee, and given the efforts and techniques Dr. Brandon has so meticulously employed, I could see no reasonable alternative but to withdraw life support and let nature take its course."

The Judge and all present in the courtroom heard the whispered words from the Douglas camp.

"You bastard!"

Judge Bolstein wisely kept the proceedings moving and avoided another outburst and confrontation with the family of his good friend Peter Douglas.

Dr. Brandon sat with his head hanging, seemingly oblivious to everything being said.

"Are there any further witnesses?"

Brian's lawyer stood. "Your Honor, Brian Douglas would like to address the court on behalf of his family."

"Mr. Douglas?" The Judge sat back in his chair. Brian turned and looked at his family before speaking. They all looked at him with pride and approval. Matt gave his brother a thumbs-up and winked.

Brian turned to face the Judge. "Your honor, the first thing I did this morning was visit my father. I'm sure it won't surprise you to know that we have been on a constant vigil since his admission to the hospital. When I'm in his room I feel his presence. He is more than a limp body lying there. Your Honor, he is still Peter Douglas. His energy and spirit are powerful and tactile. He continues to be a great source of strength to this family even in his current condition. I understand from the written briefs and the testimony here today that the odds of someone recovering from this situation are enormously weighted against him. My father, our father…" Brian fanned his arm at the Douglas bench "…has been an odds-beater all his life. If any person can overcome adversity, Peter Douglas can. We should give him every opportunity to do so. Our family has the means to support him financially. We have the courage to live with the consequences of his recovery, however slight or profound it may be. Recently, our father's dog was returned to us."

The Judge raised his eyebrows at this statement.

Zalkow squirmed in his seat.

"That was the best thing that ever happened to me in my life. I can't express how good it felt to have this small part of my father back in my arms. We sit before you, your Honor, the family of an amazing man. I speak on behalf of our sister Catherine in Paris and our mother, who at this moment is attending to her mother who has suffered a stroke in Florida. Please allow us more time to determine if we have overlooked the smallest detail which may lead to our father being returned to us. Even with his brilliance there is no way that he could have predicted what circumstance he might have ended up in or the prognosis for recovery. Although Dr. Brandon is a fine Doctor, there may still be some answers that we must take the time to find. Your Honor, please do not take our father away from us yet."

The courtroom was 'pin drop' silent for several seconds after Brian sat down. Sarah and Charlotte sniffled and Edward's eyes were glassy, staring at some distant point. Matt leaned forward and placed his hand on Brian's shoulder. The Judge broke the silence.

"Ladies and gentlemen. I have been asked to rule on the validity of the Living Will of Peter Douglas. It has certain provisions pertaining to the situation we find ourselves in today. It is not my job either to play God and deliver or take anyone's loved one from them. I received substantial written briefs from both sides represented here today. I have reviewed the laws and precedent pertaining to a matter of this sort carefully. The testimony I have heard today has been poignant and moving, but as it relates to the issue at hand, it isn't particularly relevant. Mr. Douglas has been a life-long friend of mine as well. It pains me to no end to be in the situation I find myself in today. However, I have been trained all of my life in this profession to be impartial, and that is how I shall remain, regardless of my personal relationship with or feelings toward Mr. Douglas."

Judge Bolstein took a long breath.

"My role here today is to determine whether or not the Will before me is binding, period. Mr. Douglas we all know was, is, a proud, independent and forthright man. He was never prone to making rash decisions. I have read in the written brief his Will was prepared in his usual well-thought-out manner, in consultation with some of the city's brightest advisors. It was not the act of an irrational man. According to the written testimony, Mr. Douglas made it clear when instructing his lawyers that he had led an active, healthy and fulfilling life. He has made the point most adamantly that in no way did he wish to be kept alive beyond any point at which God decided he should pass on."

Another heaving intake of oxygen slowed the delivery of the Judges oratory.

"We live in a technological era. In many ways we have become subservient to the technology we have created. We are losing touch with each other as more and more technology, not personal contact, is the medium by which we know one another. Peter Douglas would have never wanted to be a slave to a machine."

Bolstein stopped speaking. He scanned the room and rose.

"This court will recess for fifteen minutes while I prepare my final decision. Once again I must request that no one leave this room."

- Chapter 56 -

Judge Bolstein slipped into his office and settled into a high-backed leather chair which creaked under his girth. The recess was perfunctory, but it gave everyone a few minutes to let the proceedings gel. He slid open the bottom drawer of his oversized ornate wooden desk. He didn't often drink while sitting, but he felt that one jigger...no, maybe two...would settle his system. This was about to be the toughest judgment he had handed down in his long and esteemed career.

The first shot went down like a burning rag. He had definitely strained his throat this morning. The alcohol seared the already inflamed vocal chords. He picked up his pen and scratched out several sentences on white vellum before buzzing his court assistant. No words were exchanged when the paneled wooden door between the book cases swung open. His helper and friend of 22 years walked to the desk and took the paper he held out. She glanced at the stubby measuring glass on his desk.

The Judge simply nodded, indicating it was a tough morning. They exchanged more information in a few seconds of body language than most would in a lengthy conversation. When she left, he measured his second and last shot of the day and poured it down his now-anaesthetized throat.

This final drink carried even more heat than the first. His neck constricted in response to the liquid assault. A full sweat broke out over the enormous man's entire body. The temperature in the office went up about twenty degrees in five seconds.

The lights, normally adequate for reading, stung his eyes. He squinted, trying to focus on the bookcase now spinning in front of him. He barely noticed the pain that cut across his chest. He had only enough time to place both of his hands over his heart before slumping face down on his desk, forcing his sweat-soaked face to imprint itself on the leather surface.

Fifty-five minutes passed. With each agonizing minute the tension in the courtroom increased. A few nasty looks were exchanged between the camps, but no verbal assaults were launched. The competing lawyers consulted at the front of the courtroom. What appeared first like an adversarial exchange gave way to a more jovial session.

Zalkow shifted continually, apparently trying to avoid making eye contact with anyone on the Douglas side.

On several occasions the bailiffs had to remind those present that the use of a cellular telephone or PDA was prohibited while the court was in recess.

Numerous messages were exchanged between the senior bailiff and a pretty young clerk who darted soundlessly in and out of a side door.

All present snapped to attention when the eight-foot high door swung open.

"All rise. This court is now in session. Her Honor Miriam Whiteside presiding."

The scene in the courtroom for the first few seconds could have been straight out of Madame Toussaud's Wax Museum. Every individual present was frozen in caricature. Mouths gaped. Eyes fixed unblinkingly on the black-robed woman who entered the court and settled into the lofty perch formerly occupied by Judge Harold Bolstein.

"You may be seated." The Judge scanned the room to acquaint herself with those present, referring to a seating plan hastily prepared by the ubiquitous clerk. Lawyers on both sides exchanged looks and silently mouthed communication before rising simultaneously.

"Your Honor, may we approach the bench?"

"No." The Judge studied her notes without further comment.

The Douglases spoke amongst themselves, whispering theories.

Zalkow continued to squirm.

"I am Judge Miriam Whiteside. I have been appointed to replace His Honor Judge Harold Bolstein. I regret to inform the court that he was pronounced dead on arrival at the General Hospital approximately thirty minutes ago."

The Judge continued with dispatch, trying not to show any of the emotion swirling inside her. She could see that her audience was stunned by her pronouncement. They hung on every word presumably assuming a further explanation about the Judge's death would be forthcoming.

"Prior to these proceedings, myself and three colleagues were required to review the briefings and be prepared to sit before you this morning. Judge Bolstein drew the short lot and I drew the second. I have reviewed the transcript from this morning's proceedings and I have received Judge Bolstein's recommendation."

While Judge Miriam Whiteside spoke, she clutched the last written words of her friend Harold Bolstein. His assistant had not typed out the formal copy nor had she yet deciphered the Judge's scratching on the white paper. Only seconds after she had taken the paper from the Judge and left his chamber, she had returned to ask him a further question.

She found him dead.

His removal had been rather unceremonious, so had the speed at which Judge Whiteside had been summoned from another proceeding.

She was forced to recess a minor trial in progress in order that she might attend to the high-profile Douglas hearing. The entire courthouse would be closed for one day in memory of the senior Judge. A full dignitary funeral would be held, but for now there was business to conclude.

She looked again at the familiar scrawl that was Harold's hallmark. She had no trouble deciphering his intent, that the Will should be found in question and a ninety-day extension granted.

"I have reviewed the briefings thoroughly and examined the law governing this situation. I have considered the testimony given this morning. I find that the Last Will and Testament of Mr. Peter Douglas is valid in the way it is prepared and executed."

Zalkow could barely hold back a wide grin.

Dr. Brandon hung his head presumably in the knowledge of what his next task would be.

Sarah and Charlotte sobbed openly while Edward, Matt and Michael huddled around them for comfort.

For Brian it was his worst nightmare coming true. He was about to lose the beacon that had guided him through life. He had been in complete denial. Now acknowledgment washed over him.

No one noticed when the Judge stood and quietly left without disturbing the mood in the room with formality. She folded Bolstein's note in her hand and slipped it into the pocket of her robe.

Unlike Harold Bolstein, she did not have a relationship with the Douglas family. She had been a colleague of his for over a decade and respected him immensely. She also understood what the word "judgment" meant. In this case, she had exercised hers to the best of her ability. It was irrelevant that it didn't agree with Judge Harold Bolstein's.

The bailiff had arranged for the dejected Douglas clan to leave from the underground garage beneath the courthouse. They decided to go to a small restaurant outside the city for some food and drinks and a chance to bolster each other's spirits. Little food was consumed, but numerous drinks were. For that short period of time, the family spent some quiet time together mourning Peter's now-inevitable passing.

Brian made a call to his mother in Florida. He was surprised that, between the stress she was enduring with her mother and perhaps the fact that she had essentially lost Peter years earlier, she responded quite calmly.

Perhaps for her it was a final act of closure on a lifetime with the man who fathered him and his siblings.

She promised to call Catherine right away to let her know what had happened in court. Brian agreed to fill in details for her the moment they were available.

Zalkow and the lawyers waded right into the media scrum waiting outside the court house. No one really knew how the media found out about the case, but the only question on the minds of the reporters was whether or not life support would be removed from Peter Douglas. Zalkow brushed away microphones when they were stuck in his face and reporters when they sprayed their questions. He had his own media outlet to feed information. He also had hot news regarding Schebb that he knew would fuel sales and speculation about the upcoming features in the Star.

– Chapter 57 –

"What the fuck…a hundred million dollars?" Zalkow continued to speed read through pages of a lengthy document that Harvey Kirkland had delivered to him in an unmarked envelope.

He read the same page three times to ensure that he had it right that Peter Douglas's death triggered a $100 million dollar gift to the trauma centre. He wrote five characters on a blank page: C H O Y ?

His laughter filled his home office. He stretched back in his chair, grinning widely, then stood up to leave.

He paused, turned toward the copy of the THE LAST WILL AND TESTAMENT OF PETER WILSON DOUGLAS, then grabbed his crotch firmly, jiggling the package toward the document.

"Ya, fuck you Peter Douglas. Fuck you. What goes around comes around."

He bent down, clicked the shredder on, and page by page watched the evidence slip into its teeth.

The bus was pulling into his driveway just as Zalkow was backing his car out. He stared in the rear view mirror then stopped immediately, jumping out to greet his daughter.

"Hello, my sweet."

"Daaaaa."

"Did you have a good day?"

"Yaaaa. Daaaa. Daaaa."

He kissed his wife quickly on the cheek.

"I've got it."

The elevator of the handicapped bus lowered the wheelchair carrying his severely crippled daughter.

"Daddy's got you, sweetie. Daddy's got you."

"Daaaa. Daaaa. Luuuv."

"I love you too, now go with Mommy. Daddy has to go to work to do some business."

He jumped back in his car, watching his wife wheel their daughter up the ramp and into the house.

Pausing, he tried. But he felt nothing. He heard the words of his therapist.

"Just keep doing it physically, Joe, and the feelings will come. Like smiling when you answer the phone. You sound happy and then you get a happy response back. She'll know, Joe. She'll know."

He would keep trying, but perhaps years of suppressing anger at God, himself and the world around him had numbed him to a point where vengeance now seemed to be his driving motivation.

Was this all that was left? Had it been so long that joy was gone for good?

He backed onto the road, then stopped with a light squeak of the tires on pavement.

His nemesis Peter Douglas and his all too perfect family again occupied his mind the way it had for years after he had been spurned for a key role in the Douglas organization over two decades earlier. A number of his friends had gotten in early and made millions on their stock options but Peter explained that Zalkow's lack of business experience made it virtually impossible to hire him and still have the respect of the others.

"Stay with medicine, Joe. You'll do fine there."

Zalkow's career floundered along and then a chance meeting with a financially strapped Harvey Kirkland led him into an undisclosed controlling interest in the City Star where this slippery slope had all started.

His motivation to let Peter Douglas slip into history had seemingly increased well beyond revenge and into self propulsion without him noticing.

He shifted the car to drive and pressed hard on the accelerator.

The hospital boardroom was filled with an intense buzz. Board members sipped coffee, speculating over rumors surrounding the Douglas family. From windows in the room they could peer down to the street where news crews, with their trucks, hovered around the front doors of the hospital. Several police cruisers were on site to keep order amongst a few dozen picketers who lined the sidewalk proclaiming views on euthanasia. Every news station had picked up leaks on the story about the court case surrounding Peter Douglas's Will and his desire not to be kept alive by artificial means.

No one had yet leaked to the media the tidy little fact that the hospital was in line for a major inheritance if his wishes were supported.

The meeting was called to order several times before all the members finally took their seats and focused on the Chairman. Peter Douglas's lawyer had sent his regrets along with the written brief outlining the requests in Peter's will. His role as Peter's executor and agent would preclude him from participating in the discussions. The session started with 45 minutes of routine housekeeping matters then two hours of final budget deliberations.

Zalkow had been called to report on the matter of a major law suit that the hospital was fighting which had seen him and the trauma centre accused of negligence, fraud and malpractice over the handling of information that positive tests for breast cancer were actually inconclusive or without justification. Many supported Zalkow, others quietly weren't so sure.

Zalkow had put on a good show even though he had inside information from court contacts that a loss to the hospital - in this case, in the tens of millions - was very likely.

The group of prominent board members was wound up extremely tight when the agenda moved on to the final, most potent item of the evening.

All but the executive committee members were asked to leave.

"It pleases me to announce that in a vote held earlier today, Dr. Joseph Zalkow was elected Chairman of the Merciful Care Committee." The Chairman fanned his hand toward Zalkow who accepted the applause of the small group.

"I humbly accept this most sensitive position. I assure all of you present today that my leadership and decisions will be tempered by the utmost in consideration and sensitivity considering the nature of the matters dealt with by the committee."

Zalkow filled the room with his ego for a few minutes longer. He felt very good about the words coming out of his mouth and the nodding responses he was getting from his audience.

"Thank you, Joe, thank you." The Chairman finally took the floor from Zalkow, who sat down reluctantly. "As hospital Chairman, I have automatic membership on all standing committees. The first order of business that Dr. Zalkow will be overseeing is the Douglas case. This is a high-profile and sensitive case. Before I continue, I must remind you that all discussions within this room are confidential to those present and those who have official access to the board and executive committee minutes. I have been informed that Peter Douglas's Will was held in court to be valid. It contains a provision which stipulates his desire not to be kept alive by artificial means. We will be referring this matter to Joe's committee for immediate deliberation. However I feel, as it is a sub-committee of this board, that we should send our recommendation on to Joe's committee in order that they may proceed with our support."

A rumble around the table broke out. Numerous small discussions commenced.

"Order. Order."

One of the board members rose. "Many of us have known Peter Douglas for years. I for one do not wish to be part of the decision regarding his life."

Several others confirmed their negative feelings around the topic; the members' voices increased again. The Chairman banged his gavel for the first time that evening.

"Order! Whether you like it or not, we members of the Hospital Board are ultimately involved and responsible for all decisions taken by this hospital. If you hadn't thought of that before, you need to think of it now. These positions come with weight, ladies and gentlemen. Perhaps you haven't felt that burden before now. Dr. Zalkow?"

"Thank you, Mr. Chairman." Zalkow stood up, buttoning his jacket. "Ladies and gentlemen, the mandate of my committee is to ensure that this hospital's care and resources are allocated in the most moral, ethical and financially appropriate manner."

"Here, here." One of Zalkow's supporters added.

"As you know, until recently this and other hospitals have doled out medical care without accountability. Resources were squandered in an unbridled fashion regardless of the potential human return. Our job now, in this hospital and as mandated by the State, is to ensure that we are allocating our resources in a manner which maximizes the human return. This may seem somewhat callous, but the reality is that the system is going broke."

There was a mumble around the board table and nodding heads.

"We are spending millions of dollars caring for people who have little or no hope of recovery. At the same time we refuse admission to adults, seniors and children who are faced with medical emergencies but have no means to pay for services. We have reached the limit of our ability to interfere in what is essentially God's work. Ladies and gentlemen, the fact is, you are involved in the process of life and death decisions."

The room was hushed.

Zalkow paused poetically and let that little pearl sink in. He knew that most board members had been sitting for years. Their roles had been simultaneously prestigious and perfunctory.

"I was present at the court case and our Chairman has a copy of the binding judgment regarding Peter Douglas. It pains me also to deal on a matter regarding one with whom I am so close."

This last sentence raised some eyebrows around the table from those who knew the level of animosity between Peter Douglas and Zalkow. He saw looks being exchanged across the table. If Zalkow had started the evening with credibility, he was quickly losing it with those in the know. Sensing the shifting breeze, he toned down his rhetoric immediately. He was an apt political sailor with a good sense for the wind direction and velocity.

"Ladies and gentlemen, the matter of Peter Douglas is out of our hands. We are merely facilitating the legal wishes of a man whom we all respect. Our only duty now is to ensure his wishes are carried out as requested. In this matter my committee really has no say other than the mechanism and timing of termination."

Zalkow instantly wished he could have retracted that word the moment it left his mouth. The winces on the faces of the board members were proof to him of that concern.

"What I mean is…"

"Thank you, Joe." The Chairman stepped in before more damage was done. Another board member stood and spoke to the Chairman.

"Is there no chance the family might appeal this decision?"

"I'm certain there is, but our duty is to carry out the business before us as mandated by the court. If a higher court changes that mandate, then we will respond accordingly. It's not our place to sit by and wait in speculation or anticipation of what might or might not happen. We must deal with the present situation. We need a motion then. Joe?"

Zalkow took the opportunity to rise again. "I move that this board direct the Committee on Merciful Care to proceed with our support in facilitating the requests of Peter Douglas's will which were bound by the judgment of this State's court."

"So moved. Second?"

One member at the back gingerly raised his hand.

"Any further discussion?"

Another member left her chair to speak. "Is there any possibility we may be in conflict of interest as a board?"

Zalkow felt his stomach sink.

He saw the Chairman's forehead begin to glisten.

Does he know what I know?

"We, and the public, all know that Peter has been an avid supporter of the hospital and that he is a man of considerable means. It wouldn't be much of a stretch for someone to assume that this hospital was in line for a healthy donation upon his demise. If the public thought our decision was in some way driven by this knowledge, we could look pretty bad."

The room started humming again with members acknowledging the point and asking each other's opinions. Several minutes went by while people chattered about the downside to their reputations if such allegations came forward.

"You make a good point. However, I contend once again that it is not our job to speculate or gossip. Money flows to us from the most obvious and least likely places. We can all cite cases in which we have unsuccessfully treated patients whose death brought this hospital financial benefit. However, if it makes everyone feel better, we can seek declarations of conflict in advance of the vote. Joe?"

"In the matter of the standing motion, do any members of this board have specific knowledge of Peter Douglas's will that would prejudice their unbiased judgment?"

The Chairman started at his left. He made eye contact with each member around the table. All eyes shifted from member to member. All shook their heads negatively in turn. Over the silence of the room a chant could be heard from the street below.

"NO MORE DEATH! LIFE IS IN OUR HANDS!
NO MORE DEATH! LIFE IS IN OUR HANDS!"

A shiver rippled up Zalkow's legs.

All eyes stopped at an elderly gentleman two from Zalkow's right. There was a pregnant pause; his head stayed motionless.

Zalkow felt his ass moisten.

"Do I have to stand to talk?" His voice was somewhat feeble.

"No. Please go ahead."

"Well, a few years ago I was at a function with Peter and got to talking about Wills and estates. Now, I don't have much of an estate myself and I can't really understand why a wealthy man like Mr. Douglas would want to talk to me about his estate, but…"

Zalkow felt the tension in the room increase.

"He did indicate at the time that it was his intention to donate a sizable portion of his worth to, I believe his words were…"

Zalkow and the Chairman leaned forward, hanging on this man's words.

"I believe his exact words were 'worthy medical causes and facilities.'"

Two sighs of relief were audible.

"Now, I don't know if that causes any problems, but I thought I should mention it just the same."

"Thank you, but no, I don't think that poses any problems."

The eyes continued their circular scrutiny.

The woman next to Zalkow shook her head.

He did the same, keeping his eyes focused on his notes.

The Chairman immediately took the floor again without actually making any head motions.

"Fine. Is everyone's conscience clear? Now back to the vote. All in favor?"

The eyes of the board circled once again, landing on each member.

Starting from the Chairman's left, an arm stuck high in the air. Zalkow counted the rising arms. He felt his spirits lift until the "ayes" got to the first woman who sat still, looking at the other members.

Everyone's eyes bore down upon her, seemingly forcing her arm to reach into the air. The next few were automatic until the man two down from Zalkow. He shook his head in the negative.

"I just think I should stand out of this one. Just in case."

Zalkow threw his arm up in the air to keep the momentum going which seemingly forced the person on his left to do the same.

He didn't want any retractions.

"Passed!"

The Chairman's gavel hit the table, startling the older members.

Peter Douglas was officially a dead man.

The meeting ended quickly and tired members left the room without much pause for conversation.

Zalkow and the Chairman exchanged looks.

He must know something, Zalkow thought.

They were the last to leave, cordially ushering everyone with dispatch.

In the hall they were stopped by Dr. Brandon.

"Dr. Brandon, what are you doing in so late?"

"I was doing some rounds Mr. Chairman, but I am also very interested in knowing the fate of my favorite patient. Also, Dr. Zalkow here wanted me nearby in case I was required to speak to the board. You know, cleanse their hands."

"Oh, our hands are clean. I can assure you of that. The matter is quite straightforward. We'll be abiding by the court's decision. Actually, it's really out of our hands."

"It may be out of our hands, but it's certainly on both of yours. I'll resign before I give up on the Douglas case."

"Well, you may find that you're an unemployed Doctor then." Zalkow eyed him with malevolence and kept walking. "I suggest we speak tomorrow after a good night's sleep."

Dr. Brandon kept quiet but knew where he stood. The men turned from each other and walked away in silence.

If it comes down to that, Dr. Brandon would come clean if necessary regardless of the cost to himself.

– Chapter 58 –

It was long before crowds of visitors and staff buzzed through the hospital corridors. The sun had just risen to another day. Winter, although officially still several weeks off, was in the air when Edward arrived at the hospital early in the morning.

He struggled; it had been a long time since he'd wheeled a baby carriage. Each time he passed the odd person, they would strain for a peek inside to see what the little bundle looked like. Ultimately they were disappointed when they saw that the blankets kept his passenger completely hidden.

Edward put his finger to his lips to indicate that the baby was sleeping. He smiled and mouthed "newborn" or "first grandchild."

He couldn't believe how effective a license the carriage actually was. People opened doors and moved aside, making way for his determined trip toward Peter's room.

"Good morning, pal! Rise and shine!"

Peter watched while Edward closed the door. He then pulled the curtains over the window before wheeling the carriage to the bedside.

Edward only had to pull the blankets back a bit to expose the damp nose of Schebb, who immediately stood up in the wobbly carriage and started to bark.

Edward quickly grabbed his mouth. "Quiet."

Schebb continued to whimper, looking curiously at Peter, then leaned forward to vigorously lick his master's dry-skinned hand.

Peter was elated to see his best friend. He laughed while Schebb continued to lick. Then, without warning, sorrow replaced Peter's laughter. The sight of Schebb brought back a flood of memories, intensifying his feeling of confinement. He wanted so badly to be free of this captivity. Symptoms of disaster mounted quickly.

"Are you okay? This equipment is going goofy."

Peter was silent.

"Peter, are you there? Can you hear me?"

Schebb moaned, Edward approached the bed and gently nudged his friend. "Peter? Peter?"

"I'm here. I felt trapped and afraid, Ed. It's scary. Sometimes, like when you arrived, I forget all about my situation. But then something like Schebb reminds me how precarious my existence is. I have to stay calm or risk..."

Edward took Peter's hand.

"...risk everything."

"I'm here with you, my friend. I'm not going anywhere, and if I have my way neither are you."

"Thank you, Edward. Thank you."

Schebb broke the exchange with a quiet bark. Peter and Edward smiled at the unusual scene.

"I guess he can't figure me out, can he? Watch this."

Peter focused his mind. He let himself fill with the love he had for his pet. Schebb immediately stopped licking and looked directly at Peter. He whined a few times, then wagged his tail, putting both front feet on the bed so he could lick Peter's face. Tears flowed out of Peter's eyes. Schebb dutifully licked the salt water.

"You can talk to animals too?"

"Not really, but I think he knows it's me."

"There's no doubt about that."

"Where did he come from?"

"We don't know for sure, but according to a note left, it seems that the trucker who saved your life had him all the time. He obviously doesn't want any publicity and said to give the reward to a charity. Schebb's in perfect health. He evidently took good care of him."

"Edward, I want you to promise me that you'll find that man and make sure he has no financial worries in the future. That's really all I can offer, but I want him to know from you. He gave me a second chance, which is worth more than any money I ever had."

"You have my word…Peter, the court ruled in favor of your Will. Brian did his best but couldn't get an extension. Your friend Harold Bolstein died in court yesterday while deliberating over your case."

"He died? In court?"

"In his office, actually. Obviously your case isn't what killed him, but the irony of it all strikes me. We were in recess, sequestered in the courtroom. He never returned. Miriam Whiteside showed up and gave the verdict. I guess she just read his notes and followed through."

"Not a chance. Those two haven't agreed on a verdict since they met."

"What are you saying?"

"I'm not saying anything except that if Whiteside found my Will valid, you can bet that Harold would have torn it to shreds. I guess we'll never know. It is ironic. The court has done exactly what I would have wanted them to do in any other circumstance but this. I've been given powers beyond any I've known or imagined, but they do have their limitations. If nothing else, I've been able to express my love for you, my good friend."

Edward went quiet, listening. Schebb had settled back into the carriage, seemingly content that he had been reunited with his master.

"In a way Edward, I'm looking forward to the freedom ahead of me. I think I've learned my lesson. I don't think judgment will be so harsh

this go-around. If I had more time though, I'd certainly put what I've learned to use over the balance of my life."

"Your lessons aren't lost on me, Peter. Perhaps one day I'll write about it after I'm no longer concerned about people questioning my sanity."

Edward and Peter laughed like there was nothing unusual about communicating this way and having a dog bedside in a hospital.

"You know, this really isn't that unusual, Peter. We seem to have always known what each other were thinking. It's just that we could talk then. I wonder how many people I'm close to; that if I really tuned in I could know their thoughts. Maybe talking is just an obstacle to real communication. After all, it is people's thoughts and actions that make good or bad deeds happen, not their words."

"I know for sure that even though Zalkow might think he's winning this round, his prospects for the future are very unpleasant. And you know, even if I could change my Will, I wouldn't. I know that some of those funds will be squandered, but most will go to help people in need. It would be nice to be revived and continue life on Earth but I really am at peace now. I'm no longer afraid to die, Ed."

"I understand, Peter. I could feel it when we traveled together. It was like in correcting one wrong you mended many. I too have learned through this process, and I thank you for that."

The two lifelong friends shared a loving silence, connected by mind and spirit.

"How long do I have? I mean now that the court has ruled?"

The question startled Edward. "Cripes Peter, I don't know. I don't want to know. It's easy to talk like this, but the thought of losing you twice scares the hell out of me. I suppose we'll hear though, and I will tell you. If you want to know."

"I'll know."

"I forgot you're a mind reader. Brian is appealing, of course."

"It won't make any difference. It's unlikely that any Judge will go against my wishes. I took great pains in drafting that Will to avoid any ambiguity."

"Zalkow and those lawyers make me sick, Peter. You should have heard Dr. Brandon going on. He has really turned out different than I thought."

"Go light on him, Ed. He's being blackmailed by Zalkow somehow. He's confused, but I think he'll come through in the end. Between Brian and you, give him whatever support he needs. I think something happened in the past and Zalkow is holding it over him. He's done his time. He's a good man, I'm sure of it."

"Is there anything you don't know? Can you tell me who's going to win the ball game today?"

"No." Peter chuckled.

"Too bad! Anyway, your family is spending lots of time together. Brian skipped the board meeting for obvious reasons. I know he was planning to leave the city for a couple of days to let his head clear. Peter, you'd have been proud of him. He reminded me so much of you when you were his age, it was uncanny. It was like you were there."

Edward stopped mid-sentence and stared at Peter. A slight chill came over him when the significance of his words sunk in.

"Peter, you weren't there...I mean, in the courtroom, were you? This isn't a joke, you know. We are going through hell on this side."

"I've been to hell. What you're going through is just life. Besides, do you really think I'd take my own life?"

"I don't know. It's getting harder to tell what 'life' is."

"Believe me, everything is going the way it should. We have to have faith that the journey has meaning."

Edward held Peter's hand and patted Schebb at the same time. No further words were exchanged. Edward watched his friend's face, reliving in his mind a lifetime of friendship. Peter was and continued to be the most significant person in Edward's life. His gratitude for the opportunity to share this special communication was boundless. Edward quietly bundled up the dog and left Peter's room, not knowing whether his friend was present or faraway.

Peter had been flashing in and out of memories while they talked. His time was measured in a way that didn't affect the continuity of their conversation. He had grown quite accustomed to visiting the past and touching up little flaws. His path had been smoothed immensely. People's lives had been altered in a way that wasn't measurable in human terms; inside, a warmer memory of Peter Douglas now existed in those individuals he had retraced his steps to see.

When Edward left, Peter was reliving the first day with his new pup and relishing in the joy they both felt to have found each other. He hadn't been completely honest with Edward either. He knew precisely who would win the ball game that day and every day forward.

Chapter 59

"We're in a lot of shit here, pal."

Dr. Brandon entered Peter's room wearing casual clothes covered by a white lab coat. He was without his usual entourage of interns and nurses or his ever-present clip board and stethoscope.

He had Peter's full attention.

"There's very little doubt that this joint is going to shut you down. First of all, that's what you've asked for and the court has ruled in favor of your request. Secondly, your buddy Zalkow is now running the committee that decides these things. He and I suspect that fucking wormy Chairman of the Board, have their greedy eyes on the money they believe you're leaving to the hospital."

Peter remembered Choy's words.

How did she know all of this?

"Now, I've had a suspicion from the start that you're awake inside there. Call me crazy, but it's a hunch I've had since you got here. I've had some feedback from our equipment to support my feelings, but not nearly enough to prove anything. I'm being fucked over by Zalkow for something that happened years ago. I've done my time, Mr. Douglas. The problem is that if he goes public with my file or lets it leak to the media, I'm finished."

Peter's hunch had been right.

"You know people don't read the small print, just the headlines. I need your help here. I know we're all just puppets being orchestrated from above. If it was my choice I'd keep you here forever. Who knows, you might just wake up. But we're dealing with reality here and the reality is that I can't prove you're in there. For all I know, keeping your body alive may be the worst thing I can do for you. If you want me to try to stop this, you have to give me something real to work with. Something I can show some people. Something that will get them to listen. Are you in there or not? Can you hear me?"

Peter watched and listened. He was confused like the rest of them about his prospects for the future. Was it possible that his tampering could leave him a life trapped in a useless body?

Death, at least, would bring some certainty, wouldn't it?

Dr. Brandon was getting even more anxious. He placed his hands on Peter's shoulders and shook him. "Wake up, wake up, I know you're in there, I know it."

"Talking to the dead now are we?" Dr. Brandon jumped up when he heard a voice behind him.

"How long have you been there?"

"Long enough to see you're losing it." Zalkow smiled an evil little smile. "Peter Douglas is long gone. You're talking to an empty shell. Why can't you just accept the inevitable and be happy with the result? He'd want the same thing. What if you revive him and he's a drooling invalid for the next ten or fifteen years? Do you think that's what he wants? Do you think that's what his family wants? Of course not. We're not grim reapers. We're apostles of life."

"Keep selling because I'm not buying, Joe. You've got your own motives. I'm not sure what they are, but when I find out, so will the rest of the world."

"I'm clean, Jim. It's you who has the dirt in your closet." Zalkow held up a brown envelope. He waved it in his face. "Don't worry, I have copies."

Four men in white walked into the room wheeling a cart with a variety of tools on it.

"Go ahead, gentlemen."

"Who are these guys?" .

"We're shipping this equipment back to Europe. They can chase ghosts over there."

"This is my patient, Zalkow. You have no authority here."

Zalkow handed Dr. Brandon a yellow form. "Wrong again, Dr. Brandon. Our committee now has full authority over the Douglas case. You are now the advising physician only. Duly authorized by the new Chief of Staff."

"You sleazy bastard."

"Go ahead, guys. This equipment ships out on an evening flight. Get busy."

Dr. Brandon moved back to Peter's bedside and grabbed his limp hand.

"It's up to you. The choice is yours, if you have one. Now would be a good time."

The technicians began disassembling the equipment that Dr. Brandon had hoped would be instrumental in this case. He felt an overwhelming sense of defeat.

"Fuck you, Zalkow. This isn't over."

Dr. Brandon brushed close enough to Zalkow to seem threatening, then stalked past him and out of the room.

"Is Dr. Brandon here? Something really strange is going on next door. I need to see Dr. Brandon."

Zalkow realized the young man was from the monitoring room next door. "Yes, I can help you." He took the young man's arm and moved him toward the door.

"Are you Dr. Brandon?"

Zalkow walked the technician toward the monitoring room. He looked around to see who might be listening and saw they were alone. "Yes, that's right. How can I help you?"

"It's the monitoring equipment. Something really strange is going on."

Zalkow closed the door behind them pressing the lock on the knob. When it clicked the technician looked at the door and then at Zalkow.

"This is all very confidential, you know. We don't want some orderly bursting in on us, do we?"

"I guess not…Dr. Brandon. I guess it's okay."

"So what's the problem?"

"We've had virtually nothing on the screen since we got here. Then all of a sudden a few minutes ago, all of the calibrations started to reset themselves to lower levels. Your name kept flashing on the screen. All of the data was automatically rerun with the new settings. Based on what I saw, there's been tons of activity. It was just the settings were so high that the information was being saved in memory instead of being displayed. Here, let me run it for you against the date line."

Zalkow looked back to ensure that the door was locked. The technician's fingers flew over the keys, preparing to display the captured data.

This guy may be stupid, but he knows this equipment.

"Okay, here we go. Starting from the first night. The higher the spikes, the more brain activity."

The time appeared across the bottom of the screen. It lit up with an impressive display of vertical lines. There were numerous occasions when the screen exploded with activity.

"I can't explain that, but in a conscious person I'd say it represented a pretty big burst of emotion. Now let me run the same display against a normal waking baseline."

Zalkow shivered, realizing the implications of what he was seeing. Peter's brain activity was virtually normal. If what he was seeing was true, his arch-enemy Peter Douglas may be alive.

Was he wrong that euthanasia was moral and actually helped best meet the needs of all affected?

Zalkow justified his feelings.

That's fine. That's fine. I can live with this little secret. Besides, Douglas's millions would help many others. He might never recover. The equipment was all experimental anyway. The readings might not mean a thing.

"This is fantastic. You've done a great job here. I'm going to include you in my report. What's your name?"

Zalkow dutifully wrote down the young man's name, making him swell with pride.

"How many copies of this information do we have?"

"Just one, sir. On the hard drive."

"Give me two copies. One to review and one for a back-up, then clear the hard drive of all the data. We don't want this showing up on someone else's case in Europe."

"No, sir. That's a good idea too. The back-up. It's always a good idea, just in case." The young man tapped away on the keyboard. Within minutes Joe had two data storage devices, the size of his thumb, in his pocket. He watched the man type a command to delete all data on the hard drive.

"Dr. Brandon?"

Zalkow hesitated, and then answered when he realized who he was impersonating. "Yes?"

"What about the modem?"

"The what?"

"The modem, Sir. We're online to somewhere. This was set up the first day by two off-site guys. No one knew them, but they were here with some other Doctor. The other guy who's been around a lot." The technician picked up the phone line on the floor. They both followed it to where it disappeared into a jack in the wall. "I don't know where it goes, but presumably they've got everything we have."

Zalkow paused. He knew the "other" Doctor was the one he was impersonating. He didn't know who the "two off-site guys" were and didn't really care. He had heard the rumors like everyone else, but couldn't worry about them now. "That's another back-up off site. I'd forgotten about that. We were just doing some tests with a new storage system. We won't need it now that I've got hard copies. Can you erase it from here?"

The man's fingers flew over the keys, mining into the system. He sat back in his chair, looking at a screen of gibberish that meant nothing to Zalkow. "Well, not directly, but I could send a general format code. It's sort of like dropping a match in gas. Everything will be gone. We'd wipe out whatever is on the drive at the end of this wire. Is that what you want?"

Zalkow envisioned a computer full of data somewhere in someone's office. He was about to ruin that someone's day. He figured by the time anyone would come calling, equipment, technicians and data would be long gone. And so would Peter Douglas.

"Sounds fine. It's probably dumping into a dedicated machine anyway. No problem. On my say so, go ahead."

A few more key strokes and data somewhere at the end of the telephone line would start to disappear. An alarm would sound immediately, warning of the unusual command sequence. Calls would be made. With luck, the response would be slow. By the time someone actually got to a terminal and checked out the problem it would just be another mystery. Probably chalked up to a hacker that no one would ever hear about.

"You've been really helpful. Why don't you take the rest of the day off? I'll get the guys next door to load this gear up." Zalkow reached in his pocket and pulled out a fifty dollar bill. "Here, get yourself some lunch and a few beers."

The technician took the money hesitantly and stuffed it quickly into his white pants, shook Zalkow's hand and thanked him.

"Don't mention it. Remember, everything in this room is confidential. We don't want the integrity of our experiment tainted with rumors. So no discussions unless authorized by me, got it?" Zalkow unlocked the door.

The man zipped his mouth with his fingers and smiled leaving Zalkow alone in the room.

Zalkow closed the door after him. It was very quiet except for the hum of the computer. He paused for a moment, steeled himself, then reached down to where the main power bar was plugged into the wall. With a firm jerk on the cord the computer whined to a halt. The screen went blank. The room went silent. There was no looking back now.

He instructed the workers in Peter's room to add the monitoring equipment to their list of duties, then left for his office in another wing.

Zalkow was quite amused at the way the little data storage devices extended and retracted from their slim cases with the flick of his thumb.

So much power in such a small place.

He smiled to himself, closing his office door behind him. With the flick of a pen knife from his desk he pried both devices open with barely a clicking sound to indicate they had been violated. With one more deft flick of the blade he extracted the tiny electronic contents and held each up for a close inspection.

The shredder grunted once, pausing prior to the attack on whatever it was that bulged between the sheets of paper that it normally munched on. A second later the evidence that Zalkow had extracted from the computer was well mixed with a week of shredding. While the machine hummed, awaiting its next bite, Zalkow smiled to himself for being such a brilliant strategist. He looked forward to hearing the response from his board when a check for one hundred million dollars was presented by Douglas's lawyers.

– Chapter 60 –

Michael was the only person at the table who hadn't been drinking at the previous evening's family gathering. He had offered to drive Charlotte and Sarah back to Catherine's flat after the family dined.

Sarah had gone directly to bed and left Michael talking with Charlotte. He promised to say goodnight before he left. Michael had listened quietly for some time while Charlotte poured out her feelings. She felt isolated and lonely. She felt, despite the family's efforts to involve her over the years, that she was the outsider. She worried about how they would be with her if Peter was gone.

"You've fit in so quickly, Michael. That's very rare with this family."

It started the night she was at home and unaware of Peter's accident. She had let the guilty feelings from that night consume her. She told Michael about her idea of having Peter's baby and was gratified to know he felt it was a wonderful idea. She spoke of Marion's change toward her and that she had thought of going to Florida to visit with her. Most of all she spoke about Peter, about how much she loved him and what a wonderful man he was.

"He's told me on many occasions that he wasn't always this nice." Charlotte just smiled. "It's hard to believe that someone could have really been that different."

"People can change dramatically; sometimes by choice, sometimes by circumstance. One has to have the will to change. Will it so and eventually it will be."

"I like that.'Will it so and eventually it will be.' It sounds so simple."

"It is. I believe we bring upon ourselves exactly what we wish for. We become a function, or in some cases, a victim of our wants and actions. If we have a poor relationship with everything and everyone around us, if we continually stand in judgment or see only the bad in everything or everyone, then we end up with a very poor relationship with ourselves. That's the true pain, the real loss. Eventually our life's score gets added up. In the end, I think we are our own judges. That's a harsh court. We can't hide from our own truth, a truth that has been known all along."

"Are you saying that by thinking the Douglases don't like me or blame me, I may be bringing those feelings upon myself?"

"That's what I think. Treat people the way you want them to be and for the most part they will be. It seems to me you can always find in someone exactly what you're looking for."

Charlotte nodded, letting Michael's words sink in. She leaned forward and took Michael's hands. "Thank you, Michael. I feel so much better. It all sounds so easy once you hear it. I guess it just gets a bit noisy up here." Charlotte pointed to her head.

"The simplest concepts usually bring the most profound results. Living a good and happy life here is easy. It's the unhappy life that's hard. It takes much more energy to be negative than positive. It sure is easier and more enjoyable to find the good in people rather than seeking out the evil."

Charlotte was smiling broadly now.

"What is it?"

"I was just thinking how many times today I saw the bad points in people and things I was doing. That has just changed."

They both stood. Charlotte gave Michael a motherly hug. "Where'd you learn all this at such a young age?"

Michael smiled and shrugged his shoulders. "Honestly, I have no idea, I really don't. It seems like I've always known it. Yet I get the same reaction from people all the time when they respond to such simple concepts. It gives me a great feeling to help them."

"Don't forget to say goodnight to Sarah."

"I won't."

Sarah's room was at the opposite end of Catherine's flat from the third-floor room where Charlotte was staying. When Michael walked down the hall, two cats tangled in his feet. He could hear Charlotte's distant steps walking the two floors to her room. She had extinguished all the lights but one in the foyer.

I wonder what she's thinking?

Sarah's door was left invitingly open. He approached her bed. He could hear her soft breath. A nightlight shadowed her face and hair against the pillow. Michael felt awkward about disturbing her. He leaned down to kiss her lightly on the cheek, then paused just close enough that he could smell her slumbering essence.

What am I doing? This could turn out very badly.

He stood, appreciated her beauty for a final second then turned and walked away.

- Chapter 61 -

A unique and wonderful bonding had formed amongst the group after sharing such an emotional time during the court challenge and then hospital board meeting when the ultimate decision to remove life support for Peter was made. Brian had taken Matt and Edward in the Douglas sedan and dropped them off before heading home for the evening. They discussed, with amazement, the hole carved in one's soul after experiencing what they were going through. It also left a craving in each person that needed to be fulfilled. They agreed that the challenge for them, as for anyone who suffers an emotional trauma, was to fill the hole with something good. They talked about how easy it is for people, including themselves, to cope with emotional pain by abusing alcohol, drugs, sex, work or any of the myriad of coping mechanisms our disenchanted society offered. They agreed the lucky ones would find satisfaction and growth through sharing with someone they trusted.

The Douglases comprised an immensely private and complicated collection of individuals. Each had been brought up in a similar environment, yet that common upbringing had manifested itself differently, creating markedly different personalities. By virtue of his long association with Peter, Edward was as much a Douglas as any of them, although his upbringing nowhere resembled that of the Douglas children.

After being rescued by his new foster parents, Edward had grown up a farm boy. He walked with a distinct limp and had to work hard fitting in with other kids. His foster father loved to gamble. Edward spent many weekend nights watching his father play cards until dawn; winning, then losing, then winning what appeared to be fortunes. There was always plenty to eat at home, but he remembered constant complaining by his foster mother about his Dad's gambling habit.

Edward loved cards and card tricks. He practiced and practiced when he was a young boy, watching his Dad gamble. He could do things with cards that no untrained eye could follow. This skill became his ticket to making friends, fitting in and ultimately moving on to get an education. He combined his father's knack for gambling with his own unique ability to make cards appear and disappear at will.

At age sixteen, he announced he would be leaving home and going to college. He had several thousand dollars stuffed in socks from the hundreds of games he had won while playing with his father's friends and others. Through the years he began to apply his sleight-of-hand abilities to magic tricks, with which he entertained regularly.

When Edward felt a void inside, he would sit and do magic and card tricks for hours. It reminded him how he had reached where he was. It put into perspective whatever problem was getting him down. The court hearing, his visits with Peter, and dinner with the Douglases that evening had disturbed him. Edward stayed up late, working with his cards, calming his mood. Meeting Peter Douglas at college had been one of the single most important events in his life. The thought of losing him left a hollow space he knew no magic trick would ever fill.

Brian had rattled around his apartment for a while, trying to imagine a good reason for telephoning Marjorie late on a Friday night. He had dialed her number several times before finally letting it ring through. His mood sank with disappointment when her voicemail picked up.

I wish I could un-dial that call! She must be out. Hopefully not in someone else's arms.

He paced.

They rarely spoke of their private lives and Brian didn't know if she dated anyone or not.

"This is Marjorie. I'm sorry I can't take your call right now, but please leave a message and I'll call you back."

Brian loved hearing her voice. Even though it was a recording, there was comfort in its familiarity. He wondered who called her. What messages were left? Who she called back or didn't. The beep had suddenly passed while Brian stood frozen in time. A typical warrior, he was unafraid of life's 'battle and bloodshed', but was wilting and spineless at the sound of a woman's voice. Pride and ego hurt by a woman loved were far greater punishment than any wounds the wars of life and business could inflict. He hung up...then dialed again. Much to his shock, she answered.

"Oh, ah, hi Marjorie this is Brian, Brian Douglas." He felt sixteen years old, calling a crush. "Sorry to be calling you at home but ah...I just got in. It was a long day. I thought you might want an update. I'll be up for a while if you want to call me back...I mean if this is a bad time."

Marjorie listened intently to every word. She suppressed her urge to burst her feelings into the telephone. She reminded herself several times with whom she was dealing and waited until the last possible moment.

"Hello, Brian. Can you hold on for a second...? I just got in. Let me get my coat and shoes off."

Marjorie stood in her nightgown and let ten seconds pass before she put the phone to her mouth. "Sorry about that. How are you?"

Just got in? I wonder where she was...and with whom?

Her inquisitive tones were comforting to him and he longed to be in her arms, pouring his feelings out. "Well, sorry I didn't get back to you. I just wanted to keep you informed."

"Of course, I appreciate that."

"Yes. Good then, uhmm…perhaps I could fill you in over a coffee…but I guess you just got in…"

"No no it's okay, let me see…I'll tell you what…I'll put on a fresh pot. You've never seen my place. You could come by here and tell me in person."

Brian felt like he rose about three feet off the floor. He tried to contain his elation at her invitation. "I wouldn't want to impose…but if that's okay, I could leave here in thirty minutes. I have a few things to tidy up." He was ready to bolt out the door without hanging up, but felt he'd done an adequate job of sounding interested but in control.

He changed his shirt and tie three times.

Marjorie took her second bath of the day and dressed appropriately seductive without being obvious.

She lived directly across the Boston Commons in a town-house near the State building. It was no more than a fifteen minute walk. Brian figured he'd rather spend the extra time in the park than pacing around his flat. He crossed Arlington Street. Traffic was light. He walked slowly through the wrought-iron fence. The evening lights shimmered on sidewalks wetted from melting snow; he could see his breath in the evening air. The trees had long since released their leaves in the annual ritual of self re-creation. He stopped on the bridge that crosses the pond where thousands of tourists rode the swan boats each year which had long since been stored for another season.

He heard the approaching clip-clop of horses' hooves. The sound rose, fell and rose again when a single mounted officer passed beneath the bridge on which Brian stood. The two nodded to each other when the officer looked up.

Brian recognized the wispy sound of the horse's tail swishing from one haunch to the other.

He continued his circuitous route through the park, stopping at the bronze statue of a mother duck to quietly count her bronze ducklings while he rested his shoe on her head. He retied both his laces.

"One, two, three, four, five, six, seven, eight. Eight baby bronze ducklings."

Which nursery story was that?

"Eight, seven, six, five, four, three, two, one."

The Duckling's way? No.

This time he pointed at each one he counted, "One, two, three, four, five, six, seven, eight."

I can remember, Jack, Mack, Quack…ahh…forget it.

He looked at his watch, then angled his excursion toward Frog Pond.

Ten more minutes passed. The duck story still occupied his mind.

He could see her building: a compressed, three-story town house like his sister's. One of thousands in the area, each one similar on the outside but unique to their occupants. He wondered what Marjorie's would look and smell like. He imagined her living room, dining room, kitchen… and bedroom.

Soft music played in the background, candles flickering to its beat cast shadows on the muted wall. She realized she had forgotten to put the coffee on the moment she opened her door.

"It's nice to see you."

"It's nice to see you."

A waft of fragrance swept over Brian when they greeted each other awkwardly, yet with tenderness. No more words were spoken, allowing an undeniable force to pull them together.

The embrace and kiss were gentle at first while each tested the other's waters. Passion increased dramatically; they felt the acknowledgment of the other.

This was right. This was exactly where they wanted to be.

Brian felt the void inside him fill instantly. All problems vanished into a haze of affection.

Marjorie loved this man.

It seemed she had loved him forever.

His arms were strong around her, his lips soft and wet. His cologne rising on his body heat dizzied her.

They paused for a breath but stayed clutched together.

He whispered to her, "What is the name of the book about those bronze ducks in the park?"

"What? She leaned her head away and looked at him confused.

"You know, in the Public Garden, the baby ducks."

"It's Make Way For The Ducklings. Why, would you like me to read it to you?"

"You have a copy?"

"Yes."

"Nooo."

"Yes...," she pressed her mouth to his ear, "their names are Jack, Kack, Lack, Mack, Nack, Quack, Pa..."

He smiled at her broadly then her mouth went silent as his met hers to pick up where they had left off.

Both kissers were smiling.

Two drifting souls were now united.

- Chapter 62 -

When she entered his room, Sarah was struck by how bare it seemed. She didn't immediately realize the monitoring equipment had been removed. The significance of its absence finally dawned on her. She pulled the curtains to create some privacy and went to Peter's bedside.

"Good morning, Daddy."

Peter loved it when she called him Daddy. It seemed to preserve both their youthfulness. He couldn't help notice the brightness of her face. Energy was radiating about her. Peter listened while his daughter rambled on nervously. The significance of the court hearing had not settled on Sarah. Michael's words had made her an optimist. She wasn't dwelling on losing her father. Instead she was appreciating him while she had him; he could wake up tomorrow or he could be gone tomorrow. She would deal with that when it happened. For now, she had news to share. Michael's presence in her life seemed to have made all of this much easier.

"I mean I have to go back to school at some point. I'm so far behind it will take weeks to get caught up. I've got exams coming up and there is no way I'll be ready for them. I don't really like the school. I'm thinking of coming home to go to school here. I guess I'll have to talk that over with everyone, though. I know you sent me there to improve my study habits and keep me focused on school. The fact is I can get into just as much trouble up there as I can at home. Once you learn the rules it's only a matter of time before you learn how to break them."

Sarah's buoyant mood suddenly waned. "Please don't leave us…"

"Hey, Sis." Sarah spun around.

"Oh, hi, you scared me."

"Do I look that bad in the morning?" Matt put his arm around Sarah's shoulder. He kissed her on the head; they looked at their father. "He looks tired. I guess he's been through a lot, hasn't he? It's sure going to hurt if we lose him."

"Matt, you shouldn't talk like that. What if he *can* hear us?"

"You're right. Sorry, Dad."

"Daddy, Matthew's here to see you." Sarah picked up her father's hand and placed her brother's hand on it. She put her arm around her brother's shoulder.

Matt looked around, recognizing the significance of the missing equipment. They stood in silence looking at their father, listening to him breathe. The air rattled as it flowed in and out through his mouth tubes. He'd seen the nurses clear his throat periodically with a long straw-like suction device to keep his breathing clear.

Sarah rubbed her hand over her father's forehead and smoothed his hair. "It's okay. We're here with you."

She felt her brother's body tense.

She heard his first small sob, then he let go of her hand and turned to walk toward the window. Sarah followed her brother and held him.

All his barriers were down.

His soul mingled with hers in a warm, tearful and loving exchange.

"I hope you're not dripping all over my clean shirt!" Sarah chuckled through her tears.

"Now you'll have matching stains on both sides."

Matt reached over to the window sill for a box of tissue and handed some to Sarah. Both blew together.

"It takes a lot to get us Douglases going, but when you do, watch out." Matt's voice was nasal with stuffed up sinuses. "See what you've done to us, Dad? We're a mess here because we both love you very much. You've been a great father. We hope you come back to us soon."

Sarah had never heard her brother speak like that. She wondered if it was for her benefit or if he really felt that way.

"By the way, Dad, I haven't seen Terri around. What did you do? Tell her the truth about me?"

"Who's Terri?"

"It's a long story. I'll tell you some other time." Matt continued, "I'm taking your daughter to Bermuda with me. Don't worry, I'll have her back before you know it. Hey, for all I know, you may be coming with us."

Sarah looked at Matt inquisitively.

"Another long story. I'll tell you on the trip."

Peter watched his two children with pride. He was pleased Matt was getting closer to Sarah. He could feel a genuine love between them.

Two nurses came in and explained it was time to give Peter a bath and turn him on his side. Peter's muscles had been kept supple with electric stimulators, but he still needed to be turned every four hours. They explained this was to avoid bed sores which were caused from lack of blood circulation to pressure points his body rested on.

Matt and Sarah said their good-byes and kissed their father. Sarah had never seen Matt kiss their father. She was touched by his gesture watching his lips make contact with Peter's forehead.

In the hallway they met Mrs. Rossi moving her cleaning cart along the corridor. She looked directly at Sarah and spoke. "You must be Sarah. Your father has told me so much about you."

Sarah looked at Matt hesitantly, then back at Mrs. Rossi. Matt spoke immediately as if someone had put the words in his mouth. "I have to make a quick call, Sarah. I'll be right back."

Mrs. Rossi took Sarah's hand in her worn, warm ones. When the old woman looked at her through the eyes of ages, Sarah felt like a mild trance had come over her. The significance of this woman suddenly seemed obvious.

"I know your father well, my child. He is very special man. He loves you and all his children. He wants you to know that he has been called to do work of angels. You must understand this is God's way. He not suffering. He sees and hears you the way I do. Speak to him gently, child. Give him strength for his journey. My calling has also come. I will soon fly in the path of angels too."

Sarah stood dazed.

When she returned to reality she found she was standing alone. She closed her eyes for a few seconds, trying to recall what she could. Her focus on the elderly cleaning woman was broken when Matt placed his hand on her shoulder.

"Where'd she go?" Sarah asked.

"Where'd who go?"

"The cleaning woman who was just here when we came out of Daddy's room."

"What are you talking about? I said 'wait here, I have to make a call.' You were alone, Sis."

Sarah shook her head, seeming to know there was no point trying to convince her brother that the experience was real.

"He loves us and he wanted us to know that."

Matt recalled the Bermuda experience and wondered if Sarah had something similar happen when he was gone. "I know, sis. I know that." Matt put his arm around her and walked past the Douglas security guard toward the elevator.

"The car's waiting. Bob's got the plane fueled and ready to go. Let's pick up our things and get out of here for a few days. We can be back in two hours if anything happens. Sound good?"

While Matt spoke in the elevator, Sarah folded Michael's card different ways until, unconsciously, she folded the card in such a way that it formed a perfect pyramid. A small protrusion on one end when folded tucked inside the three dimensional triangle and held the little structure together. Each side displayed one of the words BODY, MIND and SPIRIT. The base of the pyramid carried the word HARMONY.

"I get it!" Sarah interrupted Matt mid-sentence.

"Get what?"

"Michael's card. Did you figure it out?"

"The way it folds into a pyramid and sits nice and stable on the desk? Sure I got it. It's just hard to keep it."

"What?"

"Never mind."

"Hmmm, I thought I was onto something of my own but I guess you have already figured it out."

"I can tell you Sis that folding the card is a hell of a lot easier than following its prescription. But now that you've discovered its answer you can impress Michael, I'm sure."

"I don't think he's that easily impressed. He's one guy who isn't falling all over me."

"Well maybe the guys in Bermuda will be." Matt nudged his elbow into her bony ribs.

"Just wait and see, Mr. Matthew Douglas. I can hold my own with you."

Sarah held the little pyramid between her fingers so she could spin it by flicking it with her free hand.

"Well, I guess we'll see won't we?"

"You're on. Are you going to call Sus…"

"Sarah."

"What I was just…"

"Sar…"

"Okay, okay I can't imagine what interest any woman would have in you anyway."

Matt grabbed his sister and tickled her, defending himself with a list of attractive qualities. "I'm tall, I'm good looking, I'm smart and funny. I'm in great shape. I'm very sexy."

Sarah burst into laughter. "Matthew, you're my brother. Brothers aren't sexy."

"Great. So much for self-confidence. Are you this tough on all your men?"

Sarah paused at this comment.

"Yes."

The elevator door opened. Bermuda awaited.

- Chapter 63 -

Although Edward was arriving quite a bit later than he had the previous time, he wasn't concerned about having his little ruse discovered. Today he was feeling confident about his strategy for bringing Schebb into the hospital and, like before, people smiled and peered into the baby carriage.

"Good morning." They would say with big knowing smiles. "Lovely day to be a new father. Congratulations."

Schebb was well covered and well behaved.

Edward knew Peter would be glad to see his best friend again. He waited alone near an elevator. He was pleased that he ended up with an empty car to himself. When the doors closed he pressed a button for Peter's floor and relaxed against the bronze mirrored wall.

"Good boy. Stay quiet now, we're almost there."

Schebb whimpered faintly.

Their solitude was short-lived. When the elevator stopped, the door opened and six nurses, holding trays, looked in at the tall stranger with the baby carriage.

There were a few seconds of hesitation. Edward tried to will them to wait for another car.

Please no, don't get on. Please no, don't get on.

Edward smiled unconsciously, which seemed to cause the six nurses to step aboard. Each was carrying a tray of food fresh from the cafeteria. The aroma made Edward's mouth water. The nurses stood three on each side of the carriage, their trays at waist level. Edward tried to pull the carriage back, but had only a few inches to move. When the doors closed, the smell of food intensified.

Oh shit. Houston, we have a problem.

A brown nose poked out from under the covers to sniff the air.

Edward made eye contact with Schebb, urging him to stay low. He reached in and adjusted the covers.

"Good boy. We'll eat in a few minutes."

"We must be making him hungry," one of the nurses commented.

"Is he eating solids yet?"

Another proceeded with a story about her youngster. Edward's face color darkened with embarrassment.

C'mon elevator, keep going. Keep going.

The momentary distraction allowed Schebb to poke his head from under his covers without anyone noticing.

A second later, Schebb edged forward. With his long nose he reached out and gobbled a piece of bacon off the nearest tray.

The cab exploded with screams when the woman spotted a hairy beast emerging from beneath the pink wool blanket.

Schebb barked in response to their screams causing six trays to simultaneously launch upward, projecting eggs, bacon, toast, jam, coffee, juice, yogurt and fruit onto the ceiling and mirrored walls.

Schebb leapt in the air to catch a flying piece of bacon, forcing six screaming nurses into one corner.

He gracefully caught and gulped down the first piece of bacon in mid air. He then lunged out of his carriage onto the floor to start gobbling the breakfasts now splattered on the tile.

Edward reached down to grab Schebb who growled back at him. He jumped back with the group of nurses, whose crisp white uniforms were now drenched with food and liquid.

"Schebb, sit."

He reached again for the ravenous dog who had already consumed most of the solid food, putting him slightly off balance when the elevator doors slid open.

At the first light of freedom, Schebb bolted from the chaos of the elevator into the corridors of the hospital floor.

Edward paused, quickly pressed a button for another floor and stepped with his carriage into the hall. He glanced back at the stunned nurses who watched with shock as the doors closed in front of them.

Edward's distress took only a second to convert to laughter, realizing the silliness of the scene. Several people had gathered to wait for the next car.

Edward faced them, wiping egg from his face.

"Has anyone seen a dog running through the halls?"

Without waiting for an answer he wheeled the carriage to the nearest washroom, where he cleaned himself up before heading to Peter's room.

When he arrived and peered through the window, he sighed with relief.

Schebb had gone immediately to his master's side. Except for the Douglas security guard, Schebb had apparently escaped notice. Now he lay beside Peter on the bed, alternately licking his master's hand and the remnants of breakfast from his fur.

Edward pulled the curtains, blocking out the view from the hall then closed securely.

Schebb looked up at Edward and whimpered a bit while he licked his chops.

"Hello, boss. I've brought a visitor for you again!"

Peter basked in the honest affection emanating from Schebb. He was delighted to see Edward arrive. They laughed together with Edward telling the tale of Schebb's misadventure.

"I wonder what the penalty is for bringing animals into the hospital?"

"He's a pretty smart puppy. He knew exactly where your room was." Edward carefully rubbed Schebb's head, trying to avoid getting egg and coffee on his hands.

"I guess I should have fed him more this morning. He lapped up those breakfasts like he hadn't eaten in a week!"

Edward mused for a moment, then his face went neutral focusing on Peter.

"This is going to be another tough week, Peter. Did I tell you that Brian is trying to appeal Judge Whiteside's decision on Monday?"

"I almost wish he wouldn't."

"He wants a hold put on your request, Peter. He feels more time is needed for testing to see if there's a chance you can be brought back. Peter, don't take this the wrong way, but I get the feeling that he's holding on to you for the wrong reason. He's heard how slim the chances are and knows the risk of your ending up conscious but in very bad shape. I can't help but think his motives are personally driven. We all have to grow up sooner or later. Losing parents is kind of a rite of passage that symbolizes we are no longer children. There's no one left to blame or to run to in times of need. We're finally out there on our own, making our own decisions and living with the consequences. It's too bad it's so hard to become an adult when our parents are still alive."

"So much has happened since I've been here. I'm okay with all of this. I really am excited about where I'm going. Something is changing; I'm no longer afraid. I'm not so prone to panicking and feeling confined. I've been blessed with the chance to fix a few things. I almost feel ready. I know the loss on your side will be painful...I've seen and felt the love from my kids. I know they'll miss me. And I'll miss them."

Edward turned away to walk toward the window. "Are you saying you want to die?"

"I'm saying that I've come to accept the inevitable. It's the way it should be, Ed, you can't fight that."

Edward felt his frustration rise. "Peter, you used to be such a fighter. You can't just give up."

"I feel there is an important place waiting for me. I'll be fighting new battles and watching over all of you. So you better watch your step, pal."

They shared an uneasy chuckle before Edward moved back to the bedside and stroked Schebb. "This guy's gonna miss you, that's for sure."

"He's been an amazing friend. I wish he could talk and tell us about the accident. By the way, any luck yet locating the trucker?"

"Nothing yet. He seems to have just disappeared. He hasn't been working, and no one along his regular route has seen him recently. He's probably holed up somewhere. We'll keep looking for him."

"Promise me you'll find him. Take care of him, Ed. The man gave me the greatest gift and probably at great personal risk. I remember nothing about the whole event. I know I was watching, but it's all a blur. I haven't been able to revisit that time. Perhaps it's too fragile and any tampering could result in worsening the outcome."

"What do you mean?"

"I mean I could already be long gone."

"Oh." His head swiveled at the sound of a knock on the door.

"Just a moment, please." Edward opened the door a crack to see Charlotte's face peering at him. "Charlotte, it's you, come in, come in. Wow...you look stunning as usual."

"Why is the door locked, Edward? Oh! Schebb?"

"Yep."

"You naughty dog. Where've you been and how'd you get in here? I heard we had him back. He looks great. I was always jealous of the time Peter spent with him instead of me, but it's great to see him. I bet he's had quite an adventure."

She eyed the baby carriage while patting Schebb. She looked at Edward. "In this?"

"You'll never believe just how exciting pushing a baby carriage can be."

"Really?" She looked at Peter. "How's he doing?"

"He seems about the same. A brilliant man trapped in a useless body."

"What do you mean by that?"

"Charlotte, there're lots of things in this world we can't explain. I believe that Peter's in there, but we just can't prove it by conventional means. This week, this hospital is going to take away my best friend, your husband and a wonderful man."

Edward completely lost his composure. His face crumpled, he wrapped his arms around Charlotte. They stood, holding each other, sharing sorrow.

Peter returned from another experience to the sight of his best friend and wife standing over him. The view prompted many memories of the three of them spending time together. Instantly he departed to relive some of those memories.

"Edward, I've been in discussion with several Doctors here at the hospital. We're going to try to extract sperm from Peter."

Charlotte had Edward's complete attention. She continued without emotion, hoping her bravado would last. "His body has continued to produce sperm. He has ejaculated on two occasions. Tests have shown normal counts. Edward, this would mean that I could have a child by Peter. We were about to start trying when the accident occurred. It would fulfill a dream we both had and allow me to hang onto Peter even if he is gone. The people from the fertility clinic are coming down this morning to assist."

"It sounds bizarre and wonderful at the same time. Have you spoken to any of the kids about it?"

"No, and I don't see the need. This is between Peter and me. I mean, we didn't call them every time we planned to make love. Peter would want this. I know he would."

"How is it done?"

Charlotte lost her composure. "This part is a bit embarrassing, but it is possible for me to...to try...to try to..." She rushed her next few sentences. "To stimulate him to the point of ejaculation. The sperm is collected and immediately frozen. The other way is that the Doctors can penetrate with a syringe and try to extract it."

Edward winced. He felt his own testicles retract.

A syringe? I don't think so. No sir.

"But it's very difficult to get a useful sample that way."

"The first way sounds good to me, Charlotte."

"It also has the highest level of success, and I have to assume that time isn't on my side. It seems a bit morbid, but if I focus on the goal of bearing his child I think I can do it."

Edward stood silently.

"What do you think of all this?"

There was no communication from Peter, so Edward assumed he probably wasn't listening or if he was he was too embarrassed to comment. Peter never talked about his love life, even in college. He always said there was no upside to kissing and telling.

"I have a few props here to create a mood." Charlotte opened a drawer in the bedside table and displayed some items she had left on her previous romantic encounter. She reached in the bag and took out a small bottle of red wine.

Edward raised his eyebrows and checked his watch, hinting he'd probably rather not be having this conversation.

"And this," Charlotte held up a condom-like device shrink-wrapped in plastic. "Romantic, huh?"

"I won't even ask, Charlotte."

She chuckled, "I know, bizarre isn't it.? But it's important to me. Edward?

"Yes?" He knew something was coming next.

"You're a dear friend. How'd you like to be a Godfather?"

He breathed a sign of relief. "I'd be honored Charlotte. Truly honored. Now…well…I mean…I'll just leave you two kids alone now okay?" Edward was smiling awkwardly. He turned, then paused and turned back. "You'd better be careful if you light those candles. You might send the whole place up in flames!"

"I know. The Doctors told me after the last time to turn off the oxygen and everything would be fine."

Edward raised his eyebrows toward the ceiling. "'The last time?' You mean you…?"

"Uh, huh."

Edward shook his head, thinking about Charlotte lighting matches near Peter's bed with pure oxygen flowing in his face.

"They also said that creating the proper mood may help Peter respond even though he's not aware."

Edward's smile broadened.

It's not morbid at all. Peter will know what's going on, and even though Charlotte doesn't know it, they will be sharing a truly unique experience; one that might just produce a child and make me a Godfather.

"You're incredible, Charlotte. Now really I better get going. You've got a date!" Edward gave her a big hug, then loaded Schebb into the carriage just as a firm knock banged at the door.

"Just a minute!" Charlotte stalled the knocker.

Edward tucked Schebb into the carriage and raised the top to reduce his exposure.

When Charlotte opened the door a crack, she recognized two Doctors from the fertility laboratory.

"Hello, Mrs. Douglas."

"Just a moment please." Charlotte eased the door closed. "Ready yet?"

"We're outta here." Edward wheeled his carriage past Charlotte like a pro. They exchanged kisses on the cheek. "Good luck."

"Edward?"

"Yes."

"It might be better for now if this was just between you and me. It might upset the children, and I'm sure Marion wouldn't be impressed."

"About what? Charlotte, I'm not sure what you're talking about."

Charlotte looked at Edward in disbelief before she realized what he was doing. "Thank you," she mouthed.

She opened the door and Edward wheeled passed the two Doctors. They both smiled at the carriage the same way everyone else did.

"The moment you're ready, ring us downstairs. We'll take it from there. We'll do a quick count under the microscope, then assuming it meets our criteria we'll immediately freeze the sperm."

The second Doctor spoke up. "We're breaking new ground here, Mrs. Douglas. We hope that if everything goes well you'll assist us in publishing the results. It could help many in the future who find themselves in your situation."

"It would also help us with funding for more research."

Charlotte's patience was thinning. She couldn't decide if these two were insensitive or just numb from years in the trauma center.

"You can assist us anonymously. That will be your choice of course. If the results are positive there will be substantial notoriety."

"This is very sensitive to me. I'd like to take things one step at a time. Now if there is nothing else…"

"Yes, of course. Of course."

Both Doctors quickly backed up, bumping into each other. The door was closed and bolted. Charlotte was finally alone with her husband.

"Hello, darling. Remember that date we had planned the night you didn't come home? We're going to try again."

- Chapter 64 -

Peter had returned. He watched while his wife moved about the room, thinking how incredible she looked.

Charlotte closed the curtains to the outside world. She reached behind the bed and turned off the oxygen before removing the clear tube that fed it to his nose. She set two candles on the bedside table and lit them with a small plastic lighter. She pulled the chain to extinguish the remaining artificial light in the room. She smoothed Peter's hair and looked at him in the glint of the candles.

"You look as handsome as ever." She kissed his forehead, leaving a trace of color from her lipstick. Pulling a chair close to the bed, she opened the bottle of wine and poured two small glasses. She toasted Peter and let the first glass slip down her throat. The alcohol heated her body and lightened her mood. She dipped her finger in Peter's glass and wet his lips.

"I hate to drink alone. Won't you join me?"

Charlotte took a long draw on his glass of wine. A sense of euphoria gradually came over her. She started the tiny music player and the dull and sterile hospital room was alive with the sounds of Peter and Charlotte's favorite music. Wine glass in hand, Charlotte mimed a dance with her husband, singing words to a love song that filled their bedroom so often.

Peter watched with pleasure and he was whisked away to the bedroom of their home. He remembered the evening Charlotte had set a romantic mood for lovemaking, hoping to conceive a child. He was relaxed in bed, listening to the sounds of his wife bathing. When he had awoken, it was well into the night. The candles were gone, the music was silenced. His wife was asleep at the far side of their bed. This time it would be different.

Charlotte reached under the covers to replace the condom catheter with a new, sterile one just like the nurses had shown her. It was really quite simple.

She was surprised to find Peter's penis was partially erect. The low lights, wine, music and contact with her husband's body made her flesh tighten and her thighs warm. The act of touching her husband without his knowledge was strangely erotic. It gave her a momentary window into some of the sexual perversions that haunt people's minds.

This was different. She was neither perverted nor weird. She was with her husband, trying to make a child with him. It was that loving thought that justified her means and made her actions seem natural. She now understood how partners could still be very intimate even if one was disabled somehow. Love truly overcame any obstacle.

She tucked the sheets under Peter's chin. His body's outline was visible in the candlelight. She ran her hands over his chest and down both legs.

"Let's make a baby, Peter."

Charlotte stood bedside and closed her eyes, letting the wine and music envelop her. Her mind instantly slipped back to the same time Peter was visiting.

She let the warm water of her bath and bubbles wash over her body while she thought of her husband waiting in bed outside the door. The same music played like it had that evening. Candles burned, wine lightened their spirits.

Peter waited, this time without fear of sleeping. He knew this special gift was his to give and that the result would be a lasting companion for his wife.

When she got out of the tub she dried herself with a thick white towel before letting it drop to the floor. She unpinned her hair, letting it fall in long spirals around her shoulders. A mist of perfume cooled her skin when it evaporated. She dropped a white, mid-thigh silk slip over her head and down onto her body. It shimmered into place, sticking where water still clung to her skin. She breezed into their bedroom, the gossamer material clinging to her body, outlining its form and highlighting her breasts.

Peter was wide awake.

She approached him, admiring his physique. The sheets were pulled down to his waist. His chest was firm and well defined, covered with a light mat of brown hair. Peter had great shoulders and wonderful arms which she loved to watch flex when he held her.

Sexual tension was thick in the air, naturally pulling these life partners and lovers together.

Peter welcomed her into his arms with a kiss. They melted together, rolled and intertwined. Both were ready. Charlotte's legs tensed against the bed frame. Her hands wrapped tightly into his buttocks. She hung from his body like they were one, falling from the earth, never to return.

Peter was on fire from head to toe. Their lovemaking heightened every sense. His body stiffened, a long moaning sigh of relief flowed from within his wife. Peter crushed her toward him; a sigh of longing exhaling from her mouth. Her body pulsed in rhythm with his surges.

Her face darkened and twisted with intensity.

They were frozen in time.

Motionless, yet spinning, crystal clear in a perfect haze of affection.

Charlotte opened her eyes. She stood completely still, unable to move for many seconds. Her body quivered, her knees were weak and she realized that her hand was trapped, pressured between her pelvis and the bed. She removed it slowly and eased into the bedside chair. She closed her eyes again to relive what had just happened, but it was gone. What had seemed like hours had taken only seconds.

She gingerly stood and looked at her husband. His face was soaked with sweat. The sheets absorbed the perspiration from his body. She stroked his face dry and leaned in to kiss him. She slid her hand down to feel a slightly less than erect penis beneath the bed linen and its latex companion enlarged with warm fluid.

She smiled through tears, overwhelmed by the intensity of her dream and the reality of the results. She looked at Peter's quiet face. She recalled the words Edward had spoken earlier about him being inside.

Could he be in there? What does Edward know?

Charlotte had no explanation for what had happened and within a few minutes the memory had all but faded. There would be no possible way of explaining it. She felt the marvel she just experienced was for her and Peter alone to have shared. She would conceive his child. She felt certain that what she was doing was meant to be and hoped it would be successful.

Charlotte tidied herself a bit before brushing a few more kisses across Peter's face. "Thank you, my love. If you are in there, know that I love you. I will always be thinking of you." Her tears fell onto the sheets.

"What I just experienced was beyond this world. That is where I now think you are, watching over me like an angel. You have given me your love, the greatest gift I could ask you for. In return, I will bear you a child and you may watch over him. I love you, Peter."

Charlotte now had to call the Doctors. She hated to break the mood in the room, but knew it was imperative. She drew back the curtains and let the sun pour in. She blew out the candles and emptied the remainder of the wine in the sink. The bottle would be kept as a memento.

She pressed three digits on the telephone.

By the time she hung up and unlatched the door, the Doctors were standing there in anticipation. She was all business now.

"You'll find the sample there, Doctors; please call me at home when you have the results."

Once they were gone, she did not let the sterile environment of the hospital tear the memory from her. She would secret it out of the building and home to a sacred place.

The next day she would drive out to their house in the country to be surrounded by all of the things that meant "Peter" to her. She would know by then what hope, if any, she had for the possibility of a pregnancy with her husband's child.

– Chapter 65 –

What was supposed to be a quick stop to pick up a few things en route to the airport turned into a 45-minute argument.

Susan stood in her doorway after the car carrying Matt and Sarah had driven away.

Matt spent most of the drive to the airport in silence.

Sarah respected the silence and listened to music with her earphones.

Out of sheer habit, Matt had feigned innocence when Susan challenged him about his reasons for being in Bermuda. He wanted to tell Susan everything, but he figured if he opened that Pandora's Box Bermuda would be off the agenda for much longer than he was willing to wait. He would level with Susan the moment things were firmed up with Cara.

Susan told him they were through if he didn't make a commitment.

"If you won't, I will find it somewhere else."

He knew that Susan played the game well; after all, she'd been taught by the master.

What she didn't tell Matt was that she had already found it somewhere else. Finally, one of the many offers she'd received over the years looked attractive enough to nurture. She wanted to be sure where Matt stood before she fanned a new fire. Even though she did love him and she hoped he might turn out to be perfect for her, she knew she had to look out for herself.

He was caught off guard. She had never confronted Matt so vigorously in all the time she knew him. He didn't even think Susan would be home. He'd already written another note in his head, one of hundreds he'd left over the years when he took advantage of her busy schedule to satisfy his.

Minutes after parting, Matt and Susan picked up their telephones. They knew they should have called each other but they each made the classic mistake of turning away from the obvious answer. They sought that which only they could give each other from someone else.

Matt was unable to reach Cara, but the effort to do so and the lift-off of the plane seemed to lighten his mood. He slipped back a double vodka tonic, yanked on his sisters' earphones and started to talk.

Old habits die hard. Sobriety would be paused for a moment.

When he heard himself talking out loud, Matt realized just how much he had grown to like Cara. Up to that point, she had been kept a secret like so many of his previous short-term girlfriends. Cara was different. Or perhaps he had changed, for this time he sensed deep feelings for her. He confided in Sarah about his not-so-perfect past and proclaimed that he was now ready to commit to someone.

He noticed that Sarah didn't ask about Susan right away but she did listen eagerly about Cara. Matt assumed that she found it interesting to hear her older brother talk about his substantially younger girlfriend. Perhaps she would avoid guys like him.

"What about Susan? She seems perfect."

She was surprised at how quickly and simply her brother responded.

"She is."

Sarah wasn't sure what his answer meant. She didn't press Matt as he poured another double.

"You want one?"

"Nope."

"All pure are we now?'

"Yep." She smiled when Matt thumbed his nose at her while taking a long sip.

She had a hard time imagining her brother having sex with someone, but she was curious to meet the woman who had apparently swept him off his feet. Especially since she was only five years her senior.

Matt made several calls to the hotel but had yet to reach Cara. On each successive call he had something else sent to the room. Two orders of flowers and a bottle of champagne later, the jet touched down on the sun-scorched tarmac.

The humid air of Bermuda filled the cabin when the customs officer stuck his head in the door of the jet.

"Hello, Mr. Douglas. Welcome back to Bermuda." The uniformed man spoke with a beautiful British accent.

"Devon, this is my baby sister Sarah."

Sarah was model perfect in stylish clothes and dark glasses. Devon removed his peaked cap. His smooth dark face stretched wide to accommodate his grin. His eyes twinkled with sincerity. "Welcome to Bermuda, Miss Douglas. My title is actually Officer Devonshire Whitmore but you, like your brother, may always refer to me as Devon. That's what they call me here on the world's most beautiful island. You are our most honored guest, and your host is one of the nicest gentlemen to visit our island. Enjoy your stay." Devon withdrew from the aircraft after a cursory look in the cabin.

"Is that it? They come right to your door?" Sarah asked.

"Uh huh."

"I'm used to those customs lineups at Logan. I like this Bermuda place already."

"Nice, huh?" Matt grinned. He was in his realm now. "Keep her warm Bob, in case we get a call."

Sister and brother popped into a white Mercedes cab and drove directly to the Sands Hotel. Matt pointed out how each house had a roof designed to collect rain water for storage in a basement cistern.

"You wash your hair and it seems like the soap just won't rinse out. The water here is like velvet."

"I love the pastels."

Several large cruise ships could be seen on the ocean while they followed South Road to Elbow Beach. The liners were cruising to the Front street piers of Hamilton on the other side of the island. They would dump several thousand tourists into the island's main city to shop, dine and party for two days before weighing anchor and heading back to the U.S. mainland.

"I love this island." She let the wind whip her hair back. "Sure beats damp and dreary old Boston."

When the car pulled up under the hotel portico, Matt was greeted by name and welcomed back.

"C'mon, Sis, let's see if Cara's back. We won't call up. We'll just surprise her."

"Hello, Mr. Douglas." Sandy Dugas' familiar voice came from the concierge desk. Matt waved, but Sandy motioned him toward her.

"I'll call you from the room. This is my sister Sarah." He pointed to her as they walked toward the elevator, feeling that he should deflect any thoughts that he might be bringing in a new "guest." Matt recalled a favorite saying of his father's: "Guilt rests only in the guilty one's mind." He figured his social history would have people assuming that he was with another young woman.

Sandy had a look of protest on her face, but let him go.

Matt was filled with childish enthusiasm as he slipped the card key into the door and swung it wide open. "Cara?"

Matt stopped in his tracks to survey his room. Sarah fell in directly behind. To her it was just another hotel suite, but

Matt felt the world fall from beneath him when he surveyed his domain.

Flowers, more flowers, champagne, bed perfectly made without a cover ruffled. The sliding glass doors were open. The curtains flew inward the way they had the first time he and Cara had laid on the bed together. His expectations rose and sank again when he saw that the balcony, too, was vacant.

The oversized bathroom was equally in order. A white envelope on the black marble vanity was the only non-standard item in the entire place.

Not a trace of Cara remained.

Matt picked up the envelope with a shaking hand.

He walked to the balcony. It was identical to the one where he had nearly killed a young man over his love for the girl whose handwriting was on the envelope. He tore it open then sat in one of the wicker chairs to read.

Dearest Matthew:

How does one start an end, but with a new beginning? I find myself lifted on a new breeze. The need to spread my wings and fly is taking me on a new path. I depart knowing that I have been blessed with time spent in the arms and heart of an incredible man. Can I ever convince you how much you have meant to me and how I will always, always, hold you in my heart? My soul has been graced because it connected with yours, but I feel that you and I have done that which we were brought together to do.

When you read these words I know that you will wonder why this has happened. I do not have an answer to that question. I do have faith that our lives are continuing to unfold the way they are intended. Matthew, you are a kind, gentle, caring and loving man. I wish for you everything that will fill the emptiness inside of which you so often spoke. I only hope that my feelings for you will be a few drops in the torrent of love that I am sure will find you. Someday our paths may cross again. I'll miss everything about you.

Loving you always,
Cara.

"FUCK!"

Matt crumpled the paper. He felt as though someone had gouged a chunk out of his chest. His stomach tightened to the point of vomiting. His whole world seemed to crumple into the ball he now squeezed in his fist.

"FUCK ME."

Was there even more to Cara than he had thought?

I was too busy trying to fuck her and didn't even get to know her.

He was hurt but not surprised. His pain was more about himself than Cara. Her letter mostly acted like a mirror in which he now viewed himself. It all seemed too easy. All the talk, all the feelings. All too good to be true.

I saw this coming but I ignored the warning signs. Those vacant looks when she was bored. Her envy of people her age as they'd drive by in a group, having fun.

It was crystal clear to him now.

When they were alone, when the real world was held at bay with infatuation, everything seemed perfect, but reality was always waiting. Matt just pretended it didn't exist. Cara had many hours to think. He couldn't keep up the high maintenance. Distractions were ever present. Her independence was one of the many qualities he loved about her, and in the end it was this quality which pulled her away. She wanted to live her own life, not someone else's. She wasn't anywhere near ready to be one-half of a full-time partnership. It was clear. It was very clear now. All this said and acknowledged, it still hurt like hell.

"Bad news?" Sarah's hands rested on his shoulders.

"The worst." Matt wiped his face with his sleeve. "Hey, I'm glad you're here."

"It must really hurt. I've never seen you like this."

"Stick around. You'll find out that your big, tough brother is no tougher than you."

"None of us are tough, Matt. We only pretend to be. Besides, we were made to feel, not to not feel."

"Oh, you're a philosopher too now. How so wise at such a young age?"

"I've had some tutoring."

"Michael? He's a good guy, Sarah. You may want to hang on to him."

"He says that you can't possess love. You can only give it and receive it with those you care about. It is a fluid commodity, ebbing and flowing like the waters of the oceans. We have to swim in it when the tide is high and sit in admiration of it when the tides of love recede."

"Hey, that's pretty good Sis. So young, so wise. I feel a little better already. Let's go for a walk on the beach and then I'll take you out for a nice supper. We can fly home in the morning."

"Sounds great. We can talk more about this."

"Do I have to?"

"Yes!"

The telephone rang.

Maybe it's Cara.

He reached. He knew better.

Sandy Dugas' voice quickly punctured his balloon of hope.

He promised himself not to let that happen again.

"Sorry about Cara. I wanted to let you know before you went up. Is there anything I can do to help?"

"Sure, find me another one."

The telephone was silent. Matt broke it with a chuckle.

"Mr. Douglas...Matt, if you have a few minutes, there's something I'd like to discuss."

"About Cara?"

"No, I really have no idea where she went or with whom."

Matt figured she was lying. He respected her for it, though.

"It's another matter. Do you have a few minutes before you go out? In private?"

"Sure Sandy, why don't we take a walk on the grounds? You can tour me through the new landscaping."

- Chapter 66 -

Matt paused in the lobby to make a telephone call. The instant he heard Cara's voice mail he knew it had been a mistake to call. He hung up quickly, resigned himself to her absence, then dialed Susan's number. He felt his palm go wet and before the phone rang he dropped the receiver back in its cradle. He stood silently for a moment with closed eyes then took a deep breath and ambled over to see Sandy.

He noticed she was agitated when he arrived at her concierge desk. Few words were exchanged while they wandered out through the patio area of the hotel onto manicured grounds.

Matt's curiosity was peaking.

"Mr. Douglas."

"Sandy, please."

"Matt, I have something to tell you about the night you found Cara in your suite with Jason."

Sandy had Matt's full attention; a small rush of adrenaline heightened his senses. She spoke in small bursts.

"Well, you know I had taken Cara to the party. It all started out a bit of a joke once we met those guys."

"You were with them?"

Sandy held up her hand in protest. "We decided to get Cara drunk. There was some coke and things got carried away and someone must have spiked her drink with a roofie or something given she has no recollection."

"Roofie? Coke? At Houston's place?"

477

"Ya...it's pretty common. In fact it's at every party if you are into it. I'm not...usually but...anyway...goodness this is hard...anyway at first I thought we were just going for a boat ride. It was stupid to even get in the boat with them, but once we were off shore there wasn't much I could do. I was pretty drunk and...and...and a bit more and nothing was registering too clearly. I had no idea Cara was in the kind of shape she was in. Then the accident happened. We were all scared and didn't know what to do. We brought Cara back to the hotel and I let them into your room. I don't think Jason meant any harm. I'm sure he's more than learned his lesson."

Sandy let her speech settle in. She took a breath.

"So, you were there the whole evening with Cara?"

"Yes. The point is that none of them mentioned my name when they were questioned. No one other than Cara, the guys and now you know I was there. I felt I owed you that after what you did for me when you wrote the letter to Mr. Merck. That saved my job and probably my career."

Matt was interested in how she found out about his personal note to Merck, but would save that for another time.

"It's a wonder none of you were killed. Did you really think he was just putting her to bed in the hotel?"

"Matt, he was so scared there's no way his intentions were otherwise. I know he got fresh with her on the boat, but it was so dark and we were moving so fast I didn't see much. Everyone was pretty drunk. That's no excuse of course, but it is the fact."

Sandy kept the story simple. There was no point speculating on what might have happened if circumstances had been different.

Flashes of the evening when he'd nearly killed the young man with his bare hands haunted Matt. "What are you proposing we do, Sandy?"

She was silent for a while.

"Obviously I was wrong to be involved. Some bad things did happen. I thought by bringing Cara back here she'd be safe. If you hadn't shown up she probably would have slept it off and possibly not even remembered what happened. Neither of you would have been involved at all. She's gone now…"

Matt wanted to interrupt and grill Sandy but decided not to paste his heart to his sleeve.

"…and it looks like everyone is going to be okay. The police aren't pressing any charges. It's unlikely that the boys would re-open this mess by bringing me into it."

There was another long pause. Sandy stopped and turned toward Matt. She was very close.

"My hope is that this can stay between you and me."

She held Matt's eyes while her request settled in.

I'm being had here, he thought, asking more questions won't bring Cara back.

He'd had enough heartache for one day. He let enough silence linger, hoping it was at least painful for Sandy. He started to walk slowly again before he spoke.

"I guess I can agree to that, but that's two markers I now have to call on when I need a favor."

She stopped walking and stepped in front of him again. This time he saw her pretty white smile brightened her beautiful face.

Matt looked down at Sandy and felt his face tighten in a broad grin. The area around his scar tingled like it always did when his blood pressure increased.

"What's that look for?" Sandy asked.

"You remember the time you were giving me a tour of one of the suites and Mr. Merck interrupted us, don't you?"

He saw Sandy's face turn crimson.

"Yes. Vividly, why?"

"Well, did you want to finish what you were about to do that day?"

Matt couldn't believe his own boldness. All thoughts of Cara and Susan disappeared for those few seconds his brain stopped thinking. He felt the thick field of sensuousness stirred between them.

Sandy glanced to her right, then left, before leaning up to greet his mouth as it pressed down on hers. Their arms wrapped around each other and they kissed.

She was tiny. He could feel her body warm against his.

For Matt, that bit of passion poured into a gaping void. It was momentary gratification. Neither seemed to care.

Bodies melted there in the garden for a few minutes in a shared experience that would not be repeated, a melting pot of miniature sins culminating in a kiss, rich with life and wet with desire.

Sarah smiled slightly and shook her head while she watched her heart-broken brother nursing his wounds in the garden beneath her balcony.

Matt took the stairs up to his suite. The vacancy within had returned. He fought his feelings. He told himself over and over that everything would be fine, that the Cara thing had happened for a reason he was yet to know.

I've had a great life and it has gotten better and better with each experience. Something great is coming. It must be. I just need to get my shit together.

He put on a brave face and opened the door. When he entered the room, his step did have substantially more spring than when he had left.

He smiled when he saw Sarah reclining on the balcony.

They concluded the day by strolling the beach and shopping in various hotel boutiques. He continued to be impressed with her maturity and insight. She had successfully kept his mind off Cara, for which he rewarded her with dinner and a show at the Princess Hotel. On the way home in the taxi she convinced

Matt to detour through town. That was step one of a two-step ploy to get him dancing at a night club she'd heard about. The second step took some convincing, but Matt relented. They danced and drank for two more hours before Matt finally called it a night. They laughed at everything and talked about nothing during the taxi ride home. Both concluded it was the best evening they had ever spent together and that they should make a habit of it.

Matt opened the door to the suite. "Just think, Sarah, two or three more years and I can date your girlfriends!" Sarah screamed and punched Matt.

She took three giant strides, went air borne and flopped on the king-sized bed.

"Just for that, you get the cot."

Matt chuckled out loud while he pulled the mattress from the single bed that had been delivered and threw it on the floor.

He'd had a terrific time with his little sister.

He looked at her watching the fan spin overhead. She was every bit a woman, lacking only experience in life that time would provide. He saw a lot of himself in her. He knew that she came by her gregarious nature honestly. She was a beautiful young woman. Men craned their necks when she passed. He was relieved that the attention didn't faze her. Being her brother, it was hard for him to see her as a sexual being, but her physical attributes and way of dressing exuded sensuality.

She told him she really admired Michael which got Matt's attention. In the end he concluded that the guy was just doing his job and that Sarah likely felt a bit better hearing his type of message from a stranger rather than a family member.

Matt knew the influence that a man can have on a younger woman and felt Michael's could be very positive, especially considering this little girl was about to lose her father. Matt had known too many women who had hooked up with the wrong type of guy when they were young. As victims of their own naiveté, it often took years before they came out the other end of a negative or even abusive relationship. Luckily that wasn't to be the case with Michael.

A knock sounded at their door. Matt looked through the peephole but could see no one and wondered if it was just a mistake. He heard the quiet shuffle as a white envelope slipped under the door at his feet. A uniformed desk clerk rose into the distorted view lines.

He recognized the stationery immediately from Sandy Dugas. He assumed that it was a follow-up note from their afternoon meeting. He tossed the envelope on his mattress for bedtime reading and headed to the bathroom.

"What was that?" Sarah asked.

"Just a note from the concierge. Probably confirming a few questions I asked."

Sarah raised her eyebrows and smiled. "Oh I see. It seems that you get pretty good service around this place."

"They treat everyone well here Sarah. That's what we pay for."

Matt retreated from the conversation and headed to the bathroom. He had the distinct feeling that Sarah knew more than she was letting on, but chalked it up to women's intuition.

She couldn't resist a parting comment. "That's good. You certainly seem to be getting your money's worth!"

The two Douglases settled onto their respective sleeping surfaces. Matt immediately wondered why he'd been so generous with his sister. After bidding each other goodnight, the lights went out except for a small reading lamp Matt positioned near his mattress. The white envelope reflected the light and beckoned his attention, but ended up being the sole star on a spot-lit stage, for Matt quickly dozed off while contemplating his encounter with Sandy.

- Chapter 67 -

When Matt opened his eyes, his first view was out the balcony doors to the naked back of his tall, slim, sister. She stood soaking in the early morning sun without a hint of modesty. For an instant he saw her in the abstract and not like his sister. He appreciated the beauty of his parent's creation. That lasted only a second.

"Saaaraah."

She spun around and walked into the room, seemingly oblivious to the fact that she was now standing nude in front of her brother. Her body was immaculate, with youthful skin stretched perfectly smooth over her young bones. Her breasts were awakened by the morning breeze. Her tousled blond hair frolicked down over her shoulders. Her long, toned legs met at a sparse patch of tufted blond hair.

"Sarah, put some freakin' clothes on." Matt pulled his own covers up and rolled away from his sister to avoid staring, hoping that she would heed his command quickly.

"I'm your sister, what's the big deal? It's not like you haven't seen a nude woman before."

"That's exactly the big deal. You are my sister and you're standing on my balcony in the buff. Now please put some clothes on."

Sarah obliged by pulling on a pair of white cotton briefs and a tank top before stepping back onto the balcony to soak in more sun and let the morning breeze fill her lungs. Matt rolled out of bed and pulled himself up from the floor. He was pretty stiff from a restless night.

"You get the cot next time."

Matt stretched his frame and then joined Sarah to overlook the gardens and ocean. He took a couple of sideways looks in the wall mirrors, trying to convince himself that he still had what it took to attract a replacement for Cara. His muscular legs in patterned boxer shorts highlighted his slim waist and strong chest. He was built like his father and shared the same shapely arms and shoulders. Sarah gave him the once-over, then pinched an inch on his waist and started to taunt him.

"Don't you think you should have a shirt and pants on? What would the neighbors think? What would that concierge friend of yours think?" She raised her eyebrows and looked down toward the gardens.

Immediately he realized the view from the balcony of his new suite looked directly over the place where he and Sandy had exchanged affections. He assumed Sarah had observed the whole thing and quickly changed subjects. Sarah gave her brother a friendly jab in the stomach. "Pretty good shape for a man your age."

Again, Matt stayed neutral and let her have fun at his expense until Sarah finally left the balcony to shower.

Matt strolled back into the room, spotting the white envelope sticking out from beneath an ejected pillow near his mattress. He flopped down on the floor with the sound of the shower spraying in the background.

How weird. A week ago that was Cara. Today it's my little sister. Okay, I am listening, up there. I get it. I get it. What an odd journey life can be.

He tore open the envelope; half expecting some sort of complimentary words coming from Sandy which resulted in intensifying the shock he felt when he absorbed the handwritten note.

Dear Matthew:

I apologize for not reaching you sooner, but we had no idea where you and your sister had gone last night. I did not want to leave a voice mail for such a personal message.

Your sister Catherine called from Paris to inform you that your grandmother in Florida has passed away. Catherine is en route to join your mother in Florida. You are to call her there immediately. Please accept my sincere condolences for the loss you must feel. If there is anything I or the staff of the Sands can do to assist you, we are at your service. I will also inform Mr. Merck of the situation.

Warmest Regards,

Sandra Dugas

Head Concierge

Matt lay stunned.

He could not believe the news he just read. He felt terrible that he was getting it many hours later than he should have. Thoughts of his father, Cara, his mother and his grandmother swirled into an emotional soup. He buried his face into the pillow, numbed with grief, a deluge of feelings flooded out. Specific sources of the feelings could not possibly be isolated. It wasn't because he was so close to his grandmother that he felt the depth of remorse that he did. The cumulative effects of many years of denial had finally caught up to him. Now, an emotional catharsis had commenced that would continue until it was complete.

Sarah emerged from the bathroom wrapped in towels.

Is he back in bed? Hey, he's crying.

"Hey, are you okay? What is it?" She knelt down beside him and rubbed his shoulders.

He kept his head buried in his pillow, handing Sarah the crumpled letter.

She read it in silence.

He felt her melt down beside him and wrap her arm over his shoulder. They cried together like two infants huddled in a ball of security. Sarah cried mostly because her brother was upset, which in turn triggered raw feelings about their father.

Matt's stew of emotional baggage, that he continued to stir each day with his life style, boiled within him overflowing at the least provocation.

Matt was first to regain his composure.

"Cap…it's Matt. It's Emily. In Florida. She's gone, Cap. She's gone…Yes. Please…about thirty minutes."

"Mom…Matt…yes, yes, I am very sorry we were out, no cell phones and when we…yes, Sarah and I, she's here with me…yes well anyway we got back…well never mind. How are you?"

He wasn't surprised to find out that, between his brother Brian and super-sister Catherine, arrangements for transportation and the funeral were underway. He was continually amazed at how organized and driven his two siblings were. It seemed that Matt's only chore was to get Sarah and himself home safely.

He made a third call to someone else. Sarah couldn't tell who it was, but she presumed by the tone that he was speaking to a woman. She could have guessed but chose not to ask considering her brother's state.

Matt and his sister scurried around the room collecting items that had been scattered about. Matt called for Sandy, but learned she was off for the next two days. His call was forwarded to Steven Merck's office where he was immediately connected with his longtime friend.

"Matt, what can I say? You're having the time from hell it appears. May I express my condolences for your grandmother and let you know that I'm there for anything you might need?"

"Thanks, Steven. We're holding up okay. I've got my sister Sarah here. She's a rock."

Matt put his arm around Sarah who was sitting beside him on the bed and squeezed her shoulder.

"I know what you mean, pal. We men only act like rocks, right Steven?"

"Listen Matt, Andy Houston has offered his jet helicopter to get you back to the mainland. He can drop it right on the beach and probably save you 45 minutes. It's state of the art. Safe as an ark."

"Thanks Steven, and thank Andy, but Bob's ready to go. Our arrival isn't that time-sensitive. I'll take a rain check for a junket sometime when you can join us."

When Sarah and Matt walked into the main lobby, they were overwhelmed by a large crowd of the Sands staff who'd gathered to see them off. The senior doorman who had bid welcome and farewell to Matt so many times shook his hand and Sarah's, expressing his condolences. He handed Matt a card signed by all of the staff. In his formal British way he expressed a reminder to Matt that sorrow is the sword that carves in one's soul a place for joy. Matt thanked him and waved to the group, though they blurred in his vision.

Slipping into the limousine beside Sarah, he stared straight ahead, holding his sister's hand. Matt was overwhelmed by the kindness these strangers were expressing. He found it interesting how powerful unexpected kindness was.

The world needs more of that. I need to do more of that.

- Chapter 68 -

They were awaiting the arrival of the funeral director from the firm with which Emily had made pre-arrangements. Brian, Marjorie and Edward were all seated at the Douglas boardroom table. The strain was showing on all of them although they all agreed that this forethought on her part was not only progressive but extremely considerate, saving the grieving family the task of orchestrating decisions concerning a loved one's internment.

Brian took a call from Catherine who was with their mother in Florida. A Douglas lawyer had been dispatched to facilitate the paperwork to move Emily from the State of Florida to Massachusetts. A charter company would jet Emily's casket, Marion and Catherine home the next morning.

Matt called from the plane to let everyone know he and Sarah were en route. A family dinner had been planned for the evening. When Brian spoke on the telephone to his brother, he felt his foot nudge up against the leg of the boardroom table. It took several minutes before he realized that he was actually rubbing his shoe against Marjorie's foot. He gave her an exasperated look, feeling his face flushed.

She returned with a "Hey, you're the one with the roving feet" look.

While they waited, Edward reported on the search for Fuzzy. They had his correct name now and statements from a number of truckers confirming he had been seen with the dog.

They still didn't know they were looking for a clean-shaven, well-dressed man. For now, Fuzzy had shaken them.

"It doesn't appear that any crime was committed. If he doesn't want the reward or his privacy invaded, perhaps we should let him be. You never know, he just may surface on his own." Edward had a further theory that he would share if necessary but for now he would keep it to himself. He felt certain that if Peter died that Fuzzy would be at the funeral.

Brian listened to Edward.

Is this another example of me chasing something for the purpose of pure pursuit? Am I missing something here? Edward's got it figured out. I hope I get it one day.

He looked at Edward and nodded.

"How about I leave that one up to you, Edward? I'm sure you'll make the right decisions."

Edward returned a silent acknowledgment.

Brian started his review of the material for his appeal in the morning. He had acknowledged that it was a long shot but felt it was worth the attempt. This time though, he would try harder to feel the direction he should go in rather than think it.

"You know I'm a great believer in fate, don't you?" Edward asked.

Brian nodded.

"And normally when something is going in a direction that it shouldn't, I feel very uneasy. Well, I've been in to see your father many times since he's been in the hospital and I get a tremendous sense of peace coming from him. It's hard to explain, but this feels like nature taking its course."

"And…?" Brian looked to Marjorie for support but she was looking at Edward, listening intently.

"And…as odd as the events surrounding us have been, and as difficult as this is to contemplate, I feel that your dad's passing is happening the way it should."

Brian looked at Edward, not really sure where he was coming from with this speech.

"Brian, just think of the opportunity his circumstance has provided for all of us to come to grips with our feelings toward him. I know when I'm in his room I speak openly to him, and I believe with certainty that he knows I'm there. I never leave the room feeling remorseful. In fact, if anything, I feel joyful having spent time there."

Brian listened carefully.

I know he's right. I know he's right. Why can't I let go?

"Look at how his circumstance has brought this family closer together; I've never seen you kids more open and loving in all the time I've known you. Remember, out of hardship springs opportunity. Anyway, I'm blabbing on as usual, but I just wanted to get that off my chest. This family has been blessed in more ways than we can count and I've been blessed to be a part of it. I think it's important to keep all that in mind when we face the next few days. If our faith prevails, we will all emerge from this stronger, wiser and more loving than we entered."

"Are you saying I shouldn't be trying to overturn his wishes?"

"No, you'll follow the path that you feel is best. The result will be the one that should be. I'm just saying that we need to be graceful in our acceptance of that which we can't control."

Marjorie was quiet, but her thoughts were completely on Brian and any potential the future might hold for them. She felt selfish thinking it, but in some ways, if Mr. Douglas was destined to pass his departure may allow a place in Brian's heart for her to fill. She knew his nature and that any pressure or obvious movement forward would spook him. She would stay neutral, hard as that would be, and create a place within her for him. Hopefully he would allow himself to be drawn to it. She felt, after many years of being at his side, she would be a perfect partner in life. She only hoped he would also see that.

The security desk announced the arrival of the gentleman from the funeral home. The group spent the next several hours in discussion about the arrangements. Catherine and Marion were brought onto the conference telephone so they could participate fully. Matt and Sarah had been contacted but deferred to the wisdom of the group. Sarah asked if she could do a reading at the service if there was time. Both brothers expressed surprise at her bravado and gladly endorsed her offer.

Emily was well known in the West Palm Beach area. The decision to hold her funeral in Boston was not taken lightly. If Peter Douglas was alive and well or dead, there would not have been any discussion around the location. She was to be buried in the Douglas family plot, although services would have been held in West Palm. Marion's father was buried in Idaho and an engraving on his headstone would recognize Emily's passing. There were no friends or family left in Idaho and Emily had made the decision to be buried with Marion's family, knowing that it is the spirit that rises and not the bones. She believed she would join her husband just as quickly, no matter where her body was.

The Douglases decided to charter a plane and offer complimentary transportation to any of Emily's friends who wished to attend the service. They also realized there would be hundreds of well-wishers resulting from her relationship with their family. It was agreed with the funeral director that everything reasonable would be done to personalize the services, both at his funeral home and their church.

He explained that it was now very common to have photographs and objects representing the life of the deceased around the casket and the viewing room. They would definitely have a closed casket, except for any private viewing the family wished to arrange. Marion, Catherine and the housekeeper would handle the task of selecting appropriate photographs and personal items for display. Emily always wore a floppy white hat with embroidered flowers on it. That's how people in West Palm knew her and how they recognized her. It was decided that the hat resting on the casket where her head would be was the best possible way to remind people of the person she was. It all seemed too ironic that the very week Peter Douglas's life might be terminated, the family would actually be mourning the loss of another dear family member.

Marion would feel the worst of it since she was so close to her mother and had lived with her in Florida. The Douglas children all loved their grandmother, but had not been particularly close since the divorce. They mostly felt for Marion and the sorrow and loss she would have to endure with the possibility of bidding farewell to two of the most influential people in her life looming over her.

Catherine had spoken to Brian regarding Marion's tendency to turn to alcohol or prescription drugs at times like this. There was a real concern that she might lose her sanity and in a moment of grief try to take her own life to avoid facing the pain. Catherine assured Brian that she'd stay close to Marion until they were up north. She and their mother were planning to attend at least one get-together of a group called "Grieving Families." It had been recommended by a close friend who had recently lost her husband to suicide. She felt it was important to be with people they could relate to and share their loss.

The group wrapped up their meeting quickly and casually, seemingly growing numb to crisis. They just dealt with whatever came their way. Somewhere down the line each of them would have a major come-down. That was why it was important for them to work and stick together as a family. Because of their high profile, many on the outside would love to see things fall apart for the Douglases. Such was the nature of success.

Peter Douglas had always pointed out that the public rooted you on in your striving for the top, but once there the same public delighted in your descent.

Edward left the boardroom with the funeral director, chatting about pre-planning his own funeral since he didn't have any family in the area.

"You've got more family than you can handle, Edward."

"Touché young man, touché."

Marjorie and Brian were frozen in time once the room was vacated. They avoided eye contact, hoping the other would speak first.

Brian finally burst. "This is silly."

"It is."

"I'm sure we are thinking exactly the same thing."

"We are."

"So what are we doing?"

"I don't know."

"That's a lot of help!"

"Sorry."

"Don't be." Brian stepped toward her. She returned his advance. Their embrace was delicious to them; two became one.

"This is hard for me," Brian admitted.

"I know."

"You know?"

"I've always known."

"You have?"

"You've always trusted me haven't you?"

Brian nodded.

"Then don't change. I'm on your side."

"You are?"

"Yes. Now shut up and kiss me."

Her lips became a blur to him but her words were magic.

Brian held Marjorie tightly. He felt her hands caress his shoulders and back. Her face pressed into his neck. He drew in the scent of her.

"This is where I want to be," she said.

"This is where I want you to be too."

- Chapter 69 -

No warning came prior to the explosion in the Douglas corporate jet. There were no vibrations, no noisy alarms in the cockpit, no fire or smoke.

The event had actually been precipitated several weeks earlier. During a standard roll out on take-off, a small stone lying on the runway had popped into the air when a nose wheel ran over it at an absolutely perfect angle. The plane was moving forward at about 120 miles per hour just prior to lift off. Both jet fans were whining at full power. The small stone was sucked in and through the right-hand turbine. When it passed through the titanium blades, its force of contact caused a micro fracture to one of the fan blades. Bob always did a visual inspection prior to each take-off, but even his trained eye would not have noticed this subtle imperfection. The fracture was a time bomb waiting to explode as the continuing forces of high speed revolutions strained the blades enormously. The instant of fracture could have just as easily taken place on the ground as in the air.

When the single blade finally torqued in half, it was only milliseconds before a loose metal piece jammed in the fan spinning at 12,000 revolutions per minute. The remaining blades sheared off, one at a time, unleashing razor sharp pieces in all directions. One of those pieces sliced through a metal casing, shearing a pressurized fuel line which provided the aviation gas to the thirsty engine. The subsequent spray of loose fuel ignited, causing the entire right engine to explode. The first blast ripped an outer casing from the engine, damaging the joints where the engine attaches to the fuselage of the aircraft. The damaged engine was now exposed to the full might of a four hundred mile-per-hour wind. As the force of the air ripped the remnants from the outer skin of the plane, it left a hole the size of a small garbage can and severed a portion of the tail which helped steer the craft.

Such aircraft fly at 30,000 feet or more. A plane is much like a balloon full of air. Like a punctured balloon, the greatest desire of the air inside is to get out as quickly as possible. In the case of an aircraft, any loose articles inside tend to get sucked out when the cabin loses its air pressure. When an incident of this sort occurs, many things are designed to happen automatically: numerous alarms start ringing in the cockpit; the plane immediately releases its autopilot system to manual control; oxygen masks are deployed from the ceiling for passengers; a ruptured fuel line is sealed by a mechanical valve. In short, a once subdued cabin becomes an emergency zone of activity.

Matt's plane veered sharply right when the force from the remaining left-hand engine now pushed it in that direction. A loss of steering control resulting from the damage threw the craft into a high banking turn, causing its nose to point downward. Sarah and Matt were seated side by side in the middle of the plane. When Matt flew by himself he loved to stretch out on a wide bench seat at the rear of the cabin. Had that been the case during this flight, his head would now have been adjacent to a three-foot hole. He would be undergoing a direct assault from a barrage of magazines, glassware, hand baggage and other miscellaneous items that were being sucked out of the cabin.

Neither Matt nor Sarah had seat belts on, but the overstuffed leather seats protected them from being pulled by forces of the air rushing past. The cabin de-pressurized in seconds. Other than having been showered with papers and some clothing, both were unharmed. Matt grabbed Sarah in his arms. The event had taken place so fast that both were silent with shock.

Bob had been reviewing a chart with his co-pilot. They had been on a standard course flown by auto pilot. He'd often told Matt, "This plane has done the route so often it can fly itself."

Now the instrument panel lit up with red and yellow warning lights. Alarms sounded in several different areas. The auto-pilot system released to manual control, allowing the craft to plunge downward without influence. Bob grabbed the yoke with both hands. The altimeter spun in a blur while the plane lost altitude. Ten thousand feet were gone in seconds while the ocean came rushing up toward them. Bob's co-pilot put on his oxygen mask, then reached over and pulled one over Bob's face while he struggled to gain control of the plane.

A deafening alarm resulted from the failure of a mechanism designed to stop free-flowing fuel from a ruptured line. Several attempts at overriding it failed so it continued to wail. The right wing-mounted fuel tank was draining into the sky, causing two problems. As the plane's weight continued to become more dominant on its left-hand side, it would be even harder to control. Massive fuel loss could mean that even if Bob got his plane under control, they would fly short of their destination.

Matt and Sarah could do nothing but wait in each other's arms. The violent wind resulting from de-pressurization had ceased, but a loud howl caused by the gaping hole in the cabin made it impossible to hear anything. Matt and Sarah pulled on their oxygen masks and huddled.

Their world seemed to go into slow motion.

Would she ever see her mother or father again? Or anyone?

Please God save my Daddy and get Mom and him back together. Michael if you can hear me please speak to God and help us.

I've been such a fucking idiot. What am I doing with my life? God please bless all of my family and friends and if we survive I promise…I promise to get it right. I know you must be pissed at me and I don't blame you but I am not ready to die and not with Sarah. Please God another chance.

"Power down seventy-five percent!" Bob wrestled with the controls trying to determine what responded and what didn't.

The co-pilot reached instantly and pulled the throttle back. This first action substantially reduced forces on all control surfaces so the plane was now slightly more like a diving glider than a rocket. The ailerons, on the trailing edges of the wing surfaces, adjusted by turning the yoke right or left and changed the airflow over the wing surfaces causing the wing to rise or fall. They responded normally, and Bob was able to level the plane relative to the earth. It was still diving, but at least it was diving straight.

Two floor pedals that control the tall part of a plane's tail that helped steer it right or left also worked, but turning right or left was not an issue at this point. When Bob pushed or pulled on the yoke, the flat surface of the tail called the elevator was supposed to raise or lower, causing the nose of the plane to rise or fall. The explosion had completely eliminated the right hand section of the elevator. When Bob pulled back violently on the yoke, the normal response would be that the plane would pull out of a dive and head skyward. Since only half was functioning, the effect of pulling hard on the elevator accomplished little. The plane continued its dive.

Bob was a very experienced pilot who had seen many emergencies in military and civilian service. A pilot has many ways to manipulate the control surfaces to achieve a desired result. Bob's task in the seconds ahead was to determine which combination of actions would at least level his plane. He had to be right the first time.

"Power down to ten percent! Full air brakes! Flaps five degrees!"

The plane decelerated rapidly, pressing both pilots hard against their seat harnesses. Matt and Sarah were thrown forward into the back of the seat in front of them. They landed together on the floor and huddled, frozen, waiting for the end, knowing their plane would surely smash onto the ocean's surface in seconds.

"More flaps. We're leveling."

Panels on the rear edges of the wings extended slowly when the co-pilot responded to Bob's command.

The view out of Bob's window was normally that of blue sky, but now it was the black blue of an ocean that filled the space.

The plane had all its extra surfaces extended. Metal air brakes were propped up on its wings like erect panels. Flaps hung fully extended out of the trailing edge of the wings. Bob hoped that if he could get the plane slowed down enough, the remaining portion of the elevator in combination with wing control surfaces could level the plane. He pulled again on the yoke, and although the result was less violent, the speed of descent was still too great. He had to dump more speed.

"We've only got one option left."

Brian Douglas had watched a special program on television about safety devices for private aircraft. He was so taken by the documentary that he asked Bob to install the emergency parachutes, featured in the show, on the entire Douglas fleet.

The purpose of these chutes was to stop a plane in the event that normal braking mechanisms on the ground failed. It had been reported that a high percentage of corporate jet accidents occurred when they were unable to stop on the ground due to mechanical failure or high speed landing on short runways. These short runways were mostly found in secluded places where corporate executives liked to be flown.

"They're just a gimmick Boss, save your money," had been Bob's response.

A small explosion ripped through the plane as a powerful charge inflated the chute out of its tail.

Deceleration was instant.

The plane now hung suspended from a chute that was never designed to be deployed during flight.

Matt and Sarah were once again jammed against the seat in front of them while their plane lost speed.

The result of the deployment could have been a relatively soft landing in the ocean and slow death by drowning, failure of the chute to sustain the strain of high speed inflation and a continued plunge to death or an effective deceleration of the plummeting jet.

The latter held true.

"She's holding, by God, she's holding. Speed reducing."

"It won't hold long."

"Power up five percent. Controls seem responsive."

The plane's nose started to rise, but the plane was still losing altitude from the increased drag.

They had plummeted to 10,000 feet.

Bob nursed the controls and called for further increases in power. He could feel the tremendous pull of the chute and knew that any sudden change could result in an unpredictable and devastating end.

The forces on the aircraft produced other-worldly sounds. The lonely remaining engine whined under overloaded conditions, wind whipped through a normally sedate and luxurious cabin.

Degree by degree, the plane leveled.

"C'mon baby. C'mon. We can do it. C'mon."

He could feel the air thicken, smell the salt mist and feel the buffeting of the ocean winds.

His co-pilot had silenced the fuel alarm by manually turning a lever in a floor panel, stopping the flow of fuel to the missing engine. His eyes were now glued to the altimeter watching it spin through 5,000 feet. The rate of descent had declined dramatically, but the plane continued to lose altitude.

"We're level at 1,500. Add five percent more power...no hold that...maintain power, eject the chute." The co-pilot hesitated. He looked at his captain.

"Eject it, damn it. Let it go, I've got the controls."

Bob's knuckles were bone white on the steering yoke. He was drenched in sweat. His heart pounded in his headset.

Without further hesitation the co-pilot punched a red plunger with the heel of his hand. Behind the aircraft a silky billow of fabric stalled instantly in mid air and began a playful trip to the ocean below on spider threads of nylon.

The plane lunged forward, throwing Matt and Sarah backwards this time. Both cried out, startled by the sudden change of force.

"900 feet, Captain."

Bob wrestled with the controls and the new freedom his aircraft felt, having dropped its anchor.

"Level at 600 feet, Captain. Speed one four zero knots. Flaps forty-five degrees. Air brakes one hundred percent. Temperature RED. Oil pressure RED. Fuel RED. Captain, we're shy on juice."

Six hundred feet is about the height of a sixty story building. If you jumped from its roof, it would take less than five seconds to hit the ground. Bob continued to navigate over the ocean's surface at about 170 miles per hour.

"You okay?" Matt yelled over the wind noise, relaxing his grip on Sarah when he realized they were no longer plummeting.

They pulled off their oxygen masks and eased themselves onto the leather chairs. "Matthew, we're almost in the water!"

Matt reached over and buckled her seat belt. He then pulled a life vest from beneath the seat and forced it over her head.

"Where are you going?"

"To check with Bob, I'll be right back."

She looked at him tearfully, patting her life vest to signal that he should put one on also. Matt forced a smile and reached beneath his seat, then he pulled it over his head and tightened the straps.

"Don't worry, we can swim from here."

"Matthew." Sarah yelled half laughing and half crying.

Sarah looked out her window at the white-capped ocean below. The knuckle of her thumb automatically found her mouth; an old habit long broken.

Matt stumbled his way to the front and poked his head in between his pilots. "How does it look, Cap?"

"We're still in the air, kid, were still in the air. I'm going to gain some altitude and assess whether we can make it to the mainland. You'd better buckle in beside your sister. It'll be a rough ride. Matt? If we go in, there's a raft at each exit. You and Sarah take the rear. We'll take the front. The doors will open automatically on contact with the water.

"Do you think we'll make it?"

"I'm the pig, remember!"

Matt moved back to his sister.

Bob liked to tell a war story about the difference between the officers who did all the planning and the pilots and troops who did all the fighting and risked their lives in war. "It's like ham and eggs," he'd say. "The chickens are interested, but the pigs are committed."

Matt buckled himself in beside Sarah and squeezed her hand. "Bob says we're going to make it." Sarah buried her face in his shoulder.

"Okay Cap," Matt yelled forward. "It's all up to you now. Do us proud."

"Retract air brakes one hundred percent!"

Resistance on the plane abated immediately as the stiff metal panels settled flush onto the wing surfaces.

"Climbing now at one hundred feet per minute!" Bob eased back on the yoke to gain altitude at a faster rate. "Increase power ten percent!"

The engine revolutions increased with normalcy now that they were free of the effects of two main sources of drag. "Climbing now at three hundred feet per minute. Bring power up to fifty percent."

"Captain, we're pressing the red lines on all gauges. I suggest we hold here for now."

Bob's first reaction was to overrule his second in command, but he hesitated.

"Maintain power."

"Thanks, Captain."

"Hey, we're a team right?"

"Right."

Minute by agonizing minute passed while the aircraft gained precious altitude. At 10,000 feet Bob leveled off. The flaps were fully retracted and except for the unorthodox method he was using to steer the plane it was flying straight and level.

The cabin was cold. Matt and Sarah huddled together.

The overhead speaker crackled to life. "We're level at ten thousand feet. I'm going to get you two home, so stay buckled in. If you've got any pull upstairs, now would be a good time to use it."

Dad? It's Matt. Now would be a good time.

Bob was in radio contact with the mainland who revised his course to steer to Logan International Airport. Its runway 27 extended East out into the ocean and they had the most modern equipment for assisting in emergency landings. They had estimated twenty-seven minutes to visual contact. Fortunately the air was clear and winds were light.

All traffic into the airport was re-routed. All other flights were grounded while preparations were made. Two yellow trucks foamed a lengthy stretch of runway 27. A crew erected a net at the end of the runway to catch whatever made it through the foam, which was both a fire retardant and a medium to slow the plane down.

Two ambulance crews raced to the target runway followed by a full fire brigade in four trucks. The chief traffic controller took a seat in front of a green radar screen. After a quick briefing, he made contact with Bob.

The co-pilot also kept in constant contact with his captain. Everything they said had to be yelled to overcome the noise in their cockpit.

"I have visual contact, Captain. Everything's still red-lining. It's amazing that number one is still turning."

"How's our fuel?"

"We must be on fumes. The needle is pinned."

"Can you cross over from the starboard tank?"

"I can, but if I re-open the valve to allow a cross over we'll start blowin' fuel out our ass end again. It could go up, Captain."

"Switch to battery. Radio only. Take the generator off line. Commence fuel crossover."

The co-pilot flipped several switches and breakers, cutting all but the most essential power. That would eliminate any possibility of a shorting wire sparking a fire when he re-opened the fuel line. He knew the left engine had consumed fuel at an astonishing rate, resulting from the extra load it was pushing. The damaged electrical systems could no longer properly control the flow of fuel through the sensitive turbine.

"What's the load on starboard?"

The co-pilot read from the gauges and estimated the gallonage.

Bob did a quick calculation. He figured that even if twenty five percent of the right hand fuel tank got pumped to the empty left one servicing the engine they'd have enough to make it to the mainland. They would definitely not have enough fuel for anything other than one direct approach.

Nostrils flared as the smell of jet fuel permeated the cabin. The co-pilot had been right. When he opened the valve to pump fuel from the one tank to the other, a steady stream flowed out of the torn fuel line where the engine was once attached. Passing winds blew gallons of fuel in through the hole and into the rear of the plane. The cabin filled with fumes as the volatile liquid evaporated. It took only a second or so before both pilots smelled the same fumes. Neither said a word. They had made their choice. They now had to live with it.

It's not that rare for a disabled aircraft to come wobbling out of the sky, onto a runway and into waiting arms of a safety crew. In most places in the world a bird crashes and a mess just gets swept up. American airports boast the finest safety standards in the world. This combined with highly trained crews and modern equipment gives them an ability to rack up a high rate of success. The public rarely hears of these successes, but always hears about the failures since exploding jets and charred bodies make for good headline news. The airport crews were ready, but not overly excited. This was not routine, but it was not unusual either.

The tower now had visual contact.

The chief controller watched a monitor display the approaching plane in crystal clear resolution.

Bob was now in combat mode and spoke clearly and confidently. Only further mechanical failure would foul his mission.

"We've got a visual for runway 27."

"Dump fuel at two miles," the tower commanded.

"We won't have a thimbleful when we mark two miles, tower."

"Shake your tank then, Captain, shake your tank." The controller tried to keep a serious situation light by suggesting that

Bob use every drop to cover the distance. "We've got a frosty one waiting for you. Make that two…I presume you have a Co…?"

"Roger that. Crossing two miles tower. On course."

Matt and Sarah could clearly see people on boats below. Town houses and condos on the shoreline were quite distinct.

Matt cleared his throat. "If I've never told you, you're a great sister and I love you very much. I'd do anything for you."

Sarah's eyes filled with tears until she could no longer hold back. She hugged Matt.

"You're the best brother in the world and I love you very much too."

Normally Bob would have extended flaps, dropped his landing gear and reduced speed in preparation for landing. This time he would only be lowering his landing gear at the last possible minute. He did not want to risk any sudden changes that might take him off course. If the gear didn't lock, he'd have to land anyway and put his hopes in the hands of the ground crews.

"Crossing one mile tower. Gear down now!" The auxiliary batteries were nearly consumed extending the landing gears, but one by one three green lights came on, indicating that all wheels were locked in place.

"Gear down and locked tower. We're high but sinking fast." The drag of the wheels had slowed the aircraft, disrupting the sensitive balance.

"Power up fifteen percent."

The co-pilot's left hand was glued with sweat to a palm-sized handle that gave or retracted power from the engines. He pressed the lever forward.

The four people on board inhaled at exactly the same moment the left hand engine went silent. Only a whistling sound of wind in their cabin filled the air.

"We've flamed out on one, Captain. Restarting."

A restart sequence was attempted using the remaining battery power, but without success. Even with more battery power an engine can run on fumes for only so long.

"Tower, we're gliding. We've got full engine failure. Repeat, full engine failure. Visual looks fair at one half mile."

Bob wanted to retract the landing gear to reduce drag on his plane and improve his glide profile but he now figured that the batteries would not support any further demand. He needed to use the tiny amount of remaining power for radio contact.

The tower did the same calculations Bob had already done in his head. Without some unforeseen force acting in concert with the plane's forward motion, it would not make the runway. The speaker in the cabin crackled on battery power.

"We'll make it, kids, but it's going to be a rough landing. Buckle up tight and bend down."

Bob knew that whether his prediction was true or not was irrelevant. He had to have everyone believe it.

Bob and his co-pilot could just barely see their touchdown point when he had to start easing the nose of his aircraft up to maintain altitude.

Tower staff and rescue crews watched quietly while the plane drifted in over the bay.

Boats in the harbor stopped, having seen the activity on the nearby runway. People stood on their decks and craned their necks to ogle at the tiny plane gliding downward.

Flashing lights and sirens had alerted residents of the area and those who were walking on shorelines near the airport that something was happening.

One by one and pair by pair, hundreds had stopped to focus their curiosity and hope on the tiny white bird trying to make it home.

Cameras were capturing the scene that would instantly end up on the internet and newscasts that evening.

Even the seagulls, as though by intuition, had all settled on the ground to make room for this giant mechanical cousin.

Bob knew that, by the numbers, the little jet plane couldn't have made the glide from the time the engine flamed out. It was hopeless; he was about to come up a few hundred feet short of the runway.

His thoughts steeled. At this low altitude a turn to the right or left would leave no time to level off and thus he'd bank his craft into the cold and salty waters of Boston harbor which would break up the plane and certainly kill its occupants.

Bob looked back over his shoulder to Sarah and Matt, who were bent over in their seats, arms wrapped around each other.

Both were silent.

He contemplated yelling something to them, but decided that a silent prayer was his best tribute. He was a captain who would go down with his ship if it came to that.

Quickly considering his remaining options, he realized if he nosed down and could skim along the water's surface like a flat stone the Douglas kids would think they were landing. The plane might stop or could smash into the concrete pilings that supported the runway jetty. Death would be instant. Sarah and Matt would not suffer. A crumpled mess, like a crushed soup can, would sink to the bottom of the bay, taking four dead occupants with it.

In that moment it seemed to him like the collective consciousness of the hundreds of people looking up, the gulls on the ground who gave their loft away, the safety crews and tower staff, Sarah, Matt, his co-pilot and, of course, God combined to provide a gentle tail breeze and extra lift that glided the jet a few hundred extra feet to cross the jetty's edge, over a fence with only inches to spare and onto the grass preceding runway 27.

Bob could feel the subtle shift in the air and the subsequent lift when he squeezed the grips firmly and pulled back on the yoke. The nose of his plane rose, blocking his view while he willed his craft to its target.

A stall alarm screamed out through the cabin.

The four passengers held their breath while their metal cocoon slipped noiselessly through the air.

Suddenly, the wheels made solid contact with the dirt and rolled a few yards before screeching onto the pavement.

Their cabin went dim and silent as their plane coasted into the marshmallow softness of white foam.

There was complete silence.

The plane had stopped.

They were safe.

All news media were alive that evening with stories about the Douglas family and their near disaster that occurred that day. Emily's passing and speculation about Schebb's return were also getting some play, but there was no co-operation from the Douglas front to confirm or deny any of the material. The media were well aware of the Douglas Corporation's ability to punish any firm that stepped too far into the realm of speculation or disrespect and thus they governed themselves accordingly…for now.

Matt, Sarah, Bob and his co-pilot had evacuated their jet unharmed. After an on-site check over by paramedics, they were released with a clean bill of health and a few bandages for minor cuts and bruises. They were advised if any pain or headaches occurred, they should go to their physician or to a hospital for further examination. Bob and his co-pilot were required to attend a debriefing with Federal Aviation Association officials. The Douglas jet was removed from the runway and placed in a warehouse to be examined for the cause of the explosion.

- Chapter 70 -

Much to Brian's embarrassment, Edward had tracked him down at Marjorie's home. The moment he found out the reason for the intrusion he summoned a Douglas car so he and Edward could pick up his brother and sister from a separate terminal far from the hustle of the international airport.

All press were barred from the premises.

Other than being shaken up and exhausted by their experience, Sarah and Matt were enjoying somewhat of a celebrity status. Crews and passengers of private jets shook their hands and asked for some of their good luck. They signed numerous autographs in aircraft manifests and rubbed a number of aircraft key chains in attempt to pass on their good fortune. The Douglas car pulled into a hanger attached to the small terminal. Matt and Sarah were greeted with hugs from Edward and Brian and they were forced to tell their whole story on the way back to the city.

"You guys are something."

"Thanks, Uncle Edward."

"You know for many people, an event of this nature would have been a monumental event in their lives. But for you Douglases, and in particular your father, the monumental seems normal and the absurd is just plain routine."

The mood lightened in the car and everyone had a good chuckle.

"I guess you can archive this ho hum near-fatal crash alongside an extensive list of exceptional circumstances this family has found itself in over the years."

Matt jumped in and asked the driver to drop him at an address he wrote out on a piece of paper.

When the car pulled up in front of the house of his on-again, off-again fiancée Susan, no one ventured a word other than "goodbye" and "call us in the morning."

Edward was dropped back at his home. Sarah rode to Catherine's place.

"You okay, Sis?"

"Ya...I've got some things to think about. I am going to give Michael a call and invite him for a coffee. I want to tell him how much he's meant to me and our family."

"Really? Anything I should know?"

"Not that way, Brian. I have a lot of growing to do before I get serious about a man. But...if I were going to get serious, I think he has set the bar pretty high."

"You sure you're okay?"

"Sure...Brian? Do you think one day I could maybe work with you in the business? I mean if I get serious about school and stop, you know, partying and stuff?"

"That would be awesome if you're interested. Hey, maybe next summer you could do a stint at one of our affiliates and see if you like it?"

"I was sort of thinking I might want your job."

"My job? Oh, okay Miss Douglas...right away Miss Douglas...I will get Marjorie to get you some business cards."

The two had a good laugh.

Sarah gave Brian a big hug and kiss on the cheek when he opened the door for her. He watched her bounce up the sidewalk to his sisters flat.

Sarah Douglas, President and CEO. Hmm...I like it. So would Dad.

Once alone in the car, he directed the driver to take a long route back to where he had started. He telephoned Marjorie to make sure she was still enthusiastic about him being there. He was very pleased to hear her welcoming tone. His car snaked its way up the constricted streets of Beacon Hill. Trees overhung the streets. A light rain had started to fall. The constant radiance of the gas lamps played in the trickle of raindrops on the car windows.

"I like the red ones."

"Pardon, Sir?"

"The red ones. I like them."

"Yes, Sir. So do I."

At night these effulgent red beacons, which stood tall on black cast iron poles marking fire pulls, gave the street an eerie look. He watched residents dart to and from their flats carrying shopping bags and umbrellas. He peered into the lighted windows and wondered what stories each told from within. He toured the length of Charles Street and did several loops of the Common, passing his home twice before pulling up to Marjorie's.

"Shall I pick you up, Sir?" Brian wondered if the driver was prying. He was simply asking the requisite question.

"No. No, thanks. I can just walk home. Have a good night."

"Sir?"

Brian stuck his head back into the car.

"I'm happy for you and your family that things worked out today. I used to drive for your Dad. Hell of a thing, that."

Brian was moved by this simple gesture. He looked into the elderly man's pleasant face. "Thank you. That's very kind. Goodnight."

Brian closed the door softly and watched the taillights disappear down the hill. The rain had stopped. He stood at the bottom of her steps, letting the major event of the day sink in a bit further.

The thought that he had nearly lost his brother and sister affected him profoundly at that moment. He realized it was the strength his family provided that allowed him to deal with his father's situation. When that was cast in relief against the prospect of losing Sarah and Matt, he found a new peace and acceptance around the prospect of losing Peter. He had come to realize that the young must accept the burden passed on by their parents and carry on. They must take their parents' wisdom and hard-earned lessons and move forward. They must try to improve upon what they were given and in turn pass it on to the next generation to do the same.

Peter Douglas had not been a perfect father, but Brian now realized he had done the best job he could with the skills he had. That is all his father had ever asked of anyone. Brian was realizing that the point in life seemed to have arisen too suddenly when one understands that their parents aren't perfect but human, with all the same strengths, frailties and fears their children have. Brian knew his Dad made many mistakes, but Peter Douglas was a very forgiving man toward the mistakes of others. Brian could feel the mantle of adulthood lowering onto his shoulders. He now knew, as his father had forgiven him for the many mistakes he'd made, that he must do the same for his father and accept his father for who and what he was.

The man Brian looked to for all the answers, in the end, had just as many questions as he did. It was sobering to realize that, in a sense, he and his peers were now taking charge of the world in which they lived.

How did I get here so quickly? It seems like only yesterday I was a kid. Now people look to me for advice and listen to my opinions.

As he stood, the words of his father sounded in his head.

"Life flies by, doesn't it? You'd better enjoy every day, because they don't come around again."

- Chapter 71 -

It was a sunny morning.

Their single lawyer followed at a respectful distance while Brian and Edward climbed the steps of the old entrance to the Boston Public Library.

Edward paused with Brian when he stopped outside the doors of this iconic building to scan Copley Square and Trinity Church across the street. They each absorbed a few beams of radiance from the morning sun.

"You go on ahead, okay?" Brian said to the lawyer.

"Yes, Sir, Mr. Douglas."

"'Sir?' Edward. Everyone's calling me 'Sir' these days."

"Get used to it old man. Get used to it."

"I remember when I was a little boy I couldn't wait to get older Brian."

"And now?"

"Now I wish I was a little boy." Edward put his hand on Brian's shoulder but said nothing. He would wait with him.

This was one of Brian's favorite places in the city. Trinity Church stood proudly in the square across from the library, supported for hundreds of years on wooden pillars that kept it from sinking into the landfill that comprised most of the city. Landfill carted from surrounding hills, one horse drawn wagon at a time, by soldiers long dead.

He marveled at the seventy-story John Hancock tower and wondered why it didn't sink into oblivion. He used to love taking visitors to the top of the massive, mirrored building where they could get a spectacular view of the city and watch a miniature re-enactment of the historic events leading up to Boston's present. That little joy ended after the terror attacks of 9-11 when they subsequently closed the visitor gallery.

The rumble of the underground subway seemed to shake him back to the moment.

"Let's go," Brian said. "Thanks for waiting."

Edward just smiled a knowing smile.

The two men entered the building and crossed the marble floor of the library foyer. They nodded at the security guard, who was busy checking a student's backpack and walked through the metal detector.

They climbed slowly while Edward worked with his cane.

After they ascended the well-worn steps of the central staircase, Edward turned left and Brian turned right, rounding the huge carved marble lions that faced each other, protecting the confines. They met on the second level and stood overlooking the lobby below. A massive chandelier hung overhead. The few sounds that morning echoed loudly as they ricocheted off the stone walls and high, ornate, vaulted ceilings.

Two more flights of twenty stairs led them to the entrance of the Cheverus Room.

"Is there no elevator in this damn place?"

Brian only smiled. He knew Edward was spryer than he let on.

They were to have met in Judge Bolstein's chambers, but a last-minute call changed the location.

"Good morning, gentlemen. I'm Judge O'Reilly." The Judge was in his gown. He closed the two heavy bronze doors after he entered the room, which was currently displaying children's books in long glass cases. "You all know that I preside over the State appeals division."

His thick Irish accent was almost comical. Its tone was comforting, but Brian reminded himself that he hadn't become Chief Justice of the State Appeals Court by being a pushover.

"I appreciate you gentlemen meeting me here. I'm on a very tight schedule so I have to be back in my own court in thirty minutes. I just happened to be over here on another matter and I knew it would be more convenient for all of us."

O'Reilly moved directly to the end of the room and sat on a wooden table. The light from the window produced an aura around his head and shoulders. Brian and Edward tried to adjust their positions to ease the impact of the sun which streamed into the room onto their faces.

Brian knew the "sun at the back" trick and wondered if O'Reilly did too. He did a quick calculation and realized, when he factored in travel time for the Judge, that he was about to get approximately ten minutes of this man's time.

He felt queasy and his throat was dry.

"You must be Brian. You look just like your father when he was your age."

Not a good sign. Another "old friend" of dad's.

He shook his hand and made an innocuous comment then introduced Edward as his father's long-time best friend, hoping to balance out the old-boy thing with his own ace. He introduced his lawyer, but kept talking so the Judge could see this was a family matter and not a legal matter. His words bounced off the walls of the square room. Much to Brian's dismay, Judge O'Reilly held up his hands and stopped Brian's stream of verbiage.

"Son."

I'm done right here, right now. Fuck.

He let his eyes slide to the books in their cases and read their titles to himself in an attempt to maintain his composure. The Big Heart, How Much is a Million?, The Tale of Peter Rabbit, Jemima Puddle Duck.

I wish I was six again.

"Most people sitting in this town's courts have followed your dad's progress throughout their careers. There aren't many of us who haven't at one time or another been retained by him to provide legal or advisory services. We all monitored JB's proceedings..."

What is this a club? He's calling the dead Judge JB now?

"... closely. Your father is a man of honor and integrity. To my knowledge he has never made a major decision without seeking the counsel of intelligent and able advisors."

Brian recognized this speech. He felt like throwing his papers on the floor and walking out.

"Your father drafted his Will with very specific instructions pertaining to his current situation. He now finds himself precisely the way he had anticipated. Not unusual for your dad, Brian. Peter had an uncanny knack for predicting the future and planning for all contingencies."

Brian tried to speak, but the Judge held up one hand and kept talking. "That is why he has been so successful in business. The reason I wanted to meet with you prior to our hearing was to let you know in advance that, as a loyal friend to your father and as a Judge, I intend to maintain that loyalty and uphold the law. His Will is valid. Miriam Whiteside's decision is valid and I will not overturn it. I admire your love and loyalty to your father, but I want you to search inside and question your motives for arguing against his wishes. Are you trying to do him a favor or are you reluctant to let him go for your own selfish reasons?"

Brian could feel his pulse quicken. His face went red while this astute stranger pressed directly on sensitive buttons.

"His wishes cement some certainty around his life here. We don't know what, if anything, comes next. Neither does your father. We do feel that the likelihood of him surviving and living a life the way he knew it is negligible. By holding onto him, you risk bringing him back to a life that he has clearly rejected. He wants to die the way he lived: with dignity and grace. He doesn't want to spend the rest of life on earth in chronic care or sitting in a wheelchair, having others do everything for him. I should further tell you that there probably isn't a Judge in this state, and perhaps not at the federal level either, who will think differently."

The Judge continued to preach.

Brian drifted. Am I being selfish?

"We've become a warehouse society, gentlemen. We store our elderly in homes. We store our children in daycare centers. We store our poor in ghettos and slums…"

Please give me some guidance.

"…we've plugged those roadside storage lockers with enough extra stuff to fill about half as many homes as we have in this country. Each day most Americans shuffle themselves to and fro in mobile storage containers called buses, trains and cars…"

Am I afraid to go it alone? Father? You listening?

"…they spend a good part of their day battling to make it through this society that we've clogged with so called progress."

The Judge's voice grew louder and his accent stronger with his enthusiasm.

Brian's mind drifted through thoughts of family and Marjorie.

"Times are about to change. We've spent billions on drugs and services to keep people alive regardless of the quality of that life. Your father, as usual, is setting an example I'm sure others will follow. He is saying no to being stuffed away in a warehouse until we decide it's time for him to go. He is saying 'Please give me death with dignity.' It's the way of the future gentlemen, and you heard it here first. Those three words,

death with dignity, will dominate the landscape socially, politi-
cally and economically in the years ahead, mark my words."

O'Reilly finished in measured and certain tones. "Listen
son…"

Call me son one more time and I'm walking out of this
place.

"…he did the best he could to influence his fate while he
was alive. I will not take that privilege away from him at this
most critical time."

The force and intent of his convictions was impressively
filling the thirty-by-thirty foot room.

A crystal silence now hung for ten seconds or more while
Judge O'Reilly made eye contact with Brian, Edward and the
lawyer before speaking.

"Is there anything else, gentlemen?"

Brian looked casually at his watch, realizing that the Judge
could have breakfast and still make it in plenty of time for his
next sitting.

Edward cleared his throat and stepped forward.

"Judge. Your Honor. I couldn't agree more fully with what
you have stated, but could we explore a hypothetical situation?"

Edward felt he was about to step clearly from the trunk to
the limb. He wanted to test its resilience cautiously. O'Reilly
looked at his watch and sat back.

"Sure."

"Suppose, just suppose, that everything we know about
Peter's condition is true. And that all the best medical people in
the world and their equipment confirm what we believe."

"Sir, we don't need to suppose what is already fact."

"Stay with me, please. Suppose there was something going
on at a level that couldn't be measured or determined conven-
tionally. And suppose that by letting Peter go, based upon what
we know today, we really are letting go of Peter. In a word,

killing him. Suppose that Peter is indeed alive, but trapped in his body."

Judge O'Reilly was not moved. He answered without hesitation. "How would we prove this and who could give me facts to support your hypothesis?"

"Let's say that a person, any person…" Edward paused to choose his words carefully, "…gifted with special skills, was able to communicate with him?"

Brian's mouth had opened while Edward talked. It now dropped further.

"First of all, I'd say that person should enjoy the time communicating with him while they can. Secondly, I don't think it's safe to assume that just because we allow his body to lapse, that his spirit will also lapse, but that gets down to some pretty subjective discussions around faith."

"So what you are saying is that if you could go into that hospital room today and have a conversation with Peter Douglas and he told you not to execute his wishes, you would anyway?"

"Those are your words. Here are mine. We exist here the way we do. We are governed by rules that are based upon what we know and what we believe. If the spirit world exists, and I'm not saying it does or doesn't, we can only presume that there are rules to govern it also…rules which we would have no way of knowing or understanding. I would not want to have a ghost come in to my courtroom and try to influence how I make decisions in this world. Nor, if given the chance, would I try to tamper with a world I know little or nothing about. We have to accept what is dealt and make the best decisions we can. I'm sure we've all had inexplicable experiences. Some people allow those experiences to rule their life. I guess others, like me, accept them as a gift and a signal that faith is well founded. We then continue on until our time here is done."

Edward stood quietly, nodding, thinking.

Maybe this Irishman wasn't a stranger to the paranormal or unexplainable. Perhaps he is right. I should relish this opportunity to be with my friend in such an intimate way. Perhaps this is my test of faith.

"Gentlemen, if there's nothing else, please let my clerk know if you intend to proceed with your application." There was a pregnant pause; Judge O'Reilly looked again at each of the men present.

No words were spoken.

After the Judge stood, he softened his demeanor and looked at Brian.

"I have no doubt this is one of the most difficult times you have faced in your life. The more you care, the more it hurts. You will get through this, just like your father managed through his hardships. You will be wiser for the experience. Your loss is shared by me and my colleagues. I want you to know that we have the utmost respect for your father and his family."

The Judge's hand poked from beneath the ample sleeve of his black robe and extended toward Brian, who shook it firmly. The Judge placed his other hand on Brian's shoulder.

Inside, Brian reluctantly agreed with this man. He was also rethinking the notion that he was, in any way, in charge of the world in which he lived. O'Reilly quickly disappeared, leaving the three men standing in silence.

Brian walked to one of the high windows. He pulled aimlessly at the string of the venetian blinds. One blind dropped, startling them all momentarily. A cloud of dust hovered in the rays of sun that broke through the slats.

Brian sneezed. Then sneezed twice again.

"Let's get out of here. I think I'm allergic to something in this room."

Walking toward the door Brian managed a small, crooked smile. "Well, I guess that's that. What do you two think?"

Edward put his arm around Brian's shoulder and started the descent of the forty steps.

Brian counted out loud. "One, two, three…"

"Ever heard about the monkey in the tree?"

Brian stopped counting.

"What?" Brian looked at Edward curiously. He continued counting the steps silently while he listened.

"Well, you see, there was this monkey sitting in a very tall tree in a jungle, overlooking a river. He had a great view of the surroundings in all directions. He heard a splash below and noticed that a young tribesman had fallen into the river. The man was a good swimmer, but the current was strong. He watched while the man swam with all his might against the current, trying to get up-river and back to where he had fallen. The monkey screamed advice to the man, but he wouldn't listen. He kept swimming hard against the current."

Brian had tuned in to the story now.

"After many minutes of struggling, the man started to tire. The powerful current forced his mouth full of water. He coughed and sputtered, trying to breathe. When he did, the current took him even further downstream, making him struggle harder. The monkey kept screaming at the man, but he continued to struggle against the rushing water. Eventually, and much to the monkey's dismay, the man tired to a point where he could no longer struggle. He let the water engulf him. He gasped as it filled his lungs and he drowned."

Edward looked to Brian who was obviously hanging on the words of the story teller. He smiled and continued.

"The monkey watched while the body of the man, now free from its struggle, floated quickly down river. It rounded a small bend and floated onto a shallow beach where the sun was shining and the current was still. The monkey had swung from tree to tree, following the floating body down river. He climbed down and ran along the beach to where the man's body lay and poked to see if he was alive, but he was not. The monkey was saddened that his words had gone unheard."

"'You should have listened,' he said. 'I was trying to tell you to swim with the current, not against it. You would have been safe that way.'"

"Thirty-nine. Forty." Brian looked at Edward. "Do you think I'm swimming against the current?"

"I don't know that. I do know that if we can rise above this or any situation, we can see it from a higher perspective. From there we have a better chance of making a good decision. It's difficult to see the elephant when your face is planted in its leg."

"The current hasn't exactly been flowing with us, has it?"

"No."

"Perhaps all of the signs we are getting are coming from people with a better perspective?"

"Perhaps."

"If we ignore the signals we're getting, we could risk drowning in our own desire, when just around the corner is a sunny beach?"

"You're close enough."

The three men walked in silence.

Brian looked at his lawyer, who had politely stayed a couple of steps back. "Call the court clerk and tell her..." His throat tightened. "...Tell her that we won't be proceeding with the appeal."

The lawyer didn't hesitate. He faded off at his master's command.

Edward and Brian continued together past one of the marble lions. Brian stroked its smooth back and sculptured mane.

His body felt like rubber.

Until that moment he refused to imagine that he would lose his father. Now he contemplated life without Peter Douglas.

In the middle of the landing he surveyed the cool halls of the ancient library - a place of weighty thought and, no doubt, weighty decisions. He could have cried, but he didn't.

He collected his faculties and looked at Edward.

"One life ends…and another begins…I hope…let's go."

- Chapter 72 -

Taking in the view that his office in the GBC Tower provided Carl Nathan rose from his desk and walked to the glass wall. He just hung up the phone from Marion, having explained his reason for not flying to Florida. She agreed.

Carl gathered his thoughts and picked up a well-read copy of the City Star. At the last minute he slipped on his suit jacket before entering the boardroom connected to his office. Carl was not a nervous man, but for his upcoming performance he wanted no signs of weakness. Wet underarms were always a dead giveaway.

He made a point of getting his adversaries to remove their jackets during negotiations. Carl made a habit of wearing a T-shirt under his dress shirt on any days that he would be employing his astute negotiating skills.

When he entered the boardroom, Harvey Kirkland and Joseph Zalkow nervously got up from their chairs.

"Good morning, gentlemen."

Carl put his copy of the City Star on the table and walked over to get a cup of coffee. "Gentlemen, coffee?"

"No thanks." They answered together.

A grim-faced woman entered from a different door and took a seat at the end of the table.

"You don't mind if I take a few notes, do you?"

Both men looked at each other then shook their heads in unison indicating it was okay.

Carl was toying with them. The woman's looks belied her sagacity. This morning Carl was enjoying his position of power as Chairman of the GBC News Corporation. His secretary had called both men at home long before they woke to request their presence at a meeting in his office. The mere fact that he knew both of their private residence telephone numbers was no small indicator of Carl's ability to meddle with their lives if he chose.

"It makes me very unhappy that the City Star is about to attempt to embarrass and disgrace the Douglas Family in an upcoming 'extravaganza,' I believe you called it. All this in an attempt to sell a few extra papers. Gentlemen, I'm disappointed." Carl flipped a few pages of the Star to display the offending headline. "I have asked you here this morning to politely request that you refrain from featuring any uncomplimentary pictures or articles of Peter Douglas or his family."

The men listened to the soft words coming from Carl Nathan's mouth. They had already discussed this and figured he wouldn't ask if he didn't have a large club to back his 'request' with.

They knew the trick was to try and find out how big the club was. They needed to determine whether the number of papers they could sell, resulting from George's work, would outweigh the size of the blow he might inflict upon them. Kirkland started the negotiations.

"Carl, I admire your loyalty to Peter. He's a friend of ours too, but the people want to know what's happening in the lives of our public citizens. If we don't tell them, someone else will."

"I don't think so."

Those were the only words Kirkland needed to remind him that between GBC and Douglas, there was no media in the region that was outside their influence if one got overzealous. The Internet was another story, but in terms of front page news they had a virtual lock on what working men and woman saw in the newsstands when they walked to work. The Star was the last of the independent newspapers.

"You have no reason to concern yourself. This will come and be gone. We'll have sold a few papers and we'll be on to our next story."

"I'm asking that you move on to your next story now."

"Is there an offer behind this benevolence toward your friend? Are you willing, say, to offset our lost revenue if we take a pass on this one?"

"I'm asking it as a professional courtesy. Maybe one day GBC can return a favor."

"No deal, Carl. This is worth untold dollars to us. The interest in this family is huge. There may be a book and movie deal. By the time you or anyone can stop us it will be too late. The spoils will have been taken. In fact, as a little guy, having your big corporation chase us could actually be good for business."

Kirkland sat back in his chair and let his little speech sink in.

Zalkow was still wondering why he had been called.

"I was worried that you might not respond positively to my request. That's why I invited Joe along. Perhaps, as a major shareholder in your paper…"

Zalkow felt his ass begin sticking to the leather chair. His shareholdings in the Star were highly secretive. His face puckered when he considered the potential consequences.

"… you'll respond to his request. After all, he claims to be a good friend of Peter's. I'm sure he feels the same way I do. Joe?"

"Carl, I don't know what to say." He chose not to pretend innocence on the ownership issue. "Of course, Peter and I were very close, but I have a duty to support my investments and the people who manage them. I can't really interfere in Harvey's business. I really have no say over what happens at the Star. I'm merely a silent investor. I wish I could help you."

"I'm disappointed in you, Joe. Maybe I can help you change your mind." Carl motioned to his assistant who started flicking switches in a recessed panel in the table. It was the same set-up as Peter Douglas's; they both loved gimmicky technology.

Blinds closed automatically over the exterior windows. Pot lights dimmed and cast a subtle illumination throughout the room.

Kirkland and Zalkow shuffled nervously in their seats, exchanging glances.

A screen slipped quietly down from a slot in the high ceiling. Carl nodded to the woman controlling the devices. The screen came alive with the familiar logos and theme music of the GBC News Corporation.

"We interrupt our regular programming to bring you this special news feature." The picture cut away to one of GBC's familiar news faces standing in front of the hospital.

"I'm standing in front of the Boston Trauma Center. Inside, a news conference is underway, disclosing the fraudulent and perhaps criminal activities of Dr. Joseph Zalkow. He has been implicated in the blackmailing of the physician in charge of Peter Douglas's medical case. He is also accused of willful misrepresentation to the Board of Directors of the Trauma Center. Both actions appear to have led to the premature death of Peter Douglas. It is suspected that Dr. Zalkow will be forced to resign the positions he holds on various medical boards. It is also likely that he will be banned from practicing medicine while a criminal investigation takes place. It has been disclosed that Dr. Zalkow is a major financial partner in the tabloid newspaper The City Star. The independent newspaper has recently run a series of unauthorized photos and news articles on the well-known Douglas family. If Zalkow is found guilty of causing Douglas's death, he could face a lengthy prison term."

"Okay, okay, turn it off." Zalkow was on his feet by the time the lights came up.

"How dare you drag me into this? What are you trying to pull, Carl? You have no information to back up those lies. I'm merely a shareholder in The Star and even that isn't common knowledge. I have nothing to do with the Douglas case except in my officially sanctioned role."

Carl signaled to his assistant who, with the flick of another switch, started screening a slide and audio presentation. The pictures of Peter Douglas were ominous. The soundtrack was bizarre in the context of the corporate boardroom. Zalkow and Kirkland huddled. Carl watched the show, wondering what their next move might be. Both men rose from the table.

"We're not playing this game, Carl. You can't pin any of this on us. We don't care who your sources are."

Kirkland and Zalkow froze in place when a series of photos showing them standing in front of tall glass windows and talking in Harvey Kirkland's office, started to play across the screen. It was then obvious that they had been photographed from the office tower facing his.

Kirkland's mind raced, trying to place the event. He didn't have to think any longer when the audio track played from speakers hidden throughout the room. The quality of the sound and placement of the speakers was such that they felt like they were in Kirkland's office when the recording had taken place.

Their voices were clear and unmistakable. The electronic bug that Carl had Roxanne plant in Kirkland's boardroom had worked perfectly.

"…and you, my sleazy little journalist friend, are in for the news ride of your career."

"I'll take that as a compliment coming from you, Joe. If it wasn't so early I'd offer you a drink to toast our good fortune. How does that saying go? 'One man's curse is another man's blessing?'"

"If all else fails, Harvey, I'll pull the fucking plug myself. I can't stand that bastard Douglas. He's blocked me at every turn in this incestuous town and every promotion at the hospital."

Kirkland and Zalkow took their seats. Zalkow held up his hand, requesting that the show stop. With a nod from Carl, the screen went blank.

"Okay, Carl, you win."

Kirkland sat upright and protested. "Joe! Not so quick. Let's discuss this. Maybe there's a compromise."

"Shut the fuck up, Harvey. You'll do what I say."

Harvey settled back into his seat like a little boy who had been scolded by his parent. Carl spoke with an even tone.

"No stories on the Douglas family without my approval. Now or in the future."

Kirkland winced while he listened to the biggest payday of his career go out the window.

"No more contact with Dr. Jim Brandon. No pressure. No blackmail. No comment. Got it?"

Zalkow nodded submissively.

"Anything else?" Kirkland asked indignantly.

"As a matter of fact, there is."

Carl glanced to his stage partner. She opened a well-camouflaged door in the wall of the boardroom. From a spacious waiting area behind the door George and Roxanne emerged. Both were impeccably dressed. George actually looked quite handsome. Roxanne had obviously had some makeover tips; gone was the 'tarty' look. Carl's assistant beamed at her two new protégés like a proud mother. They had buffed up nicely, but that could only hide their lack of experience and professionalism for a period. Carl wanted the pair groomed for his "research" department.

Kirkland bristled at the sight, "You little prick." He looked at George with disdain who simply returned a nervous smile at him.

"Just want to play on a winning team. Didn't you get the memo that I had been traded?"

Carl's next words stung where it hurt most for Kirkland.

"Harvey, you'll write a severance check to Roxanne and George for $35,000 and give them both glowing reference letters. Not one bad move against either of them."

"C'mon, Carl, that's blackmail! Those traitors don't deserve a plug nickel."

Zalkow just looked at Kirkland.

Carl smiled. Presumably the stupidity of what Harvey had just said dawned on him.

"We'll give them ten grand and that's it."

"Twenty-five." Carl quickly replied.

"Twenty."

"Deal. And the references."

The negotiating happened so fast that neither Kirkland nor Zalkow realized that their tactics had been anticipated long in advance. They looked at each other hopelessly and skulked from the room in silence. Once the door closed behind the deflated men, the air in the board room lightened considerably. Carl patted both Roxanne and George on their backs and laughed out loud.

"Well, that's probably the quickest twenty thousand you've ever made."

"Thanks. What's next, boss?"

– Chapter 73 –

It had once been a rare occasion that the entire Douglas family gathered in one place for more than a brief visit. Since Peter's accident it was becoming a habit.

Catherine continued to direct her caterers on how to set up for the evening while her flat filled with people. A long table was formally set in her spacious living room. Wonderful aromas of food drifted out from her kitchen and down the hall. Catherine did not like to cook but she loved to entertain. She loved the idea of making two telephone calls to complete all the arrangements necessary for her evening agenda.

Catherine and her mother had flown in from Florida that morning. Marion's mother had lived a long, full life and although everyone was suffering a loss, they weren't dealing with tragedy. The funeral director met them at the airport and had taken complete charge from that point. Marion and Catherine did not have to witness Emily's casket being removed from the plane or deal with any paperwork. The simplicity of the transfer allowed them to maintain buoyancy that would otherwise have been difficult. They could put matters aside for a while and face the full assault at the wake tomorrow. Tonight was a gathering in honor of Peter Douglas and an early Thanksgiving dinner for the whole family. Emotions were raw, but the new closeness of the family seemed to keep everyone's spirits charged.

Charlotte arrived alone from her country home. Although she was tentative at first, she quickly relaxed when Marion and

Catherine greeted her warmly. Within minutes the women were chatting away like three old friends, chipping in their services to help the caterers get organized.

Sarah retreated to her room to freshen up.

Edward arrived unannounced but quickly made himself at home. Within minutes he was in the midst of the senior Douglas women, joking and teasing like he'd been with them all afternoon. He carried a deck of cards that bulged in his pocket just in case he got called upon to entertain the group with a new trick or two.

The clock was pressing hard on dinner time. Brian and Matt had already missed the social hour while everyone lounged by the fire and chatted.

The sound of the front door opening captured everyone's attention. It was obviously Matt or Brian since there was no one else expected and they were the only two who would enter without ringing. It took a few seconds for everyone to recognize who it was that filled the doorway to the living room. The attractive woman paused abruptly. All eyes looked at her inquisitively. She motioned for her escort to hurry. Brian's beaming face joined her and the context of his presence quickly identified the woman to be Marjorie.

Brian cleared his throat. "Hi everyone, sorry we're tardy. I had to do a little convincing to get a date for the evening. You all know Marjorie, of course. I don't have to tell you that we've known each other for a long time, and we've decided to get to know each other a little better."

Brian's hand slipped around Marjorie's waist. Her hand moved to meet his then he kissed her on the cheek in a symbolic public display of affection.

There was just enough pause from everyone to make the room momentarily uncomfortable. Edward, in his inimitable way, jumped up and moved quickly to support Marjorie. He gave her a big hug and whispered in her ear as he faked a kiss to her cheek, "Good work. Hang onto him."

Sarah gushed at Brian who promptly stuck his tongue out in brotherly fashion and gave her a look as if to say, "You're not the only one with romance in your life."

Then, as if on cue, Marion, Charlotte and Catherine surged forward and grabbed Marjorie. They dragged her out of the room and down the hall toward the kitchen under the guise of getting her a drink. Their tittering trailed away while the four women scurried out of sight to inculcate this novice member of the inner Douglas circle.

Brian threw his hands up in mock surrender. He kissed his sister, made a quick joke about getting some balance in his life, and settled in beside Edward.

Catherine finally announced they would be commencing dinner even though Matt had yet to arrive. Her caterer had implored her to do so or risk serving food that was well over-cooked from being kept warm while they waited. Protests were subdued since everyone was hungry and ready to eat. All seats at the luxuriously set table were taken, since Marjorie sat in the chair intended for Matt.

Brian wanted to make sure the entire family knew the most recent, pertinent details regarding Peter. He had decided that rather than lead the conversation in that direction, he would give everyone the choice of talking about it over dinner or getting together early in the morning for another family meeting. He hoped Matt would arrive before he made the suggestion and chose to open the evening with a simple toast.

Brian had automatically gravitated toward the seat at the head of the table. It wasn't purposeful, though the symbolism was apropos. When he proposed a toast, everyone went silent. Both white-jacketed servers stopped and backed discreetly away from the table.

"I'd like to dedicate this evening to two of the people without whom we wouldn't be here. Our grandmother Emily now rests peacefully, having given us our mother."

Marion nodded and smiled; her children beamed at her.

"She was a loving grandmother, a faithful wife, a friend to every one of us when we needed one and a heck of a good gin rummy player according to the West Palm gossip circuit."

A chuckle softened the mood.

"May she rest in peace. May she continue to bless us and watch over us."

Everyone nodded unconsciously with Brian while he continued.

"The second person I'd like to toast, of course, is the man without whom we certainly would not be here. We pray that Father also continues in his own way to rest peacefully while we speak of him and we pray that he feels our love the way we have felt his love for us."

Eyes around the table were glassy. "To Emily and Peter." Brian raised his glass.

The group raised their glasses. The crystal rang; each toasting the other.

"To Emily and Peter."

No one heard the door open while everyone drank. Like before, it took a few seconds to recognize the woman who stood politely in the doorway to the dining area. She looked hesitant scanning the table and twice checked back over her shoulder to see that her escort wasn't far behind. Catherine was the first to call out her name.

"Susan! Susan, come in, it's so good to see you. Where's our delinquent brother?"

Matt's frame darkened the door, but his bright, wide smile beamed into the room full of family. He was obviously very happy, wrapping himself around Susan in a rare public display of affection. He and Brian exchanged glances. His older brother raised an eyebrow. Matt's answer was reflected in a quick nod toward Marjorie as though to say, "Who are you to ask about dates?"

Catherine asked the caterer to set two more places. She looked at Matt and Susan. "Of course you're staying for supper."

While Susan and the others sat, Matt stayed on his feet. "Before I settle in, I'd like to say a few words."

He ducked when a bun flew past his head. Brian was chuckling, but Matt threw him a look that doubled the one his mother had just given him.

Brian realized that there was something serious going on.

Marjorie was amused that Brian was just another brother when it came to family gatherings.

"For once I'm serious. I hope you're all as pleased as I am to see Susan here tonight."

Susan's face went crimson at all the smiles of approval.

"I stopped by her house today after our airborne mishap and presented her with something I'd written for her yesterday; coincidentally before the plane ride. If you'd like, you can all read it later.

I don't want to sound cliché, but when one comes close to death, life's priorities seem to order themselves with unique clarity. It was very clear during the whole ordeal that Susan and our life together was a priority to me. I've spent a lifetime chasing something I have now realized I can never catch, and that's myself. I've looked everywhere to find me when all the while I only had to look inside and there I was. I don't want to continue this journey alone. I know in my heart that the partner I've been searching for has been there all the time. I've been indecisive in the past with Susan and I'm surprised that she hasn't told me to go to hell before now. Actually, she did the other day, but I think I've convinced her to recant."

A light chuckle rippled through the room and Matt's tension eased several notches. "I no longer wish to take that risk. Tonight, I've asked her to set a date to marry me. I want all of you to be my witnesses when I present her with this token of my sincerity."

There was a slight gasp when Matt removed a navy-blue box from his jacket pocket and opened it. A single diamond, the size of his baby finger nail, glimmered in the light from the chandelier. The stone was not set. It lay loosely in its velvet bed. Matt picked it up between finger and thumb and looked through it toward Susan.

"Please accept this stone as my promise to be one half of a lifetime partnership with you."

He extended his arm and the stone dropped with some weight onto her open palms. The eyes of every woman at the table were glazed as they watched the romantic theater playing out before them. Brian hoisted his glass. "A toast! To Matt and Susan. A lifetime of happiness."

The family stood together and toasted the couple.

"To Matt and Susan."

The mood around the table was positively jovial.

The women gushed at Susan.

Brian and Edward walked around to Matt's side to give him hugs of congratulations.

"Quite a day." Brian smiled at his younger brother.

"Your Dad would be proud of both of you." Edward wrapped his arms around both brothers and hugged them like they were his own sons.

Catherine , the hostess, spoke up, "Can we please eat? And, please, no more announcements tonight."

The group smiled and laughed loudly; holding for a moment, the oddity and trauma of their circumstances at bay.

- Chapter 74 -

The exit from the hospital parking lot seemed like the most subtle place to park his mother's sedan so Fuzzy eased it into an available space well away from the building. The late model vehicle had been a gift from Fuzzy to his mother on her birthday. Their family had always owned only one car which meant any time his father was away, his mother was stranded in their rural setting. His parents' resistance to accepting such a generous gift had been high, but Fuzzy won in the end by explaining that he would also use it instead of his expensive rig when he came to visit. Both Wilma and Anton took that as a sign that their son might visit more often, and accepted the gift. They didn't anticipate that the next time their son would visit, he'd be doing so to hide out.

Fuzzy had left their house well before dawn.

He did not see anyone when he walked along the hospital corridor to the elevators. His dress slacks, button-down collar and pullover sweater would not draw any attention. He had kept his face clean-shaven and his short hair was smoothly combed.

He convinced his mother to call the hospital and get Peter Douglas's room number under the guise of wanting to send flowers. When Fuzzy left the elevator, he passed by Peter's corridor once to see if there was anyone that might question his early morning visit. At first he was rattled to see a uniformed security guard, but relaxed when he observed that the lad was sound asleep. The hospital wings were designed like ladders. They had two long outside halls lined with rooms. Service and non-patient rooms ran down the middle of the wing, with many short passages joining the two long halls.

The guard was positioned such that he could clearly see down one of the halls to Peter's room. Fuzzy took the unattended hall and hoped for the best. The nursing station was quiet. Two nurses behind the counter were too busy with their morning paperwork to notice Fuzzy slip by on the outside wall. He glanced over his shoulder turning left to cross to Peter's side of the wing and plowed square into a utility rack waiting for pick-up.

At the instant of the clamoring both nurses jumped up to see what happened. Fuzzy bolted through the crossover to Peter's hall. He made a quick right, reading the numbers on the rooms. He then immediately ducked left. When he entered the opened door he heard a young male voice behind him.

"Hey, you there. Wait a minute."

The sight of Peter Douglas and the thought of being caught made Fuzzy break into a sweat. He froze in his tracks and tried to think of a quick story to tell the young security guard who was trotting toward the room to investigate. Both nurses were still busy trying to find the source of the calamity on the opposite side of the wing.

"Excuse me, sir."

Fuzzy turned on the spot to face the Douglas security guard, but before Fuzzy spoke the guard's face relaxed. "Oh Mr. Douglas, it's you. I'm sorry; I didn't recognize you from the distance. Sorry to bother you, sir."

Fuzzy was about to speak, when a voice sounded in his head. *"Just let him go."*

Startled at the sound of the voice, Fuzzy said nothing. The security guard backed up as if on command. He closed the door and left without another word. Fuzzy stood still, amazed at what he had just witnessed.

"*Good morning, Wilton. I've been expecting you.*"

Fuzzy looked down at the man he rescued. "Mr. Douglas, is that you?"

"*Yes, and I have you to thank for that. Did you know I was calling you?*"

"Well, no, but I've dreamt of you for the last couple of nights and I am here against my better judgment. What happened to the security guy? Did you do that?"

"*You don't need to speak, but then you already know that, don't you?*"

Fuzzy's lips no longer moved. "*Some things have happened to me.*"

"*You've had the gift all your life, but you've never used it. Why not?*"

"*No one would have understood. It's been more of a burden than a gift. I've known things all my life before they happened. I've always understood a person the moment I met them, but somehow I knew that I wasn't to interfere. When I came upon you, it was the first time in my life that I knew I had to do something. I've always just let things happen the way they did and watch when I might have made a change for the better.*"

"*Or perhaps for the worse.*"

"*That's true. I knew long before I got to that corner that you would be there. When I saw your spirit leave the car though, I didn't understand if I should continue trying to save you. I hope I did the right thing. Did I?*"

"*What you did has given me a gift of indescribable proportion. I am a new man and I am ready for my destiny. I truly thank you for what you have done.*"

"*But you are going to die, aren't you?*"

"*Apparently*"

"*Are you afraid?*"

"*I have lived my life twice, Wilton. I no longer fear the future. Please stay a while. You are safe here.*"

"*What if someone comes in? I guess you know I'm a wanted man.*"

"*I can handle that.*"

"Like you handled the security guard?"

"Something like that. Tell me, how did you and Schebb get along and where did you go?"

When Fuzzy told his story in detail, Peter was finally able to return to the accident and watch the entire incident unfold. He saw his car fly into the air. He watched Schebb climb the bank to the highway. He watched while Fuzzy stopped his truck and risked his life to save him. Peter had met his hero and found a man who shared his ability to move through time and participate in people's thoughts. Travelling together, Fuzzy recounted his experience from the time he first thought of Peter.

At first it was a bit awkward, like learning to dance with a new partner. However, after a few tries, Fuzzy and Peter played smoothly through shared events in time. The two men talked and learned about each other's lives. They had crossed paths many times but had never connected.

Fuzzy explained that he had met many people with similar talents to his, but had never opened up to them. He could tell when he walked in a room if there was anyone there with similar skills. Invariably the individual would make eye contact in a familiar way, but it never went any further. Fuzzy experienced out of body traveling from an early age and simply accepted it for what it was: a unique experience. Peter asked him if he had any idea why he had these talents. Fuzzy did not and had never questioned it. He said it was like he was unable to even formulate questions in his mind about the topic.

Peter wondered aloud how many people lived like this, harboring exceptional talents but unable or unwilling to explore them. He now believed that most of what happens and really counts in life can't be seen or explained. It was just there to be appreciated. This affair had confirmed for him the need to participate fully in life's everyday events as they happened. To him, that was the only true way to really comprehend what life was all about.

He explained his thought that too many people were like him, putting off enjoying life until some further goal was achieved.

"When I get a better job..."

"When we have a child..."

"I can't wait until next year..."

"I can't wait until Friday..."

"If only I had more money, time, things, holidays...my life would be better."

He was disturbed by how much time he had willed away during his life, waiting for something better to come or the future to arrive sooner. He speculated that most can't accept that life at its richest is happening every hour they are healthy and alive. He expressed his new understanding of what he now called "the miracle of the moment."

"Wilton, or shall I call you Fuzzy?"

"Fuzzy would be good."

" I now appreciate just how much is happening while each second of life ticks by. It's all there for us if we just take the time to appreciate the goodness around us and stop dwelling on the negative. I've learned that some people have figured out that life is always sending signals and post-ing road markers. Like the little everyday coincidences we encounter, the voices we hear in our minds or the unusual people we meet for no appar-ent reason. These signs are there to be followed. We only have to choose to open our minds to that possibility. There is much knowledge to be gained from understanding that what we can't see may be more important than what we can."

"Mrs. Rossi is right. You have learned much."

Not even that comment fazed Peter. He now accepted that life beyond vision existed, that this unseen world could be fully participated in. One only needed the will and the acceptance to believe in and act upon the signs that mark the path of our everyday journey down life's highway.

Peter had a taste of that life and regretted only that he hadn't figured it all out sooner.

"Perhaps that was the point," he mused. *"Perhaps we're all here until we figure that puzzle out. Then it's time to leave."*

Fuzzy checked his watch then stood up. He had to look a second time to believe that only a few minutes had passed since he arrived. It seemed like hours. In normal terms it would have taken hours to exchange the knowledge these men had shared. Peter's hand disappeared when Fuzzy wrapped his massive paw around it. The big man stood silently for a few real minutes, looking at the man he had pulled from the wreck.

"Thank you for bringing Schebb back. I know you took some risks to do that. It was great to see him."

"He was in here?"

"Twice."

Fuzzy smiled.

"It was a pleasure to have him with me and every bit worth the small risks I took."

"I'd like you to get to know my family after I'm gone, especially my friend Edward. He'll understand you."

"You mean?" Fuzzy tapped his temple.

"Yes. He'll understand."

Fuzzy shook Peter's hand again and spoke out loud. "I feel like I've known you a lifetime. I'll never forget this day. Perhaps you'll come and visit sometime. I'll watch for the signs."

"I have no idea what's next, but if I can, I will."

Fuzzy set Peter's hand down. He found nothing odd about this exchange. He felt gratified to have played a helpful role in this man's life. Walking to the elevators, he wondered how long it might be before he met another like himself. Perhaps his work was done, perhaps not. He would live in hope that he would be called to put his "gift" to use again soon.

It was like he was invisible when he walked by several nurses and the Douglas security guard, who didn't so much as look up when he passed by. People were oblivious to him when he rode the elevator down to the ground floor, but when he left the hospital and emerged into the morning sun he was even more surprised when he was greeted by one of the Doctors who stood talking on the sidewalk. "Good morning, Dr. Brandon."

- Chapter 75 -

D r. Brandon's black foreign sedan was elegant but not flashy, and when he pulled up to her steps Catherine was waiting anxiously to see what his visit was about. She greeted him wearily. The family gathering had lasted well into the night and everyone in her house was still sleeping. Catherine received his message early that morning asking to come by. She feared the worst.

When she got into the car, Catherine leaned over and kissed his cheek. "Good morning, Doctor."

His smile was strained. "Welcome home. What a terrible time for your family this must be. I'm sorry to hear about your grandmother, and I just couldn't believe the news about the plane incident. Thank God no one was hurt."

"Yes, it's amazing. It obviously could have been disastrous. Sarah and Matt were pretty shaken up but by last night they seemed to have put it behind them. In fact, Matt formalized his engagement to his fiancée, Susan. I think the brush with death cast a mortal light on him."

"Astonishing what a good scare will do for a man."

"As for Grandmother, she lived a good, long life. We're sad to lose her, but it's not tragic. It's just life. With Dad, we've all had some time now to try to accept what has happened. Our biggest concern is that he doesn't partially recover and end up living feebly for the rest of his life. He was far too independent and proud. That's one thing the whole family agrees upon. In many ways, it would have been worse if he'd died in the car accident. All of us have had time to make our peace with him. I'm really happy that Sarah has been involved in all of this from the beginning. It's painful, but I think it will be healthier for her in the long run."

"Are you at peace with this, Catherine?"

"I think so."

They drove in silence.

"So what is it, Jim? News about Father?"

He pulled the car off Storrow Drive into a park along the river and stopped.

"No, actually it's about me. Catherine, there are some things I need to tell you. I thought it would be easier if we were alone; somewhere neutral rather than at the hospital."

Her fatigue from lack of sleep vanished when she felt the weight of his voice. "Sure, if you'd like."

He exited the car and met her at the passenger's side as she was getting out. She could see the tension on his face but rather than say anything she fell in step beside him and started walking.

It was a beautiful fall morning. The Charles River was flat and reflected, in perfect detail, the university buildings on the opposite side. A few joggers and dog walkers were out. Rowers powered their boats silently through the still waters.

"It's nice to have some room and fresh air around us for a change."

"...and?"

He dove in.

"Catherine, eighteen years ago I was charged with sexually assaulting a female patient."

He had Catherine's full attention now.

"It was very early in the days when I had just opened a practice. I was doing one of my first physical examinations on a young woman. We were alone in the examination room and I made the first and biggest mistake of my medical career. While

I was doing an internal exam, I commented on how attractive she was. She was nervous and I was only trying to break the tension. I could have easily said what a beautiful day it was, and I should have. She took offense and jumped up while I was still examining her and ran out of my office screaming, bleeding and scared. My assistant tried to calm her, but she insisted on calling the police and pressing charges. The medical board was notified. Several senior people at the hospital and university were informed. My career was about to go out the window and then I got a call from Dr. Joseph Zalkow."

"The same man my father has battled all these years?"

"Yes. He offered me assistance. He also informed me of his connections with the City Star."

"The City Star?"

"Yes. He said with his paper he could not only clear my name, but could enhance my credibility with some glowing reports. I knew the woman was wrong. I knew I certainly hadn't sexually assaulted her. So I did a second wrong, hoping it would right the first, and agreed. Like magic, the charges were dropped. Outstanding reports about my academic performance and new practice appeared in the paper. My world was mine again. Or so I thought."

"It wasn't until years later when I started specializing in the field I excelled in at school that I was contacted by people claiming to have been sent by Dr. Zalkow. They knew I was an expert in coma patients and I was asked to pass on information about certain patient's likelihood of survival. I'm not sure what they did with the information but I cooperated out of fear of what Zalkow might do. Then your Dad came along and I brought in that special monitoring equipment from Europe to test. I have since discovered from one of the technicians that someone tampered with the settings and I think that someone was Zalkow. It turns out that your father has displayed the most unusual brain activity I have ever seen from someone in his condition. I can't explain it, but if I were guessing I'd say he's alive inside and can't get out."

Catherine stopped walking.

"Alive? You mean he's conscious, but trapped in his body? Can't you test for that?"

"I'm afraid not. The information we gathered is gone. It's been erased and the equipment has been flown back to Europe. It was about mid way through the monitoring that Zalkow started blackmailing me and forced me into testifying in court and at the hospital board that your Dad's case was hopeless. Somehow, Zalkow found out that your Dad's Will provides one hundred million dollars to the hospital when he dies. The fact that he requests in his Will not to be kept alive plays right into his, or their, hands."

"Theirs? What do you mean…are there others?"

"I don't know. This is way beyond me now."

"Jim, this…"

"Catherine, I promise you, I will go public with all this information regardless of the personal cost to myself if you want me to. My medical opinion is that the likelihood of your father recovering is very, very small. Your Dad, in his own way, is pre-empting any chance of recovery. Even if he is aware, we have no known treatment to even recommend. We could be tampering with a natural process we know nothing about."

"Wow. That's a lot to hear this early in the morning."

"I know. I'm so sorry. I have wanted to tell you this for weeks but…"

"Thank you. I can only imagine how difficult this must have been for you."

"Thank you, Catherine; I honestly wasn't sure who to turn to."

"Jim, forgetting all the stuff about Dr. Zalkow, I do agree that tampering with my Dad's life based upon speculation about things we don't understand and can't prove would be cruel and risky. His life, like ours, will follow the path it's supposed to. Sometimes that's good, sometimes not, but that just seems to be the way it is…"

He nodded, listening intently to Catherine.

"…that's not based on any faith or spiritual stuff. Just an observation. Despite how hard I've tried to avoid this notion, I always seem to end up where I knew I would whether I wanted to or not. We'll just have to deal with whatever happens, when it happens. Beyond that, let's decide how to use this information to best suit your needs and my family's needs. Now, can we get some breakfast? Then I'll call Brian if that's okay with you."

Dr. Brandon's steps lightened markedly. Once again he had learned the value of truth.

How many times do I have to learn this lesson? Truth always surfaces. Always sets us free. It's just sometimes very painful getting to it.

"Catherine, thank you."

- Chapter 76 -

The conversation was subdued. Several yawns triggered a round of open mouths from the rest of the group. Brian, Matt, Marion, Catherine, Charlotte and Edward were assembled in the hospital boardroom. Recent events and the previous evening were taking their toll.

Brian had chosen not to discuss their father's situation the previous night. Everyone was enjoying the company of friends and family. Matt's announcement and the enthusiasm around Marjorie's arrival on the scene had given everyone a few hours of respite from their stress-filled lives. Brian and Marion sorted out a few last minute details about Emily's funeral over the telephone. The first wake was to be that evening.

Dr. Zalkow entered the room with the Chairman of the Hospital Board. Catherine eyed Zalkow suspiciously. She had decided not to tell Brian and would wait to determine what to do with the information Dr. Brandon had confided in her.

They took seats at the head of the table. Introductions were not necessary. The Chairman spoke without pausing for small talk.

"On behalf of the hospital, may I extend our condolences on the passing of your mother and Grandmother. I wish today's meeting could be postponed or forgotten altogether, but that would not change the outcome."

"I understand and thank you for your comments."

"You all know that Mr. Douglas has made a provision in his Will that no life support is to be used to hamper a natural death process. You have challenged the authority of the will and it has been held to be valid. I have a copy of the court judgment. The lead Doctor on the case, Dr. Jim Brandon, is one of the best in the world. I have his report indicating that the prospects of a healthy survival are virtually zero. Notwithstanding these two facts, we have kept Mr. Douglas on life support until today. I suspect if he'd had his say, we would not have done so. Mr. Douglas is a valued friend to his community and to all of us. There is no one in this room, I am sure, who wishes to lose him." He looked toward Zalkow, trying to shift the focus of this group's gaze. "Dr. Zalkow is the Chairman of the committee that actually gives the directive to remove life support. That directive has been given and duly authorized by the Hospital Board. At four p.m. today, the Doctor in charge will be instructed to disconnect the nutritional life support and monitoring equipment to allow nature to take its course."

The Chairman took a long breath.

Catherine and Brian stared at Zalkow with ice in their eyes. If looks could kill, he would be dead. Zalkow sat frozen in place and avoided eye contact with any of the family.

"Are there any questions?"

"You're a cold son of a bitch!" Matt moved toward the Chairman. Edward and Brian intercepted him, but Matt continued his outburst.

"If that was your father, it would be a different story. How'd you like me to kill your fucking father!"

"Sir, excuse me, but this is your father's request, not mine. We are merely obeying his wishes and the law."

"He's right, Matt. Sit down." Brian eased his brother back into his chair. Zalkow and the Chairman quickly headed toward the door.

"Brian, you've been the spokesperson for the family to date, I assume that will continue?" Brian nodded, watching the two men leave the room.

Marion and Charlotte were in tears and comforting each other.

Catherine replayed her morning with Dr. Brandon.

Edward broke the silence.

"I guess I've known Peter longer than anyone in the room. Marion is a close second." Edward reached across the table and held Marion's hand. "I think I know him pretty well. I have to tell you that when I'm in the room with him, I swear he's right there with me. If it makes any of you feel any better, I believe we are doing what Peter would want. I believe that he's ready for his next step. If he could talk to all of us, I think he would tell us that."

Brian was still a bit perplexed.

What did Edward's speech at the courthouse mean exactly? What does he know that he's not sharing?

"He's done a great job here, but now he's being called for more important work."

Reluctant nods went around the table while Edward spoke.

Matt interjected with some distaste. "Thanks Edward. Those are comforting words. From Dad's longest and closest friend, they carry a great deal of meaning. It still doesn't take away the hurt or take away the fact that he'll be gone."

"I know that. I know that."

"You all know that Edward and I met with the Chief Justice of the State Appeals Division yesterday. He is a long-time friend of Dad's. The bottom line with him is that there is no way an appeal will fly in his court, or any other court for that matter. It seems every one of Dad's longtime friends agree on one thing: Dad was a man who knew what he wanted and knew how to get it. I haven't found any support for going against his wishes. Sometimes I feel like I'm fighting my own battle and not his."

"Brian, your Dad would be proud of you and all the efforts you are making on his behalf. I know you don't want to lose him. None of us do. It hurt to lose my mother though we spent a long, healthy life together. Death hurts at any age, but we'll get through this together."

"I think we've all been touched in a very special way since Dad arrived here. None of us has said so specifically, but I know that each of us has experienced a new level of connection with that guy, that seems…well, seems beyond this world or at least anything we've known."

Everyone agreed silently with Matt, each acknowledging and remembering how strange and wonderful their time had been with Peter Douglas while he lay, apparently sleeping, in his hospital bed.

Charlotte was bursting to tell her news, but felt she should defer her comments and let Peter's family share these few intimate moments.

"I plan to meet with Dr. Brandon just before four o'clock. I'll find out what we can expect in terms of time once the support systems are disconnected. I know we have the wake tonight, but perhaps the entire family should be downstairs at three thirty. It would be nice if we could all be together with Dad for a few minutes. Any objections?"

Everyone shook their heads. Brian had naturally taken over as leader of the family. The transition had been imperceptible.

"Matt, will you bring Sarah? I am sure she'll want to be there. Tell her Michael is welcome too, as long as we are all okay with that. She seems to have made a great connection with him which has been good for her."

"Sure, I'll let her know."

- Chapter 77 -

"I've just been before the Merciful Care Committee…"
Dr. Brandon addressed the waiting group. "… and I
have received the order I know you were made aware
of this morning. I have told the committee that I will not perform the order without the consent of the family. I would rather
resign my position and give up medicine than do this without
your support."

The room was full to capacity with Douglas family members, extended family, Edward, Michael and Marjorie.

The room was silent; the decision hung in the air.

Brian took the lead, "It seems I have ended up spokesperson for this family. That is unusual for a group like this with no
lack of opinions. Dr. Brandon, we appreciate everything you
have done for our father. I know that it must pain you to face
this decision. Life as we live it here is precious. It is hard to
imagine there could be anything better, but dad wants to move
on and find out. Hopefully he'll send us a message and alleviate
our fears. As a family we support his wishes, although I'm sure
each of us has come to that point from a different direction. We
are all behind you and hope that you too support our father's
request."

Dr. Brandon looked at each of the people present. He could
feel the love and compassion emanating from them, now they
supported each other and reached out to help him in this difficult circumstance. He spoke quietly, "Thank you." He raised
his hand and wiped his eyes.

"Dr. Brandon, how long will we have with him?" Edward asked, breaking the stillness.

"That is impossible to say. His body could react quickly and negatively once the nutrition stops, or he could linger for days. We are under orders not to resuscitate if something goes wrong. I would suggest you make the best of this time while you have it. I've always believed that the patient knows I'm there and can hear my words, regardless of their condition. I'm sure Peter has heard and appreciated all of your visits."

"I can assure you there will be no pain for your father. He has been getting morphine every four hours today and we'll continue to provide that until…" Dr. Brandon paused and searched for words, "…until he no longer needs it. I will return in a few minutes to answer any other questions."

Dr. Brandon started to leave, but then turned back. "Sometimes friends or family wish to be present at the time of disconnection. They see it as a symbolic moment. If you wish, I can make the arrangements."

A few seconds passed in silence while solemn glances were exchanged.

"It's a simple procedure. There will be no apparent reaction. He should be resting quite peacefully," Dr. Brandon assured them, hoping to put their imaginations at ease.

Edward was the first. "I'd like to be there."

"Me too," Marion followed.

One by one the entire gathering chose to be with Peter when his life support was removed. As each person in the room acknowledged in the affirmative they took the hand of the person beside them and held it firmly. When Dr. Brandon left the room eleven people stood in silence holding hands, all moved by the unity of their love for Peter Douglas at that moment.

Dr. Brandon was alone with Peter when he made the final notations on a report. He didn't want any mistakes. He had kept original copies of all his reports since Peter's arrival. He hoped he'd never have to use them.

"Well Mr. Douglas, I have a feeling you know more about this than you're letting on. I only hope we're doing the right thing by letting you go. The decision has been made. Your request is being granted. Your family all want to be here when I take this stuff out of you."

Dr. Brandon fingered the wires and IV tubes. "You have an incredible family, Mr. Douglas."

Peter listened while Dr. Brandon spoke. He was pleased; pleased and relieved. He knew he would not miss his family because he would be with them all the time.

A nurse appeared to tell the group that Dr. Brandon was ready in Mr. Douglas' room.

In heavy silence they proceeded en masse down the hall. All were feeling emotions that were unfamiliar. Each person wore a unique look, but their faces did not tell the whole story. For the non-family members, it was a rare opportunity to see the dynamics of the entire Douglas family together.

What a rare occurrence this was.

Barriers that often impeded smooth relations amongst themselves and the outside world were set down temporarily. For now, inter-family grudges, jealousies and friction had vanished. Their true characters shone through while each drew strength from one another.

For those who weren't Douglases, this moment was affirmation enough that they had chosen well in tying their life to the family Peter Douglas had led.

Peter lay quietly on his back, a fresh sheet folded at his chest. His arms were outside the covers resting at his side. His hair was neatly combed, his face clean-shaven. He looked slightly gaunt, but handsome never the less. His room was vacant and tidy except for a few vases of flowers. The equipment was gone.

All monitors had been removed. Only a single pole with a bag dripping life into his arm remained.

Peter watched and was overwhelmed by the feelings this group poured into him. He saw Edward looking at him directly. *"I guess this is it pal. We fought the good battle but I am ready to go and I hope you are too."*

Tears began to roll down Edward's cheeks. He had heard Peter in his mind but chose not to respond.

What was there to say? Perhaps this was all in his mind anyway. Just an old man trying to hang onto a dying friend.

"Good bye my friend."

"Not good bye Edward. Not good bye."

Dr. Brandon stepped forward. "I will now remove the intravenous. I doubt that any changes will occur for a while. I'll leave and let you spend some time with him."

The group backed away from the bed when Dr. Brandon pulled the tape that held the IV attachment to Peter's arm.

Sarah buried her face in Matt's shoulder.

The tape clung to Peter's skin, which stretched when Dr. Brandon pulled on it.

Peter could feel a slight physical sensation when the needle started to slip from his vein. Everyone's eyes were riveted on the point at which the needle entered his arm.

Dr. Brandon extracted it slowly.

The silver shaft lengthened drawing a trickle of blood with it. When the sharp tip finally emerged from Peter's vein a small rivulet of bluish red liquid drained from the puncture point across his forearm and onto the sheet.

Catherine fainted and fell to the floor, cushioned by those around her as she crumpled.

Dr. Brandon hit the intercom button and barked a code. Within seconds two nurses were over her. One nurse slipped a pillow under her head and raised her legs.

The second nurse swabbed her forehead with a cool cloth. "Poor thing she's white as a ghost."

Catherine sat with her father in front of their summer home by the ocean. It was a childhood setting, but their ages were current. The place was exactly the way she remembered it even though it had been years since it was sold. Everything seemed so normal when he greeted her.

"Hello Catherine. I'm glad we have these few minutes to talk."

"Daddy, where have you been? We've missed you."

"I know, darling. I've been traveling. I miss all of you too."

"Are you coming home? Are you coming back to see us?"

Her father paused and looked directly at her. He took her hand, something he hadn't done since she was a little girl. "I want you to know that I love you very much. I love our whole family. I tried my best to be a good father to all of you, but now I'm being called away. I'll miss all of you and I know you'll miss me, but don't be sad. Be happy. This journey is wonderful. One day you will all join me. I'll be waiting for you then."

"But why are you going so soon?"

"I don't know that yet. I'm not afraid. I feel peaceful and know that this is right."

The image of her father started to fade. "Catherine?"

"Yes. Where are you? Where are you, father?"

"Dr. Brandon is a good man..."

"Catherine? Catherine? Can you hear me? Catherine?"

Darkness faded to light and the blurry image of Dr. Brandon filled her vision.

She felt wet and clammy.

Everyone stared down at her.

Dr. Brandon put his arm under her back and helped her to her feet. She shivered and felt lightheaded.

"You gave us a scare." He walked her to the bathroom where she rinsed her face and straightened her hair.

She returned to hugs in the hospital room and walked to her father's bedside. Only a small speck of crusty blood marked the needle's track. A towel covered the stained sheet.

She looked at her father and he looked back at her from behind closed eyes. She bent down to kiss his cheek.

"Thank you, Daddy, thank you."

When Marion suggested they all hold hands and say a prayer, it seemed like the most natural thing to do. The family ringed the bed while they stood with hands clasped and looked down upon Peter.

"Our Father, who art in heaven, hallowed be Thy name…."

No one member of the Douglas family could have recited the prayer on their own but, in concert, the words flowed like they knew them well. At first they spoke in low tones.

"…Thy Kingdom come…"

Matt looked across at Catherine and they simultaneously placed their hands on Peter's shoulders to include him in the circle of prayer. When they did, it was like a switch had been thrown. The circle was complete and the energy flowed uninterrupted. The words flowed easier and louder. Peter joined in.

"…Thy will be done on earth as it is in heaven. Give us this day our daily bread; and forgive us our trespasses as we forgive those who trespass against us…"

While the prayer rang out through the hospital room, people's lives were changing. The power of love and faith was upon them. Matt felt the force of their actions in that hospital room. A door was being opened for him to a world he had never known or believed in.

Everyone's spirits connected and united.

Quiet tears dampened cheeks while the final phrases rolled off their lips.

"…and lead us not into temptation, but deliver us from evil. For Thine is the Kingdom, The Power and the Glory forever and ever. AMEN."

Eleven people united by a bond of pain and love stood silently, staring down at Peter. There seemed to be an expectation that something was about to happen. Perhaps he would expire on the spot or his spirit would rise from his bed.

The power of the moment subsided, hands fell. Matt and Catherine reluctantly removed their hands from Peter's shoulders. Matt leaned down and choked on his words, quietly speaking to his father. He called him the way he had when he was a tiny boy: "Goodbye Poppa. I love you."

Peter looked on with Edward standing at the foot of the bed, holding his feet through the sheets. "You're free to go, my friend. You've done your work here. We'll miss you, but we'll be okay."

The assembly had fractured into smaller groups that stood consoling each other. The reality that Peter would be gone soon settled hard on everyone.

Brian spoke, his mouth stringy with saliva. "The hardest thing for me isn't that I won't see him. I haven't seen him that much lately. It's just that the option to see him or talk to him will no longer exist. I took a lot of comfort knowing that I could always pick up the telephone and call."

Eleven people standing in silence levitated simultaneously when the telephone behind Matt rang. Its ring was obviously designed to alert even the deafest patient. It rang a second time before Matt grabbed it and answered abruptly.

"Matt Douglas, who the hell is this? … Oh, sorry, just a minute." Matt held the receiver out to Brian. "It's your security chief at the office. He says it's absolutely urgent."

Brian took the receiver while his family backed away from the bed.

Brian listened without talking then hung up, promising to call back. "Apparently the story about Dad has leaked out. The office is inundated with calls and faxes requesting visiting privileges. Security has posted city police here at the hospital and arranged escorts for any of us concerned about being hassled by the media."

Edward stuck his head out the door. "There are two of the city's finest standing at the end of the corridor and one right outside the door," he reported.

"Matt, Edward, work out a plan to get everyone out of here without being hassled. We can return one at a time to be with Dad. There's another lounge across the hall. See if we can use it for a few days."

Watching his son taking charge, Peter felt affirmed he had made the correct decision letting Brian lead the business. Matt was growing, but in a different way than he expected.

- Chapter 78 -

The telephone was ringing when Brian entered the lounge. He grabbed it on the final ring before the party on the other end hung up. She introduced herself as first assistant to Federal Appeals Court Judge Waltmire and said she had an urgent and confidential message for Brian Douglas. Brian recognized the name of the Judge but couldn't place him.

In the process of confirming Brian's identity, she asked how many fish he caught at Poplar Lake when he fished there on a camping trip with his father. Brian knew immediately who the Judge was and remembered he caught six small mouthed bass, the most he ever caught in his life. He remembered how his father had to bribe him to go away with him and the Judge for the weekend. He'd grown to detest weekends with his Dad since Peter would invariably work the entire time on the telephone or with whatever guest he had invited. The Judge had intervened and promised Brian that if he didn't catch his limit he'd pay him one hundred dollars. That tipped the scales, and Brian had one of the best weekends of his childhood. Years later he learned that the Judge was never in jeopardy of losing his money. He stocked the lake.

Convinced that Brian was who he said he was, the diligent assistant asked him to hold. A man's voice boomed down the telephone line "Brian, is that you?"

"Yes, Judge. I think you know that."

"Just checking. I'm very sorry to hear about your Dad and my condolences for your grandmother. You're having a hell of a time out there."

"It's been a challenge."

"Brian, I'll be brief. You know your Dad and I were close friends. I've tried not to let that influence my review of his case. He's too good a man to let go on a whim if there is any possibility that he might recover. What's the word down there? What are the odds, Brian?"

"They seemed pretty slim, Sir. His life support has been removed."

"Son of a bitch." There was a pause on the line. "Well, I'll leave this up to you and I ask that you not repeat this conversation to anyone. You know I have a lot of respect for your Dad and your family Brian."

I know they all respect my Dad, but if respect were medicine, he would be better by now.

The Judge's voice continued to bellow down the line. Brian could not believe what he was hearing. "Brian, I have reviewed the facts in the case regarding your father's Will. In my opinion there is substantial ambiguity surrounding this situation. I am willing to overturn Judge Whiteside's decision. I would propose an agreed-to period of time for further medical investigations to take place. That would allow for further testing to determine whether the current medical state of Peter Douglas warrants his voluntary expiration under the terms of the will."

Voluntary expiration. Who invents these candy-coated terms for death anyway?

"It's up to you. I just want you to know that you have an option. Otherwise this conversation never happened."

"Thank you, Judge. I appreciate your call."

"You'll have to take the normal channels now. If the appeal application lands up here, I'll have it steered to my court."

"Thank you."

The assistant's voice was on the line again. Judge Waltmire was gone. Brian wondered if she had been listening the whole time or whether that was the way he ended all his calls. She offered some advice on expediting the paperwork for an appeal and gave him her direct number for any further assistance he might require. She was obviously under direct instructions to help any way she could.

Brian hung up and sat stunned in disbelief. A weight of giant proportion now rested on his shoulders. He fiddled with the paper where he had scrawled notes during the conversation. What would his father do?

He could let him slip away peacefully or he could rally an appeal and get life support reinstated while "further medical investigations" took him down an unknown road to an unpredictable end.

Brian sat quietly weighing the significance of the Judge's call; suddenly the overhead speaker startled him.

"Code 169 blue, Dr. Brandon 169 blue."

Brian had now spent enough time at the hospital to know that the call meant his father was in trouble. He bolted from the lounge in time to see Dr. Brandon enter Peter's room. Two nurses with an emergency crash cart were right behind him. While Brian ran the length of the hall, Marion, Catherine and Edward were ejected from Peter's room with the door closed and curtain drawn behind them.

Edward explained that Peter suddenly started to convulse and choke on his own fluid. Marion and Catherine were white with grief while they stood silently and stared at Brian.

"Well I'm not standing out here while he dies!"

Brian pushed the door open with such force that an orderly who was leaning against it was moved several feet.

Neither Dr. Brandon nor the nurses looked up from their tasks. One nurse was withdrawing a suction device from well down in Peter's throat. A second nurse applied a manual aspirator and started pumping air into Peter's lungs. Dr. Brandon filled a syringe and slid it into a vein in Peter's arm, emptying its contents in a single squeeze of the plunger.

He then placed his stethoscope on Peter's chest and listened while the air was pumped into his lungs. Brian stood at the end of the bed holding his Dad's toes in his fingers.

Hang on Dad, hang on.

Seconds ticked by like minutes.

Dr. Brandon suddenly held his hand up, signaling for the nurse to stop.

He nodded and said only two words.

To Brian, they were two of the most important words he'd ever heard.

"He's okay."

The nurses packed up their gear and rolled the cart into the hall. The orderly opened the door and Marion, Catherine, and Edward pressed their way in.

"Peter's lungs had some sort of spasm and he was choking on his own fluids. Without assistance he would have drowned. I am not supposed to intervene. I did so because I know you need some more time. Please use this time wisely. The staff are under strict orders not to resuscitate. If I wasn't on the floor..."

He paused and looked at Catherine while he picked his words. "Well, things would be different now."

Brian squeezed the paper in his pocket that had the notes he jotted down while listening to Judge Waltmire.

He squeezed his father's toes.

Dad? If you can hear me, I could use your advice.

- Chapter 79 -

There had been a steady stream of friends, business associates and well-known people all night. Most Sarah had never heard of or didn't recognize, so she was the first person to leave her grandmother's wake. She had positioned herself that night between her brothers, who kept her informed about who was who, but tired quickly of having people she didn't know expressing their sympathies for someone they didn't know.

She was told the next day would be even busier when people rushed to catch the last wake and the plane arrived from West Palm Beach.

Brian didn't care, but Marion was upset that many people who weren't even friends of Emily's were taking the opportunity for a free ride to Boston. A member of the press had made his way into the receiving line and actually asked Brian a couple of veiled questions about Peter. Brian had him quickly removed by the security people.

Sarah had never seen him so angry. Was he going to beat the man right there in the viewing room?

This had been Sarah's first wake. She couldn't have imagined standing beside an open casket all night. She was pleased that Emily was represented by her floppy, floral hat and a flattering eleven by fourteen blow-up. She was amazed at how jovial the whole affair was. People laughed and chatted. They loved the photos and memorabilia she and her sister put on display to present a brief perspective of Emily's life.

There were a few tears and prayers, but overall people commented on what a long and happy life her grandmother had lived.

Sarah had done a mental subtraction of her age from her grandmother's and got a funny feeling in her stomach. It was the first time that she'd ever measured the likely distance of her life in years relative to someone she was related to. It was her first glimpse of mortality. She didn't like it one bit.

Michael had dropped Sarah at the hospital. She wanted to go in by herself. He agreed to wait for her no matter how long she needed. The halls were quiet and lights were dimmed. The security people recognized her and nodded when she passed. A nurse who had just left Peter's room smiled at her, which she took as a good sign.

Peter's room was still, illuminated only by exterior sources. Sarah walked to the window and looked down on Michael's car in the parking lot below. She reached into her black leather shoulder bag and pulled out a small, dog-eared rabbit.

A little girl had come to see her father. "Hi, Daddy. It's me, Sarah. Look who's here to see you. It's BUNNY!" Sarah pulled back the sheet from her father's shoulders and slipped the well-loved rabbit in beside his chin. "He'll keep you company. I don't need him anymore."

Peter saw and heard that, with these words and gesture, his little girl had transcended childhood into womanhood. Sitting by her father, she placed her arms on the bed rails and rested her head between them.

She didn't talk any more.

She cried steadily; sometimes quietly, sometimes gasping with sobs. It seemed she was giving up her childhood and father at once. The transition was painful.

Peter struggled to stay calm. He tried desperately to reach out to his precious daughter, but had to accept that the flow of feeling was only in one direction. Sarah wasn't yet ready for that sort of experience.

He knew he had to avoid getting agitated if he wanted to prolong his valuable time. He was fully aware it was now very limited. He could already feel his presence continuing to wane now that the life-giving fluids no longer flowed into his arm.

"I want you to know that I love you, and thank you for all the nice things you did for me. You haven't told me you loved me in a long time, but I know you do. I know you do. I was at Grandma's wake tonight, and I'm so glad it wasn't you. I'm not ready yet. I know you're going to a nice place, though. I had a dream about it. You'll continue watching over me and one day I'll see you again. I know you'll always be there."

Sarah stood and looked down her father.

He knew that soon she would be standing at a wake for him. He hoped it wasn't too soon.

She leaned down and kissed Bunny, then kissed her father on the cheek.

Her words choked in her throat. "Good bye. I love you."

"*I love you too, sweetheart.*"

Charlotte was waiting outside in the hall and greeted Sarah with a long hug. "Are you okay, honey?"

"Yes, but I'm going to miss him."

Both women held each other while they gained some composure. A policeman stationed outside the room used Charlotte's presence as an opportunity to take a quick break. Now he waited at a respectful distance until the women separated and noticed him standing down the hall. The gray-haired, slightly overweight officer had a kind manner about him. He tipped his hat, took his seat, but said nothing.

Charlotte and Sarah hugged one more time before parting, then Charlotte slipped into Peter's room.

"Hello, darling." She picked up his hand and held it in both of hers. "I have some wonderful news, Peter. I'm going to have your baby. At least I'm going to try. The test results were excellent. You may be asleep, but you're still a virile man. If I have a boy, Peter, I'm going to name him after you."

Peter was overjoyed. He had been reluctant to father a child at his age, but now nothing pleased him more than to think he might live on in the womb of his wife.

"Peter, I guess we did the best we could. If we'd known we only had a few years together, things would have been different. We wouldn't have argued over petty issues. We'd have spent more time together. We'd have made love more often. If only we'd known. If I had it to do again I'd treat every day with you as though it were my last. Or my first. Remember how inseparable we were when we met? What happened, Peter? Did we just take life and health and love for granted? What a mistake."

Charlotte sat in silence for a few minutes, but Peter was stirring. He was moved by her words, but he felt a longing inside him like he was being pulled from his body again. He wondered if the lack of nutrition was affecting him more rapidly than anticipated. His name exploded through his being.

P EEEE T EEER ! P EEE T EEE R !

There was sudden wrench of gravity and he felt himself accelerate through a burst of misty light. An instant later his view was clear. He was floating above a woman who was bent over a figure lying on a floor mat. Candles burned everywhere. He could smell incense wafting through the shadowy room. When the woman turned the limp body over, Peter called out her name.

"CHOY!"

Madame Wong spoke to him without looking at him or moving her lips. *"You have come. That is good. I have been calling you, but your spirit has been blocked."*

"*There have been people with me constantly. I was with them. I didn't know. What has happened?*"

"*The spirits are taking her. She has been here for several days in a trance too deep for her. She was not ready.*"

"*Is she dying?*"

"*You must know better by now.*" Madame scorned him as though he had learned nothing yet. Peter did not respond. He did know better, but his faith was being tested.

"*Choy. Choy. It's Peter. Can you hear me?*"

Madame held Choy's head with her thumbs placed gently on her temples. Madame's mouth opened and a hideous sound flowed out, like a thousand people wailing and dying. Peter had heard the sound only once before, just prior to waking up in the hospital. It was like the pain of all the ages waiting to receive its next guest. Madame's body stiffened as she held Choy's head. Peter hovered above them, helpless to do anything but watch. Choy's eyes opened and she looked directly into his. She gasped his name.

"*PETER!*"

A fading smile brushed across her beautiful face and her eyes fell shut. Peter became wrapped in a powerful mist of her likeness as it rose from her body and enraptured him. An ear-shattering cry burst forth from Madame Wong as Choy's spirit flowed through her to Peter. For an instant, Peter felt Choy's entire being within him. He felt her love, her pain, her knowledge and her experience. He heard her call his name in a fading voice repeating the words "*the will, the will.*"

Then there was nothing but the lingering sensation of the love she felt for him and a question surrounding the meaning of her final words.

Madame steadied herself, then made her way down the hall into a lounge. She dialed the telephone and spoke in short quiet bursts of Chinese, then replaced the receiver on its cradle.

Charlotte was kissing his forehead when the hospital room came into dull focus. "I love you, darling. And I'll love our son Peter."

Peter could tell his body continued to undergo changes while he was apart from it. His vision was a bit weaker. Images were slightly blurred. The sound of his heart was less robust. He knew he was dying and hoped it would come quickly and quietly. Visions of Choy seemed only dreamlike. The import of her final words, which now carried many meanings, faded. He felt vexed, existing somewhere between the spirit and the human world, ripped from one to the other. His need for certainty was paramount.

- Chapter 80 -

It was late when Matt made his way down the hospital corridor. He had dropped Susan off after Emily's wake, and though he was tired he was filled with his new commitment. He felt like a huge burden of uncertainty had been lifted. The new feelings he was sharing with Susan lightened the weight of dealing with the loss he was facing. He now had something tangible to build upon. He was excited to share his news. He closed the door behind him and went directly to his Father's side.

"Dad, it's Matt."

Peter looked at his son through hazy eyes. He felt happiness coming from him, but it lacked the intensity of a few days earlier. Peter's senses had continued to weaken. He conserved his strength by trying not to reach out.

"I'm marrying Susan. I know I've said it before, but this time it's for real. I know it's something you've wanted for me, so I'm sure it will make you happy. We're doing it when this is all over. Sorry, I didn't mean it that way. I just meant we're not going to wait. I think she's smart to keep me moving, don't you? That way I won't get cold feet. Right? We're going to have kids too. Just like you always wanted. You'll be a grandfather. I know that idea thrills you." Matt chuckled at that line, but then became serious.

"Dad, I know that being the father of this clan must have been hard. You are leaving us a pretty big pair of shoes to fill. There've been lots of times I wasn't the best son...and I know there've been plenty of times when I didn't appreciate you too. That's all behind now. You'll move on and leave it up to us to try and do it better. I know that will be quite a challenge. It's hard enough managing a relationship without thinking about a business and four kids like us. Listen to me. 'A relationship.' Like I'd know. I've been at it. Let's see…" Matt looked at his watch and smiled when he finished his sentence."…oh about…well, not very long!"

Matt rubbed his father's shoulder through the sheets. He moved his hand toward Peter's head but hesitated. He couldn't bring himself to do what others had done and actually rub his hand through his hair. He wanted to. It looked so kind and loving when he'd seen others do it, but he could not bring himself to make contact with the bare skin.

While he talked, he massaged Peter's shoulder without thinking. He stood in silence and let memories of life with his father play in his mind. His bottom lip started to quiver. He bit down hard on it. A host of life's and other events merged to flood and lighten his charge.

The renewal which had started in Bermuda continued. Matt wondered where all the tears came from. He had cried more in the last few weeks than in his whole adult life.

Maybe this was the trick: Cry less, but more often. That would be a change.

He wet his lips before he spoke. "See what's happening here? I'm losing my toughness. I'm getting emotional in my old age. Seriously Dad, my life is almost half over. Isn't that a nice thought?"

Forty. How the heck did that happen? Well, at least with Susan I won't have to lie any more.

"Well Dad, I guess I'll go home. You'd better be here tomorrow."

What if he dies tonight? What if the next time I see him he's dead?

Matt reached out and brushed his fingers through his father's hair for the first time in his adult life. It felt soft and warm. He could feel his firm scalp beneath the hair. He combed it with his fingers, then leaned down and kissed his father's cheek and his forehead. "Goodnight, Dad. You've been a good Poppa. Thank you for everything."

Several of Matt's tears dripped on his father's face.

Matt smiled, wiping them with his fingers. When he looked up, he noticed a face in a slight gap in the curtains. He could not make it out in the dim light, so he moved quickly to the door to see who was peering in on him. He wondered why the guard would allow someone to stand there.

His mother's wet and blotchy face looked toward him. "Mom, it's you. I wondered who…why didn't you come in?"

Marion braced herself with one hand against the glass while she attempted to take a step. Her legs wobbled so Matt stepped closer, only to be overwhelmed by the heavy aroma of alcohol. Marion was very drunk.

"Mom…" Matt reached out for her and spoke sympathetically.

Marion had been under constant watch, resulting from the Douglas siblings agreeing that she would need the support. She never held her liquor well under the best of circumstances. She wasn't the type of person to get slobbery drunk, but she did drink every day if given the chance.

Marion threw her arms around her son.

"I'm all alone, Matthew. I'm all alone now."

"No you're not. You've got us. We'll be with you."

"You're just starting your lives and mine is over. I'm old and alone."

Matt knew that trying to reason with her in this state was impossible and that she wouldn't remember most of what happened anyway.

"Do you want to go in and see Dad?"

"No, he can't see me like this."

"Wait here a minute." Matt propped his mother against the wall and went into Peter's room to open the curtains. He hurried back out and together they looked at Peter.

"He looks so peaceful, Matthew. He looks so peaceful. I wish it was me."

Matt squeezed Marion in his arms while she continued to oscillate from anger to fear and on to love and hate.

"Do you think he can hear us, Matthew? Do you think he knows we're here?"

Matt didn't know what to answer. "What do you think, Mom?"

"I think he's watching us all the time, the bastard. Watching us be miserable over him."

"Mother."

"I'm sorry, honey. He's your father. It's just that he hurt me so badly and now I'm all alone. I love him and I hate him. No one can replace him. Not even..."

"What Mom.?"

Some self-protective mechanism that hadn't been completely impaired stopped her from blurting out what Matt assumed was Carl's name.

"...I guess that's the way it always was. He's one of a kind. If I had the chance, I'd do it all again. You should have seen us when we were young..."

Suddenly, like a switch had been flicked, Marion freed herself of any negativity and jaunted off on a lengthy romantic tangent about her life with Peter. She started when they first got engaged.

She paused only to say goodbye through the glass, barely breaking her stream of consciousness when Matt turned her away and walked her to the lounge. He sat on the couch with her for a longtime while she talked, then paused, then talked some more. Her night ended happily and that was important. He hoped rumors of Carl were true and that he would quickly fill the place that waited.

His mother dozed off in his arms. He eased her down and slipped her shoes from her feet. He turned off all but one tiny reading light and tried to get comfortable the best he could on the daybed.

Morning would come quickly.

Based upon what his mother remembered then, he would fill in only the most positive details.

The rest would vanish.

- Chapter 81 -

The funeral director managed a small smile when he spoke. "Gentlemen, we're all cleaned up. My paperwork is done for the next three days and the coffee pot is empty. I'm afraid I have to leave and that means you two should be doing the same. This isn't the place to spend a night if you don't have to."

Brian assumed, like every other business, that there was a plethora of jokes that went with the funeral industry. He wasn't interested in hearing any of them. He looked at his watch and couldn't believe how late it was. He and Edward remained after everyone had left the wake. Several hours of reminiscing and philosophizing passed. Brian had been waiting for the right moment to tell Edward about the call from Judge Waltmire.

Walking to the car, he stopped in the dark parking lot. "Edward, I've been trying to tell you something all evening, but I haven't been able to bring myself to do it. I guess it's now or never."

"What is it, Brian?"

"I haven't mentioned this to anyone and I'm not sure what to do about it, but I got a call today from Judge Waltmire of the Federal Court."

"Waltmire? I know him. He was a great friend of your Dad's."

"So I understand. He told me that if I make an appeal to his court he'll at least give us an extension on Dad's will to do more medical testing. I'd just come to grips with the whole notion that we were losing him and now I've got this looming over me. I wanted to get your take on it."

"We'd better get in the car. It's freezing out here."

Brian started the motor, but left the lights off. He and Edward sat in darkness, barely illuminated by the dash.

"If I seek an appeal, I could put everything on hold for sixty to ninety days while we give him more time to recover."

"Or delay the inevitable and put everyone, possibly including your Dad, through hell."

"Do you think he's suffering?"

"I can only presume that being trapped halfway between here and the next place can't be any fun."

"Edward, is there something you're not telling me? You seem to have a pretty good idea about all this. Do you know something I don't know?"

"Brian, there are so many things in this world that we accept, but we can't explain, including why we are even here in the first place. That's what I call faith... When I'm with your father it's like we are actually talking together. I think things and he seems to respond. I ask questions and he seems to answer. I think about our past together and I dream in Technicolor, like we were right there doing it all over. Now, I can't prove anything. I have no way of knowing whether I'm hearing what I want to hear or if your Dad is actually communicating with me somehow. I haven't questioned it. I've just accepted it as a gift. I can tell you that I believe that your Dad is ready to move on. Anything we do to tamper with that process now probably isn't in his best interest. I could be completely wrong, but that's the feeling I have."

Brian let Edward's words sink in.

He understood Edward's experiences with his Dad. He replayed the call from Judge Waltmire over and over in his head. He remembered the Judge's final words about the call not happening.

Should he try to prolong the process for ninety days only to possibly go through all this again? What if his Dad partially recovered and had to live in a way he clearly rejected? Why had Dad written those words? Maybe Judge O'Reilly was right about trying to hang onto to someone for selfish reasons.

"Why don't you drive me home and you can sleep on it. You can't do anything about it tonight. You'll most likely have an answer in the morning. We didn't have this conversation, if that concerns you."

"Not you too?"

"What?"

"Nothing." This was the second conversation of the day he hadn't had.

The two men stared ahead while Brian drove, both residing in their own thoughts. The streets were quiet. The neighborhoods were settled in for the night. A few Christmas lights had appeared. Brian smiled to himself, thinking of Christmas when he was a child. He looked forward to being a Dad on Christmas some day.

He guided the car to Edward's door. The two men shook hands and shared a brief hug. Brian watched while Edward worked his way up the stairs to his house. His limp was exaggerated presumably from fatigue. He was about to drive away when he realized that Edward was still waiting in front of his door. He watched him checking each pocket of his overcoat then suit jacket and pants. Brian let the power window on the passenger side drop.

"You looking for these?" He jingled Edward's key ring, grinning. "Stay there." Brian jumped from his car and bounded up the steps.

"Nice legs kid. I wish I had'em. Damn keys."

Marjorie invited Brian to stay with her, but he decided that an uninterrupted sleep would help clear his thoughts. He drove by her flat a couple times testing his resolve, but in the end pragmatism won out.

In bed he read his notes again. He listened, in his head, time and again to Bolstein's, O'Reilly's and Waltmire's words.

Then, just like he had done so many times when he was a child, he carefully folded the notes and slipped them under his pillow, hoping that someone would come in the night and leave an answer for him.

- Chapter 82 -

A sack of fried chicken shared the grip on Edward's cane. Today his step was less labored, after a full night's rest, when he arrived at Peter's room carrying lunch and a garment bag.

Edward was disappointed by how poorly his friend appeared. He was in total agreement with letting Peter go. He just hoped this process would be easy. Brian said nothing about the appeal that day, so Edward didn't know if it was proceeding or not. He felt that Brian might very well do the appeal on his own and only let his family know if the results were positive, or perhaps he would present it as an option but let the decision be theirs.

He cherished this time alone with his friend and the fact that the Douglases had decided to deny all requests for visits. Those people would have to live with what they already knew and remembered of Peter. Edward had seen the list of names. He felt most were unnecessary and many were probably self-serving. In the end, treating everyone the same was the fairest approach.

He knew the previous day had been hard on the family with two wakes and dealing with a plane load of wrinkled Floridians. He realized that most of them didn't actually know Marion's gregarious, but private, mother personally.

He closed the door and curtains, hung his garment bag and sat down beside Peter's bed to enjoy a quiet lunch before leaving for Emily's funeral.

"Hello pal, I'm back again. This time I brought some food. I'm running a bit late and the chicken store beside the dry cleaners smelled too good to resist. I've finally figured out why my clothes smell so funny when I take them out of the plastic. It's a wonder stray dogs don't chase me down the street." Edward then chuckled to himself.

He was waiting for Peter to make a comment about his eating or dressing habits, but he heard nothing.

"You'd be proud of me today. I've got a whole new outfit and I just got the suit pressed. I bought them this morning. New suit, new shoes, new shirt, tie, some socks and six pairs of new briefs. Took me about fifteen minutes to pick out. The clerk said he'd never seen anyone shop so fast."

Edward chuckled again while he opened the grease-stained bag and took out his lunch. Watching Peter closely, he took a big bite out of a chicken leg.

He noticed that Peter's eyes appeared to have sunk into his head substantially, but a faint pulse showed at his temple.

It's a sign of life, at least.

"So, are you going to talk to me today or are you off on one of your trips? Hey, I guess you didn't hear the news about your buddy Zalkow. Son of a bitch was in a car crash last night! Seems he was boozing it up pretty good downstairs at that strip place and the idiot decided to drive home. Bastard fell asleep at the wheel and bam, two parked cars and a telephone pole. He wasn't wearing a seat belt. Broke both his legs. Cut his face up pretty bad...should've...never mind, hold that thought...anyway he's been charged with DWI and probably won't be driving for a while. Carl's having a field day with his papers. He's got Zalkow's picture all over them with the full story. He's even got pictures of him coming out from the strip bar. I'd say he's finished around here for a while. Couldn't happen to a nicer guy, don't you think?" Edward continued to smile broadly and chew in unison.

Peter could just make out Edward through his gray, clouded vision. He could see his friend's mouth moving, but the words all flowed together. Each slow pulse of his heart advanced through his body with steadily declining significance. Peter was slipping away and he knew it. He tried to reach out to his friend, but couldn't summon enough energy.

The previous day when Brian and Catherine had come to visit, he could hear their words but could not respond or take them out of body with him the way he had done before. Whatever powers he had been given were quickly draining away. Brian had held his hand and told him about his friend Judge Waltmire's telephone call. He'd asked Peter and God for a sign to help him make a decision. Peter hoped that he'd heard from God, because he knew he was unable to help him. It saddened him to be slipping away so uneventfully. After all he had been through; he felt the end would be more spectacular when he made one final transition to the next place.

Based upon his experiences, since the time of his accident, his confidence in the future was high. He felt he'd paid his dues. He had used this opportunity to correct some wrongs in his life. He'd earned his passage to the positive place he'd had a glimpse of just prior to waking up in the hospital. Yet laying there he felt a tremendous pull of darkness upon him. He recognized the feeling of the dark side from before. Its unmistakable coldness and emptiness was like a black hole that sucked anything in that came close. It gave nothing in return.

Peter shuddered to think of life in the darkness, and prayed that his judgment would be kind.

A loud disturbance brought Peter's focus back to his hospital room. He could not see his friend Edward anywhere. He listened, hearing the unmistakable noises of someone choking. A repetitious, soundless heaving was coming from somewhere below his bed. Peter realized that the armchair had fallen on its side. He felt his bed shake then Edward's hunched body appeared at its foot. Edward tried to rise and looked at Peter. Death was facing death, these two lifelong friends regarding each other, helpless to do anything about the other's predicament.

Edward's face was turning gray from lack of oxygen. The veins in his neck and his bloodshot eyes bulged as he fought for air. He still held part of a chicken drumstick in his hand.

He turned and lunged toward the bathroom, catching himself on the edge of the sink. He tried to splash water in his open mouth to dislodge the dry chicken caught in his windpipe.

His energy was fading with time, edging onto sixty seconds without a breath. Each precious second was a tick closer to death with oxygen reserves being consumed at an increasing rate.

Peter began to panic while he watched his friend struggling.

"Press the call button. Go into the hall."

Edward heard nothing but his heart thumping in his ears.

Why had he thought he could just cough or take a drink of water and clear his throat? For the first thirty seconds he had plenty of oxygen in his lungs to think and function while he tried without success to clear his windpipe.

Then the next thirty seconds had passed and panic began to set in when the percentage of carbon dioxide in his system increased without fresh air.

The panic had continued to increase so Edward tried to leave his chair but fell onto the floor. The exertion of getting up spent another five seconds. The ratio of carbon dioxide to the life-giving oxygen in his lungs continued to rise with every effort.

By the time Edward lunged for the bathroom, his ability to reason had been almost totally impaired.

His brain was now suffering from hypoxia.

Now, he was acting on survival instincts alone.

Peter could feel his own heart rate increasing. The force of its beat rose painfully in his head. His vision cleared. He had regained some focus. He had watched when Edward threw himself against the sink in an effort to force the air out of his lungs and eject the obstacle. He heard the thud of bone against porcelain before Edward stumbled and fell to the floor.

Edward pounded his chest with his fists, then constricted his hands around his throat trying to create some pressure and push the obstruction out. His entire body was numb. His brain no longer functioned. His muscles burned trying to work without oxygen.

In another effort, he rolled onto his stomach and raised himself to his knees. He let himself fall forward, flat onto the floor. When he fell, he pulled his hands into a ball and clasped them at the V in his rib cage. He landed squarely on his already bruised ribs, sending a dizzying pain through his chest like a hot sword had been driven into it.

He managed to writhe onto his back.

Everything went black.

Peter screamed for help now, hoping somehow the energy he was able to summon and project would be enough to get attention from someone. He knew from before that this exertion could send his own body into convulsions which, without assistance, would quickly kill him. He was prepared to risk everything to save his friend.

There were no monitors to tell anyone outside his room that there was problem. The door and curtains were closed. Peter's world continued to darken while he thrashed within himself, trying somehow to assist Edward. His body started to convulse on the bed, causing his blood pressure rise. Blasts of bursting colors returned; everything he'd experienced spun out in front of him in a kaleidoscope of his life.

This movie was now familiar.

The pull of death too real.

Two men, two best friends. Dying alone, together.

Peter's body ran with sweat. His eyes danced and bulged under his eyelids.

"HELP, HELP."

His words carried out into unfathomable distance. He lost contact with reality and slipped into a familiar void. Instantly all was quiet; he levitated above his writhing body. He looked down at Edward, his life ebbing on the floor, his anxiety dissipating. He floated there; a passive observer.

"Hello, Peter." He turned to face a smiling Mrs. Rossi.

"Peter, it's so good to see you." Emily appeared beside Mrs. Rossi. Another man and woman came into focus. It was his parents when they were a young couple.

Peter was surprised yet expectant. He felt no intense emotions when greeting each person. It felt like it should. It all seemed normal that he would see these important people in his life now. From behind, he heard an unmistakable voice sing his name with a soft Asian accent.

"Choy! It is wonderful to see you."

Others from his past continued to appear, but Mrs. Rossi came forward and spoke.

"Peter, we are happy to see you, but perhaps you are not so happy. Your friend is dying, and you want to help him."

"How can I? Tell me. I'll do anything."

The group stared down while a white haze started to form around Edward.

"We do not have long. It is not his time. That is why we have come. If you help him, there is no certainty of his or your future. If you do not, you will join us now. Edward will be on his own journey."

"Will he die? Will he join us later? Can you tell me that?"

"We know none of that, only of where we will return to, with or without you."

"Where is that?"

"You do not have time. You must decide now."

Peter felt shaken in the midst of the serenity of the others. He looked at each of them, gathered peacefully together. They were watching Edward die with a feeling that they had seen death many times before. There was no emotion. Just quiet, respectful observation.

"Let me try! I'll do anything to help him."

Peter stared in shock.

The eyes of his bedridden body slammed open like someone had plugged him into a wall outlet. Everyone shifted their focus from Edward to Peter. His body had stopped convulsing on the bed. It stiffened, and muscles throughout the passive limbs flexed.

While they stared, a sound began to emanate from each of them. It was a hum that vibrated the air, and one by one they harmonized. The flow of their energy to his body was visible. Without warning, a tremendous spiraling gust sucked him in and hurled him in a slow circular fashion toward the body from which he had risen. The faces were gone. His hospital room had reappeared.

Peter sat up unsteadily and looked at his friend lying lifeless on the floor. Driven by an instinctual force alone, Peter swung his shaky legs to the floor. A sliver of blood oozed, then trickled, from the IV puncture.

He shuffled gingerly along his bedside. Edward lay on his back halfway between the foot of the bed and the bathroom. Peter released his grip on the bed rail and took a couple of fragile steps in Edward's direction.

He responded to the only instinct he had and allowed his entire body weight to fall and land squarely on Edward's chest with all the force gravity could provide.

When Peter's weight compressed Edward's body, the remaining air in his lungs expanded out against his ribcage. Ribs and chest muscles strained, trying to contain Edward's lungs which had inflated dramatically under Peter's weight.

Suddenly there was an explosion out of Edward's mouth, spewing saliva high into the air. Through the spray, a clot of mucous-coated chicken accelerated upward, arcing away from Edward and landing unceremoniously on the floor.

The force of the fall could not be resisted by Peter's weak muscles. His head banged on the floor with a solid thud that sent a shock wave through his brain when his skull sustained the impact.

Peter's body lay draped across Edward's.

Friends through life. Friends through death.

– Chapter 83 –

A full police motorcade and several black limousines waited on St. James Avenue. Hundreds of well-dressed people filed into the historic Trinity Church, across from the Boston Public Library, to pay their respects to the Douglas family. Expensive, well-shone cars lined the streets for blocks, jockeying for position in the funeral procession.

Across the square, camouflaged by the trees and a fountain, Wilton "Fuzzy" Polonski sat in his gleaming rig. He hoped his presence would not cause any disruptions. He doubted that anyone would be looking for him today. His plan was to be the last vehicle in what was going to be a long line of cars. He knew from calling the funeral home that the procession would wind its way to a small cemetery near Westwood. The burial would be in the Douglas family plot that sat high on a knoll, overlooking the pond where ducks and geese swam year round.

There, Fuzzy hoped to get his first look at the members of Peter Douglas's family.

Inside the church the mourners were surrounded by the beauty of one of Boston's most visited monuments. Conversations reflected off the high central ceiling, creating a dull murmur of non-decipherable noise. The backdrop for the pulpit was seven massive stained-glass windows set in a semi-circular wall. A tall golden cross hung from the ceiling at the front for all to see and revere. More beautifully detailed stained glass windows ringed the upper walls of the church, wrapping around its entire perimeter. A massive pipe organ elevated on a balcony at the rear towered over the throng. This was indeed a place for meetings of veneration.

Organ music began filling the huge chamber. Brilliant sunlight cast vibrant colors on the church's interior splaying them through the elaborate windows high at the back. People in the hard oak pews started to settle. Feet shuffled while they positioned the tiny embroidered knee stools which had replaced the long hard kneeling rails.

This was the funeral service for Emily Parkin, although talk among those present was primarily about Peter Douglas. Many wondered if the family would delay his funeral for a while to absorb this loss before trying to grieve a second one. The mood was not celebratory.

The Douglas family filed in at the front of the church from a small staging room. Michael, Susan and Marjorie entered with them. Each of the group wore a black ribbon. Their faces were solemn. They passed Emily's casket below the raised pulpit. Flowers were tastefully arranged on its top and at the base. Eight pall bearers were seated to the left. The first rows on the right were reserved for this final group.

Waiting to enter the church, the Douglases had asked amongst themselves about Edward. When Brian told them he had been with Peter, it was assumed he would enter through the main door.

Walking into this church full of people staring at them had distracted any of the Douglas family from looking for Edward while they took their seats.

This was Emily's day.

The rumble of conversation quieted when a gray haired man, in lavish robes, took his place at the front of the church.

The Douglases had no attachment to any church in the city. They were rare visitors at best. The funeral home made all the arrangements including this august but traditionally dry and dogmatic speaker.

"Let us pray."

Heads bowed while he recited The Lord's Prayer.

Sarah was the first to start crying when she remembered saying the same prayer over her dying father. Where was her tiny rabbit? Still tucked under his chin?

Sarah's tears triggered her mother, who in turn started Catherine. By the end of the prayer the entire family was holding hands.

Some wept. Some held back stoically.

The minister looked at the family with kindly eyes. He would be the sole speaker today.

"We are joined here today to celebrate the life of Emily Louise Parkin, who leaves this world we know so well. She departs to a world we know little about except through the teachings of Jesus Christ, who promises us...."

He spoke in monotone for many minutes about the path that Emily was now on. He spoke of the faithful life she lived which guided her successful passing from this world to the next.

Michael couldn't help but wish he knew the Douglases better. He would have offered instead, a vibrant and uplifting service that would reach all the people present in one way or another. He noticed many were already dosing off while the speaker used this opportunity to praise the faithful and castigate the sinners, presumably hoping to reach at least one new person who might promise his or her life to Jesus and fill one of the many empty seats of the fading church flock.

"...The road of the Lord is pitted with trials and tribulations. The faithful must see these as tests to prove their love of God. Although the way around the challenges God puts before us appears easier, it is a road to damnation that tempts us from our rightful path to His House. He that so believeth in God shall be loved by God and blessed with miracles..."The droning continued.

A long, creaking sound ran the length of the Church as the carved wooden door slowly opened. A broad swath of sunlight flooded down the aisle. It illuminated the face of the minister, who squinted while he continued to preach. Late arrivals usually slipped in quietly from one of two side doors to avoid interrupting the service. The Reverend felt a twinge of annoyance, but calmed himself knowing he had another soul in his midst to try and save.

Glancing up again from his reading he was pleased to see when he looked at the backlit figures in the doorway that he had more than one new soul to save.

"...Yes my friends, miracles are what God is about. Look around us at the wonder of daily life. Look at the phenomenon of birth and of death. Of course, we live these miracles on the basis of the first miracle, The Resurrection...."

The wooden door boomed softly shut.

Two men proceeded up the aisle. Their faces and bodies were in plain view now that the door, once again, blocked the sun. The Reverend refocused on the sight before him in astonishment; one by one the people in the church turned to look. Many gasped. A rumble of conversation rippled through the pews.

Brian closed his eyes, slipping his hand into his pocket to crumple a well-worn piece of paper in his fist.

A girl cried out. Leaping up from her seat, she ran down the aisle toward the man sitting in a wheel chair which Edward and Dr. Brandon were gingerly pushing toward the front of the awe-filled church.

"Daddy! Daddy!" Sarah fell to her knees at the feet of her father. She wrapped her arms around his legs. Peter was feeble and gaunt, but managed a smile, gingerly raising his arms to hold her. Rivulets of tears turned to small rivers running down Sarah's cheeks when she spotted the head of her stuffed and over loved bunny peeking out from beneath the top of the blanket covering her father's legs.

One by one, people in the pews began to stand up.

The Reverend watched in admiration of the spectacle he was witnessing. Waves of people were rising, their movement spreading throughout the church.

Then it started, with a single clap of two frail hands from far in the back. Another pair joined, then several more. The sound was infectious, reverberating throughout the massive chamber. Within seconds of its commencement, a sole pair of hands had created a celebration of applause that filled the air. The mood of elation lifted each person there, with Emily leaving this world and Peter being welcomed back. The miracle of life and death brought together as one.

Edward and Dr. Brandon, flanked by a beaming Sarah, wheeled Peter ahead toward the Douglas family who moved forward, in raptured silence, to join them.

- Epilogue -

The door clicked somewhere back in his mind as Matt sat back and wistfully watched the blinking light. When it stopped he removed the tiny data storage device from his laptop and explored its exterior, holding it in front of him.

Feeling a pair of warm hands on his shoulders, a tiny ribbon of electricity ran the length of his body. He smiled but continued to look over the screen of his computer to a brilliant blue ocean. Its warm breeze had been his friend for many months while he hopped back and forth between Boston and Bermuda. It continued to blow gently in his face the way it had over the duration while he attempted to write his first novel.

"How is it going, sweetie?"

Matt reached over his shoulder, without looking back, and handed the tiny black plastic device to his fiancée.

"Done…I'm finished…it's ready for editing."

He turned from the screen to face her, feeling tired and a bit distant. What had started out as a lark had become a full-time, all-consuming project.

At first, he couldn't even remember his characters' names. Then his story continued to write itself and now he had become intimately involved in the life of every person in his book. He knew everything about them; what they looked like, how they thought, their history, their plans and their dreams. Most importantly, Matt now knew himself better since each character in his story had grown from a seed within him.

He stood and Susan pressed her body against his. She attempted to kiss him. This time his lips yielded a wet and rugged response. For the first time in weeks Matt leaned into her. He had told her that his nervousness about completing his story had been draining him emotionally.

Susan leaned back and smiled at him. "I guess you're finished."

"I guess you're right." He walked her backward through the sheer curtains then pressed her onto their bed and knelt over her.

What will they think? Wouldn't Brian and his father, in fact everyone, be surprised when he dropped the manuscript in front of them?

No one knew. No one would suspect that he was even capable of starting a novel, let alone finishing. He no longer cared if it was good or bad. He'd started. He'd finished. That, in itself, was his greatest accomplishment.

It had been difficult many times, but he'd managed to keep the project a secret thus far. He hadn't wanted to risk pre-announcing something that might never be finished, but now he could finally come clean. New talents were surfacing and he wanted to continue exploring them. He could now unleash some of the creativity that he had diverted into other, less fulfilling activities over the years.

Matt's mind filled with images of his favorite character, Cara, while he undressed Susan and flung his own clothes aside.

"Let's make a baby, Matthew."

When he pressed his body against Susan's he felt the wind of the overhead fan on his back.

He closed his eyes, pushing Cara's face and the others from his mind, and then made love to Susan for the first time in weeks.

Matt felt completely happy. For once in his life he'd finally accomplished something that hadn't been given to him and now he was ready to do the same with Susan.

Share the Journey of

CRITICAL CARE

Email info@criticalcare.ca, fax 613-546-9191 or snail mail
Grace Media Inc., 844 Division St. Kingston, Ont. K7K 4C3 this form.

Send a book worth thinking about to a friend

Your Name: _____

Address: _____

City: _____ State/Province: _____

Zip/Postal Code: _____ Phone: _____

Email *(will not be shared)*: _____

Ship To: *(if different from above)*

Friend's Name: _____

Address: _____

City: _____ State/Province: _____

Zip/Postal Code: _____ Phone: _____

Email *(will not be shared)*: _____

Quantity Order: _____ x $24.95 = _____

Plus applicable taxes and $9.95 per book shipping and handling

Card Type : Visa ☐   Mastercard ☐

Card Number: _____

Expiry Date Month: _____ Year: _____

Name on Card: _____